# COLONY EAST

## THE TOUCAN TRILOGY
## BOOK 2

Scott Cramer

*Colony East—Toucan Trilogy—Book 2*

Copyright 2013 Scott Cramer
www.facebook.com/AuthorScottCramer

ISBN-13: 978-0-9898128-1-8

Cover artist Silviya Yordanova
www.facebook.com/MyBeautifulDarkness

Editorial
http://laurakingsley.yolasite.com

Formatting by Polgarus Studio
http://www.polgarusstudio.com

This book is a work of fiction. Any references to real people, events, and organizations are used fictitiously. All dialog, names, incidents, and characters are drawn from the author's imagination and are not construed as real.

# DEDICATION

For V, Megumi, J-girl, Harry & Misty-Duck

# RETURN TO CASTINE ISLAND

# CHAPTER ONE

Awake for two days straight and recovering from the epidemic that had killed most of the world's adults, Abby felt herself sinking deeper into the mattress of winter jackets she'd piled on the floor.

Fearing that someone might try to enter the house, she roused herself by rolling onto her sunburned arm. Someone had to keep watch. Even though her mother's house was one of thousands abandoned since the night of the purple moon, Abby knew the mainland was a dangerous place.

She ached to breathe the salty air of Castine Island again. Twenty miles east of Portland, Maine, her island home was about a hundred miles from Boston as the crow flies. She missed her sister, Toucan, while those on the island approaching adolescence were counting on her and her brother, Jordan, to return with antibiotic pills. The pills were the only cure for the deadly bacteria.

The comet had streaked by Earth a year ago. Dust from its long tail had penetrated the atmosphere, turning the sky, sun, and moon purple. The dust also contained germs that attacked the human hormones first produced during puberty. Adults and older teens died within hours. The comet left a planet of children in its wake, with the oldest survivors living with a ticking time bomb of approaching adolescence. Scientists, in quarantine at the Centers for Disease Control, after many delays, had finally developed an antibiotic to defeat the bacteria, and were now in the early days of distributing the pills across the country.

1

Abby twisted her head to glance at the others in the living room. Moonlight outlined Jordan on the couch with only his shaggy mop of brown curls for a pillow. Her brother always looked agreeable in sleep. Abby's blood chilled when she recalled just how close he had come to dying. She'd never complain about his stubborn streak again.

Mandy and Timmy, the mainland kids, shared a cushioned chair. Nine-year-old Timmy had survived the past year all on his own. With a cowlick and bright grin, he seemed to bounce from tragedy to tragedy, as if racing from one thrilling roller coaster ride to the next.

Mandy, fourteen, looked so peaceful snuggled next to Timmy, nothing like the tough girl with multiple piercings and choppy blonde hair, whose glare at an adversary was as lethal as the long knife she carried.

Through the window, Abby saw the full moon high in the sky and guessed it was one or two o'clock. It was quiet outside except for dogs barking in the distance and the hum of crickets chirping in the overgrown lawns.

Her nose crinkled from the pungent smoke coming through the broken windowpanes. It smelled like burning rubber and chemicals. A fire must be raging in Boston or maybe somewhere in Cambridge. Another building or city block turning to ash.

She scraped the scaly tip of her tongue against her teeth and tried to swallow. Despite her overpowering thirst, the effort to crawl to the can of beer sitting on the table ten feet away was too great.

They all needed food and water, and Mel was their best bet. Abby's best friend since the second grade, Mel lived on Pearl Street, two blocks away— at least that was where she used to live. Abby hadn't seen her in over a year. Before the epidemic, they'd team up and torment Jordan whenever he annoyed them, which was always. Mel was faster and stronger than any boy she knew.

Yesterday Abby had stopped by Mel's and found laundry hanging in the yard, but it might have belonged to squatters. She had scratched a note on the front door just in case, to let Mel know that she and Jordan were at their mother's house.

Would Mel share? Many kids hoarded food and water because they believed it was the only way to survive. Abby, on the other hand, believed that caring for every individual made the group stronger. That was how they tried to live on Castine Island. She realized the epidemic changed people, but thought her friend would help them if she could.

Staring upward, Abby felt a deep fatigue set in and began seeing images on the ceiling; she was sailing home and had entered the calm waters of Castine Harbor. She fixed her eyes on the tip of the mile-long jetty that stretched into the mouth of the harbor. It was her favorite place to be alone on the island. She imagined that the noxious smoke from the distant fire was the rich, raw scent of seaweed at low tide. Abby's eyelids drooped as a sense of peace settled over her like mist on a pond.

~ ~ ~

Abby jolted awake. Feet slapped the pavement outside. Someone was sprinting down Pearl Street. Blinking the grit from her eyes, she sat up, but dizziness slapped her back down. She turned to the window. The moon, dirtied by waves of smoke, hovered just above the rooftops across the street. It would soon be dawn.

The runner came closer. Adrenaline pumped through Abby's body as he came closer and closer until she thought he was going to charge up the steps and enter the house. Should she wake up the others?

All of a sudden it was silent, except for the drumbeat in her temples. She wondered if the runner had stopped or was moving quietly through the tall grass. She held her breath and listened for creaks or scuffs on wood, anything that would announce he was climbing the steps.

Abby heard more runners approaching. It sounded like a whole pack of kids. Maybe they were chasing the first runner, or some larger group was chasing all of them. The strong chasing the weak was all too common on the mainland.

Once more, she considered waking the others. Not sensing any danger, though, she decided to let them sleep. They were invisible, she told herself. Her mom's house, plundered long ago, was no different from any of the other houses on the street. Even if they were discovered, they had nothing of value, except half a can of beer.

Abby swallowed hard, remembering Mandy's motorcycle. She and Mandy had rolled it behind the bushes by the side of the house. The motorcycle was extremely valuable to them because it offered a fast way to scout boats in Boston Harbor and to get the antibiotic pills at the airport. She had to hope they had hidden it well.

"Which way?" a boy shouted. Abby noted that he had a deep voice. He must be her age, if not older.

"That way," another boy said.

"Wait here," a girl said.

"She's gone," Deep Voice said, this time angrily. "We lost her."

Abby realized the runner was a girl.

The kids stopped to catch their breath. As they stood there huffing and talking, their voices drifted through the broken window. They must be standing on the street right out front. Sitting up, Abby braced herself as the walls started spinning. She concentrated on the voices.

"Trust me, she's around here," the girl said. "She's hiding. I know it."

"Or else… " Abby couldn't make out the rest of the sentence.

They swore at each other and talked about where they might find the runner. Abby counted four voices: two girls, two boys. They all sounded as if they were thirteen or fourteen. The boy with the man's voice had to be at least that old.

She still saw no reason to wake the others. Whatever was going on outside wasn't any of their business. Her priority was to return to the island.

Jordan grunted loudly and thrashed his arms. Chills rippled down Abby's spine. It wasn't her brother's first nightmare of the night, and luckily he settled quickly. Abby held her breath, worried the gang heard the outburst.

"I need a pill now," Deep Voice bellowed.

"Brad, stop whining," the girl snapped. "We all need them."

Still shaking, Abby realized the kids were sick, and who could blame them for being anxious. The illness was horrific: a month of high fever, loss of appetite, hallucinations in the latter stage, and a painful rash that devoured the skin in the final days leading up to death. The antibiotic was the only cure.

"How do we know she even has pills?" the other boy asked.

"Why else would she run," the girl said.

Abby wanted to shout, go to the airport like everyone else. Boston was a Phase I distribution center, one of a handful of cities across the country receiving the first shipment of the pills. Scientists were handing out the antibiotic at Logan Airport.

"Brad, I don't get you," the girl said. "She might have shared them with us."

"You got a problem with me?" Brad fired back.

"It was stupid what you did," the girl accused. "They didn't do anything to you."

Brad growled, "Don't look at me like that."

"What are you going to do? Bash my brains in too?"

"I snapped, okay?" Brad said.

Cringing, Abby crawled to the window and leaned against the wall just below the sill. Cool, smoky air from outside cascaded over her like a polluted waterfall. She did not dare raise her head for fear they'd see movement.

"Let's split up and meet back here in ten minutes," the girl suggested.

"She's probably a mile away by now," Brad said.

Abby hoped that was true for her sake, and for the nameless runner.

"Hey, what's that?"

Brad's voice jarred Abby. He had moved closer to the window. Much closer.

"We're wasting time," the other boy said.

Brad wheezed, "Over here." He was breathing deeply through his mouth.

Brad was now so close that she could have reached out and touched him. Abby heard them chattering back and forth.

"I don't believe it. A motorcycle."

"It's chained."

"You think it has gas?"

"The cap's locked."

"Are you surprised?"

"Do you know how to ride one?"

"How hard can it be?"

5

"It has a Maine license plate." Brad spoke in a hushed tone. "They came from Maine to get the pills. They're inside. They have pills. I know it."

They stopped talking and turned on a flashlight. Abby's hand shot to her mouth to stifle her gasp. Batteries were scarce, and only the most violent gangs had them.

Light glinted on the shards of glass in the windowpanes. The beam danced on the ceiling above her, darting back and forth like the eyes of a hungry predator. Then the light snapped off.

Abby knew they'd enter the house at any moment and demand the keys to the padlocked chain on the motorcycle. If it were up to her, she'd let them have it. The motorcycle was not a necessity, not worth sacrificing their lives for. But Mandy lived by another code. She'd fight for it.

The gang would also demand pills. Abby had crushed the last pill they had and pushed the powder down Jordan's throat. They'd never believe any of that, and then what might happen? Desperate people did unpredictable things, and from what she'd heard it sounded like Brad had already bashed somebody's brains in.

They were no match for Brad's gang. Even though it was four against four—if she had counted the voices correctly—she and Jordan were recovering and lucky to have the combined strength of one, and Timmy only weighed fifty pounds soaking wet. That left Mandy. Wielding her knife, Mandy could take on two at once, but that still left two.

Abby wondered if she could reason with them. She'd explain that the line for pills at the airport moved slowly, but at least it moved.

If that failed, she could always try bluffing. A gang with a motorcycle must be particularly vicious, right? She'd convince them that the members of her gang outnumbered them, and that they, the hunter, were about to become the prey. Unfortunately, Abby knew she couldn't lie to save her life.

Weighed down with doubt, she pressed against the wall, ready to do something that she hoped would frighten them—buying her precious seconds to wake the others.

She shot to her feet, waving her arms wildly and shouting. The shouts came out as pathetic croaks, and a fresh wave of dizziness seized her. She gripped the sill to steady herself.

Shocked, she gaped out the window. The gang had already retreated to the other side of the street. Grateful for her parched throat, Abby quickly ducked out of sight.

Peering out the window, careful to avoid a shard of glass inches from her nose, she saw four shapes close to each other. One kid stood a foot taller. He had to be Brad.

As Abby moved from the window, something rustled outside. "It's her," Brad shouted.

The flashlight flicked on, and the beam locked onto a girl coming out of the shrubs across the street. She wore a green jacket and had long hair. She ran straight at them, like a bull charging a matador. Then she veered away at the last second and dashed down Pearl Street. Like lions after a gazelle, the four kids broke after her.

It made no sense. Why did the girl run at them? Abby chalked it up to the craziness of the mainland.

Expecting Brad's gang to come back for the motorcycle and to demand pills if they didn't catch the girl, Abby jiggled Jordan's shoulder. "Hey, wake up."

He grunted, folded his arms and rolled over.

The stories of what her brother could sleep through were legendary. Fire engines. Fog horns. Screaming toddlers. "Jordie, c'mon." When she jiggled him again, he swatted her hand away.

Accepting defeat, she moved to the others. It tugged at her heartstrings to see Mandy sucking her thumb, and Timmy clasping Mandy's free hand with both of his. Abby shuddered when she recalled Mandy's tearful admission, but it helped her understand why Mandy, who had only known Timmy for a matter of hours, was acting like his fierce protector. Even huddled together in the chair, they looked cold, so she covered them with a jacket.

Deciding to let all of them sleep, Abby grabbed their only beer and tilted the can to her lips. It was a special purple brew, made to celebrate the comet. She took a tiny sip, which barely moistened her swollen tongue, and closed her eyes, savoring the pale wash of flavor. She wanted to throw her head back and guzzle the rest to quench her powerful thirst, but she saved the rest for the others.

She slid the piano bench beside the window to keep watch. The eastern sky showed a trace of light through the hazy smoke. She eyed front yards where she had once played, while her mind replayed the voices of neighbors who died the night of the purple moon. She had grown numb to the staggering loss of people who had once been part of her life.

Daffodils bloomed in the garden below the window. The sob came without warning, along with tears that Abby couldn't believe she had left. They trickled down her cheeks. She had helped her mom plant the daffodil bulbs three years ago.

Abby's feelings about her mother were still raw. She and Jordan had buried Dad last year. They, along with Toucan, had grieved as a family. But Mom was here in the house, right upstairs in bed, undisturbed for the past year.

Jordan had gone to her bedroom. "Mom looks so peaceful. Abby, go see her."

Abby was holding on to a special image in her mind—her mom on the Castine Island ferry, healthy and happy, red hair blowing in the wind, waving from the deck. Abby wanted to preserve that memory of her mother.

Dawn broke and swept away the shadows and her dark thoughts. Tall weeds sprouted from cracks in the sidewalk, and a carpet of oak and maple leaves covered the street. Nature was reclaiming the city. Abby wondered if, someday, Cambridge would resemble an ancient Mayan city swallowed up by jungle, or would kids, with help from the few remaining adults, preserve and rebuild it.

The sky brightened to a burnished gray as billows of black smoke boiled up in the distance. The smoke was so thick and black that it blotted out the sun. Would this fire alter their plans? Could they get to the airport by taking the route she knew, or would they have to find a different way?

That and other problems weighed heavily on her mind, and soon, Abby could no longer stand being alone, no matter how much the others needed rest. She looked up and down the street a final time, then turned to the scene of sleeping kids.

"Hey, time to get up." Abby pressed her hand on Jordan's shoulder. Once again he slapped her hand away. He was living up to his reputation of being a grumpy, hibernating bear. She considered dragging him off the couch, which would serve him right.

The front doorknob clicked and Abby froze.

How stupid could she be? Brad's gang had doubled back. They'd been watching her at the window all this time and made their move the moment she stepped away.

Her heart boomed. She rushed to Mandy and squeezed her arm. Mandy's eyes shot open. Abby put a finger to her lips and pointed in the direction of the door.

Mandy understood instantly. She pulled Timmy's head close and placed her hand over his mouth. "Shhhh," she whispered in his ear.

The door squeaked.

Abby held up four fingers, showing Mandy the number of kids they had to fight. Then she held up one finger with her hand raised to show that one of the kids was a monster. Mandy nodded and removed her knife from its sheath. The sight of the long blade sent a chill down Abby's spine.

Mandy set the sheath on the floor. Then she tapped Timmy and pointed to a corner of the room, wanting the boy a safe distance away. Timmy stood his ground, ready to take on any threat. Mandy narrowed her eyes and shot him a look. He tiptoed to the corner with a scowl.

When the door clicked shut, Abby feared the gang was inside.

Should she try to wake Jordan? If she spoke up now, she'd put them all in jeopardy. She took a deep breath and focused on the hallway. The blood pounding in her ears drowned out all sounds.

Mandy plastered herself against the wall, ready to strike with sudden force. Gripping the knife, she motioned Abby to swing wide. Not wanting to veer too far from Jordan but trusting Mandy's instincts, Abby moved to a spot beside the piano where she had a good view of the hallway. Movement caught her eye. She tensed. Timmy was inching forward.

As the girl with the green jacket rounded the corner, Mandy raised the knife and reared back. In one motion, she twisted her torso and drove the blade forward.

"Stop, I know her!" Abby cried.

Just as the knifepoint came in contact with the girl's jacket, Mandy jerked in surprise. She opened her hand, and the knife tumbled to the floor.

Abby threw her arms around her friend, Mel, and wept in utter relief.

# CHAPTER TWO

Jordan jerked upright when the motorcycle engine fired up. His head started spinning, and he swung his arm over the back of the couch for support. He was alone in a room he knew all too well. Memories trickled in. The house in Cambridge. He had grown up here. At the age of nine, he moved to Castine Island with Abby, Toucan, and Dad, but Mom stayed behind because of her job in Boston. Now Mom was ready to join the family on the island.

No, all the adults, including his mother, had died a year ago. An ache pulsed deep inside his heart. Last night, he had found her body upstairs. To say his final goodbye, he had reached out and touched her arm under the blanket. Jordan clenched his fists and grunted, trying to force the sad memories from his brain.

He vaguely remembered arriving. Abby had helped him up the steps and inside. She had steered him to the couch. It was all coming back to him. Leaving him alone in the house, Abby had gone to the airport to get pills. One thing seemed certain. She must have succeeded—otherwise he wouldn't be asking any questions.

Jordan let out a sigh of relief when he saw a makeshift bed of jackets on the floor. Maybe Abby was out front with the person on the motorcycle? The sound of it idling agitated him for some reason.

"A-Aaa…" His attempt to call out sputtered in his dry throat.

He wanted to go to the window, but with the room spinning the way it was, he'd fall on his face before he took more than one step.

He dragged his sleeve across his eyes, wondering if he was hallucinating. A can of beer sat on the table. He reached for the can, but knocked it over. Purple beer dribbled over the edge of the table. Mopping his tongue across the dusty tabletop, he tried in vain to lap the beer up—then slumped back on the couch and cursed himself.

The motorcycle engine revved. Jordan flushed with rage, suddenly remembering the gang who had abandoned him and Abby in New Hampshire. Mandy, Jerry, and their leader, Kenny, had been taking them from Portland to Boston to get pills. Jordan would never forget the roar of their bikes as they sped off, leaving him and Abby to die by the side of the road.

A hard lump formed in his throat when he spotted the knife sheath on the floor. He recognized it immediately. He'd never seen Mandy without the long knife dangling from her belt.

How could Mandy be here? And why? Abby must have run into her somewhere and offered her a place to stay. It was like his sister to be so forgiving. It was also like Abby to do something that stupid.

A cold wave of fear traveled through him. Mandy might have stabbed Abby. She was capable of anything. He scanned the room and thankfully saw no blood, but that didn't mean Abby was safe.

He jumped up and immediately lost his balance, crumpling to one knee. He fixed his gaze on a painting above the piano. It was a watercolor of sailboats in Castine Harbor. Using the painting as a visual anchor, he stood up and wobbled as if he had drunk the whole can of beer, but he managed to stay on his feet.

Going to the window was a waste of time. He couldn't defend Abby with his eyes. He needed a weapon.

He headed for the kitchen to arm himself with a knife. Plowing through waves of dizziness and nausea, he stumbled three steps to the wall between the hall and the living room. From there, scraping his shoulder against the wall, he shuffled into the hallway where he stopped to take aim at his next goal, the kitchen counter. If he could make it to the counter, he would have support all the way to the knife drawer. In the drawer was a meat cleaver his mom had always used to chop up chicken.

He pitched forward and grabbed the counter. Hand over hand, step-by-step, he worked his way around the perimeter, past the stove, the spice cabinet, the onion drawer, the toaster on its side, the sink, a broken glass, an empty cereal box. The journey seemed endless.

He yanked open the knife drawer and swallowed a sob. The meat cleaver was gone. The carving knives were missing too. He realized that scavengers had taken every big knife.

He grabbed a paring knife, which had a narrow, three-inch blade. It was the sharpest item in the drawer. Better than nothing, he sighed.

Gripping the knife, he took a step toward the front door and teetered. Flailing his arms to maintain his balance, he veered to the left. He shifted his weight, careened right and plunged forward. He crashed on the floor, bouncing hard on his shoulder.

Jordan rose to his knees and crawled in a zigzag pattern, avoiding the broken glass scattered on the floor. Reaching the door, he grabbed blindly for the knob and quickly drew his hand back when his palm found jagged glass in the smashed door window. Blood trickled down his arm.

He transferred the knife to the hand with the cut and squeezed the handle to stem the flow of blood. In one motion, he stood and flung open the door.

"Jordie!"

He jumped back. Abby stood before him. Her cheeks were sunken. Grime caked her sunburned skin. Her red curls hung limply. She looked half-dead. A young boy was also on the porch beside her, along with another girl about Abby's age. The girl stared blankly as if she were in shock, deep sadness reflected in her eyes.

Just then, Mandy rode down Pearl Street on her motorcycle.

Jordan blurted. "Did Mandy hurt you?"

"Hurt me?" Abby shook her head. "She saved our lives."

"Huh?" The knife dropped from his hand, and the new boy trotted down the steps to the sidewalk. "Mandy's gang left us to die," Jordan said.

A look of concern flashed across his sister's face. "Mandy gave us pills."

What made him gasp in astonishment were Abby's eyes. For the first time in weeks, they were bright and filled with optimism. Mandy must have tricked her. "I don't care what she gave us. We shouldn't trust her."

Abby reached out and inspected the cut in his hand. It measured about two inches near the base of his thumb. He grimaced as she probed with her fingertip to check for signs of any foreign bodies like splintered glass. "We need to clean and bandage that."

"Where did Mandy go?" he asked.

"She's hiding the motorcycle."

"Abby, she's dangerous."

She scrunched her brow. "A lot has happened that you need to hear about."

"Who are they?" he asked, gesturing to the strangers.

Abby nodded to the boy on the sidewalk. "I met Timmy on the way to the airport, and you remember Mel."

"Mel?" Jordan's jaw dropped. Was this the same girl who'd get him in a headlock until he begged for mercy? Mel Ladwick, Abby's best friend, whom he loved to tease and see if he could outrun, though Mel always caught him. She ran like a lion. Now Mel was a ghost of her former self. Something was very wrong with her.

Abby took him by the elbow. "Let's go to the kitchen." He resisted her effort to turn him and stepped past her onto the porch. The sky was dark overhead and even darker to the south. The neighborhood was silent and deserted. Jordan had the eerie impression that a large bomb had gone off, and everybody had fled. Coughing from the smoke, he looked warily down the street. He didn't know why Mandy was hiding her motorcycle, and he didn't care. Before she returned, he would have to tell his sister a thing or two about trusting the wrong people.

# CHAPTER THREE

Abby faced three immediate problems.

Since Mel had come within a whisker of Mandy stabbing her, she had followed Abby like a shadow and not spoken a word. Abby had seen kids in shock before. Some stopped eating, others cried non-stop, and some, like Mel, retreated into themselves. The best approach, Abby thought, was to back off and give Mel time to recover.

Jordan had apparently forgotten everything she had told him after she, Timmy, and Mandy returned from the airport last night. He only remembered Mandy as the girl who, along with her gang members, had tried to steal their supplies in Portland, and then abandoned them in New Hampshire. Abby would tell him what happened again, but her first priority was to take care of his wound.

Finally, Brad's gang was out there somewhere. She hoped the gang had forgotten about them, but, as a precaution, they needed to prepare for Brad's return.

Abby sat opposite Mel and Jordan at the kitchen table.

"Mel's not feeling well." Abby told Jordan about Brad's gang and what had happened. "Stay with her. I'm going to look for bandages and something to clean your cut."

He rolled his eyes. "I'm fine."

Abby glowed inside. Stubbornness was a Leigh family trait, and Jordan's attitude proved he was getting stronger. She had never seen her brother more agreeable than when he had been close to death.

"You can't let it get infected," she said. "The illness might have weakened your immune system. Even a small cut could be dangerous."

He shook his head. "Abby, I can't believe Mandy is here."

She narrowed her eyes, wishing that he would be a little less stubborn.

Soap was almost as valuable as food and water, Abby thought, as she groped inside the dark cabinets below the sink, where her mom had often kept a spare bottle of dish liquid. No luck. Next, she checked the laundry room. On the island, they used detergent for bathing, saving one brand for their monthly shampoos because it stung the eyes less. Finding nothing, she looked inside the washing machine, but the well was clean of detergent residue.

Abby knew that alcohol killed germs. Remembering where her mother kept liquor, she rushed to the closet and reached up to the top shelf. She cursed the scavengers who had already found the whiskey.

Head down in near defeat, she entered the bathroom, not expecting to find much. Kids would have looked here first for medicines and toilet paper. Catching her reflection in the mirror, Abby gulped. She felt so much stronger than the ragged girl who stared back. She bared her teeth, and amused herself with the thought that she could scare Brad's gang away with this face.

She swung open the medicine cabinet door and grabbed the only item on the shelf, which she quickly tossed on the floor. They didn't have much use for an earwax removal kit.

All of a sudden, Abby's knees buckled, and she gripped the sink to steady herself. The toilet was in one piece. Few toilets had survived the winter on Castine Island. The water in the bowl turned to ice and the expansion cracked the porcelain. How strange that a toilet could stir such a flood of emotions.

It reminded her of Kevin, the boy she had loved. Three months earlier, Kevin Patel had told the survivors on Castine Island that the water in toilet tanks was safe to drink. Not long after that, he had died from the epidemic.

Tingles bubbled deep inside and boiled over, and she erupted in a fit of giggles and sobs. Doubled over at the waist, Abby laughed so hard her stomach ached and cried so hard she felt her lungs might burst. Tears of absurdity mixed with tears of sorrow streamed down her cheeks.

A hand squeezed her shoulder. "What's wrong?" Deep creases cut across Jordan's brow.

Wiping away tears, Abby caught her breath and simply shook her head. He'd never believe her. "We need something to drink, and…"

He lowered his eyes. "I spilled the beer."

"What?"

"It was an accident," Jordan shot back.

Abby removed the tank lid. "We have plenty to drink."

His eyes widened. "Kevin!"

Maybe now he'd understand her strange outburst. She cupped some water from the tank and brought her nose close to it. Dejected, she opened her fingers and let the water dribble out. "Bleach."

Jordan pointed out the dispenser hooked over the lip of the tank. "Mom used these all the time. I'm sure the upstairs toilet has one too."

Then she lit up with an idea. "Jordan, stick your hand in. The bleach will kill the germs."

He immersed his cut. Blood dissolved in the water, turning it red.

Abby peered into the tank. "Is it working? Do you feel anything?"

"Does stinging count?"

She winked. "Mom's looking out for us." She quickly looked away because further eye contact with her brother would lead to more tears.

"Abby, I'm sorry about the beer."

"Forget it. There wasn't much left anyway. I've been thinking we could drink from the Charles River." The river separated Boston from Cambridge. It was a half mile away.

Jordan swished his hand back and forth, making little wavelets. "Dad used to say that if you fell in the Charles, you'd need a tetanus shot."

Abby smiled sadly. "The polluters are gone. I saw lots of kids camped along the river." Then she swung the bathroom door closed and lowered her voice. "I need to talk to you about Mandy before she comes back."

Jordan scoffed. "She left us to die. What more do I need to know?"

"When I went to the airport, there were thousands of kids ahead of me in line. Do you remember me going?"

He nodded reluctantly.

"I wasn't sure I could live long enough to get a pill for myself. And if I did get pills, I had no idea how I'd get back to Cambridge. Jordan, you were dying." He lowered his eyes, and she saw his lip quivering. "I met Timmy outside the airport. He came up to me and took my hand. We stuck together the whole time we waited. Later on, I heard motorcycles. Kenny rode by first. Then Mandy stopped and gave me two pills. One for me and one for you."

Jordan chuckled coldly. "What, did she feel guilty that she left us to die?"

Abby ignored the comment. "She brought Timmy and me here on her motorcycle. We found you on the couch, and you weren't breathing. I crushed the pill and put the powder into your mouth. We did CPR. I pumped your chest while Mandy gave you mouth-to-mouth resuscitation." Abby paused to let that sink in. "She saved our lives."

Jordan was silent for a few seconds. "Why would she give up pills? It makes no sense." He shook his head. "Abby, there's something she wants from us. Don't be so gullible"

Abby took a deep breath. The only way Jordan would understand Mandy's motivation was if she shared Mandy's secret. The one she had confessed just before they left the airport.

"Jordan, after the night of the purple moon, the mainland was very different from Castine Island. Everyone panicked. Mandy was no exception." Abby struggled to get the words out. "Mandy left her little brother in the woods."

He cocked his head. "What's that supposed to mean?"

"He was three years old. She took him into the woods and left him there, because the older kids in her gang thought anyone under the age of nine was too hard to care for."

Jordan pulled his hand from the tank. "She murdered him!" he cried. "No!"

"Fine," he hissed sarcastically. "She just left him in the woods to starve to death. Wait, was it in the winter? Then she left him to freeze to death.

Abby, are you crazy? What more do you need to know? Did we abandon Toucan? What about Clive and Chloe? They were babies. Were they too hard to care for?"

"The mainland was different."

Jordan glared. "If you and I had lived in Portland, would we have taken Touk out to the woods?" he muttered and looked away. "You know the answer."

"Mandy will never forgive herself. Ever."

"Good," he fired back.

"Jordan, she made a mistake."

"Some mistake."

Even though Jordan had tuned her out, Abby had to finish telling him why she thought Mandy had changed, why she trusted her.

"Mandy gave us the pills because Timmy was with me. I saw the way she looked at Timmy. Mandy has a big heart and something about Timmy touched her. She'll protect him. I know it."

"She'll leave him just the way she left her brother," Jordan stammered.

Abby realized the revelation had intensified Jordan's hatred of Mandy. Was her brother right? She couldn't know for sure how Mandy would react in the future.

"Think what you want," she said. "We need Mandy to make it to Castine Island. We all need to work as a team."

He nodded. "We'll use Mandy to help us find a boat, but there's no way she's going with us to the island. Timmy and Mel are welcome. I'm not inviting someone who murdered her own brother."

Jordan opened the door and immediately jumped back. Mandy was standing right outside.

Abby gasped for breath, feeling as if all the air had been sucked out of the room. How long had she been standing there?

Mandy raised her hand. In it was a small knife. "I found this on the floor." Her voice bled with sadness. All of a sudden she fixed an icy stare on Jordan, and he stared back. Abby saw that his hands were shaking until he anchored them against his legs. A chill rippled through Abby from the pure hatred in both their eyes. Mandy tossed the knife on the floor, turned and left.

Jordan gave her a knowing look. "Convinced now?" He picked up the knife and slipped it into his back pocket.

Of all the problems Abby was facing, Brad's gang just fell to the bottom of the list.

# CHAPTER FOUR

Jordan pressed back against the wall. Mandy perched on the kitchen counter to his right, higher up than he was. He figured she had chosen the spot to intimidate him. He avoided looking at her.

Sitting on the floor nearby, Timmy was building a tower of wooden blocks. The boy had found Jenga upstairs in Jordan's old bedroom.

Mel sat mute at the table opposite Jordan, sniffling every now and then. He still found it hard to believe it was really Mel Ladwick. The most striking difference was her eyes. They were just haunted. What had she seen?

Abby was in the dining room looking for something to bandage his hand. He wished she'd hurry up.

Jordan looked at the bottle of murky water on the table and licked his lips. Mandy had supposedly collected rainwater from a blowup swimming pool in the yard where she'd hidden her motorcycle, but he had yet to take a drink. Even Mel, with her crazy eyes, too traumatized to talk, had taken a sip, but he refused to accept water from the girl who had murdered her little brother.

Jordan watched his hand slide forward as if it had a mind of its own. The pull of the water proved greater than his distrust of Mandy. He wrapped his fingers around the bottle and brought it to his lips. The sip pooled beneath his tongue and dirt stuck in the cracks between his teeth. He tilted his head back and let the muddy water sluice down his throat. It only nibbled at his thirst, and he wanted more, but he wouldn't give Mandy the satisfaction.

He turned his attention to the pile of mostly dead bugs—an assortment of wings, legs, heads, and bodies of squished crickets and grasshoppers that Timmy had pulled from his pocket in two fistfuls. Timmy had collected the bugs in the front yard, which he called cricket heaven. Jordan thought how the epidemic had destroyed much of the human population, but other species were thriving as a result. A grasshopper leg twitched. He put a pinch of unmoving parts in his mouth and started chewing. Disgusting! But the protein would make him stronger. He swallowed too soon and felt spiny appendages sticking in the back of his throat.

With an aftertaste of insects lingering, Jordan glanced at the basement door and thrilled at a sudden memory of creamy chocolate, sugary raisins, chewy fillings. He nearly blurted out that he knew about a candy stash. Two Halloweens ago, he had gotten a large haul—two pillowcases filled to the brim—and worried that Mom would confiscate the candy, he had hidden some in a shoebox in the one place that she refused to enter: the messy basement. Candy was way better than bugs, but with Mandy around, he'd keep the stash a secret for now.

"Look!" Timmy shouted. With gleaming eyes, he added a new Jenga block to the tower. At least three feet tall, the tower wobbled and then toppled. "Anyone want to play with me?"

Mandy hopped off the counter and sat next to Timmy. Jordan shook his head, seeing Mandy's red-rimmed eyes and wet cheeks. Instead of staring him down as he imagined, she'd been crying. She wiped her eyes and added a block to the tower. Something inside Jordan softened, and he felt the pull to join them. Then he tightened his stomach and pushed back in his chair, reminding himself what Mandy had done to her brother.

Abby returned with a strip of cloth and a safety pin. As she wrapped his wound, Jordan's thoughts returned to the candy in the basement. How could he get it and then share it with everyone except Mandy?

Abby addressed the group. "I don't think we should stay here. The kids who chased Mel might come back. We can go to the O'Brien's house next door."

"Nobody's going to mess with us," Mandy said.

"Abby, you're right." Jordan nodded to his sister. "We should switch houses."

Mandy shook her head. "There are gangs everywhere. Anytime we move, they might see us. I'm not worried about four kids."

He faced her and blurted, "We'll go, you stay here." He spoke without thinking. How then would he get the candy in the basement?

"We're staying together," Abby spat as she shot Jordan a nasty look. "Someone should keep a lookout."

"I'll do it." Timmy playfully knocked over the tower of blocks and skipped away to the front door.

Mandy took a seat beside Jordan. "How's your hand feel?"

He slid his chair a few inches away and ignored her question. "Abby, we need to get pills, right? We have to go to the airport."

Mel choked on a sudden sob. They all waited to see if she had something to say, but Mel just lowered her eyes.

"After we get the pills, we need to find a boat," Jordan continued.

"I can't swim," Timmy shouted from his post.

"I'll teach you," Jordan told him.

Abby gave Timmy a reassuring smile. "Jordan's a good sailor. We won't capsize."

"You should wear a life jacket," Mandy said in a concerned tone.

Jordan sneered, making sure Mandy saw his cold expression. Her comment smacked of incredible insincerity. She leaves her baby brother in the woods to starve or freeze to death, and now she wants to make sure Timmy wears a life jacket. Maybe Abby was right. The guilt was eating Mandy alive. *Eat away!*

He turned to Abby. "The first place to check for a boat is the Charlestown Yacht Club." They had both taken sailing lessons there. "Some people used to put their boats in the water in March, and one of those would be perfect, because I need to find one with a hull that ice hasn't damaged. They stored sails inside the club, and some of the boats might have a spare mainsail below deck too. We won't get far without a good mainsail."

"Can you take Jordan on your motorcycle?" Abby asked Mandy. "Charlestown's about four miles from here."

"I'll walk," Jordan grunted.

"Don't be stubborn," Abby fired back, zapping him with an angry, big-sister look.

He twisted his mouth and looked away, knowing Abby was right. Walking to the yacht club would take a long time, and it would be exhausting. He needed to save his energy to fix a boat.

Jordan inhaled and turned to Mandy. Surprised, he paused. What had happened to the tough-talking member of a motorcycle gang? Biting her lip and hunched over, she looked like a sad, frightened ten-year-old.

It was at this moment he began to believe Abby. Mandy had saved their lives. It still freaked him out that she gave him CPR, though.

Jordan tried to imagine what had gone through her mind when she abandoned her brother. He understood that peer pressure could be strong, and he did not doubt that Kenny, the leader of Mandy's gang, could be persuasive. After all, Kenny had tricked him into revealing where the scientists were handing out the pills.

"Fine, Mandy can give me a ride, but she's not coming with us to the island."

Timmy blurted out, "Why not?" He appeared to be on the verge of tears.

He heard sniffling, and this time it wasn't Mel. Mandy was crying.

Jordan gave a little snort. "Oh, all right, she can come with us."

Abby thanked him with her eyes. Then his sister placed her hand on Mel's.

"Do you live with anyone? They can come with us, too."

Jordan shot forward. "We won't have room on the boat without capsizing it. We can't invite half the city."

Mel burst into tears and buried her face in her hands. Jordan could have kicked himself. Everyone was crying, or about to cry, because of him. He felt bad, not for what he'd said, but for how he'd said it. Mel was in a fragile state, and the truth was, they'd be lucky to find a boat big enough to hold five of them.

"Hey, your friends can come to the island," he said. "Really. My friend Eddie and I will sail back. We'll make as many trips as it takes. It won't take long." He wanted to change the topic. "Shouldn't we go to the airport to get pills?"

All of a sudden Mel snapped her head up, eyes shining with wild terror. The hair on the back of Jordan's neck stood up. Mel cried out, "The airport's on fire."

# CHAPTER FIVE

Mel's words struck Abby like a sledgehammer. Nobody said anything.

Abby's eyes darted around the room. Jordan just sat there, pressing his palms against his forehead. Mandy had wrapped her arms around Timmy.

Mel stared right through Abby and spoke in a low, halting voice. "Two jets collided. One was taking off, the other was landing."

Timmy's face brightened. "The jet was bringing pills, right?"

Mandy pulled him closer.

"There was a huge explosion," Mel continued, ignoring Timmy's question. Abby wondered if Mel was even aware of who was in the room with her. "The flames spread, and then there was a chain reaction. Fuel trucks exploded one after another."

Jordan leaned forward. "Can you believe that all this smoke is from the airport? Logan is five miles away, but I knew I smelled oil burning."

"All the terminal buildings caught fire," Mel said. "It happened so fast."

Abby gasped. "The adults were in one of the buildings, and so many kids! Did anyone get out?"

Mel looked straight ahead with a deeply creased brow, as if she were watching the horrible event play out on a movie screen.

Abby squeezed Mel's hand. "When the terminal caught fire, were people able to get out?"

Mel paused a long moment. "I don't think anyone escaped."

They peppered Mel with questions all at once. "What did you do?" "What else did you see?" "Did you get hurt?" Abby was about to ask Mel if she got pills, but she caught herself. If Mel had enough pills, they might avoid a trip to the airport, but Abby told herself that she should first focus on her friend. Mel spoke in a lifeless tone. "I was leaving the airport when the jets crashed. I just stood there as everything exploded. Lots of smoke drifted over and I started choking. I took off my shirt to breathe through it. Then I thought about Steph and Alex."

Abby's jaw dropped. "Steph Simpson?" Steph was one of her best friends. They'd been in the same sixth grade class at the Monroe School.

Mel hiccupped and started crying. "Steph and Alex are my housemates. I needed to get Steph a pill. She was really sick. I entered the tunnel as fast as I could, and the smoke thinned out, so I was able to breathe. I ran the whole way through it. When I got out the other side, I noticed four kids were following me. One of them was really tall."

A lump formed in Abby's throat. Brad and his gang. "Timmy, look out the door, please."

The boy crossed his arms defiantly. "I took a turn already."

Mandy gave him a little smile. "Go on. We need to talk about what happened. I'll join you in a minute."

Timmy shuffled his feet to the door.

"Mel, why did they follow you?" Jordan asked.

"They figured she had pills." Mandy said. "Mel, did you hide the bag?"

Mel's lip trembled. "They saw it."

Jordan shrugged. "Well, other kids had pills, too."

Mandy smirked. "She looks like an easy mark."

Abby shuddered at Mandy's cold, calculating perspective, but it didn't seem to bother Mel at all.

Anger flooded Mel's voice as she continued. "They chased me down Mass. Ave. It was dark, but I could see where I was going in the moonlight. I cut through backyards, and I thought I lost them." Mel's eyes glassed over and her tone softened. "Abby, when I got home and saw your note, I couldn't believe that you and Jordan were really here."

The hard edge in her voice returned, and rage filled her eyes. "I went through the front door. It was dark inside. I called out for Steph and Alex.

When nobody answered, I went straight upstairs. Steph's fever had been keeping her in bed. But neither of them was up there. I started to panic. Then I figured that Alex might have moved her to the basement. It was cooler down there."

Mel paused and squeezed her hands together so hard it made her knuckles white. "I heard Alex shout something. She sounded frightened. Then I heard a thud that made me sick to my stomach." Mel's breathing quickened. "When I got to the top of the stairs, I saw a flashlight and heard strange voices. They were just coming up from the basement. I went down a few steps. Whoever had the flashlight, shined it on Alex's face. Alex wasn't moving, and there was a lot of blood. The beam moved to Steph. She was on the floor, too. Then I saw a boy holding a brick." Mel pounded the table with her fist. Abby's heart, already racing, jumped to her throat. "There was blood all over it, but he just tossed it on the floor like it was nothing.

"I ran into my bedroom and locked the door. Then I opened the window. We had practiced what to do if intruders got in our house. I lowered a rope out the window with one end tied to the radiator. The boy kicked the door open just as I swung my leg out. I let go of the rope and fell into a pile of leaves we'd made. He leaned out the window and shouted. Then a girl and a boy came around the corner and started chasing me. I ran straight here. When I got to your neighborhood, I realized I had led them here. First I led them to my house, then here to you. So I hid in the bushes across the street. For a while, I didn't think they'd find me. Then they saw your motorcycle."

Abby was trembling. "I saw you, Mel. You ran straight at them. You wanted them to chase you."

Mel clenched her jaw and nodded. "I ran for miles until I lost them for good."

Mandy placed her knife on the table. "You're certainly not as weak as you look, but the gang will be back. Abby, you were right. We should go to a new house."

"I hope they come back," Mel said through gritted teeth. Then she reached into her pocket and placed a bag of pills on the table.

Abby couldn't take her eyes off of the clear plastic bag with the CDC logo. Each tiny blue pill inside could save a life, yet they had already caused so much sorrow. A chill rippled through her. Would greed and fear cause more sadness and death before they could make it back to Castine Island with the pills?

# CHAPTER SIX

Jordan watched in shock as Mandy picked up the bag of pills and slipped it into her jacket pocket. He shot to his feet. "What are you doing?"

"They're safer with me," she replied in a matter-of-fact tone.

He turned to Abby. "Say something!"

Abby, who was comforting Mel, glared at him. "Can we stop fighting?" She had a sharp edge to her voice.

Heat flared in Jordan's cheeks. His sister's reaction agitated him, but what Mandy had just done put every life on Castine Island at risk. "They're not yours," he stammered. "The pills belong to Mel." He feared Mandy heard his voice shaking.

She patted her knife. "Nobody's going to mess with me. Don't worry."

Blood pounded in his ears as he cursed his stupidity. He had let his guard down, and Mandy had made her move. Now, the pills were even more valuable than before.

He felt for the tiny paring knife in his back pocket. Then he quickly withdrew his hand, knowing he was no match for Mandy and her long blade.

What if she rode off and took the pills? Jordan thought of those on Castine Island who would require the antibiotic soon. Toby was probably the most at risk. Whiskers had sprouted from his chin and his voice was cracking, sure signs he had entered puberty. Jordan worried about his girlfriend, Emily, too.

Mandy held Emily's future in the palm of her hand, or more precisely, inside her jacket pocket closest to the knife dangling from her belt.

"They're back," Timmy cried.

Abby rushed to the door, with Mel and Mandy right behind.

Jordan gripped the back of a chair and lifted it an inch to gauge its weight. If he swung it hard enough, he could do serious damage. His heart pounded in his throat as he contemplated what to do.

"Oh my God," Abby cried.

"It's not them," Mel said, sounding disappointed.

Mandy put her arm around Timmy's shoulder and pulled him close. "Those are the kids coming back from the airport. They never got any pills."

Jordan released his grip. He might strike Timmy. Even if Timmy stepped away, Jordan didn't think he could do it. Nor could he live with himself if Mandy left with the pills.

Jordan joined the others. His eyes widened at the sight of kids trudging down Pearl Street in a line that extended as far down the street as he could see. With their heads lowered, they looked like zombies, or like soldiers returning from a battle, which they had lost.

Although a few younger kids were in the mix, most seemed to be over twelve. The older ones were walking the slowest. Some kids moved in groups of three to six, but others walked alone, stragglers who were unable to keep up with the pack.

Abby sniffled. "There must be something we can do for them."

Jordan had a sudden sinking feeling. He knew the tone all too well. His sister wanted to save the world. Abby might well present a bigger threat to the survival of their friends on Castine Island than Mandy.

Abby, her cheeks wet from tears, moved into the living room to watch out the window. They all followed her.

"Take a good look at them," Mandy said. "That's how we should act when we go outside. If you walk like you're sick, nobody will think you have pills."

Jordan had to admit that was a good idea.

Several kids broke from the line and climbed the steps of a house across the street from them. Jordan stuck his head out the window, careful to avoid the glass shards, and saw more kids entering houses further up the street. "I didn't think anyone lived around here."

"They're going home," Mel said. "Home to die."

Abby paced. "We have to do something."

"There's nothing we can do," he said. "Do you see how many of them are out there?"

"Jordan, that was us two days ago." Her eyes pleaded. "We were that sick."

Jordan put himself between Abby and the window, trying to block her view. "What's the most important thing? Getting home to Toucan, right?" He shot Mandy a quick glance. "Taking the pills to our friends."

Abby stepped around him and answered with a gasp.

A boy who'd been stumbling along, now veered onto the sidewalk in front of their house. He was taking awkward strides, but, somehow, he stayed on his feet. Jordan's legs tensed and twitched, as if he were the one losing his balance. The boy braced himself against a telephone pole briefly, then placed both hands on his knees. He was wearing black rubber rain boots, and a bottle of water dangled like a pendulum from a loop of rope around his neck. He was making a horrible wheezing noise.

"We need to get him," Abby said in a determined tone.

Instead of blocking her view, Jordan moved between her and the door to block her from going outside. "There are thousands like him."

Abby held out her hand to Mandy. "Give me a pill."

Mandy shook her head. "He's too far gone."

Jordan hoped the boy would die quickly to end his suffering.

Abby's eyes flared with anger. "We saved Jordan. We can save the boy. Mandy, give me a pill."

Mandy kept her hands by her side.

"Give me a pill," Abby shrieked. Then she lunged and grabbed at Mandy's pocket.

Jordan wrapped his arms around his sister. She struggled weakly. His own lack of strength surprised him, and he wondered if he could hold on. Pressed against her, he felt both their hearts racing.

Just then, the boy crumpled to his knees. Abby cried out and went limp. Jordan released her. If any of the marchers heard his sister's cry, they showed no curiosity. Nobody stopped to help the dying boy, either.

"I'm going outside, with or without you," Abby told him.

He grabbed her wrist. "Abby, he can get pills in Portland." He hated himself for lying. The CDC had designated Portland, Maine a Phase II city. The scientists said they would distribute pills there in a month. If he and Abby never made it back, the Castine Island survivors were planning to get pills in Portland, but that boy would not survive another hour, much less a day, and Abby knew it. Jordan also hated himself for deciding who would get the pills—who would live and who would die—but he held onto her wrist. She drilled him with such an accusing look of horror and disgust that he had to look away.

Mandy wrapped her arms around Abby and drew her close, and suddenly Abby started to cry. Only then did Jordan let go.

The front door opened. Adrenaline flooded through his body. Mandy craned her neck, eyes wild with panic. "Where's Timmy?" she cried. The boy was gone. She pulled out her knife and ran to the door.

Looking through the window, Jordan saw Timmy skip down the steps. When Timmy was halfway to the sidewalk, he launched into the air and landed in a crouched position. Scampering over to the dying boy, he removed the water bottle from around his neck. Then, with no waste of time, he raced back to the stairs with his bounty, where Mandy met him, knife drawn.

Jordan watched in horror as others swooped in and stripped the dying boy of his valuables. Two different kids pulled off his boots, and each headed off with a single boot.

Jordan took a deep breath, fighting back tears. It didn't help that Abby was weeping beside him. Had his decision to hold her wrist led to the gruesome scene outside? No, the boy was too far gone. He would keep telling himself that until he believed it. Then he surrendered to his tears and sobbed openly.

# CHAPTER SEVEN

Abby rifled through the kitchen cabinets in search of containers with lids. They needed to store water for the trip home, and she had suggested they could get water from the kiddie pool down the street where Mandy had filled her bottle. Nobody had argued with her, but then again, nobody had said it was a good idea either.

Jordan was staring out the front door, Mel was slumped on the couch, Mandy sat at the kitchen table with a deeply furrowed brow, and Timmy was playing Jenga.

The busier Abby kept her hands, the less time she spent thinking. She couldn't shake the image of the dying boy. If they had moved him inside and given him a pill, he might have been recovering now. On the other hand, he might have died anyway. They would never know.

She understood why Jordan and Mandy had stopped her from going outside. Help one kid, turn around, and there's another kid just as desperate, and another... The boy was a grain of sand in the desert, and if she had saved that single grain, they would have had one less pill for their friends on the island.

She didn't blame Timmy for what he had done, either. He was living by the rules of the mainland, the same rules which he had been following since the night of the purple moon. Survival of the fittest. Or was it survival of the cruelest? Abby's mind could make sense of these things, but not her heart.

She reached deeper into the cabinet until her shoulder bumped against the frame. Patting her hand along the shelf, she felt a spaghetti strainer, then a waffle maker. Memories of family dinners and her mom cooking breakfast exploded in her mind like dazzling fireworks. Her mouth watered, reminding her of how badly they needed more than bugs to eat.

She swept aside mouse droppings, and her fingers followed an electric cord to a blender. Her pulse quickened when she brushed a metal clasp. In the far corner of the shelf, behind a curtain of sticky cobwebs, she felt a lunch box and another one beside it.

In the second grade, she had proudly carried her peanut butter and jelly sandwiches to school in the Teenage Mutant Ninja Turtles lunch box. Jordan had lugged a Power Rangers lunch box, believing that it gave him superpowers. How they could use those superpowers now!

She flipped open the clasp of her lunch box and removed the thermos. She did the same for Jordan's. If they filled both thermoses and Mandy's bottle, the five of them would have enough water to survive three days at sea.

She stood before the others. Timmy was the only one not moping or lost in thought, he was having too much fun adding blocks to his teetering tower.

"Mandy, you and Jordan can get water," Abby said. "We'll stay here and catch more bugs for the trip home."

She couldn't make Jordan and Mandy be friends, but if they worked together, she hoped they would start to forge a bond of trust.

"I'll go and take Timmy," Mandy said.

Jordan sprang to life. "Timmy should stay here."

"Why?" Mandy asked. "He can come with me."

"He's better at catching crickets," Jordan replied.

"We'll ask Timmy." Mandy got down on one knee. "Want to come with me?"

"Sure," Timmy said.

Abby muttered in agitation. A simple suggestion had turned into a major dispute.

Jordan moved closer to Timmy. "You want some candy?"

Timmy's face lit up. "What kind?"

"All kinds!"

"Twizzlers?" Timmy cried.

"Yeah, lots of Twizzlers," Jordan said.

Mandy furrowed her brow, and Abby felt just as confused. What was her brother talking about?

Jordan told them about the candy he had hidden in the basement two Halloweens ago. Abby thought it sounded like something he would do.

Mandy put her hands on her hips. "Go get it."

"Sorry," he replied with a shrug. "Timmy and I have to hunt for it."

Muttering under her breath, Mandy grabbed the thermoses and headed for the door.

"Wait," Abby jumped up. "I'll go with you."

# CHAPTER EIGHT

Convinced he had found a way to secure the pills, Jordan watched Mandy and Abby step out of the house. Timmy was the answer. He'd watched how Mandy treated the boy and figured that Abby was right. Mandy saw herself as Timmy's protector. He didn't care why she felt that way. All that mattered was that Mandy would not leave without Timmy. Jordan knew that he or Abby had to stay with the boy at all times.

He handed the paring knife to Mel. "Timmy and I are going to the basement. Shout if you need us."

She gripped the handle. "I hope they come back."

He knew she meant Brad's gang. "Mel, just shout if anyone comes, okay?"

He waited until she nodded, which took more than a few seconds.

In the dining room, Jordan found Timmy playing with a deck of cards. That annoyed him. He had asked him to search for a butane lighter or a book of matches in the drawers of the sideboard. "Did you find matches?"

Timmy shook his head and gathered up the cards. "Can I have these?"

"Yes. Let's keep looking."

Timmy crammed the deck into his pocket, where it probably shared space with bug parts and who knew what else.

A moment later, Timmy lifted a photo from a drawer. "Who's that?"

A lump formed in Jordan's throat. "My mom and dad." He held the photo. His parents had been in Paris on their honeymoon, the Eifel Tower in the background. He guessed they were in their mid-twenties, and they looked so happy. It was strange to think they would go on to raise a family and then their lives would end abruptly just because a stupid comet passed by the Earth.

"My dad's in the army."

Timmy's voice startled Jordan.

"The army, huh?"

Timmy saluted. "The U.S. Army. He's a sergeant. He's coming home after he wins the war."

Many survivors spoke about their parents as if they were traveling or working in a different city or visiting a relative; they'd be home any day now. Jordan had known kids to even make up what their parents did. Timmy's father might have been a stockbroker. Jordan certainly didn't fault him for making up stories. He had his own fantasies to cope with the loss of loved ones.

"The army has special tents that keep the germs out," Timmy added. "Soldiers sleep in tents."

"Guess we're going to have to find the candy in the dark," Jordan said, steering the conversation back to the main topic.

They stood before the pitch-black opening to the basement.

Jordan's heart raced. "When did you eat your last candy bar?" He wasn't quite ready to go down the steps. When he was five or six years old, Abby had told him that monsters lurked in the basement. Now his mind was cooking up some pretty terrible things.

"December second."

Jordan squinted with a smile. "You remember the date?"

"That's my birthday. I turned nine."

Jordan held out his hand. "Ready?"

"I'm not afraid," Timmy cried.

"I am." He winked and grabbed Timmy's hand. Clearing away spider webs with his free hand, Jordan led the way. He found the webs comforting. Their presence meant that nobody else had been down the stairs, at least not recently.

When they were halfway down the steps, the last of the light from above dimmed and disappeared, and they continued downward, one slow, careful step at a time. The familiar smell of mold and mildew stirred his imagination, and he trembled. "So what else do you eat besides grasshoppers?"

"Pigeons." Timmy's voice was rock steady.

"For real?"

"Yeah, they're easy to catch."

"Castine Island doesn't have any pigeons, but there are lots of seagulls."

"Do you eat 'em?"

Jordan planted his right foot on the concrete floor. "We eat fish. Careful." They stood next to each other in the darkness. Jordan took a step and kicked something. He tried another direction and bumped into something else. He moved Timmy's hand to the back of his shirt. "Hold on to me."

Jordan kept both hands in front of him for protection as he explored slowly. He bumped into a bicycle. He wondered if he could ride the bike to the Charlestown Yacht Club and avoid going with Mandy on her motorcycle. His hand followed the handlebar stem to the tire, which was flat. So was the back tire. Stuck with Mandy, he thought. After he took several more steps, his fingertips skittered over the smooth cover of a magazine. A pile of magazines rose to his waist. They were National Geographics, his landmark. Buried treasure was nearby.

"Can you smell the chocolate?" he asked Timmy.

"Nope. Can you?"

"I can taste it." Jordan smacked his lips loudly.

Taking sidesteps to the right and towing Timmy through the dark, he patted his hands on three more magazine piles and then reached behind the fourth pile. His heart sped up when he felt the top of the shoebox.

"Got it!" Jordan picked up the box. His stomach dropped. Something was wrong. It weighed hardly anything.

He removed the cover. The confetti of candy wrappers inside crinkled as he swished his hand back and forth. He felt the rough cardboard edges of the hole gnawed at one end. Mice had eaten everything. He brought the box to his nose. Even the odor of chocolate had disappeared.

# CHAPTER NINE

Wading through tall grass, Abby cut across the O'Brien and Pydah backyards and then onto the Sherock property. Every step sent a spray of grasshoppers exploding upward like shrapnel from a land mine.

She'd convinced Mandy this route was safer. "We won't run into Brad's gang," she'd said. That was true, but she mostly wanted to avoid seeing the kids on Pearl Street, an endless parade of faces, empty of hope.

Poking through the clouds, the sun lit up yellow dandelions in the tall grass. The scents of cherry and dogwood blossoms mingled with the fading smoke from the airport inferno.

Abby pointed to a stucco house ahead. "You know what those people kept in their bathtub? A boa constrictor. The rumor was that Mr. and Mrs. Sherock owned a traveling zoo."

Eyes forward, Mandy continued her ice queen impersonation, and vaulted over a waist-high, chain-link fence.

"They had a lion, too," Abby lied, hoping for some reaction. Getting none, she hopped the fence. "How much further?"

Mandy gestured. "The green house."

Abby nodded to herself. Three words. It was a start. As she was trying to remember who used to live in the green house, she stumbled and pitched forward. She broke her fall in the tall grass with her hands. The ground smelled sweet, and she was tempted to stay in this other world a while longer. She rolled onto her side to get up and screamed when a withered hand pressed against her cheek.

Mandy reached for her knife and assumed a crouched position.

Abby saw the rest of the corpse. It was well hidden in the forest of grass. "No, no," she croaked. "It's…" She sat down, buried her hands in her face, and wept.

She shouldn't have been surprised to find a body here. The comet had appeared at midnight, and what better place to watch the heavens turn purple than your backyard. The deadly bacteria had penetrated the atmosphere as the stargazers marveled at the beauty.

Mandy helped her up. Arm in arm, they continued on their way, albeit stepping more carefully. Even though Mandy had yet to utter a fourth word since they had left the house, something about her was different. Abby sensed Mandy was taking the first baby steps to trusting her and wanting her as a friend.

When they climbed over the next fence, they were in the backyard of the green house. Abby saw Mandy's motorcycle stowed next to the porch, concealed behind three trashcans.

Mandy pointed out the kid's pool, which had seen better days. The air had bled from the circular bladders of blue plastic. The flat, crinkled bottom held rainwater covered with a skim of green pine pollen and brown oak leaves. Abby unscrewed the Power Rangers thermos and placed it on its side; the muddy water sluiced in. Mandy lifted the edge of the pool to make the water run into the bottle faster. Then Abby filled the Mutant Ninja Turtles thermos. Finally, she cleared away the debris on the surface with her hand and drank like a horse.

"I'm sorry I didn't give you a pill," Mandy said.

"I understand."

"I'm not going to lie. I think it would have been wrong to waste a pill on a stranger. I know you don't feel that way."

"I don't know how I feel anymore."

Mandy started to continue, but then she stopped and looked away from Abby. Almost a minute passed with neither of them saying anything. Then Mandy took a deep breath. "I don't blame Jordan for the way he feels about me. I can't change what I did."

Abby bit her lip. She wanted to give Mandy time to speak her mind.

Mandy shook her head, looked away, and cursed under her breath. "I hate myself," she said finally.

Abby gave Mandy a hug. "Things are different on Castine Island. It's not like the mainland. I don't mean to say it's perfect. Kids are kids, you know. We have disagreements and everything, but at least we try to work together."

Mandy furrowed her brow. "Jordan doesn't want me to go."

"Hey, I know my brother. He says things he doesn't mean. He's frightened. He'll never admit it, but he's afraid of the trip home. I am, too. If we stick together, we'll make it. Timmy's going to love the island. There are other kids his age. It's a great place to grow up. He can act like a kid again. He won't have to steal just to eat. Besides, Timmy needs you."

"He doesn't need anyone." Mandy raised her eyebrows. "He's tough."

"Tough on the outside. Trust me, he needs you."

Mandy sighed and stared into the distance. "Maybe I need him, too." It was barely a whisper, and Abby thought Mandy might have been saying it to herself. Could Timmy help heal her shattered heart?

Abby took Mandy's hand. "I think we could both use some chocolate."

The corners of Mandy's mouth curled up, but the sadness in her eyes remained.

# CHAPTER TEN

"Look how much there was." Jordan showed the shoebox of empty wrappers to Abby and Mandy, wanting to prove he hadn't made up the Halloween story.

They were all disappointed about the candy, but they had other things to discuss.

They talked about the plan to return to the island. They had a good cache of crickets for their time at sea, and about six liters of drinking water. Jordan rattled off some useful things they could use: winter jackets, garbage bags, shoelaces. Abby, Mel, and Timmy, who would stay in the house while he went to find a boat, could hunt for the items.

Jordan grudgingly accepted that Mandy would have to take him on her motorcycle. It was the fastest way. And in this new world, speed was survival.

"We'll go to Charlestown first," he told them. "If I don't find a boat there, we'll head north. There's a port in Lynn and a really big harbor in Marblehead. Wherever I find a boat, I'll sail it back to Charlestown."

"Isn't Charlestown close to the airport?" Mel asked in a concerned tone.

"The dock's about a hundred yards from one of the runways. "I don't think the fire would have spread to the yacht club. That hundred yards is all water."

Abby wanted to know how the others would get to Charlestown. "That could be the most dangerous part of the trip. After the fire, kids will be desperate to get pills."

Mel shrugged. "We'll walk. Five miles is nothing. We'll hang our heads and shuffle."

"After I drop off Jordan, I can give the rest of you rides," Mandy offered.

Jordan's heart beat faster. He imagined a situation where it would just be Mandy and Timmy on the motorcycle. Would that tempt Mandy, who still held on to the pills, to take off? He couldn't chance it. "Timmy, come with me and Mandy. I could use a hand."

"Jordan, that's not safe," Abby said.

He made a face. "The three of you rode on the motorcycle. Timmy's small."

"I mean, it won't be safe at the yacht club."

Jordan gave the thumbs up to Timmy. "We'll watch out for each other, right? Four eyes are better than two."

Abby persisted. "Jordan, you might have to swim out to a boat. You'd leave Timmy alone on the shore."

Jordan did in fact expect he'd have to swim out to the moored boats, knowing the odds of finding a rowboat would be slim. Survivors would have found rowboats useful for fishing and would have claimed them by now.

Timmy piped up, "I'm not afraid to be alone."

Jordan let out a low whistle. "Timmy knows how to survive better than all of us combined."

"I know you're not afraid," Abby told the boy. "But none of us has to be alone, except for Jordan, and he'll be on a boat. We should always stay in pairs. It's safer."

"I can go with Jordan," Mel countered.

Jordan hung his head. His plan was sinking like a boat on the rocks. No sooner had he patched one hole than another one opened up.

Mandy shook her head. "Sorry, there's not enough room on the bike for me and two older kids."

Unknowingly, Abby shot another hole into his plan. "When Mandy comes back, she can give Timmy a ride. Mel and I will walk."

Jordan gulped, then tried his best to sound calm. "You three should walk together. Safety in numbers."

"Then Mandy would be alone," Abby pointed out.

Jordan wanted to stuff a sock in her mouth. Instead, he turned to Mandy. "If somebody is chasing you, wouldn't you rather be alone on your motorcycle."

She patted her knife. "Not too many people chase you when you know how to defend yourself."

Jordan felt like someone was holding him under water, and he only had a few molecules of oxygen left in his lungs. "Let's ask Timmy what he wants to do. Timmy, I can teach you how to rig a boat. It's really cool."

Timmy ran over to the Jenga game. "I want to stay here."

Jordan slumped back in the chair. Friends and loved ones on Castine Island might die because of a stupid game. Unless he came up with a new plan fast, Mandy could seize the opportunity and take off with Timmy, leaving them high and dry without the pills.

He had to find a way to tell Abby that without alerting Mandy. "There's something you should take with you," he told her.

From the sideboard drawer, he removed the photo of their parents on their honeymoon in Paris. Keeping his back to the others, he wrote in pencil on the back: Keep Timmy with you.

He allowed Mandy and Mel to glance at the photo. "Our mom and dad." Abby's eyes widened and glassed over with tears. When he passed her the photo, he made sure that only she saw his note. Her eyes opened wider and she gave him a stare of disbelief before nodding reluctantly.

~ ~ ~

Ten minutes after leaving the house, Jordan stood behind Mandy as she removed the trashcans blocking her motorcycle. Life surely was strange. Forty-eight hours earlier, Mandy had left him to die at the side of the road. Now they were a team of sorts.

He drank from the kiddie pool, then belched, tasting crickets, before helping Mandy push the motorcycle to the street.

His legs cramped up quickly, and his lungs burned from the exertion of pushing something so heavy. He shook his head in silent embarrassment, hoping Mandy didn't notice how weak he was. Still, he felt stronger than he had in weeks.

The kids walking down Pearl Street kept their distance. He wondered if the knife on Mandy's belt had anything to do with that.

"We need gas," Mandy said, speaking her first words since they'd left the house.

She could keep her mouth shut for the rest of the day for all he cared. He needed a ride to Charlestown and the pills, not a friend.

She produced a rubber tube and a fold-up knife from her pocket. She locked the blade in place, then, searching for a tank that held gasoline, worked her way up the line of cars parked on the street. She used the jackknife to pop open a locked lid. She unscrewed the cap and put her nose close to the opening. After striking out on the first six cars, she seemed pleased with the sniff test on a blue SUV. She wheeled the motorcycle next to it, fed one end of the tube into the gas tank of the car, gave a quick hard suck on the other end of the tube, and then inserted that end into the motorcycle tank.

Siphoning the gas seemed to take forever, and Jordan grew impatient. If they started out soon and he caught a few lucky breaks, they could all be heading to the island before dark. From the position of the sun, he guessed it was close to noon, but by the look of the gray clouds bunched up on the horizon, it might rain later on. Rain was not a huge problem. They'd be wet, cold, and miserable, but they'd survive. The biggest problem was nightfall. He needed light to rig a boat.

Mandy mounted the motorcycle, put on her helmet, and kick-started the engine. Jordan climbed on back and pointed which way to go. She shifted gears, and they were off.

He directed her through Medford Square and then toward the highway. She stayed on the streets unless a section of road became too crowded with kids, and then she didn't think twice about riding on sidewalks and lawns. Reluctantly, he had to admire her driving skills.

The four-lane highway, Route 93, was mostly free of survivors but clogged with abandoned vehicles. Mandy had no problem navigating around them with her motorcycle.

They took the Charlestown exit off the highway, leaning into the corner as they followed the off-ramp. Soon the Bunker Hill Monument came into view.

"Go to that thing," he shouted, pointing to the stone spire.

Rising from the city's highest point, the monument, which resembled a miniature Washington Monument, honored a Revolutionary War battle. Jordan couldn't remember which one, but the yacht club was a straight shot from the monument, on the other side of the hill.

At the top of the hill, he had a bird's-eye view of the airport two miles away. Wisps of black smoke rose from craters and from the terminals. A gruesome assortment of charred plane parts spread across the tarmac.

Jordan drew in a sharp breath at the scope of devastation. Until now, he had held out hope that the scientists might send more jets with pills. That hope went up in smoke as he witnessed the destruction. With all that debris, there was no way a jet could land on the runways.

When they had seen enough, Mandy coasted down the long, steep hill and took a left at the bottom. The entrance to the yacht club driveway was on the right side of the street, two blocks up. She turned in. Halfway down the driveway, Jordan spotted the first sign of trouble. There was no yacht club.

They rolled to a stop in the parking lot. The club had obviously burned long ago. One wall and a flagpole were all that remained standing. A charred flag dangled at half-mast from a rope.

Jordan climbed off the motorcycle. He half expected Mandy to leave straightaway, but she dismounted too.

When he spotted the five boats at moorings, his spirits revived. The hulls appeared to be in good shape; at least from this distance.

Then his spirits truly soared. Several boats had broken free of their moorings and had formed a boat graveyard along the shore, where they were stuck in the mud. It was a goldmine of spare parts. There had to be a set of sails in at least one of them. A mainsail would be nice, but he could make do with a jib. From all the boats available, he felt confident he could cobble together a single boat that would take them to Castine Island.

"Mandy, let me have the pills." He had nothing to lose.

She reached into her pocket, took out the bag, and held it out to him. He stared in disbelief. With one hand Mandy placed the bag in his hand, and with her other she curled his fingers around it. "They're safer with you. There are twenty-three pills left. I'm keeping one of them."

He started to speak, but the first words broke into stutter and he stopped in the middle of the unintelligible sentence.

She narrowed her eyes. "Count them if you don't believe me."

"Why?" he asked.

"Why did I keep a pill for myself?" She looked away. "In case Timmy comes with me. He'll reach puberty in a couple of years. Who knows what things will be like then?"

That wasn't his question. Ever since Abby had told him that Mandy had abandoned her brother, the question of how anyone could do that burned in his mind. He was just as curious about her sudden change of heart.

"Aren't you coming with us?"

Mandy pursed her lips and shook her head — a tense jiggle. "My grandparents lived on a lake in Northern Maine. They had a little cabin, nothing special. My mom used to take my brother and me there for Thanksgiving and Christmas. You have to go two miles down a logging road to reach the place. I don't think any survivors will be there. Timmy and I can fish, hunt and trap. Nobody will bother us." She looked away. "I hope Timmy wants to go."

Jordan stared at her, not knowing what to say.

"You and the others will always think of me as the girl who abandoned her little brother. Everyone will find out. And everyone will hate me."

"No, they won't hate..." His voice trailed off. "Mandy, how could you do it?" His voice was barely a whisper. "How..."

She looked right through him. "This is going to sound like an excuse." She spoke in a halting voice. "It's not. I take full responsibility. The morning after the moon turned purple, my mom wasn't in her room. She worked as a waitress at a fish restaurant, and she usually got home around midnight. That night, her restaurant was offering a special dinner on the terrace in honor of the comet. She told me she might be home later than normal. Sammy—my brother—was still sleeping. So I rode my bicycle to the restaurant. I don't have to tell you what it was like. The clouds were purple. The sunlight was purple. I came across cars in the road with the drivers slumped over the wheels. At the restaurant…"

Mandy paused to collect herself.

"I don't even remember riding home. Sammy and I stayed inside for the next two weeks. I had never been so scared in my life. We heard gunshots. Cars raced by. Some of the drivers were fifth and sixth graders. Then the house across the street burned down. At first I thought it was an accident. One morning I looked outside and saw some kids setting fires. I learned later that they were doing it because they thought it was cool to see a giant purple bonfire. I knew our house was next, so I grabbed Sammy's hand, and we ran to Jerry's house. Kenny was there."

A rancid mix of anger and hatred rose in Jordan's throat at the mention of the gang leader.

"Kenny was the toughest kid in my seventh grade class," Mandy continued. "He knew how to ride a motorcycle because his brother worked at a dealership. Kenny had already brought five motorcycles to Jerry's house. He made everyone feel safe. He'd go out and get us food and water. Gradually, other classmates joined us. He taught us all how to ride. He'd lead us on raids at stores like Target and Walmart. If anyone got in Kenny's way, he…"

Jordan didn't need Mandy to finish the sentence.

"We eventually moved into three houses on Berkley Street. It was Kenny's idea. He had us build a barricade at both ends of the street. We never questioned him. He had saved our lives and made us feel safe. I worshipped him. I would have done anything he asked without question.

"One day, he told us that anyone under the age of nine was nothing but a drain. They ate food and drank water, but they couldn't contribute to our survival. They couldn't fight. They were too young to steal. He told us that living with them jeopardized all of us. Of course, I knew it was wrong, but I never said anything. There were four kids under nine in our house, including Sammy. Kenny ordered the older brothers and sisters to put them on the backs of our motorcycles."

49

Tears streamed down Mandy's cheeks.

"We marched them into the woods. I told Sammy to stay there. I made up some story and said I'd come back for him soon. He kept calling for me as I walked away."

Mandy fired up the motorcycle. "I know what you're thinking, I'm a monster who murdered her baby brother. You're right. I am."

He wasn't thinking that at all. He was wondering what he would have done in the same situation. All of a sudden, Jordan didn't know.

Mandy put on her helmet, and he saw his reflection in the dark mask that hid her face. He hadn't moved a muscle while she was talking.

"Wait," he said.

She shifted the bike into gear and pulled away. The throb of the engine shrank to a pinprick of sound and then to silence.

# CHAPTER ELEVEN

Abby smiled at Timmy, sitting on the floor.

"Can I bring this with me?" he asked, clutching the Jenga game.

"Absolutely!"

"Awesome!" Timmy hurriedly stuffed the game into his backpack as if afraid she might change her mind.

She, Timmy, and Mel had moved to the O'Brien house next door soon after Mandy and Jordan left for the yacht club. Brad's gang wouldn't think to look for them there, but Abby had a second, more personal reason for suggesting they switch houses. She couldn't bring herself to go upstairs where her mother's body lay, and she didn't want Mel or Timmy to go up there, either.

Abby continued searching for items on Jordan's list. She hit the jackpot in a closet where she found a box of old ice skates. The skates produced a total of about ten feet of lacing.

She glanced out the window every few minutes. Kids still passed by in waves, but the gaps between the clumps were growing longer. Every time she spotted a tall boy, she asked Mel if it was Brad.

Together, she and Mel scrounged up about half of what Jordan wanted. Along with the laces, they found plastic garbage bags, which could serve as rain jackets, keep stuff dry, or plug a leaky hull.

Timmy caught more crickets in the backyard, and Abby ripped up a garbage bag and packed individual pouches of bugs for each of them to carry.

Hearing a motorcycle, Timmy charged out front. Abby figured it was good news that Mandy was returning so soon. She'd been gone less than an hour.

When Abby stepped onto the porch, she noticed a front door closing in the house across the street. A figure darted out of sight. She didn't get a good look at the person other than to see that he or she was wearing a baseball cap.

Mandy had dismounted her motorcycle and was speaking to Timmy. His head bobbed up and down. "Yes," he cried in response to whatever Mandy had told him. She gave him a bear hug, and he pushed back from her. She tousled his hair.

Timmy raced past Abby and Mel and into the house.

"How about 'excuse me'," Abby joked, but Timmy was already out of earshot.

"We'll have plenty of time to teach him manners," Mel said with a wry smile.

"That's her job." Abby gestured to Mandy.

Mandy stopped before them and looked away.

"Well," Abby asked. "How did it go?"

When Mandy didn't answer right away, Abby felt her stomach sink. "Did you guys find a boat?" Mandy remained silent and shifted from side-to-side. "Mandy, what's wrong?"

"Your brother found a boat. He has the pills. Timmy and I aren't going to the island with you."

Abby cocked her head. "Isn't the boat big enough to fit all of us? If not, Jordan can make two trips, remember?"

Mandy nodded. "It's big enough for you guys. I'm doing what's best for us."

Abby folded her arms, thinking of one way she could change Mandy's mind. "You care what happens to Timmy, right? Going to the island is what's best for him. We're planning to open a school for the younger kids."

"School!" Timmy blurted and made a face. "Forget it."

Abby wondered how long he'd been standing beside them. Mandy shoved her hands in her pockets and turned away.

"What if…?" Abby began.

Mandy spun around. "There is no what if. We're not going with you." Abby had seen that expression before. When she first met Mandy, she mistook it for toughness. It was really fear.

Mandy told them about her grandparents' cabin in Maine. Inside, she found a pen and paper and drew a map. "You're welcome anytime."

Abby knew then, Mandy and Timmy were leaving. She looked at the crude map. A cabin in the woods, next to a lake, far from this madness, sounded almost as good as Castine Island. She hoped Mandy would find the peace there that would allow her heart to heal.

She declined Mandy's offer to shuttle her and Mel to the yacht club, thinking if they were going to split up, it might as well be now.

Mandy handed Timmy her motorcycle helmet. "You ready?"

When he put it on, it swallowed his head and came to a rest on his shoulders. "It's too big!"

Mandy rapped the top with her knuckles. "Anybody home?" Her light-hearted tone did not match the grave doubt flickering in her eyes.

A moment later, the ultimate mainland survivors were gone, and it was just her and Mel, about to put their own survival skills to the test. Friends since the second grade, they were going after Jordan again—this time they'd greet him with a hug, not a headlock.

# CHAPTER TWELVE

Convinced that the only witness to his covert activity was the gull hovering overhead, Jordan brushed away ash at the base of the flagpole and scooped out a little hollow. He placed the bag of pills in the hole and covered it up with dirt. He didn't want to risk the pills dissolving while he swam out to a boat.

He walked to the end of the dock and stared at the cracks between the boards until his vision blurred. Mandy's words would not let go of him. Why hadn't she told him earlier the whole story of what had happened to her? He felt bad because he thought the way he had treated her was the reason she wasn't joining them.

He knelt and dipped his hand into the water. An aching sensation spread from his palm to each finger and up his arm. Boston Harbor would not warm up until the dog days of August—three months away.

The closest boat was forty yards away. He stripped to his underwear and placed his shoes and his clothing into his backpack. When he slipped into the icy water, he grunted, expelling a breath of air. With the pack on his back, he dog paddled out to his target.

The frigid water quickly sapped his energy, and he panicked. Numb from the neck down, he imagined what Abby's reaction would be when she arrived and found him doing the dead man's float. He struggled to keep his chin above the water, clawing wildly to thrust his head up enough to take each breath. By tensing up, he just sank deeper.

To break the cycle, he fixed his direction on the nearest boat and pretended he was a polar bear out for a leisurely dip. Webbing his fingers, he closed his eyes and paddled.

After a while, afraid that he might be veering away from his target, he opened his eyes, and a surge of excitement crackled through his frozen insides. The vessel, *Duke of York*, was only five feet away. He kicked his leaden legs until he reached the stern. After several failed attempts, he finally pulled himself up and rolled into the boat.

Sunshine streamed through a patch of blue, and it was tempting to lie there, tingling in the warm air. A gull cried out and water lapped against the hull. He sighed and got to work.

He guessed the sloop was about twenty-five feet long. A quick inspection revealed it had no sail, but he discovered three life jackets. He put one on, clipped the other two together, and clipped them to his. He might die of hypothermia, but he wouldn't drown.

He thought about a trick weight lifters used. They imagined that the heavy dumbbells they were about to lift were as light as a feather. Hot, cold, heavy, light—the mind could outsmart the body. Looking down at the water, he pretended it was a warm Jacuzzi he couldn't wait to jump into. The loud yell that came out of his mouth when he plunged into the icy water, indicated he had yet to master the trick.

Five minutes later, he rolled into *Stargazer*, a thirty-foot yacht that had everything they needed and then some. A canvas covering protected the sail, which was rolled on the boom. The lines were frayed, but he thought they'd hold. The hull had survived both pounding winter storms and a frozen harbor. Jordan whooped when he discovered a life raft. It came with a pressurized canister to inflate it, as well as an emergency kit of first-aid supplies, flares, an air horn, and protein bars. Jordan ripped the wrapping off a bar and tore off a hunk with his teeth. He worked the crumbs that tasted like sawdust into a paste and gagged it down.

Then Jordan entered the cabin where he discovered the skipper. The man slumped in his berth, his book open to the page he had been reading on the night of the purple moon. With blood pounding in his head, Jordan closed the book and covered the corpse with a blanket. "Thank you for letting us use your boat." He felt his throat pinch. "Once we're at sea, we'll give you a proper burial."

Jordan burst from the cabin and took a deep breath of fresh air. For a moment, he stood in awe of a single spear of light splitting the darkening clouds. Then he started to rig the *Stargazer*.

# CHAPTER THIRTEEN

Abby and Mel limped down the O'Brien's front steps. On the sidewalk, they dropped chins to their chests and joined the slow flow of kids moving down Pearl, pretending they, too, were walking to their graves. Mel had turned her jacket inside out, showing the white side to reduce the odds that Brad's gang might recognize her. She had also smeared dirt on it and tied her hair up as an added precaution.

Abby did not have to change her appearance to look like she belonged in the death march. She slung a garbage bag over her shoulder, which held diapers, lacings, and more garbage bags. Bug packets bulged in their pockets, and each of them carried a thermos. As Abby passed her mom's house, she lifted her eyes to the second floor, to her mom's bedroom window, knowing it was probably the last time she would see the house. She started to tear up, so she quickly returned her gaze to the ground.

They turned right on Massachusetts Avenue and headed for the Charles River, six blocks away. Abby had visited the Charlestown Yacht Club more times than she could remember, but, naturally, she had never walked there from Cambridge. Unfortunately, she had never paid attention to the route they took when her mother or father drove her there either.

They planned to follow the river to where it emptied into Boston Harbor, just past the Museum of Science. They would cross the highway and then start to look for the Bunker Hill Monument. Abby felt confident that, using it as a landmark, she could lead them to the yacht club.

Of the many dangers they might encounter, nighttime worried her the most. She wanted to reach the club before the sun set. They might never find Jordan in the dark, and she dreaded the idea of spending the night outside. With six hours of daylight remaining, she thought they could make it. If it meant they had to stop their fake limps and walk fast, that was just a risk they would have to take.

Mel looked back while Abby shifted her gaze left and right. Together, they kept a complete watch on their surroundings.

Squatters had moved into a deli, furniture store, nightclub, and Chinese restaurant along Mass. Ave. The smell of roasting meat wafted through the broken windows of the post office in Central Square. Kids had built an urban campsite inside Sky Dry Cleaners, complete with a wood stove, several mattresses, and a full-length mirror. It was protected by barbed wire. Abby saw bedding and pots and pans in several cars. Laundry hung out of the windows of a yellow school bus, parked half on the sidewalk. In what used to be her favorite park, boys and girls were playing soccer.

Nearing the river, they encountered an increasing number of survivors. The younger kids demonstrated the most energy. The teens looked sick and moved more slowly.

Ahead, a motley pack of dogs were chowing down on something, all tugging at the object and growling. Such an odd collection: a poodle, a Chihuahua, several mutts, a German shepherd, and a Lab. Abby had no interest in seeing what the dogs had found for a meal.

They encountered kids lugging drinking water two blocks from the river. Then Abby saw 'The Charles'. It was a mile across by the Mass. Ave. Bridge. Makeshift shelters crowded both banks. On the other side, Boston's skyscrapers, some rising like charred stalks of corn, formed a saw-toothed pattern against a darkening sky.

A storm was approaching, but Abby looked forward to the rain. It would protect her and Mel by making them look even more bedraggled.

On Memorial Drive, halfway between the bridge and the Museum of Science, Mel squeezed her arm and whispered, "We're being followed."

Eyes straight, they continued walking as Mel described the girl who she said had maintained the same distance behind them for the past quarter mile. "Black leather jacket, torn jeans, short hair. She's wearing a baseball cap. Thirteen or fourteen."

Abby wanted to ask Mel why she had waited so long to say anything. "Maybe she's not following us."

"I know when someone is following me."

Abby sighed, realizing that being on constant guard was a skill one needed on the mainland. She yearned for the peace and security of Castine Island where such skills were not necessary. "Let's look back fast on the count of three."

Mel agreed and Abby counted.

The girl looked vaguely familiar. She stood twenty yards away. She had stopped as they had. There was one thing Mel had failed to mention. A knife hung from the girl's belt.

"What do you think she wants?" Mel asked.

At that moment, a tall boy stepped out from behind a tree and moved next to the girl. Mel gasped. "It's them."

Even if Mel had remained silent, Abby would have known it was Brad. He towered over the girl. He had a Mohawk haircut and long arms. He had a knife attached to his belt too. Cocking his head to the side, he glared at them as if she and Mel were hunks of raw meat, and he was a hungry wolf.

Now Abby recognized the girl. She was the one wearing the baseball cap who had ducked inside the house across from the O'Brien's house. Throughout the night and most of the day, Abby thought, the girl had been spying on them.

Soon, the other gang members caught up. They reminded Abby of desperate predators. She understood what had weakened them—the illness, a lack of sleep, chasing Mel over half the city—but that only made them more dangerous. They would stop at nothing to get the pills, which of course, neither she nor Mel had.

"What can they do to us?" Abby whispered.

"Run," Mel cried and bolted.

Abby dropped her sack and ran after her friend. In a blur of thoughts, one cut the deepest. It was incredibly stupid to have dropped the bag. They needed those supplies, but it was too late to go back. She tightened her grip on the thermos.

Pumping her arms and lifting her knees, she dodged a kid on a skateboard, hopped over a corpse, and veered around a group of kids that were milling about. She felt the first drops of rain.

When the downpour started, many on the street and sidewalk scurried to their plywood shelters. It was now possible to run in a straight line, but Brad enjoyed the same advantage. Abby turned and saw that he was gaining on her. The drumbeat of his plodding feet grew louder. She expected him to pounce at any moment. If he tackled her, she'd try to gouge his eyes out. She'd have to fight him and his gang alone because Mel had just disappeared from view. Any fight would probably end quickly and not in her favor.

Abby huffed through her mouth, sucking in as much air as possible and then blowing out hard. In. Out. In. Out. Gulping oxygen, she inhaled until her lungs inflated to capacity and it felt like they were about to explode in her chest. Then she forcefully expelled the air out until her lungs felt as empty as shredded balloons.

Her pace slowed as the effort to lift her legs increased with every stride. On the Museum of Science grounds, she stumbled from a spasm in her right thigh. Immediately, she felt the spasm jump to her left thigh so both were trembling, a warning that she was about to collapse. Hobbling, she moved more and more slowly. She stumbled again, caught herself, and continued awkwardly.

Abby lost her footing on the slick pavement, and this time, she didn't think she could recover. Pitching forward, she turned an ankle. She cried out and tensed up for a crash landing on the grass.

Mel appeared out of nowhere and caught her in her arms. Long strands of hair plastered Mel's face, and water trickled off her chin and nose. She was a mess, but Abby had never been so happy to be face to face with a friend impersonating a drowning rat.

Abby gasped for breath. "Mel, slow down!"

"Sorry."

Abby turned around to see a beautiful sight. The gang had also stopped. They had lost ground, too, though they were still dangerously close. Brad was wheezing. The other boy was on one knee, holding his sides. One of the girls was puking. The one with a baseball cap was hugging a light post.

Abby and Mel locked arms and continued. Abby was limping for real now. The gang immediately followed them at the same pace. It was now a race among turtles.

They crossed the McGrath-O'Brien Highway. Cars and trucks, all with skeletons behind their wheels, sat where they had crashed and come to rest a little over a year ago.

"Mel, I'm going to tell you how to find the yacht club. If I can't make it…"

"Abby, shut up."

"Seriously," Abby said.

"Shut. Up."

In a muddy lot, Mel scooped up two fist-sized rocks. "I'm going to kill them if I get a chance."

"Mel, shut up."

Mel held out one of the rocks. Abby accepted it reluctantly.

They took turns looking back. Coming down like liquid drills, raindrops smashed the pavement and splattered up, obscuring the view. Abby thought their chance of losing the gang completely was getting better when one of the girls fell behind and then stopped. Brad slumped over, half running, half walking in an erratic zigzag pattern.

A moment later, Mel tugged at her arm. "Faster!"

Abby turned to see that, incredibly, Brad was gaining on them again. Water exploded from the puddles that he stepped into. She tried to speed up, but she felt as if she were dragging an anchor.

Ahead, a pack of kids had sought shelter under a bridge. When she and Mel stepped out of the deluge, some of the kids eyed them with suspicion, but most with boredom.

"See those kids behind us," Mel told them, "they have pills."

Heads turned, and some of the kids stood. Abby saw a blade flash in one boy's hand. Sad regret pumped through her veins. What Brad's gang had done to Mel's friends was unspeakable, but why put others in danger? Mel had changed more than Abby had imagined since the night of the purple moon.

They stepped out from under the bridge and into the drenching rain. Abby craned her neck when she heard a scream. One kid was on the ground. Brad was throwing wild punches and kicks. The other kids scattered, allowing Brad to continue chasing them.

Abby opened her hand and dropped her rock.

Brad was now twenty feet away. His glistening knife blade swung back and forth with every awkward stride he took. The clap of his footsteps rose above the rush of rain beating down.

Anger crackled like furious lightning in Mel's eyes. "Hurry." She almost pulled Abby's arm off.

They continued, gaining and losing ground to Brad, both parties slowing down to a marathon of caterpillars.

When Abby spotted the Bunker Hill Monument, she knew that the yacht club was a quarter mile away. "We're almost there."

"How far can you run?" Mel asked.

Run? "About twenty yards."

Mel scoffed. "If your life depended on it, you could only run twenty yards?"

Her life did depend on it, and Abby had first thought ten yards, but she had doubled her answer.

"I don't think so," Mel continued. "You can run for half a mile. Tell me when we have a half-mile to go."

Abby's lungs screamed for oxygen. She staggered because of cramping muscles. She was afraid of Brad, but she was just as afraid that her body would simply give out.

The bike path was just ahead. It hugged the harbor and passed close to the yacht club. They only had about two hundred yards to go, which was a lot less than the half-mile warning that Mel had asked for. Abby gritted her teeth and imagined a pack of wild animals was chasing her. The only way to escape them was to become like them, unthinking and focused, fueled by the most powerful instinct of all, the drive to survive. Did animals ever collapse from exhaustion? She was about to find out.

"Now," Abby shouted.

# CHAPTER FOURTEEN

Jordan reefed *Stargazer's* sail, an action that involved rolling some of the sail around the boom to reduce the surface area of the canvas. He would sacrifice speed for safety. Salt air corroded clips and hasps, reducing the strength of the rope, and by not raising the sail fully, he would put less stress on the gear.

The boat was as ready as it was going to be. To get underway, all Jordan had to do was cut the line tied to the mooring buoy.

He inflated the raft and climbed in. The raft would hold three passengers safely. If Timmy was with Abby and Mel, Jordan would make two trips. He fixed the oars in the oarlocks, dipped the blades in the water, and pulled.

Fuzzy plumes hovered over the city. The rain looked like coal dust between the dark clouds and building tops. The wind stiffened from the approaching squall.

When the raft scraped the bottom, Jordan hopped out and sank to his ankles in silky mud. The rain was now coming down steadily, and clouds of steam boiled up at the airport. He dragged the raft toward the beach and flipped it over to prevent the wind from blowing it away. He didn't want to have to explain to Abby that the tiny yellow dot halfway across the harbor was their raft.

He retrieved the pills from the base of the flagpole and pushed the bag deep into his wet pocket.

Just then, two people appeared at the end of the driveway. Jordan blinked and wiped his eyes. With the rain coming down harder, he couldn't tell who they were. Except for how slowly they were approaching him, they looked like they were running—pumping arms and leaning forward. Waving the paddle in the air, Jordan ran to meet them. He saw it was Abby and Mel.

Abby, wide-eyed and panicking, gasped, "Brad's coming!"

Jordan loped beside them, wondering if he might have to carry Abby. She stumbled and fell twice before they reached the raft. As he dragged the raft into the water, he didn't see anyone coming down the driveway. He pointed to *Stargazer*. "That's our way home." When he was knee-deep, he instructed them to climb in. He pushed the raft until he was up to his waist. Then he jumped up, hugged the side, and rolled in.

He handed an oar to Abby. Admitting she was too weak to row, she passed it to Mel. With the wind at their backs, they moved at a good pace toward *Stargazer*. Gusts sent dark shivers pulsing across the water as rain pooled at their feet.

"Look!" Abby's voice trembled. "It's Brad. Can they get us?"

Two boys and a girl limped across the muddy beach and stood at the water's edge.

Jordan gauged the receding shore and made some quick calculations. "We're safe," he told his sister, knowing that even if Brad was a strong swimmer he posed no threat to them.

The wind carried a sound that nearly caused Jordan to let go of the paddle. He traded glances with Abby and Mel. The gargling throb of the motorcycle grew louder.

"Mandy and Timmy," Abby cried. "They changed their minds."

Jordan watched in stunned disbelief as Mandy rode to the end of the yacht club driveway and came to a stop before the docks. Timmy hopped off the back and took off his helmet. The gang members started for them, fanning out in a semi-circle.

"Get on the bike," Jordan said mostly to himself. "Go. We'll wait for you."

"Mandy never backs down." Abby's voice had a tone of resignation.

When Mandy took out her knife, each gang member produced a weapon. Timmy handed his backpack to Mandy, who raised her knife in one hand and held the backpack in the other. Jordan figured she'd use the pack to blunt an attack.

Timmy balled his fists, looking ready to take on anyone.

"Jordan, we have to go back," Abby cried.

"I'm taking you and Mel to the boat," he told them. "The raft won't hold everyone. I'll go back for them." He wondered how long Mandy could keep the gang at bay.

He and Mel paddled for all they were worth until they were beside *Stargazer*. He maneuvered the raft to the stern where it would be easier for them to climb out. He held the rudder to steady the raft as Mel went first. From *Stargazer*, she helped Abby.

"Put these in the cabin." Jordan handed Abby the bag of pills. Then he shoved off.

He wished that he had asked Mel for the paring knife. A puny weapon was better than his bare hands alone. It was too late to go back.

Squinting in the windblast, he reached out and dug the oar blade deep. He sank the shaft until his hand touched the water and then, twisting his torso for power, pulled the blade until it splashed out of the water. He thought the oar could double as a weapon.

Lowering his head, he stroked until his shoulders and upper back burned from fatigue. The raft, collecting rain, was riding lower in the water with the weight. It felt like he was paddling a sinking boat.

He nearly cried out in defeat when he looked back and saw that he'd only gone twenty feet or so. Abby, waving her arms and shouting, appeared to be a mime. The wind ripped the words from her lips and blew them in the opposite direction.

When he turned back toward shore, he saw Mandy swing her knife at Brad, who jumped back. The tall boy sneered. He seemed content to retreat and advance as part of a pack.

Jordan bent forward at the waist to lower his profile in the headwind and took shallower strokes. When he saw he was making progress with this new paddling technique, he got a boost of strength from somewhere.

Thinking he was in waist-deep water, he grabbed the raft's towline and jumped out. He sank into the icy depths, the water going over his head.

Pushing off the bottom, he broke the surface of the water and gulped air before he sank again. Leaning forward as far as buoyancy allowed, he bounced on his toes and inched toward shore.

He beached the raft on the wet mud and flipped it over. Both oars were missing; they must have tumbled out. He scanned the water, but didn't see either one. They'd have to paddle with their hands.

As the wind threw sheets of rain down that almost blinded him, Jordan cupped his hand over his eyes. Mandy, with Timmy at her side, was waving her knife back and forth as the menacing gang inched closer.

Jordan gulped at the sight of the gang's arsenal. Brad and the girl each gripped knives with blades as long and lethal as Mandy's. The other boy held a length of heavy chain, which he swung back and forth like a pendulum.

Jordan put one hand behind his back as if he were about to produce a weapon.

"Take Timmy." Mandy threw him a look that allowed no argument.

*Yeah, right!* He was not about to make two trips in a raft without oars.

Jordan waved them over. "Let's go."

Mandy gave the boy a tiny shove. "Go to Jordan!"

Timmy snapped back to her like an elastic band, clenching his jaw in defiance.

The girl with the knife started for Jordan. He stepped back by instinct. Not completely thawed out from his plunge, he was numb from the waist down, and he almost lost his balance and fell over. Emboldened by his retreat, she came at him faster. He kept his hand behind his back and held his ground. Then he locked eyes with her and took a step forward. She backed away, her eyes darting with doubt.

"He doesn't have any pills," Mandy told them. "I got 'em."

Jordan shook his head. Did he hear her clearly? Then he realized that Mandy wanted to make sure Timmy got to *Stargazer* safely. She was planning to hold off the gang single-handedly.

The boy with the heavy chain approached Mandy. Wearing a smirk, he started swinging the chain in a circle. Then he charged and swung it at her.

Mandy ducked just in time. The chain, completing its arc, whistled an inch above Timmy's head. Chain Boy grunted in disappointment and cocked his arm back, ready to swing the chain in the opposite direction.

Mandy saw her opportunity and lunged, stabbing him in the chest.

Chain Boy dropped the chain and stumbled back, clutching his chest. When he took his hands away, he discovered that the knife tip hadn't gone through his leather jacket. Soaked in fright, it took him a moment to realize how lucky he was. "Ooooh, she bites," he said with a forced grin. He scuttled to pick up his chain.

At that moment, Timmy charged at Chain Boy and attempted to land a kick. Chain Boy stepped aside and laughed.

Something flashed in the corner of Jordan's eye. The girl was streaking toward the raft. Before he could take his first step, she slashed the raft with her knife. Then she started for him. Realizing she could see that he didn't have a weapon, he backpedaled.

He tripped and fell on his back in the soft mud. Pelting rain blurred his vision, and he wiped it away desperately. The girl was now looming above him. She was twelve or thirteen years old, with a diamond nose piercing and brown eyes. A scar extended from an eyebrow to the start of her hairline. He shouted as she reared back to strike him with the knife and raised his hands in a futile attempt to defend himself. Just as the girl drove the knife forward, Mandy thrust the backpack forward to block the blade. The knife fell to the mud. Then Mandy stabbed the girl in the shoulder. The girl screamed as blood, thinning to pink in the rain, sheeted down her arm.

"Watch out," Jordan cried to Mandy.

Chain Boy swung his chain at her from behind. She turned and raised an arm, but the chain caught the side of her head. She buckled to her knees with a stunned look in her eyes. Timmy ran to her side, shielding her head with his body. To stop Chain Boy from striking her a second time, Jordan picked up the girl's knife and crawled beside them. When he stood, Chain Boy backed up.

Mandy was groaning. "Take Timmy and go. Please," she begged.

Jordan wondered if Mandy understood that they had no raft. Or had the chain dazed her? Jordan thought he could swim to the boat, but it wouldn't be easy. Timmy would never survive the frigid water. Then Jordan remembered the boy didn't even know how to swim. Out of the corner of his eye, he saw movement. Jordan snapped his head around. Brad, with a cold, blank expression, was closing in.

They jerked their heads at the sound of metal on metal. Chain Boy had knocked over Mandy's motorcycle and was lashing it with his chain, busting up whatever he could.

"I'm staying with you," Timmy cried, wrapping his arms tightly around Mandy.

"That makes two of us," Jordan added, keeping an eye on Brad.

Mandy got to her knees. Without warning, she slapped Timmy in the face, hard. "Leave! Go with Jordan. I don't want you with me anymore."

Timmy puffed out his chest defiantly as he fought back tears. She shoved him toward Jordan.

Brad inched closer, waving his knife. Then, as fast as a bolt of lightning, he lunged. Jordan barely reacted in time, pulling Timmy out of the way. The blade passed within an inch of where Timmy's face had been.

Mandy jumped to her feet, and wildly waving her knife back and forth, sliced nothing but raindrops, but that was enough to make Brad back off. Jordan realized that they could not beat the gang. Timmy was too much of a liability. It had nothing to do with the boy's courage and determination. It boiled down to inches and pounds. Timmy was too young, too small, too weak.

Jordan swallowed hard. He and Mandy locked eyes. She seemed to read his mind.

"Don't look back," she said. "I know it's not easy, but do it for me. Just turn and go."

Fighting tears, he gave Mandy the girl's knife and grabbed Timmy's hand, yanking him toward the water. Timmy stumbled and barely stayed on his feet. Jordan kept dragging him into the water.

He couldn't see the fight, but the wind delivered each grunt, curse, and shout. Jordan knew that Mandy didn't stand a chance. He wished the wind would change direction to spare Timmy from hearing the screams.

Knee-deep in the water, Timmy thrashed and shouted. He wanted to go back to save Mandy. Jordan squeezed his hand harder, forcing him into the deeper water. If the gang discovered Mandy didn't have the pills, they might think that he or Timmy had them.

Timmy couldn't shout as easily when the water was up to his chin, but he continued to kick and flail his arms just as much.

A terrifying silence stopped both of them. Timmy's blue lips trembled, and his face contorted in tears. Jordan knew that Mandy was dead. The girl he had thought a monster, was braver than anyone he'd ever known. Determined to honor her final request, Jordan wrapped his arm across Timmy's small chest, and started to swim toward *Stargazer*.

# CHAPTER FIFTEEN

The wind and rain buffeted Abby as she gripped the rail next to Mel. She had put on a lifejacket for warmth, but her teeth chattered. She wasn't trembling from the cold. She pulled her eyes away from the gruesome scene on the muddy beach, knowing Mandy's sacrifice would haunt her forever.

With a slate-gray sky, it was hard to see the boys in the choppy water. They had gone about twenty yards and had another thirty to go. They were so close together their heads appeared to be one.

She knew how hard Jordan was working to keep Timmy's head above the water while moving the boy forward. Timmy was flailing his arms.

Timmy was at risk of succumbing to hypothermia—though that might not be so bad. While it would put his health in danger it should also make him go limp, making it easier for Jordan to swim with him.

Abby kicked off her sneakers and cinched her lifejacket just in case she had to go in and help. She shouted encouragement to them, but realized that her shouts were as wasted as her prayers. She felt as if the wind was literally pushing the words back down her throat.

"I want to kill that son of a bitch," Mel said, fixing her gaze onshore.

The gang, which had apparently finished going through Mandy's pockets, had split up. The girl and the boy were surveying the motorcycle, on its side. Brad was standing at the water's edge.

He stared out at them, the rain obscuring his expression. Abby couldn't imagine what he was thinking. A moment ago, he had delivered a fatal knife thrust, but he still found himself in the same situation, sick and dying, needing a pill to survive.

Sheets of rain slapped the water, and droplets, in the hard gusts of wind, stung Abby's face like bees. Halyards clacked and beat against the metal mast, and the rush of wind past a small opening somewhere produced a piercing whistle.

The direction of the wind worked in Jordan and Timmy's favor, pushing them closer to the boat. However, the gusting wind created a different danger for them. *Stargazer's* bow pointed directly toward the shore, straining against the mooring line. If the line snapped, Jordan and Timmy would find themselves stranded as *Stargazer* beached itself on the opposite shore.

"Look for rope," Abby shouted to Mel. "We can throw it to Jordan." She started for the cabin.

Mel's eyes suddenly opened wide. Abby turned and gasped. Brad was charging into the water. He waded up to his waist and dived in. He splashed wildly as if he were swimming the last leg of a race.

While Mel tried to untie a rope wrapped around the boom, Abby stepped into the cabin. Because the two dirty portholes let in only a little light, it was difficult to see much of anything. She started in one corner and searched with her hands as much as she did with her eyes. Her hands found a pair of pliers and grabbed them greedily. Then she came to a blanket, an unexpected gift. She pulled it back, revealing the body of the man it was covering. She looked behind and all around the corpse for rope or anything else they might use. Grimacing, she undid his belt buckle and left with the belt, the blanket, and the pliers.

Mel was struggling to untie the knot. Swollen and salt encrusted—the rope fibers had fused together. Abby handed her the pliers.

Abby coiled the belt around her hand and crawled to the bow. The rain pelted her, and spray exploded upward from the wind-whipped waves that were crashing against the hull. The mooring buoy line was fraying where it rubbed against the railing.

The three swimmers were a blur. She wiped the water out of her eyes and saw how much Brad had closed the distance between himself and Jordan and Timmy.

Timmy had gone limp. Jordan not only had to tow him, but he also had to keep Timmy's head above the water.

"Mel, I need you," Abby cried.

Mel lay on her belly beside her, ready to help her bring the boys on board. The tiny fibers of the mooring line were snapping, and Abby wondered how much longer the rope could withstand the force of wind and waves.

Jordan and Timmy were now several feet from the mooring buoy, with Brad right behind them. One or two strokes and he would be on top of them. Jordan threw one arm over the buoy and held on to Timmy with his other. Abby shouted as Brad reached out, but, as with all her other warnings, the wind blew her words to the other shore.

Brad grabbed Jordan's hair.

Jordan released Timmy and pushed him toward the bow. The boy floated on his belly with his face in the water. Brad slammed his other hand across Jordan's face, forcing him under.

Abby tossed Mel the belt and dived through the air. The headwind made her feel, for a moment, that she was flying, suspended between sky and sea.

She landed on her belly, outstretched. The icy water smashed into her, knocking her breath away. Her momentum carried her to Timmy. She quickly rolled him over, cradled an arm across his chest, and took several hard strokes and frog kicks toward the boat. The buoyancy of her life jacket helped keep both of them above the water. Timmy's eyes were shut, and his face was blue. He appeared to be in a deep sleep.

Behind her, Jordan and Brad fought. She did her best to ignore their brutal grunts and shouts as she focused on Timmy, knowing how close he was to death.

Gripping the rail with one hand, Mel stretched out her other arm and unfurled the belt. She had to do it twice more before Abby managed to grab the buckle. Mel pulled with all her strength, and soon Abby and Timmy were at the side of the boat. Abby shook the boy and yelled, "Timmy. Timmy. Open your eyes."

Two slits appeared. He was alive but just barely.

Mel grabbed one of Timmy's hands, and Abby found the other and held it up for Mel who pulled Timmy's limp body out of the water slowly, inch by inch. When Mel had Timmy onboard, Abby spun around and gasped. Brad had a headlock on Jordan who was clutching the hook on top of the mooring buoy to keep Brad from pulling him under. Jordan's gray face was twisted into a grimace, and he was gulping for air against the white noise of the rainstorm.

All of a sudden, Jordan let go of the buoy hook, and both boys disappeared. A moment later, one breached the surface, and then the other. They rolled over and disappeared again. Abby realized that Jordan wanted to take Brad under. It was the only way to break Brad's grip.

Abby pushed away from the boat. "Jordan!" A wave cut her cry short, and she gagged from the salty water that went down her throat. From behind, a hand pushed down on her shoulder, and she thrashed forward. She turned, ready to gouge Brad's eyes. Abby caught herself, seeing it was Jordan, his chin barely above the water. She wrapped her arms around him. The lifejacket kept them afloat.

Brad surfaced near the buoy, which he promptly hugged. Exhausted, he pressed his face against it. His cheeks were bluish and his eyes dark. He closed his eyes for a long moment. Already weak from the illness and chasing them for hours, the final battle had completely drained him. The hatred of Brad she had held in her heart dissolved into deep sadness for him and everyone else involved.

Abby kicked until she and Jordan were beside the boat. Mel tried pulling Jordan into *Stargazer*. He hooked his fingers over the rail, but that was as far as he got. He was too heavy for her to lift, and too weak to pull himself up.

"The stern," Jordan said before taking in a mouthful of water.

Abby reached up." "M-m-el, g-g-give me your hand." Her teeth chattered uncontrollably. "Drag us to the back of the boat."

Mel disappeared and returned with the belt. Abby grabbed the buckle with one hand and held on to Jordan's shirt with her other. Mel towed them to the stern. Every wave bashed them against the hull. Abby's arms were numb. She concentrated all her energy on keeping her fingers welded to Jordan and the belt.

Behind the stern, the hull shielded them from the brunt of the waves and wind. Abby maneuvered her brother closer until Mel had hold of his hair. That stirred him, and he took Mel's hand. Bobbing up and down in the rough water, he tried to pull himself up, and on his third try, he was able to hook his leg over the rail. Mel rolled him onto the boat.

Then the two of them dragged Abby onboard.

"Jordan, go to the cabin. You need to get warm."

He shook his head. "The mooring line won't hold much longer."

Abby gave him a lifejacket for warmth. Slipping it on, he grabbed the pliers and headed for the bow.

She went to check on Timmy in the cabin. He was shivering, which was a good sign. His body was starting to generate heat. She wrapped him more tightly in the blanket and returned to the deck.

Looking back over the rail she saw Brad, still clinging to the mooring float, but just barely. They made eye contact. No longer a monster, he was a frightened child. Abby sensed her fingers unsnapping the clips of her life jacket.

Brad seemed to read her mind, and he pushed away from the buoy and slowly treaded water, coming toward her.

She removed her life jacket. At the side of the boat now, Brad reached up and held on to the rail. His fingers curled around the railing. His sudden strength surprised her, and she stepped back.

Before the night of the purple moon, he might have been a good basketball player, popular, with lots of friends. Or maybe he had grown fast and was gangly and had never had friends. Through no fault of his own, the epidemic had changed the course of his life. He still bore responsibility for his actions, but it was unlikely that he would have turned into a killer under better circumstances.

Abby believed that a kind act sometimes set off ripples that spread out and eventually inspired other kind acts. She held out her life jacket.

In a blur of motion, Mel slammed Brad's fingers with the rock she had picked up earlier. He screamed, flopped back, and disappeared beneath a swirl of bubbles.

"Hold on," Jordan shouted at that moment and snipped the mooring line with the jaws of the pliers. *Stargazer* lurched and they started drifting sideways toward the other shore. He scrambled to the tiller and pushed it all the way to the port side. When he pulled in the mainsheet, the sail puffed out. *Stargazer* heeled from the harnessed wind and cut a straight line through the chop.

Abby fixed her gaze on the spot where Brad had gone under and a shiver passed through her when she realized he wasn't coming up. Mel was staring at the splatter of blood on the rail, and Abby put her arm around her friend. She didn't think she could ever kill like that, but she understood Mel's rage and fear. Abby wondered just how far she, herself, would go to protect the people she loved most. Turning to the bow, she hoped she'd never have to find out.

# ONE YEAR LATER

# CHAPTER ONE
# COLONY EAST

Lieutenant Mark Dawson squinted against the rays of morning light streaming through his room at the Biltmore Hotel. After five years of submarine duty, he found it strange waking to sunshine.

A lump formed in his throat as he thought back to that moment on the *USS Seawolf*, two years ago, when Admiral Samuels' voice had crackled through the squawk box, changing his life forever. "A catastrophic epidemic has swept the planet. We will remain submerged until further notice."

Dawson had stood next to his bunk, paralyzed with fear, thinking about his wife and baby daughter at home as the admiral delivered the chilling news.

As it passed by the Earth, a comet had deposited bacteria into the atmosphere, which attacked the human hormones testosterone and estrogen. Except for scientists in quarantine in Atlanta and on-duty members of the U.S. Naval submarine fleet, every adult and post-pubescent teen in the country had perished. Other countries had fared worse.

In the months that followed, Dawson struggled with constant anxiety about his daughter, Sarah, as the wait for the handful of remaining scientists to develop an antibiotic to defeat the bacteria dragged on.

Seven months later, the CDC had developed the antibiotic and distributed the pills to Navy personnel, and then the two organizations worked together to distribute the pills to the millions of survivors who were still dying when they entered adolescence. Fighting time, and with little experience in the logistics of such an operation, they had tried to do too much with too few resources and their efforts failed miserably. The fiery tragedy at Logan Airport, in Boston, proved to be the first of many. Now, the CDC, with support from the Navy, had embarked on a new strategy to rebuild society.

Dawson rolled onto his side and fixed his gaze on the picture of Sarah on the table next to his bed. She'd turn three years old next month, on May twenty-third. He fanned the ember of hope that she was alive and an older child who had survived the epidemic was taking care of her.

He shot up in bed when a muffled cry came from down the hallway. Dawson craned his ears but heard only silence. One of the younger cadets must have been having a nightmare.

Doctor Perkins, the colony's chief scientist, had counseled company leaders to take no action for nightmares. "Horrible memories fester in the subconscious, and dreams help the children process what they experienced during the epidemic. It's the healthiest way for them to cope with losing loved ones."

Dawson didn't always agree with Doctor Perkins, but thought he was probably right about the dreams. Still, every cry and scream he heard in the night felt like a punch in the gut.

He dropped to the floor and stiff as a plank of wood, cranked off one hundred pushups. It was a daily routine since his freshman year at the Naval Academy. He started a second set, knowing he would probably do a third one as well. He would keep going until the ache of oxygen-starved muscles burned away his anguish.

Three hundred and sixty-two pushups later, Dawson popped to his feet and entered the bathroom. Looking at himself in the mirror, he realized a visit to the barber was in order to keep his wavy, black hair within grooming standards. The crook on the bridge of his nose triggered a memory of John Collins, his roommate at the Academy. JC had accidentally spiked a ball in his face, in a game of volleyball. Sadly, Collins had accepted an assignment in a carrier group and died during the epidemic. He always wondered if

Collins had done him a favor, though. Dawson's wife had told him that his broken nose made him look handsome.

He turned on the tap and splashed cold water on his face, trying to put loved ones and his former roommate out of his mind.

After a week-long interruption, the water was running again. The repair crew, who made daily descents into New York City's underground labyrinth of pipes and cabling, had finally found the leaky pipe that fed Biltmore Company. He didn't envy the sewer crew. One chief petty officer claimed to have seen rats the size of raccoons.

Dawson exited the bathroom and picked up the envelope stamped CONFIDENTIAL from the floor where an ensign had slipped it under the door in the early morning hours. The other company leaders at the Hilton, the Sheraton, and the Four Seasons, would also have received the daily memorandum.

He committed the day's activities and items of interest to memory:

*Lecture on the lifecycle of the honeybee at Carnegie Hall, 1500 hours ... Two-way traffic on Broadway ... Power out in sectors 2 and 7 ... Local area network access restored at the Chrysler Building ... Subway operational from Wall Street to Times Square ... Seeking volunteers at the United Nations chicken coop.*

He tensed when he saw the Code 4.

*Code 4: Stay alert for children who experience any combination of the following symptoms: Increased appetite, fever above 101 degrees, breathing disorders, hallucinations. Report cases to Medical Clinic 17.*

He read the section a second time and then filed the memorandum.

He had forty-five minutes of unscheduled time before reveille. He put on his running shorts and shirt and laced up his sneakers. He walked down the plush red-and-gold carpet and entered the stairwell through the fire-exit door. He sprinted up forty flights to the top floor and stepped into what was formerly the restaurant at the Biltmore Hotel. He couldn't help but imagine the scene that had taken place here a little more than two years ago.

He'd gleaned from a menu that *coq au vin with sautéed asparagus* was the special on the night of the purple moon. Earth had entered the comet's tail on April twentieth, a Friday night, at 11:30 p.m., and every guest received a complimentary glass of pomegranate juice. The streaking comet, which had turned the stars and moon purple, must have been a spectacular sight to the diners—dinner, a show, and then silent death.

The Body Disposal Unit (BDU) had cleared the restaurant months earlier, and the only mementos of the gala event remaining were a few tables with white linens draped over them.

The top floor offered a stunning 360-degree view of Colony East through the restaurant's tall windows. Looking to the east, Dawson faced the red orb of the rising sun, five degrees above the horizon. He didn't see any sails on the sparkling ocean this morning. The sailboats that he spotted on occasion were a source of intrigue. Some of the larger sloops were up to thirty feet in length, and once he'd seen a schooner with two masts. He thought that if he were fifteen years old and outside the colony he'd want to be at sea sailing on a schooner too.

He moved to the other side of the restaurant and eyed the Hudson River. Standing in the middle of the river, huge windmills generated electricity for Colony East. Their blades rotated slowly in the dawn breeze. Along the bank, razor wire, coiled on top of the perimeter fence, glinted in the sunlight. Abandoned cars and trucks clogged the George Washington Bridge, and a concrete barrier sealed off the Colony East side.

He took a deep breath and pivoted northward. The twisted steel beams of the Brooklyn Bridge splayed out like some sort of abstract modern sculpture; artwork fashioned courtesy of Navy demolition experts. Their handiwork had also taken down the Manhattan and Williamsburg bridges. He often wondered what the kids on the Brooklyn side of the East River thought about the extensive measures taken to keep them from entering the colony.

He placed his fingertips on the glass. The town of Mystic, Connecticut, where he had lived with his wife and daughter, was somewhere off in the horizon.

"Permission denied." The words echoed heavily in his heart.

Dawson had twice asked Admiral Samuels if he could take a few days to return home to find out what had happened to his daughter and to bury his wife, and possibly his daughter, too.

Samuels was now the colony's highest-ranking officer, the third highest in the nation behind Admiral Wilson in the Atlanta Colony, and Admiral Thomas stationed in Colony West.

"Mark, I understand what you're going through," Samuels had told him. "I'm a grandfather. A day doesn't go by that I don't think of my five grandkids, but I can't afford to let you go, not even for a day. I have three officers and one hundred and two sailors. Those are my resources to care for five hundred children and fifteen scientists. I'm sorry."

Two months later, he had asked again, making a vein pop out in the admiral's neck.

"Permission denied. Dismissed."

Dawson understood the admiral's hard-line. Military commanders had asked the men and women serving under them to make sacrifices since the dawn of time. He also understood the importance of his own crucial role in the mission. The restoration of society was at stake. Much was riding on his ability to obey orders and serve as company leader with distinction.

The sun had shucked its red husk for a direct yellow glare. Sighing, Dawson did what his father had taught him to do during times of adversity and inner turmoil. He pulled his shoulders back, stiffened his spine, and raised his chin.

He was ready for another day at Colony East.

# CHAPTER TWO
# CASTINE ISLAND

Flashlight beams danced in the harbor playground as a merry band of five- and six-year-olds scurried about. The kids giggled and chattered as they untangled lines and tapped stakes into the rocky soil. Derek Ladd, the camp leader, was attempting to teach them how to pitch tents. Even in the early evening light, Abby could see the scar on Derek's left ear from his fishing accident.

She shivered in the east wind and zipped her jacket all the way up. Surrounded by the waters of the North Atlantic, Castine Island had two seasons: icy damp and damp. It was April, the start of damp.

Waiting to pick up Toucan from survival camp, Abby walked over to the swing set where other teens were also waiting to pick up younger siblings or kids they had adopted.

"Hey, Abby, you going to Toby's?" It was Eddie, Jordan's best friend. He swept away the long blonde hair covering his eyes. Streaks of grease covered his wiry, strong arms. Eddie could fix anything. He'd hold a broken part in his hand and let his fingers do the thinking. If there had been no epidemic, Abby was certain that he would have worked as a mechanic someday. The comet had simply accelerated his career path, as it had forced every kid to grow up overnight. Eddie was the island's boat mechanic. Toby Jones was their lead negotiator, the only one who had a radio that received

The Port, the teen radio station. Many island residents gathered evenings at Toby's house to listen to The Port.

Abby shook her head. "We're going home. Jordan's monitoring the two-way. I want to know if any gypsies are coming. See what they've heard about the Pig."

Gypsies sailed from trading zone to trading zone, bartering information in return for food, water, and batteries to power their shortwave radios. The last three crews to visit the island had spoken about a strange, new illness, which they called the Pig. Victims gorged for weeks and then suddenly developed a high fever. Several had died from the illness.

"Jordan will tell you if he hears anything." Eddie paused a moment. "Are you worried about him?"

"No," she blurted, maybe a little too quickly.

Eddie raised his eyebrows. "He doesn't need you holding his hand. He's going to snap out of it."

Just then, Derek dismissed camp. "Good job, everyone." The kids scattered.

Glad for the interruption, Abby again told Eddie she was going straight home and then braced herself for the impact.

Toucan was running straight at her. The wind pushed back her sister's curly, red hair, showing a face beaming with excitement. Ounce for ounce, Touk was just as stubborn as Jordan, but she possessed twice the energy and three times the enthusiasm of Abby and Jordan combined. Toucan launched herself.

Abby caught the bundle of flying arms and legs.

"Abby, want to see my tent?"

"I'll see it tomorrow. We have to go home." Abby found Touk's hand and grimaced with concern as she felt her sister's bony fingers. Because of food rationing, everyone on the island ate less during the winter months, but Toucan was a fussy eater to begin with.

Heading home, they took a shortcut through an alley behind the hardware store and the bowling alley. Moonlight outlined the shape of garbage cans but refused to reveal potholes and other small tripping hazards. Flicking on her flashlight, Abby shook her head at the flecks of purple space dust sparkling where rains had sluiced sand and dirt into a mound. Even after two years, there was no escaping the horrible reminders of the comet. She picked out a route, memorizing the layout in her mind, and turned off the light to save batteries.

"Touk, let's go to the library tomorrow."

"I want a book about pirates."

Abby smiled bitterly. She used to enjoy reading books like *Treasure Island* aloud, but the stories of real pirates robbing victims on the mainland had soured her on the topic. "How about something new? Like, uhh, not pirates."

"Pirates," Toucan insisted so enthusiastically that Abby could only sigh. "Sure, why not?"

They exited the alley and started up Melrose, the street they lived on. Wheels rumbled as a pack of skateboarders zoomed down the island's only hill. Nighttime made the run down 'Mount Melrose' more thrilling.

"Touk, what did you eat at camp?" Abby heard the desperation in her own voice. "They gave you a box dinner, right?"

"I wasn't hungry," Toucan replied.

Abby faked a chuckle. "Fish isn't that bad." In truth, she had to pinch her nose to eat the bony, smoked mackerel.

Toucan made a face. "Yuck."

"Want me to make you some french fries?" Abby asked.

"Okay!" Touk chirped.

"You have to eat some fish first."

"No, thank you."

Abby took a deep breath. "Touk, c'mon."

"I want chocolate."

"If you eat fish and french fries, then you can have one piece of chocolate."

"Okay!"

Abby could tell from Touk's tone that she was grinning. Grinning and winning.

They saved chocolate for special occasions, but Abby thought her housemates would understand letting Touk have a nibble.

Up ahead, Abby heard rock music drifting out the window of Toby's house. The strong signal of the adult station, 98.5 FM, operated by the

Centers for Disease Control, came through clearly day and night, but they could only pick up the weaker FM 101 after the sun went down. DJ Silver, the host, called the station The Port.

The Port's mysteries played in Abby's mind. DJ Silver once mentioned he was broadcasting from Connecticut, but he didn't give the exact location. How did the station get electricity? How did teens know how to operate a radio station? Strangest of all, The Port only played music. Abby had never heard them give news flashes. It continually puzzled her.

DJ Silver's voice crackled out the window. "Silvy, can you dig it? Jimmy knows you dig him, and Jimmy knows you dig the Beatles. So, Little Miss Sugar Lumps, here's a little something that Big Jimmy thinks will start your evening off right. Keep it locked on The Port." The radio began to play "Sgt. Pepper's Lonely Hearts Club Band." DJ Silver dedicated every song. Where did he get his information for the dedications? Just one more unanswered question about The Port.

As they passed by Toby's house, Abby noted all the bikes and skateboards in the front yard. In the glowing light of lanterns, she saw kids inside, some dancing. When Abby spotted Mel standing by the window, she suspected that Timmy and Danny, her other housemates, were at Toby's as well. It meant that Jordan must be home alone.

Toucan pulled at Abby's hand, wanting to run up the steps of Toby's porch to join the party.

Abby tugged her back toward the sidewalk.

"Toby wants to kiss you," Touk said with gleaming eyes.

Abby crinkled her brow. "Who said that?"

"I'll tell you for two pieces of chocolate."

"Forget it."

"Toby told me."

"What a surprise," Abby replied flatly. Most people considered Toby annoying, which he was. These same kids pretended to be his friends because he was the island's lead negotiator. They hung out at his house every night because he shared snacks and, of course, had batteries for the radio. Abby considered him a real friend, but she wanted to keep it at that.

She picked up the pace, and they both held their breath as they walked by the fourth house up from Toby's. The backyard was this month's toilet.

With half a block to go, Touk raced ahead and flew into their house. Abby ironed the crinkles from her forehead and forced a small smile before stepping inside.

"Gypsy vessel, this is Castine Island, do you copy?" Jordan stood by the battery-powered shortwave radio in the family room, keying the mic. "Gypsy vessel, do you copy?" Her brother was lanky, like their dad, and thanks to a recent growth spurt, he now towered over Abby by a good five inches. "Gypsy vessel, do you copy?" The radio speaker emitted a crackly hiss.

Jordan looked over at her, the lantern light magnifying the sadness in his eyes. "The captain of *Lucky Me* reported they have a medical emergency onboard. She said they're near Bar Harbor, and they expect to arrive here tomorrow afternoon."

Bar Harbor, on the coast of Maine, was about a hundred miles from Castine Island.

Abby's stomach twisted into a knot. She thought it was revealing that the gypsies preferred to sail all night and much of the day to come here, rather than pull into a closer mainland port. There were scant medical resources available on the mainland, and, in her opinion, many parts were dangerous. She worried what she'd have to face as the island's medical first responder. "What type of emergency?"

Jordan gave a little shake of his head. "I don't know. The transmission cut out." He brought the mic to his lips. "Gypsy boat, do you copy?"

A broken bone? A cut requiring stitches? Appendicitis? With limited supplies and possessing virtually no experience, Abby could only try to provide comfort if the injury was serious.

Trying not to worry about a problem she couldn't deal with tonight, she lit a lantern and entered the kitchen. She cut up a potato, put the slices into a frying pan with a few drops of peanut oil and placed the pan on the wood stove. She picked out the bones from a piece of smoked fish and put it on a plate. Then she broke off a corner of a treasured candy bar and added it.

In the family room, Abby found Toucan petting Cat, the gray-and-white, domestic shorthair that had followed Abby home on the night of the purple moon. Jordan continued trying to talk to the gypsies.

After a few minutes, she returned to the kitchen and flipped the potatoes. Then she went back to the family room. Jordan shut off the two-way radio and checked his weather instruments. "The wind's out of the southwest," he said. "They'll be lucky if they get here by tomorrow night." He shot her a hard look. "They need a real doctor. When did the adults promise to open the first clinic?"

Abby let out a long exhalation, feeling the underlying tension in her brother's voice.

"Tell me, Abby. When are they opening the first clinic?"

She bit her tongue. *Let him vent.*

Jordan paced. "If I remember correctly, it was supposed to be October."

Abby said nothing, because everyone on the island knew that. Nine months ago, the robotic voice on the CDC station had announced the scientists were planning to open medical clinics to treat survivors in major cities. They would also train kids to be doctors, calling the program, 'Doctors of Tomorrow'. But not a single clinic had opened, and the CDC had yet to offer an explanation for the delay. Jordan already knew that.

"Jordan, they're going to open the clinics." She immediately regretted saying it. "The adults care about us. Remember what happened in Boston? They have as many problems as we do. They're probably waiting until the mainland is safe before they try to open a clinic."

"Pirates," Touk chirped.

"The mainland is safe," he said, rolling his eyes. Then his face turned the color of burgundy in the flickering light. "The adults have forgotten about us. I don't listen to their stupid station anymore. It's a waste of batteries. One clinic! Is that too much to ask? I bet they have a hospital in New York City. Why did they build a fence with barbed wire around the city?"

Abby leaned back in her chair, wishing he would stop. While she understood his anger, she wished he would take it out on someone else for a change. "We don't know that's true."

He gave an exaggerated nod. "Trust me, it's true. You believe every bit of news the gypsies bring until they tell you something you don't want to hear."

Abby had lost count of how many times they'd gone down this same road, each time making the same points, the conversation spiraling to the same conclusion that nobody knew what the adults were doing. The quickest way to end the conversation was just to have it and get it over with. "Only one gypsy said the fence had barbed wire."

Jordan threw his hands in the air. "Then why did the adults blow up the bridges?"

She swallowed hard. "I'm sure they had a good reason."

"Yeah," he fired back. "They don't want to help us. You know when we'll see the first adult? Guess."

"How would I know?"

"When we grow up," he chuckled coldly. "When we become adults."

Catching a mouthwatering whiff of potatoes frying, Abby saw her chance to escape her brother's wrath. "To grow up, you have to eat, right?"

Jordan jolted. He seemed to understand that he wasn't the only one with problems. He pressed his lips together and gave Abby a little nod. Then he turned to Touk. "Three meals a day. How else are you going to get strong enough to beat me at arm wrestling?" Jordan made a muscle.

Toucan made her own muscle and growled. "Bring it." The growl quickly became a giggle.

"My money's on Touk," Abby smiled.

Jordan assumed an arm wrestling position at the corner of the table. "I hate it when my sisters gang up on me." He locked hands with Toucan, ready to battle.

"I'll count," Abby said. "Jordan, no cheating. Ready? On the count of three. One, two, two-and-a-half." Abby struggled to purge her voice of tears. Toucan's grit and determination to beat Jordan were bigger than the ocean, but her arm was as frail as a toothpick. "Three."

Touk pinned Jordan's arm. "I win," she squealed, grinning with a bright face.

Jordan scrunched up his face in a mock frown. "You won't be so lucky next time."

Abby winked at him and headed to the kitchen, where she scooped golden potato slices onto a plate. Returning to the dining room, she set the meal on the table and wagged her finger at Touk. "Fish and fries before chocolate!"

"Can I have some ketchup?" Toucan's eyes begged.

Abby returned to the kitchen, thinking she was finally on the home stretch. French fries, chocolate, arm wrestling, now ketchup... whatever it took to get her sister to eat... one meal, one victory at a time.

She ladled a spoonful of pale red water into a cup. A trader at the Portland Trading Zone had come up with the idea of mashing up a few tomatoes, adding salt, gallons of water and calling it ketchup. Adding a healthy dose of imagination to the subtle flavor worked wonders.

When Abby returned to the dining room, she stopped cold. Toucan and the chocolate had disappeared and Cat was making off with the fish. Jordan, staring sadly into space, was oblivious to the heist that had just taken place under his nose.

# CHAPTER THREE
## COLONY EAST

Lieutenant Dawson stepped outside the hotel and onto Lexington Avenue to enjoy a final moment of calm before awakening the one hundred and five cadets of Biltmore Company. He wore many hats—father, mother, counselor, big brother, naval officer, math teacher, and once the day's activities began, he'd be on his toes until lights out, fourteen hours from now.

The sky was turquoise and rays of light from the rising sun blazed on the remaining glass windows of the tall buildings. He detected a whiff of salt in the canyon of skyscrapers. An east wind was blowing off the water.

He lifted his eyes to beating wings. Canada geese passed overhead in a V-formation, most likely heading to Central Park Farm or the reflecting pool in front of Rockefeller Center.

Colony East was awakening. A Navy medic jogged by on his way to the hospital. The medic saluted, and Dawson returned the salute, though he didn't recognize him. Dawson used to know most of the military personnel at the colony by sight, if not by name, but transfers from Atlanta Colony and Colony West were arriving all the time. Down the street, sailors were assembling for construction work. A van, ferrying supplies from La Guardia Airport, rounded the corner, and a scientist approached on a bicycle. She wore a white lab coat, a trademark of the CDC personnel stationed at the colony. She said nothing as she pedaled by, a snub Dawson didn't take personally. All interactions between the scientists and members of the military were strictly business.

Dawson returned to the Biltmore's lobby and unlocked the padlock of the suggestion box on the wall. He was pleased to find a card inside, but he read the note with growing concern. The anonymous author reported that Cadet Billings possessed contraband. He made a mental note to search the cadet's living quarters after the national anthem played.

He locked the box and moved behind the front desk, where he flipped the switch of the luxury hotel's intercom once reserved for emergencies, historically, fire or terrorist attacks.

"Reveille!" His voice bellowed into every room on floors one through four. "Rise and shine. It's a beautiful day. On the double, let's go."

He pictured eyes cracking open, sleepy heads lifting off pillows. He imagined a lot of groaning going on. Groaning and grumbling were good. He prescribed to the wise military saying: 'When your troops stop grumbling, start worrying.'

He drummed his fingers. How should he announce Code 4? His cadets hated going to Medical Clinic 17. Dawson could empathize. The scientists lacked bedside manner; they treated the kids like guinea pigs in an experiment, poking and prodding them without explanation, often saying nothing for long stretches as they recorded data. "Code 4," he barked, figuring honesty was the best policy. "I repeat, Code 4. If anyone feels extra hungry, or warm and achy, please see me. You'll need to go to Medical Clinic 17."

He ended with the Colony East credo that every company leader delivered twice a day. "Remember, you are Generation M, the seeds of the new society."

'M' for Magnificent. That was the official word from Doctor Perkins. From scuttlebutt among the company leaders, though, he understood that 'M' really stood for Mendel. Gregor Mendel, the father of genetics, who died in the late 1800's.

Dawson rose and faced the small American flag on the counter. "Please rise," he said and punched play on the boom box. He saluted the flag while the Star Spangled Banner played.

# CHAPTER FOUR
# CASTINE ISLAND

Abby rolled out of bed at first light, anxious to visit the harbor and keep watch for the gypsies. They might arrive earlier than expected if the winds had picked up or changed direction during the night.

She dressed in layers so she could shed one at a time as the temperature rose throughout the morning. Tiptoeing, she turned on a walkie-talkie and propped it on Mel's pillow.

Once she was downstairs, Abby ate a piece of mackerel, some rice, and drank a glass of water from the still. She took a pinch of sand from a glass on the windowsill, brushed her teeth with her finger, and spat out the gritty slop. She put a piece of fish on a plate and wrote TOUK on a sheet of paper, which she placed over the fish. On her way out the door, she stuffed her pocket with peanuts and grabbed a plastic trash bag and walkie-talkie.

When she arrived at the deserted harbor, she saw whitecaps forming beyond the jetty. To get a better view of the open ocean to the north, the direction from which the gypsies should arrive, she scrambled up the giant blocks at the base of the jetty and started for the end. Seagulls, standing in a line like soldiers, stretched their wings and stepped into the air, one by one, as she approached.

At the tip of the jetty, Abby positioned the trash bag on a flat boulder and sat with her back against the corroded metal structure of the beacon, which had remained depressingly dark since the night of the purple moon.

Wishing she'd remembered binoculars, Abby gazed out to sea. Most gypsy vessels had a mainsail and jib, and sometimes they raised a spinnaker to run with the wind.

The sun warmed her face as it moved higher in the sky. Over the next several hours, the moisture on the boulders evaporated and gulls skimmed over the water, dipping their beaks below the surface to snag herring. She closed her eyes and listened to the birds dropping clams onto the rocks.

Abby thought about her problems with Touk and Jordan. Mel had told her recently, "Your sister will eat when she's hungry." Abby kept telling herself that, but then she'd panic every time she saw Touk turn her nose up at food. Mel was probably right and Abby had to find the strength to back off, keep her mouth shut. Jordan hadn't helped the situation, accusing Abby of being domineering so often that Toucan had started to call her bossy.

Even though Jordan's problem was different, Abby thought the solution was the same. Keep her mouth shut and back off. She knew what it was like to grieve the loss of a loved one. You needed the comfort of friends, but you also couldn't help lashing out at the people you cared for the most. Jordan lashed out at her, saying some very mean things. She hoped that by serving as a punching bag she was helping him heal.

As the morning wore on, she took off her windbreaker and then peeled off her sweater. There was a hint of spring in the air. Another hour passed. At the dock, the trawler's inboard engines fired up. The island's fishing crew was preparing for their trip out to sea at Georges Banks. The cod and haddock they harvested from the rich fishing grounds was the currency that Toby spent at the Portland Trading Zone. He'd trade fish for everything from fuel to peanut oil.

Abby's heart raced when she spotted a glint of silver in the sky. The airplane flew over the island seven days a week, usually in the morning. Endless speculation about the flights always led to the same conclusion. Nobody had a clue what the airplane was doing. She liked to believe it was proof the adults were coming up with some plan to help them.

She stood and gripped a steel bar of the beacon. The plane was coming in low, very low. The roar of the four propellers sent the gulls flying.

Abby waved both arms until the belly of the plane was directly above her. They must see her, she thought excitedly.

After the plane passed over, the wings tilted back and forth. The pilot was waving back!

Abby let out a whoop. It was her first communication with an adult in over two years.

~ ~ ~

Dishes rattled. The house foundation vibrated. The bed shook. The roar rose to a loud crescendo and then faded just as quickly.

Jordan blinked and rolled onto his side. He simmered with anger. He had gone to bed angry, had violent dreams, and now the airplane was stirring his rage on a new day.

The airplane was a reminder of everything wrong with the adults. It was a total mystery, just like what the adults were doing in New York City.

They never explained anything. Never said why they hadn't opened clinics. Never mentioned why they had stopped distributing pills.

He slammed his fist into the pillow at the memory of Portland. A year ago, he had gone to Portland International Airport, where the scientists had announced over the radio they would hand out pills.

He had arrived on May twenty-ninth. It was almost six weeks after the double tragedies in Boston—the disaster at Logan Airport and the death of Mandy.

Thousands of kids, most of them sick, were already waiting at the Portland airport. Portland was a Phase II city. The scientists were supposed to distribute the antibiotic pills there on June first. Some kids, like Jordan, were there to get pills for friends.

The scientists never showed, and from what Jordan later heard from news gypsies, they had not shown up anywhere else across the country. Millions of kids, desperate for the antibiotic, had waited in vain, and every one of the unlucky ones had died.

Such large numbers of victims numbed him, but the death of a single person—the girl he loved—had shredded his soul, and he would never be the same again.

He took quick, shallow breaths. Why hadn't he insisted that she take one of the pills that he brought back from Boston?

"I'm fine," she'd told him. "Give the pills to kids who need them now. I can wait until we get more in Portland."

Jordan flopped on his back and stared at the ceiling. The ball of rage in his chest spread out and seeped into his bones the way water bleeds into sand after a wave pounds the shore.

He heard voices and laughter through the window. Touk, Timmy, and Danny were playing outside.

He dragged himself out of bed. It seemed the sadder he got, the less he cared about anything. And the less he cared, the greater his fatigue. Night after night of restless sleep caused by frightening dreams added to his fatigue, slowing his thoughts to a crawl. Exhausted and in a fog, Jordan checked the girls' bedroom. Mel was sleeping and Abby was gone. He knew how Abby's mind worked. She was keeping watch for the gypsies at the harbor. The walkie-talkie on Mel's pillow confirmed his suspicion.

He stumbled downstairs and consulted his weather instruments. Good news for the gypsies, the barometer showed fair weather. Even better news, the wind had switched direction and picked up during the night. It was blowing out of the southwest at fifteen to twenty knots. They might arrive earlier than he predicted.

He saw Abby's note to Toucan and the plate licked clean. "Can't you read," he said to Cat, eyeing him from the corner. She flicked her tail, looking not the least bit guilty.

Jordan stepped outside and found the holy trio of terror playing Jenga on the porch. Toucan, hands on hips, seemed to be in charge of the two boys, Danny and Timmy. To him it was proof that Touk had the same bossy streak as Abby. Deep down he liked the fact that his sisters were assertive; he'd just never admit it to anyone.

Six-year-old Danny sat cross-legged, his pant legs rising midway to his shins, revealing a layer of dirt baked into his skin. Because the ocean was still cold, most islanders only took one bath a month, and they jokingly called their grimy ankles 'Castine Island socks'.

Timmy ran up to Jordan. "Jordie, did you see the airplane?" He extended his arms, jumped off the steps, and made his best roaring propeller sound. Danny flew after him.

Timmy still had the ability to confront terrible things without a care in the world. Jordan wished that he knew the boy's secret.

He turned to Toucan. "Hey, did you see Abby's note. You have to eat."

"I wasn't hungry."

"Look at me!" He moved his face until they were nose to nose and her big green eyes swallowed him. "Eat!"

Touk shook her head.

He sighed. "Stubborn as me, bossy as Abby."

"Abby says I'm assertive."

"You know a big word like that, you should eat."

Touk folded her arms and shook her head.

Timmy flew back to the porch. "Can I pick mushrooms with you?"

"Me, too," Touk cried.

"Let's pick mushrooms," Danny shouted.

Jordan shook his head and headed for his bike that was leaning against the garage. The kids gazed at him with long faces. It was as if they sensed his sadness, but couldn't understand it.

He pedaled up Melrose Street. A half mile from his house, he dismounted and hid the bike behind some bushes. He walked through the woods toward the water, keeping an eye out for tiny wildflowers that bloomed in the early spring. Finding none and running out of forest fast, he knelt by a patch of moss. It was green and kind of pretty, so he dug up a small patch with his fingers.

He continued walking until he reached the desolate western shoreline, a narrow band of pebbles with a few large boulders. There he placed the moss next to the pile of dried flowers he had built over the past weeks.

Huddled next to a boulder, out of the wind, Jordan wept and, as he did most mornings, cried out her name, "Emily…"

# CHAPTER FIVE
# COLONY EAST

Once the national anthem ended, Lieutenant Dawson sprinted up to the fourth floor where the fifteen-year-old boys lived. Moving down the hall, he swelled with pride at the flurry of activity: cadets making beds, folding clothes, brushing hair. What a far cry from the undisciplined lot he'd first set eyes on when Colony East opened.

Jonzy Billings lived at the end of the hall, the last room on the right. He found the boy tucking in the last corner of the bed sheet.

"Billings!"

Jonzy snapped to attention and saluted, knocking his glasses askew. He adjusted them. "Good morning, sir."

The boy might be gangly and uncoordinated, but he had the right stuff for leadership. He was a brilliant student who radiated confidence. Conflicted, Dawson wondered if he should even document the infraction. Experience had taught him to nip problems in the bud, but he also knew that looking the other way was sometimes the best approach.

"At ease."

Jonzy relaxed.

Dawson shifted his gaze to the chest of drawers. There, according to the note, he would find the contraband in the third drawer down.

He paced, observing that Billings kept his room shipshape. Every room in the Biltmore had a king-size bed, thick carpeting, comfortable chairs, a mini-fridge, radio, and bathroom. The cadet had squared his schoolbooks on the table.

He fished a quarter out of his pocket to buy himself time while he decided what to do. He held his arm out straight, shoulder level, pinching the quarter between his fingers. "You ready?"

Jonzy pulled his shoulders back. "Yes, sir."

"You know what happens to sailors who fail to make their beds properly?"

Jonzy nodded. "Latrine duty."

He released the quarter. It bounced six inches off the mattress.

Jonzy beamed. "Good job, right Lieutenant?"

Dawson ignored the comment and took a step toward the chest of drawers, but pivoted and aimed for the bathroom. The toilet, sink, and shower were spotless. Even the crack around the tub faucet was free of mildew.

Jonzy gave him a knowing look.

"Don't get cocky, Billings. It's not like you earned the Navy Cross."

Rules and regulations were put in place for a reason, Dawson told himself and headed straight for the chest of drawers, opening the third one down. He lifted up the neatly folded pile of T-shirts and eyed the electronic components hidden beneath them. "Care to explain?"

"Those are radio parts," Jonzy's voice trembled. "Sir."

"And why do you have radio parts?"

"I'm building a radio."

Dawson pointed out the radio in the room. "What's that?"

The cadet shifted foot to foot. "It only gets the CDC station. It doesn't pick up The Port."

"You're not allowed to listen to The Port."

"Sir, nobody ever said we couldn't listen to The Port. They just made it difficult."

Technically speaking, the boy was correct. Navy technicians, at the request of Doctor Perkins, had modified the room radios so they could only pick up the CDC station, FM 98.5. To the lieutenant's knowledge, nobody had ever issued a direct order that forbade cadets from listening to the other station.

Dawson couldn't simply drop the matter. He would turn the situation into a teaching moment. He got in Jonzy's face. "I'm going to write this up and file it in my records. Consider that you have one strike against you. You know what happens if you get two strikes?"

Sweat beads blossomed on the boy's brow. "Expulsion, sir."

He paused a moment to let Jonzy marinate in fear. Dawson wasn't the least bit angry. His scowl and sharp voice were tools of the trade. He had learned it was the best way to empower a cadet to change his behavior. "I trust you'll dispose of those parts."

"Yes, sir."

He lost the scowl. "We all make errors in judgment. Learn from it." Dawson ended with the type of fatherly smile that Admiral Samuels usually gave him after a good chewing out. "Carry on."

A moment later, walking down the hallway, Dawson smiled to himself, pleased at how he had set Cadet Billings on the correct path.

# CHAPTER SIX
## CASTINE ISLAND

Abby's radio crackled to life. "This is Mel, over."

Leaning against the rusty beacon, she brought the walkie-talkie to her lips and pressed the button. "No sign of the gypsies, over."

She and Mel reviewed their plans to meet at Sal's later on. The former barbershop was the site of the island's clinic.

"Guess who came looking for you?" Mel asked.

Abby saw Toby walking across the parking lot, toward the jetty. "He just found me." Not the least bit surprised, she let out a big sigh and signed off.

Toby was wearing a leather jacket, cowboy boots, and new jeans. He had told her that it was important for a lead negotiator to dress sharply. "People respect you when you look good. You get better deals."

Abby thought there was another reason for the clothing he chose to wear. Toby blended into the crowd, an average looking boy with brown eyes that were at once shifty and pleading. He desperately wanted attention, to be accepted. Toby seemed to be forever hurting inside, and she hoped his new clothes helped him feel better about himself.

He scrambled up the boulders, and soon Abby was in his shadow. "You should have stopped by my place. I would have come with you." He gestured to the jagged rocks where the water lapped the jetty. "What if you fell?"

"Toby, were you awake at six?"

He brushed away flecks of seaweed on a flat rock and sat next to her. "Abby, I would have gotten up for you."

She smiled. "All right. Next time we have an emergency, I'll bang on your door at dawn."

"I hope the emergency is really bad," he said.

Abby lurched forward and looked at him in disbelief. "What?"

He smirked. "I don't mean life-threatening. A broken leg would be perfect." He read her grimace. "Hear me out. When you trade something, you get the best deal when the other guy needs what you have. Supply and demand. The gypsies need medical care. The more serious the problem, the more they need us. Let's make sure they tell us their news before we help them."

She shook her head vehemently. "Toby, we're not trading cod for batteries. We're talking about people here."

"Hey, it's my call. I'm the lead negotiator."

"No, it's my call. I'm the medical first responder." She narrowed her eyes. "Thanks to you, remember?"

Toby had nominated her for the position when Derek Ladd hooked himself with a triple-pronged bluefish popper, six months earlier. With the fluorescent orange popper dangling from his ear like hippie jewelry, Derek ran off the jetty screaming as a stream of blood poured down his neck. Everyone panicked, including Abby, but somehow, she managed to keep her panic bottled up. She snipped the barbs with the wire cutters and the hook fell out of his ear.

After her heroics, Toby had given a speech at the island council, arguing she should be the medical first responder. Abby had received a unanimous vote.

She glared at him until he lowered his eyes.

"We'll help them first," he muttered. "How's Touk?"

Abby gulped. His sincere tone and the look of concern in his eyes caught her by surprise. She shrugged. "I was a picky eater at her age. Maybe it runs in the family."

103

"Does she like pears?"

"Are you kidding me? She loves them."

"I'll get her a case. Some people owe me a favor. We'll keep it between us, okay?"

Abby fixed her eyes on the horizon as if that might help anchor her turbulent thoughts. She'd do almost anything to help Toucan, and now, with a simple nod of her head, she could get her what she loved most. Touk might actually eat something. The secret deal, of course, would come out because keeping secrets on Castine Island was impossible.

Even if nobody ever found out about their arrangement, Abby knew that pears for Toucan would mean the community would receive less of something else. They always tried to share equally on the island, a code of fairness that separated them from the mainland. They had worked too hard to create trust to lose it over a case of pears.

"Thanks Toby, but Touk can eat what everyone else eats."

He shrugged. "Okay."

Abby bubbled with guilt. "Can you get just a few cans?"

"No prob," he nodded enthusiastically, oblivious to her conflicted feelings.

They sat without speaking for a few moments.

Toby broke the silence. "Before the night of the purple moon, this used to be my favorite spot to hang out. I had a good view of Al's."

Al's, on Main Street, used to be the island's only tavern. They had turned it into a game room with pool and ping-pong tables.

"I could see my father stumble out," he continued. "He was usually drunk before dinner."

Abby had heard stories about Toby's father. If even half of them were true, she might be willing to admit that Toby's life was better now than before the epidemic. She knew nothing about his mother, other than that she had left the island when Toby was very young.

"It must have been rough," she said.

He didn't say anything, his eyes focused on some distant point on the horizon. All of a sudden, he shot to his feet and pointed. "Look."

Abby spotted the two sails. Nobody was going to believe it. Two boats were heading to Castine Island. She brought the walkie-talkie to her lips.

~ ~ ~

Jordan stood on the dock, watching through binoculars as the two-masted schooner executed a crisp tack, turning into the wind to change direction. It was easy to understand how Abby and Toby had first reported seeing two boats. From the snippets of conversation with the captain, Jordan had not realized that *Lucky Me* was such an incredible boat.

Several minutes later, the canvas sails spilled air and fluttered as the bow swung into the wind again. The two booms swung around and the sails billowed like cheeks puffing with air. The boat heeled high on its port side and picked up speed on its new direction. The gypsy crew were clearly expert handlers.

The schooner was about half a mile beyond the jetty, and it would have to buck a headwind of fifteen to twenty knots the rest of the way into the harbor. He estimated the gypsies would pass the tip of the jetty in thirty minutes. Once the boat moored, he and Eddie would race out to pick up the stricken gypsy. Eddie was the second-best sailor on the island, and Jordan was confident they could handle whatever came their way.

The Boston Whaler, tied to the dock cleat, had a full tank of gas. The twelve-foot powerboat with its seventy-five horse motor could fly.

Abby's voice came over the walkie-talkie. "Do you guys have germ masks?"

Jordan saw a crowd gathering outside Sal's where Abby was readying medical supplies. "What for?"

"One of them might have the Pig."

"All set, over." Jordan didn't have a mask. Abby worried too much.

"Radio the problem as soon as you find out."

"Roger that," he replied.

The crowd outside Sal's continued to grow, and a group of kids milled at the playground. A steady stream of kids on bikes and skateboards trickled down Melrose Street.

The big turnout didn't surprise him. Gypsies stopped by the island regularly, and usually residents paid them little notice. But these gypsies were different. The news had spread that this was a survival story. Survivors rooted for other survivors.

When the schooner made its final tack before entering the harbor, Jordan gave a short blast on the air horn, and Eddie burst from the crowd and sprinted toward him.

He radioed Abby and told her they were about to head out. Then he climbed down the dock ladder and into the whaler. Eddie flew over the dock boards, put on the brakes, and unfastened the mooring line from the cleat. Jordan yanked the starter cord, and the outboard motor fired up, coughing out several puffs of oily, blue smoke. Eddie shoved the bow away from the dock and jumped in.

When Jordan pushed the throttle all the way forward, the bow lifted from the surge of power. Racing toward the schooner, he squinted from the spray peppering his face.

"I think I could be a gypsy," he shouted above the roar of the outboard.

"Let's do it!" Eddie replied without a moment's hesitation. "Who should we put on the crew?"

If Jordan became a gypsy, he would go alone. He would not want any reminders of Castine Island. "Don't say anything to Abby," he told his friend.

"Yeah, she'd freak out."

As soon as the gypsies passed the tip of the jetty, they lowered their after-sail, the triangular sail closest to the stern. Jordan motored to within fifteen feet of the schooner and counted two boys and two girls on deck.

The captain, wearing a yellow rain slicker, stood at the wheel, barking commands. She had a crew cut, the latest style for gypsy captains, and her voice resonated with authority. "Secure the mainsheet. Stand by to come about." The bleary-eyed crew responded. Wet from the bow spray, they leaped, crawled, and wormed their way around the deck to perform the tasks. The schooner's lines snapped and popped against the mast. "Coming about, hard-a-lee." The captain spun the wheel and *Lucky Me* completed the tack and headed for a red mooring buoy.

Lying prone at the bow, a boy held the boat hook. He was as tall and lean as the pole in his hands. When the captain turned into the wind, the boy snagged the buoy line and secured it to a cleat. At the same time, a girl wearing a red bandana lowered the fore sail. They had made it.

Jordan motored beside the schooner and Eddie tossed a line to the captain.

"What's the problem?" Jordan asked.

"A member of my crew needs her braces removed," the captain explained.

He and Eddie traded glances. Eddie's cheeks puffed out and he burst out laughing. Jordan joined in.

Jordan started to break the news to Abby over the walkie-talkie, but then froze.

A sudden wild scream sent a chill down his spine. The tall, skinny boy and bandana girl helped a girl up from below deck. Pale and trembling, she was a writhing mess of tears and disheveled hair. She looked about twelve, and she was covering her mouth with both hands, but it did little to muffle her screams. Her two escorts each gripped an elbow firmly, or she might have collapsed.

With a trembling hand, Jordan brought the walkie-talkie to his lips once more.

# CHAPTER SEVEN
## COLONY EAST

"Compan…eee ATTEN-SHUN!"

Lieutenant Dawson's command echoed off the building opposite the Biltmore. One hundred and five cadets stood before him in ten columns. Showing how their many drills had paid off, the older ones clicked heels together and tucked chins. Dawson's sharp eye noted, however, the younger members of the company had a lot of room for improvement.

"At ease," he barked.

The cadets relaxed. Scanning the faces and postures, he looked for flushed cheeks, slumping shoulders, any signs of illness. He'd have to take anyone showing symptoms to Medical Clinic 17 straightaway. Fortunately, they all seemed healthy.

"How many minutes?" a cadet shouted.

"Did we set a new record?" someone in back asked.

The record to assemble at parade rest once the national anthem had finished stood at eighteen minutes, forty-five seconds.

He started down the first column. "You know what my commander did when we wouldn't stop talking?"

"He made you run, sir," Jonzy shouted.

"Cadet Billings is correct. Do you know how far we ran?"

"Until everyone had fat blisters on their feet." Jonzy answered.

"Is Billings the only one awake this morning?"

"No, sir," they shouted in unison.

"I can't hear you."

"No, sir!" they boomed back.

They loved this game, and most days he did too. The sudden image of his baby daughter appearing in his mind gave him pause. Sarah seemed to visit his thoughts without rhyme or reason. He might think of his daughter in the middle of showing his math students how to solve a problem, or in the evening when he was brushing his teeth. There were hundreds of thousands of children like her outside the fences of the three colonies. Would the Navy and CDC perhaps try to help them survive someday? Dawson felt the anxious heat of laser stares as eager cadets waited to hear the time. He pulled his shoulders back and glanced at his watch.

"Twenty-two minutes, ten seconds." Groans rippled through the ranks. "Tomorrow is a new day. Always strive to do better. Dis-MISSED!"

Biltmore's cadets broke into groups, some heading straight to Grand Central Station, others waiting for friends in Hilton Company to catch up. Naval architects had turned the train station into the colony's primary mess hall.

Dawson waited for Captain Hedrick, the leader of Hilton Company. One of two doctors at Colony East, she was the sole surviving member of the U.S. Army. At the onset of the epidemic, she'd been on special assignment, observing medical procedures on a submarine.

A stethoscope dangled out of the pocket of her white jacket. He guessed she was a year older than he, not yet thirty.

A Navy barber had recently done a number on her reddish blonde hair, but Dawson always found himself mesmerized by her green eyes. Whenever he spoke to her, he knew how intently she was listening because her eyes seemed to mirror his feelings. The captain led the cadets of Hilton Company with a soft touch and those caring eyes. He respected that style, even though he could never lead that way himself.

"Morning, Captain."

"Good morning, Mark."

He suppressed a smile. He liked that she called him Mark in public. He referred to her as Captain Hedrick in front of the cadets, because the higher-ups frowned on social relations among company leaders; it was an unwritten code.

They walked together, bringing up the rear of their respective companies. A plane lifting off caught his attention. The crew, he knew, was heading out to test bacteria levels across the region, as they had done every day since Colony East had first opened for business. It reminded him that everyone had a job to do, a role to play. That was the Navy way. If everyone followed orders and did what they were supposed to do, the colony would operate at peak efficiency.

A boy from Sandy's company approached them. "Sandy, I got stung by a bee," he sniffled.

She went down on one knee, held his arm and inspected the red dot. "Have you been stung before?"

He nodded, blinking back tears.

She probed the area of the sting with her fingertip and spoke to him in a gentle tone. "That's good news. It means you're not allergic to a bee sting. Ask the cook for some baking soda. Mix the baking soda with a little bit of water and put the paste on the sting."

The boy trotted off.

Dawson had witnessed hundreds of similar episodes. After surviving the epidemic, he would have thought the children of the colony should be as tough as battle-hardened soldiers. In many regards, they were that tough. Then they would become distraught over scraped knees, scratches, minor bruises and bumps. He figured they simply longed to act like kids again and the tiniest of injuries gave them an excuse to let the tears flow.

The interruptions continued.

Alexa, a Biltmore cadet, age eight, raced up to him and saluted. "Rodney tripped me!" she cried angrily.

Rodney Baker, also in Biltmore Company, was a spirited, eleven-year-old cutup.

Dawson said to Alexa, "What you're telling me is that Rodney stuck his foot out and you stumbled over it."

Alexa scowled. "That's right. He did it on purpose."

Dawson gave Sandy a secret wink. He didn't want to be in the conflict resolution business. If he started settling disputes among the cadets, he wouldn't have time to tie his own shoes. "I see." He furrowed his brow for Alexa's benefit. "Rodney tried to do it."

The feisty cadet growled. "Yes. He tried to do it."

Pursing his lips, he nodded. "Hmmm, Rodney stuck out his foot, hoping you'd fall down."

Alexa gritted her teeth. "Yes!" Then she stormed off.

"I don't envy Rodney," he told Sandy.

"What happens when Rodney comes running to you?" she replied with a smile that warmed his insides.

Dawson pointed to his ear. "Listen, listen, listen. Ears solve more conflicts than speeches, suggestions, and reprimands combined."

Sandy brushed his arm. "I'll remember that."

A moment later, a Hilton cadet reported to her that he'd forgotten his ID card. Sandy told him to run back to the hotel and get it.

"It drives me crazy when they forget their ID cards," Dawson said, thinking it was the number one infraction in his company.

Sandy rolled her eyes. "Didn't you ever forget anything important when you were a kid?"

"My father commanded a cruiser. You know what would have happened to me?"

"Let me guess. He'd make you clean the latrine?"

He chuckled. "Close. The cat litter box."

She grinned. "I bet he called you Cadet Dawson."

"Don't laugh. He called me Markie."

Sandy laughed, but he didn't mind. She looked good when she laughed.

Cadets from both companies had formed two lines at the revolving doors of Grand Central Station, egging each other on to make the doors spin faster. The doors worked like a fan, releasing a cloud of scents outside—sizzling bacon, fresh baked rolls, and fried sweet potatoes. Dawson's mouth started watering even before he stepped inside the mess hall.

Navy cooks served three meals a day. Two companies at a time ate lunch and breakfast. He silently praised the wisdom of his superiors for assigning Biltmore and Hilton to dine together. All four companies joined up for dinner.

He and Sandy waited in the chow line like everyone else. Servers gave generous portions, and cadets with soy protein shakes and their plates piled high, drifted from the galley to find seats at tables set up in the concourse.

Dawson studied the menu on a white board. Breakfast: eggs, bacon, and potatoes. Lunch: chicken cutlets, peas, and squash. Dinner: rice and salad.

"How much was grown here?" Sandy asked, quickly adding, "I know, I need to get out of the hospital more often."

Dawson winked. "You have a good excuse. You're training the doctors of tomorrow."

Then he reviewed the menu items for her. "Lettuce from the hydroponic garden. Peas from Central Park Farm. The eggs definitely came from the coop at the United Nations. I'm not sure about the chicken cutlets. Everything else was flown in from Atlanta."

Their own plates full, they moved to the officers' mess, an area cordoned off with stanchions and velvet ropes. The cadets knew to stay outside the ropes unless it was an emergency. He and Sandy sat opposite each other at the round table.

Dawson thought the din of two hundred kids laughing and chatting, and the kitchen crew banging pots and pans, would drown out his voice, but he wanted to be absolutely certain that nobody other than Sandy heard him. He leaned forward. "Did you send anyone to MC seventeen?"

She shook her head.

"Me neither." He scooped some scrambled eggs onto his fork. "You know what the Code 4's about?"

"Yes."

Stunned by her response, he set the fork on his plate. Typically, company leaders were the last people in the colony to know the motives of the scientists, and that included Sandy, despite the fact she worked alongside CDC scientists in the hospital.

When she leaned closer to him to speak, he smelled something new in the plethora of scents. Vanilla shampoo. "It's just a precaution," she said. "They've seen instances of AHA mutating."

Actinomadur halophilia-1A, or 'AHA', was the bacteria introduced into the atmosphere two years ago by the comet.

She continued, "The scientists believe the new strain attacks the hypothalamus gland. The gland secretes hormones that control the appetite."

Dawson swallowed hard as the smiling face of his daughter, Sarah, formed in the vapor of his imagination. "Is it serious?"

"The victims want to keep eating. If they survive that phase of the illness, they develop a high fever and many die from organ failure."

He wondered how doctors could act so calm and even-keeled while describing horrific medical problems. Perspiration was trickling down his neck and his head was spinning. "Why are the germs mutating?"

"Didn't you study Charles Darwin at the Naval Academy?"

"I studied Darwin in high school, but what's that got to do with bacteria from the comet."

Sandy narrowed her eyes at him, as if he should know this. "All organisms mutate. They do it to survive changes in the environment. With bacteria, most mutations die off or they're harmless to humans. The original strain of AHA attacked the pituitary gland, specifically affecting the hormones produced during puberty. But that strain is no longer a threat. Many younger kids have since developed a natural immunity to it. So this mutation gives new life to an old germ."

Suddenly, the eggs, bacon, and hash browns before him no longer looked appetizing. He took a bite of potatoes anyway, chewing mechanically. He couldn't let the cadets see him wasting food.

"All this information is preliminary," she said. "The CDC has identified the greatest number of cases in Florida. They suspect that heat or sunlight might be a contributing factor so they're collecting air samples, some from the region of the equator."

Dawson wiped his mouth with a napkin. "It's hard to believe the germs are still in the air. Why didn't they just die off, or dissolve in the ocean?"

"AHA was hardy enough to travel to Earth from a hundred million miles away. The bacteria have protective structures, as spores do, and they'll probably be in the atmosphere for the next century. The germs attach themselves to dust and pollen. They hitchhike on particles in the air."

He sniffed. "We need to stretch a giant filter across the country."

"Wishful thinking," she smiled sadly. "It used to be called the ozone layer and it covered the entire planet. Then pollution destroyed it." She took a deep breath. "The CDC is concerned about another epidemic, but they're not panicking. They already understand AHA's molecular structure. So it shouldn't take as long to develop a new antibiotic."

"How do you know all this?" He smirked. "Is Doctor Perkins your new buddy?"

She rolled her eyes. "Hardly. Perkins is a politician. He sugarcoats everything. Doctor Droznin tells it like it is." She read his puzzled expression. "Hair pulled back, glasses, serious expression."

"You just described half the CDC."

"Russian accent?"

He curled the corner of his lip. "That narrows it down. I don't think I've had the pleasure of meeting Doctor Droznin."

"She's been here from the beginning. She's on loan from the Vector Institute in Russia. Droznin helped select the kids for the colony."

Just then, the siren sounded, signaling the end of breakfast for Biltmore and Hilton Companies.

Dawson stood. "Be nice to Doctor Droznin. It's not every day a scientist tells us what's going on. Have a good day, Captain."

"You, too, Mark."

# CHAPTER EIGHT
# CASTINE ISLAND

Abby peered out the window at Sal's. The large window was the main reason that she, in her official position as medical first responder, had chosen the former barbershop to serve as the clinic. The window let in plenty of light.

Like a water ambulance, the whaler was carrying the patient to the dock from the schooner. Jordan had said her name was Nikki. He and Eddie were at the stern, and the gypsy captain and Nikki huddled close to each other at the bow. The other members of the gypsy crew were securing their boat at the mooring. A group of island kids had gathered on the dock with a wheel chair.

Abby felt bad for the gypsy girl having sore gums, but she was relieved the problem was so minor.

Mel stepped beside her and joked, "You can be the dentist after this."

"I'll leave that honor to someone else. How about Mel Ladwick?"

Mel chuckled. "Thanks, but no thanks."

"I'll nominate you," Abby said.

"Let's make a deal. I'll be the dentist if you ask Toby to get us toothpaste."

Abby rolled her eyes. "What's wrong with sand?"

"If it came in peppermint, I might like it."

"Peppermint toothpaste is a tall order," Abby said.

Mel gave her a sidelong glance. "Yeah, but the lead negotiator has a crush on you. He gets you whatever you want."

A wave of guilt washed over Abby. Did Mel know about the pears that Toby was getting for Touk?

The water started to boil on the camp stove. Happy for the distraction, Abby went over to it and lowered the flame. She was sterilizing a pair of wire cutters that might come in handy to remove the gypsy's braces.

She surveyed the splints, sutures, gauze pads, scalpels, burn cream, wild garlic paste for cuts, pain medication, and antibiotics they had set out in preparation for the unknown. What Mel had said was true. Toby got her everything she asked for.

A moment later, the crowd on the dock parted and Jordan appeared, pushing Nikki in the wheelchair. Taking one look at the girl, Abby realized this was going to be more than a routine dental visit.

Mel held the door open and Jordan wheeled Nikki in. The captain, Eddie, and Toby followed. Nikki's cheeks were sunken, and the bones beneath her eyebrows protruded to form sharp outlines in her skin that appeared to be as thin as tissue paper.

The boys looked ready to panic. Mel stared with wide eyes, and the captain looked too exhausted to react in any way. Outside, the crowd of gawkers pushed closer. Faces pressed against Sal's big window, a wall of cheeks and eyeballs. Feeling like she was in a fish tank, heat flared on Abby's cheeks and her throat constricted.

Pretending to be calm, she asked Nikki, "Can I look in your mouth?"

Nikki clutched her face and sobbed. She caught her breath, sobbed some more, and caught her breath again. The cycle kept repeating until Abby feared she'd hyperventilate and pass out.

"She hasn't eaten in two weeks," the captain offered. "A couple of days ago she came down with a fever."

"She probably has an infection." Abby kept her other thought to herself. The infection would likely worsen unless they addressed the root cause. "Get her into the chair," she told Jordan.

Three retractable barber chairs, each with red leather seats and metal footstools, faced a large mirror on the wall. Jordan wheeled Nikki to the chair closest to the door, and then he and Eddie lifted her into it.

"Stop!" Toby shouted, freezing everyone in place, including Nikki. He addressed the captain. "If she dies, you still owe us." He wiggled his fingers, like a fish trader making his final offer… "Well, do we have a deal?"

The temperature in the room seemed to rise to a thousand degrees and burn up all the oxygen.

Abby's heart pounded in her throat and her jaws clamped shut, as if sealed by glue. It didn't matter that she couldn't move her mouth because she was utterly speechless.

Nikki took a jagged breath and resumed crying.

"Get out!" Jordan shouted at Toby.

Toby folded his arms defiantly. "I'm the lead negotiator. I have the right to be here. Maybe you should leave?"

Eddie balled a fist, ready to help Jordan toss Toby out.

Abby stepped between them. "Toby, you need to go. Now!"

Confusion, then hurt flashed on his face. "Hey, I was joking."

"Let him stay," the captain said, narrowing her eyes at Toby. "You'll get your news."

Hoping to diffuse the tension, Abby gave the boys jobs. Jordan held the flashlight. Eddie lowered the back of the barber chair. Toby got the wire cutters from the pot on the camp stove.

She stood before Nikki. "We're going to help you." Abby held two pain tablets in her palm. "Take these. You'll feel better."

The girl hunched her shoulders like a turtle retreating inside its shell.

"She can't swallow," the captain said.

"We can grind them up," Abby suggested.

Next she tried peeling back Nikki's left hand to see inside her mouth, but she resisted, flailing her head back and forth. Realizing she wasn't going to be able to look into Nikki's mouth without considerable force, Abby addressed the captain. "What if we let her sleep? It's more comfortable here than on a boat. We can try again when she's feeling rested."

"She's been getting worse every hour," the captain replied in a tone of desperation. She lowered her voice to a whisper. "I don't think she can last much longer."

Abby took a deep breath and imagined shoveling dirt on her sudden urge to panic. "We have to hold her hands and keep her head steady." The calmness of her own voice surprised her, and she was amazed that she was able to think clearly. "Mel, hold the flashlight. Jordan and Eddie, stand beside Nikki. Captain, please go behind her."

"What should I do?" Toby asked sheepishly.

She told him to help the captain.

Abby moved in front of Nikki. "Be gentle," she told her helpers and nodded for them to begin. Eddie and Jordan each levered a hand away from Nikki's face. Nikki tried to tuck her chin to her chest, but the captain and Toby pulled her head back and kept it secure. Overwhelmed, Nikki went limp.

Careful to keep her finger clear of Nikki's teeth, Abby pulled down her lower lip and grimaced as yellow pus oozed out and dribbled down Nikki's chin.

Mel gagged. Eddie turned pale, looking like he might get sick. They all backed away.

"Your gums are badly infected." Abby maintained eye contact as she spoke to Nikki. "We have to remove your braces, and you need to take penicillin, otherwise... I really don't know what will happen to you. This is very serious. We can't help you unless you cooperate."

While the captain whispered privately to Nikki, Abby sent Mel on an errand, assuming they would proceed. Then she instructed Eddie to grind up two pain pills and a penicillin tablet and mix the powders together.

The captain looked up. "Let's do it."

Abby held up the wire cutters and explained her approach to Nikki. "First I'm going to snip the wires that are connected to the bands. That should release some of the tension. Are you ready?"

Nikki put her head back, squeezed her eyes, and opened her mouth a crack. Jordan and Eddie held her hands. The captain directed the flashlight beam.

Abby zeroed in on a wire along the front row of teeth. When she snipped it, Nikki cried out and sealed her lips, but only for a moment. Abby was able to snip two more wires. Slowly Nikki started to relax. After cutting the final wire, she had Nikki rinse her mouth with salt water, and then sprinkled the mixture of pain medication and penicillin onto her tongue. They took a break to let the pain pills kick in.

Mel returned with a fishhook. The steel tuna hook, made to reel in a thousand pounds of fighting fish, was four inches long and measured two inches from shaft to point. The barbed point looked like a miniature spear.

Nikki's eyes widened.

Abby patted her on the arm. "I know it looks scary. I'm going to use the point to pull down on the edge of the metal bands around each tooth."

Starting what she hoped was the final phase of the operation, Abby positioned the sharp point of the hook at the top of a band on a front, upper tooth. But the band wouldn't budge. When she applied slight pressure, Nikki cried out.

"We need something greasy," Abby said.

"Burn cream?" Mel suggested.

Abby read the directions on the tube. "For external use only."

Jordan's face lit. "Peanut oil! We have some at the house." He moved to the door.

"Wait," Toby cried. He handed Abby a stick of lip balm. "Try this."

As Jordan waited to see if it would work, Abby worked a gob of balm around the band with her finger, positioned the point of the tuna hook, and pulled down. The band moved. She slid the point on one side and then the other, wriggling the band down the tooth. When the band tumbled into Nikki's lap, a cheer rang out inside Sal's.

An hour later, Abby had removed every band but two. She was unable to reach two lower molars. Exhausted, she slumped in the barber chair next to her patient.

"Hey," Eddie exclaimed. "I think Castine Island has a new dentist!"

Abby called him over and held the hook in front of his face, the sharp tip an inch from his nostrils. "Who are you talking about?"

Eddie swallowed hard and flipped his head, hiding his eyes behind a curtain of blonde hair. "Nobody you know."

Abby sat back with a satisfied smile. "That's what I figured."

# CHAPTER NINE
## COLONY EAST

Lieutenant Dawson looked up from his desk as students filed into the Grover Cleveland Conference Room on the first floor of the Chrysler Building. Many of the cadets, including Jonzy Billings, kicked off their shoes to enjoy the oriental carpeting. He nodded to Billings, letting the boy know that he had moved on from the earlier disciplinarian action.

The bottom four floors of the Chrysler Building housed the colony's school. It was Dawson's first period trigonometry class.

At nine a.m., the short blast of the air-raid siren signaled the start of the period. Dawson broke out his attendance book and requested information on the students he noticed missing.

"Alicia?" She was a member of Sheraton Company.

"Grief counseling," a fellow Sheratonian replied.

He marked G next to Alicia's name.

"Caroline?"

Marilyn from Hilton Company reported that Caroline was at Central Park Farm.

He gave Caroline an F for farm duty.

"Max?" Cadet Max Clemson came from Four Seasons.

When nobody responded, Dawson wrote U next to Max's name for unknown.

From his satchel, he removed the stack of IQ tests, sealed in envelopes. Each envelope came marked with a barcode, the student's name, and their company affiliation. The scientists, who loved collecting data on Generation M, issued the tests quarterly to all students. The focus of today's test was abstract reasoning.

Dawson stood to address the class. "You know the drill. No talking. Finish as much as you can. Anyone need to use the facilities?" When no one raised a hand, he passed out the tests.

Once they had begun, he briefly panicked when he didn't see his fly tying kit in his satchel. He breathed a sigh of relief when he found it hiding under his germ pack. Over the next hour, he tied a Wooly Bugger, an all-purpose dry fly made with red and gold Hungarian partridge feathers. He found the concentration required to tie a fly gave him a temporary feeling of peace.

The siren sounded to announce the end of the period. It also interrupted his fantasy of landing a striped bass in the East River. He collected the tests.

During his next class, Dawson occupied himself by doing calisthenics and stretches. Nobody batted an eye. His students had grown accustomed to him exercising when they took tests.

While his third and final class of the day labored over the abstract reasoning problems, he ate lunch at his desk. Spicy brown mustard on the chicken sandwich was a new and surprising treat.

At 2:45 p.m., the school day ended, and he headed for Central Command. With every stride, he felt the two sections of his fly fishing rod in his backpack, waving back and forth like bug antennae. He weaved among the thick throng of cadets on the sidewalk. They were on their way to Carnegie Hall for the daily lecture. It was a beautiful spring day with the temperature in the high sixties, and the scent of blossoms filled the air. A haunting melody drifted down from the Empire State Building as the wind whistled past broken windows. He thought of it as the world's tallest flute.

Central Command was located in Trump Tower. Standing across the street, he waited for the light to change. No vehicles were in sight, but he wasn't about to jaywalk. With his luck, Admiral Samuels would look out his fourth-floor window the moment he took his first illegal step into the street.

Dawson's first stop was the CDC liaison office. On duty was Doctor David Levine, dressed casually in a button-down shirt, corduroy pants, and tan Hush Puppies shoes that screamed scientist. In his early fifties, with salt and pepper hair, Levine rarely made eye contact. Dawson figured he was shy, an introvert who would have preferred the seclusion of a quarantine lab, rather than dealing with the likes of company leaders. He gave Doctor Levine the bundle of completed IQ tests.

Then Dawson jogged up to the third floor and stepped into the office assigned to company leaders. Lieutenants Masters and Murphy, representing Sheraton and Four Seasons Companies, were there doing paperwork. They acknowledged his presence with slight nods.

Masters was short and muscular, built like a fire hydrant. He had been in the class ahead of Dawson at the Academy. Murphy, a landlubber from Kansas, stood as tall as the corn that once grew up to the sky in the Midwestern state. To qualify for sub duty, Dawson imagined that Murphy must have found a way to compress his joints to come under the height limitation of six feet eight inches tall.

"Max Clemson wasn't in trig today," he told Masters, hoping for an explanation.

"Medical Clinic 17," Masters said without looking up.

"Poor little bugger," Murphy said.

Masters turned to Murphy and raised his eyebrows. "Think of the bright side. It could have been Code 10."

"Ever the optimist," Murphy replied.

Dawson respected both officers, but they were a bit too casual for his taste.

"What were Max's symptoms?" he asked.

Masters shrugged. "Ask the galley hands."

"Galley hands?"

Masters nodded. "They report any kid who goes back for seconds."

"Since when?" Dawson blurted.

"Since Perkins gave the order."

Dawson frowned. Doctor Perkins would never issue a direct order to a sailor, or for that matter, an officer. The chief scientist would have asked Admiral Samuels to deliver the command. "He doesn't have the authority."

Lieutenant Murphy chimed in. "I guess he does now."

"How do you know this?"

"Levine let it slip," Masters said.

Dawson pondered the fact that David Levine had said something more than thank you and you're welcome. "Are you going to address it with the admiral?" he asked.

Master's scrunched his brow. "Address what? That one of my cadets had Code 4 symptoms that I missed? Yeah, right. I don't need Samuels chewing me out. I got enough problems."

Dawson thought he had a good point. He began doing paperwork that involved making observations on the behaviors of cadets in each of his three math classes. Since they had all taken tests and he had spent the time tying flies, exercising, and eating, he had few observations to report.

Thirty minutes later, his paperwork completed, he jogged to the South Street Seaport where he hoped to put new bacterial strains, Max, Doctor Perkins, and all other problems and concerns, even Sarah, out of his mind temporarily, and make his dream of landing a big striper come true on Pier 15.

The pier was part of a seaport complex along the East River. While many of the shops and restaurants had burned down, much of the pier remained intact. Dawson moved to a floating dock attached to the pier, where he had fished the day before. He liked the way the river flowed here, figuring the swirling eddy attracted baitfish, and baitfish attracted striped bass. He assembled his fly rod and made other preparations, including clipping on the Wooly Bugger.

Using mostly wrist, he moved the rod tip forward and backward—ten o'clock to two o'clock. The weighted line whipped out as an elongated S. He gave a final, hard snap and the Wooly Bugger landed thirty yards away. He let it rest on the surface for a moment before slowly stripping the line into the basket fixed to his waist.

Flicking his wrist, stripping line—doing this same motion over and over—Dawson felt his mind calming. He studied the windmills midway in the river, their giant blades chopping up the rays of the late afternoon sun. The Brooklyn Bridge, its middle section missing, was to his left. A freighter had crashed into one of the abutments at the time of the comet. Across the river, tents and plywood structures extended beyond the perimeter fence, while on this side, ensigns patrolled in Zodiacs. Even with heavy, powerful motors, the rigid inflatable boats could hug the shoreline.

He recalled Admiral Samuels announcing that patrol boat activity had dropped by half since the new incinerator had come online. Prior to that, kids outside the fence brazenly ventured into the East River to collect the colony's garbage.

Aware that he was facing the direction of Mystic, Dawson took a deep breath and exhaled slowly. He pictured his home at twelve Orchard Lane and started choking up. Icy chills of anxiety followed when he realized that Sarah, if she were alive, would be at risk of contracting the new illness that attacks the hypothalamus gland.

At least the scientists discovered the germ mutation early, Dawson thought. They would have time to develop an antibiotic before a full-fledged epidemic broke out.

He nearly tumbled into the river from his next idea. He would volunteer to help with the distribution of the antibiotic, making sure that survivors in Mystic received the pills. He would search for Sarah at the same time.

A fish jumped which he took as a good omen. Mirroring the ripples of water made by the splash, ripples of hope spread out from his heart. With a new zest, he moved the rod tip forward and backward—ten o'clock to two o'clock.

# CHAPTER TEN
# CASTINE ISLAND

They held the trading session at Toby's house. The gypsy contingent included the captain and a new boy, Monty, close in age to Abby. He was tall and lean and spoke with an accent she couldn't place.

Toby had steered them into a room where a single candle burned and photos of parents, older siblings, grandmothers and grandfathers, crowded the shelves of a bookcase. Most homes on the island had memory rooms to honor those who had died during the night of the purple moon. Scanning the photos, Abby was quite sure they belonged to Toby's housemates. Toby, she thought, would not want any reminders of his father.

Trading sessions usually began with both parties sharing food, and Toby had gone to the kitchen for snacks.

Sitting next to the captain, Jordan pointed out the window. "You're lucky you got here when you did. Those streaky clouds mean the wind's going to veer to the southwest. Fog will roll in."

"I'm impressed you know that," she replied.

"I'm the best sailor on the island."

Abby rubbed her chin, perplexed. It was not like her brother to boast.

Eddie nosed between the captain and Jordan. "I'm the second best sailor."

Jordan elbowed his friend out of the way. "Do you like being a news gypsy?"

The captain frowned. "Not when there's an emergency. "Otherwise, yes. I love it. Every day is an adventure."

Jordan's face lit up. "What's the farthest place you've been?"

Abby couldn't remember the last time her brother had looked so... happy.

"We've been to Florida twice."

Jordan almost fell out of his chair. "You're kidding me!"

Abby tapped him on the shoulder.

The interruption annoyed him. "What?"

"Go see what Toby's doing."

"Huh?" He narrowed his eyes. "You go."

Just then, Toby entered with a tray of snacks. The snacks were typical island fare: smoked mackerel and cold french fries with a special treat of graham crackers and peanut butter. To make sure nobody got greedy, Toby provided a toothpick to spread the peanut butter.

For the gypsy offering, the captain produced an orange from her pouch. The room quieted as the islanders stared. Abby hadn't seen an orange in more than two years. They watched her peel it then break apart the wedges. The captain passed out the wedges, along with pieces of rind. The scent of citrus mingled in the air with the waxy odor of the candle. Abby dragged the rind across her lower teeth before chewing her piece. As much as she was looking forward to hearing news, she was in no rush to eat her portion. The wedge was thin and had a tough membrane. If someone had handed her this piece before the epidemic, she would have discarded it, thinking it was too fibrous and dry. Now, it was the freshest, plumpest, juiciest, orange wedge ever. She held it under her nose and slowly inhaled. It triggered memories of walking past oranges, lemons, and limes piled high at the supermarket. She placed the wedge on her tongue and let it sit for a moment before biting down to release the juice. If this single wedge had been her only payment for removing Nikki's braces—for all the crazy drama at Sal's—Abby would have felt it was a fair trade.

Toby cleared his throat and started reviewing the trading rules.

The captain cut him off, "Don't worry. We'll tell you everything we know."

Abby glanced at Toby, but he skillfully avoided her gaze.

Typically, gypsies dribbled out tidbits at the beginning of a session, saving the most dazzling news—the big event—for last, much like a fireworks display.

The captain described kids in New Jersey who were generating electricity from solar panels. "They told us they want to trade electricity for food."

Castine Island was too foggy for solar panels, Abby thought.

"An eleven-year-old boy flew an airplane," the captain offered next.

Toby raised his hand. "Challenge."

A challenge was a polite way to ask a gypsy to elaborate or provide more evidence that a news bit, was in fact, true.

"It happened in Miami. We confirmed the story with multiple eyewitnesses. The boy took off from Miami International in a small airplane and flew over the Miami Trading Zone. The plane crashed just offshore, and he swam back to the beach."

"Figures," Jordan said. "Eleven-year-olds think they can do anything."

Toby gave a nod, indicating he was satisfied with the captain's response.

She continued, "A fuel king in Connecticut set up tolls on the main roads to the trading zones. Other kings are starting to do the same."

Fuel kings wielded a lot of power, controlling the local supplies of gasoline and diesel. Long ago, gas stations had either burned to the ground, or survivors had found ways to siphon the gasoline from their underground tanks. It left only one remaining source of fuel, the large tanks found near every port city. Toby had told Abby about Martha, the fuel king that he traded with at the Portland Zone. Martha assigned armed guards at the tanks she controlled.

The captain waited for a challenge. None came. "There was a zebra on the loose in North Carolina. Nikki spotted it."

Monty, the new boy, spoke up. "They let the animals out of the Bronx Zoo."

Abby suddenly pegged his accent. He was from New York.

Everyone accepted that a zebra was running free, she thought, because another gypsy crew had reported a camel wandering around the Providence Trading Zone.

"Do you know about the Pig?" the captain asked. They all nodded. Abby figured this topic was the big event.

"We heard about eight cases. Four in Florida, three in Georgia, one in Virginia. A boy in Connecticut died, but not from the Pig."

Toby and Jordan issued challenges at the same time.

The captain lowered her eyes and spoke in a halting voice. "The boy was seven. We talked to his older sister. They lived in a commune outside Hartford. She noticed his appetite had increased. He was hungry all the time. He became like an animal when it came to food." The captain hesitated longer and longer after each sentence, as if she were verbally struggling toward some horrific event she didn't want to describe. "He wouldn't stop eating. He gained thirty pounds in a month. He couldn't help himself. At the commune, they rationed food as everyone else does, and his sister was giving him her portions, but he still wanted more. Others at the commune wanted to kick him out. One night, the boy broke into a shed where they stored potatoes and rice." The captain took a deep, shaky breath and brought her hands to her face. Everyone in the room remained quiet.

A sourness formed in the pit of Abby's stomach. She did not want to hear the details of what happened to the infected boy, but this was important information to know. God forbid someone on the island got the Pig. "Challenge," she whispered.

The captain looked up with wet eyes. "They beat him to death."

Abby gasped, even though she expected to hear that. She had become numb to so many types of tragedy, but cruelty among survivors always bothered her. If kids shared equally and helped each other, a group became stronger over time. Why couldn't kids understand that?

The captain dragged a sleeve across her eyes and sat up straighter. "Are you ready for the big event? Monty, our newest member of the crew, lived at Colony East."

The islanders traded glances, having no idea what Colony East was.

# CHAPTER ELEVEN
# COLONY EAST

Lieutenant Dawson counted down the seconds to the top of the hour. At eight p.m., the siren wailed, putting his neck hairs on end. For half a minute, the piercing alert penetrated glass, brick, and bone. He jokingly called it 'The Colony East Lullaby.'

He had suggested to Admiral Samuels that they ring the St. Patrick's Cathedral bells at bedtime rather than rely on a siren originally intended to warn New York City residents of a nuclear attack.

Samuels had passed the idea on to Doctor Perkins, who commissioned a study. They concluded the decibel level of the bells was insufficient. "Between you and me," the admiral had confided in him, "I just think the white coats enjoy pushing the siren button."

Dawson wondered if there might have been another reason. Doctor Perkins, who often quoted from the texts of the world's great religions— who even acted like he was God on occasion—scheduled no faith-related activities for Generation M. Might the chief scientist have considered it some sort of religious endorsement if he had approved the church bells?

When the siren mercifully ended, he stepped outside the Biltmore. Two ensigns were pedaling down Lexington Ave on their way to patrol the Red Zone, north of Central Park Farm. He saw the shadowy outlines of their handguns, Navy-issued Colt 45 automatic pistols. The ensigns gave him quick salutes.

Seeing no suspicious activity, he returned to the lobby and picked up the intercom mic. "Lights out, no talking. Remember, you are Generation M, the seeds of the new society. Tomorrow is a new day. Always strive to do your best."

He jogged up to the fourth floor. "Good night," he said into the darkness of the first room.

"Good night, sir."

Greeting and being greeted, Dawson moved down the hallway. If a cadet didn't respond, he listened for the deep, steady breathing of sleep. After a grueling day of studies, IQ tests, a honeybee lecture, the consumption of four thousand calories, and possibly a work shift at Central Park Farm or the UN chicken coop, most kids conked out the minute their heads hit the pillow.

He stopped outside Cadet Billings' living quarters and saw the boy was still awake, sitting up in bed. "Good night."

"Thank you, sir. I appreciate you giving me a second chance."

Dawson's spirit soared. Billings understood he had made a mistake. It confirmed to him that Jonzy would make a fine leader someday. Leadership, however, demanded a sharp response. One must project authority at all times to maintain respect. "Who said anything about a second chance? Don't let me and your fellow cadets down again."

"Yes, sir."

Dawson breezed through the third floor and started on the second. "Good night, Daddy," a ten-year-old boy responded.

He expected more heartache. Mommy, Grandpa, Uncle, Grammy... Since the start of the colony, he figured the cadets had called him every type of family relation at least once.

Dawson's heart shattered into smaller and smaller pieces as he moved from room to room.

He dreaded the last and final floor, the wing of seven-year-old girls. Halfway down the hall, he heard whimpering, and flicked on the flashlight to identify its source. The sound was coming from the living quarters where Lily Meyers and Tabatha Williams double-bunked.

The light beam revealed Lily's empty bed. Tabatha was the one crying. Had the girls snuggled up together? He didn't see any lumps in Tabby's bed. He got down on his knees and peered under both beds. Then he checked the bathroom.

Alarmed, he went over to Tabatha, training the flashlight on the ceiling to keep the bright light out of her eyes. He noticed that her pillowcase was wet, as was the top of her nightgown, an indication she'd been crying hard for some time. "Tabby, where's Lily?"

The girl sniffled, "they came and took her away."

Dawson thought of Tabby and Lily as identical twins with dramatically different personalities. They both had big brown eyes, brown hair, and were quick to giggle. But Lily had an adventurous streak. She'd try new meals the Navy cooks concocted and, because she charged into every activity with gusto, had twice as many scraped knees, bumps, and bruises as Tabby. Tabby was studious and cautious. Not surprisingly, Tabby volunteered to work at the public library while Lily always chose the active chaos of the chicken coop at the United Nations.

"Who took her?" he asked calmly, fighting a panicky urge to shout until he had answers for Lily's disappearance.

"Two women in spacesuits," Tabby said.

He flushed with embarrassment. He'd told the younger cadets that the scary looking hazmat suits were really 'spacesuits that astronauts wore.' It was perhaps the only time he had lied as a company leader.

He realized a CDC quarantine team must have entered the Biltmore while he was saying goodnight to the cadets on the upper floors. Wondering if they had attempted to contact him, he checked his two-way radio. The volume was up. Scientists had the right to quarantine any child, using whatever means they saw fit, but they were supposed to inform him first.

"Lily's going to be fine." He soothed Tabby with his voice, hiding the building anger inside. "They took her to Medical Clinic 17 to help her get better."

Tabby opened her eyes wide with fear. "I'll never see her again!"

"Of course you will." Dawson went to give her a comforting pat on the shoulder, but drew his hand back before touching her. Regulations prohibited making any contact with a cadet without another adult present. "Crying isn't going to help anything."

Tabby hiccupped. "Sorry, sir."

He flicked off the light. "Go to sleep. Lily will be back before you know it."

Dawson feared Tabby would be up for a long time. When he returned to his living quarters, he was quite certain that sleep would elude him, as well.

# CHAPTER TWELVE
# CASTINE ISLAND

"Have you heard of Colony East?" Monty asked the group.

Jordan didn't care that the gypsy boy had lived somewhere called Colony East.

"It's in New York City," Monty continued. "The adults built a fence around Manhattan."

Jordan felt like a lightning bolt had shot through his brain. "You lived there?" he blurted out.

Monty nodded.

"Challenge," Toby said.

Ignoring protocol, Jordan asked him, "Do they have a hospital?"

Just like that, the floodgates opened and the islanders fired off questions. "Why do they call it Colony East? Is there a Colony West?" Abby joined in, asking how many adults lived there.

"Did they really blow up the Brooklyn Bridge?" Jordan practically had to shout to make himself heard. "Other gypsies told us that."

Saying nothing, Monty waited them out. In the first moment of silence, he suggested they hold their questions until he had finished telling them his story. "It looks like we'll be around here for a while. If I don't answer your question today, you can ask me later."

Abby had invited the gypsies to stay on the island while Nikki recovered. Everybody seemed to like Monty's idea.

"Monty is not my real name," the gypsy boy began. "I changed my name in case the adults try to track me down someday.

"Over a year ago, I was living in the Bronx with my younger brother, Stone, and four of our cousins. Stone isn't his name, either. We watched the adults build windmills in the East River. They parked a submarine across the river. They restored electricity to some of the buildings." He turned to Jordan. "They blew up three bridges."

The captain cleared her throat. "Monty, tell them how you got selected."

"A year and a half ago, New York City was a Phase I distribution city and the scientists handed out pills at La Guardia Airport. I waited in line for four days. There must have been half a million kids ahead of me. When I finally got inside the terminal building, a scientist asked me a bunch of questions. I have no idea why he picked me. He wanted to know my age, where I went to school, what type of student I was, where I lived.

"Then he took me to a room and gave me a test. Other kids were also taking the test. It was multiple-choice, math and vocabulary. It was super easy. After that, I got the pills and left.

"Two months later, a scientist with a weird accent showed up at my door. She said her name was Doctor Droznin. She was in charge of Colony East admissions. Two Navy dudes were with her.

"She said I'd been selected to join Colony East, but it was my choice if I wanted to live there. She told me I'd stay in a five-star hotel and go to school. I'd eat fresh fruits and vegetables. I'd be safe. She told me some crap about how I could be a seed for a new society."

Monty shrugged, "Who wouldn't want to go to a place like that? Our neighborhood was dangerous. One of us had to stay up every night to guard the house. We'd been eating pigeons and rats which was better than what some kids were eating.

"I asked Doctor Droznin if I could bring Robbie with me—"

"Stone," the captain interrupted. "Your brother's name is Stone."

Monty nodded. "Yeah, Monty and Stone. Someday I'll get used to our names. Doctor Droznin said that only I could go. I didn't think it was a big deal. I figured I could come home on the weekends. Man, I was wrong."

Monty hypnotized them with his descriptions of the colony and his daily activities. Jordan thought the stories had to be true. They were too strange to make up.

"You probably want to know why I left, right?" Monty asked them. "I missed my brother. After four months, I asked Lieutenant Masters if I could visit him. The lieutenant was my company leader." Monty grinned. "He was really cool. He let us break the rules all the time.

"He said if I left the colony, I couldn't come back. He also told me there was only one way to leave. I'd have to get kicked out by Admiral Samuels and Doctor Perkins. They were in charge of the colony. I told him I wanted out. To help me get out, Lieutenant Masters wrote a report, saying I was disobedient and nothing would change my behavior. He took me to the council. You want to meet a scary dude? Admiral Samuels looks like a pit bull ready to bite your head off. Doctor Perkins is the chief scientist. He's kind of strange. When he explains something, you don't have a clue what he's talking about.

"We met at Trump Tower. After the lieutenant finished telling them what a screw-up I was, Doctor Perkins gave me a long lecture about Generation M, and how I could play an important role in the future of the human race."

Eddie interrupted. "Generation M?"

"Generation Magnificent," Monty explained.

Jordan chuckled. "Generation Madness, I would say."

"Let him finish," Abby snapped.

Monty grinned slyly, "I thanked Doctor Perkins for wanting me to play such an important role, but I told him I hated Colony East, and I wasn't going to change my behavior. He whispered something to Admiral Samuels. Then the admiral told me they were transferring me to Biltmore Company. Lieutenant Dawson was the strictest company leader."

Abby shot Jordan a look. The way he skillfully avoided her gaze confirmed that he was thinking the same thing. Their mother's favorite television program had been Dawson's Creek. They could never watch their own shows when Dawson's Creek was on. If he made eye contact with her, it would make the memory even sadder.

Monty grinned. "I told Admiral Samuels and Doctor Perkins where they could stick it."

"Challenge," Eddie said.

Monty gestured to the candle burning and all the pictures of loved ones in the memory room. "Out of respect for the dead, I won't tell you the exact words I used, but it worked. Here I am."

# CHAPTER THIRTEEN
## COLONY EAST

The front door of Medical Clinic 17 was locked, and nobody was at the desk in the lobby. Eyeing the video camera pointed down at him, Lieutenant Dawson pressed the buzzer next to the security keypad and waited. It didn't surprise him to find the lobby empty at this hour of the morning. From what he'd heard about the work schedules of CDC personnel, he and they were polar opposites. Early to bed, early to rise... That was the motto he lived by. Sometimes, he wondered if the scientists only worked in their labs at night.

Dawson checked the time, realizing that breakfast was now underway. He'd asked Sandy to supervise his cadets at Grand Central Station. School began in ninety minutes. While he expected to make it to class on time, he had lined up Lieutenant Masters to cover first period trig just in case.

He pressed the buzzer again. What good was a video camera that nobody monitored? He walked to the sidewalk to see if, by some miracle, anyone from the CDC might be heading to Medical Clinic 17.

The five-story building was in Sector E, a two-block stretch near Times Square that offered one-stop shopping for all things medical in the colony. The dental clinic was across the street and the hospital, where Sandy worked, was next door.

MC 17 was an annex of the hospital, formerly a neonatal special care facility. Doctor Perkins had requested the enclosed bridge connecting the two buildings be walled off. Dawson had no idea why.

He spotted activity inside the lobby and jogged to the door. Two scientists had entered the lobby through interior double doors. They'd probably pulled all-nighters in a lab. Engaged in animated discussion, they opened the front door and walked past him as if he were invisible.

He stepped inside and considered his options. He could take a seat and wait for someone to show up, or he could go exploring. Squaring his shoulders, he stepped through the double doors.

He faced a long, dimly lit corridor with doors on both sides. Lily could be anywhere. He knocked on the first door on the right. When nobody responded, he peeked inside. Lots of test tubes and medical gadgets, no scientists. Knocking and turning knobs, Dawson moved in a zigzag pattern, finding no one to receive his inquiry about Lily Meyers. Halfway down the hall, he detected an odor seeping under a doorjamb, which reminded him of high school biology. His class had dissected fetal pigs, preserved in formaldehyde. The smell had made him dizzy and sick to his stomach, convincing him he wouldn't make a good doctor or funeral home director. The door to the room emitting the fumes was locked.

He continued searching until he reached the fire exit. Not the smartest design, he noted. They had no push-bars, so in case of a fire, the doors offered no escape.

Just then, a scientist entered the hall. He checked his watch, thinking it was about time someone showed up for work.

He was heading for her when a door on the left side of the corridor opened and someone wearing a hazmat suit stepped out. Dawson stepped around the person in the suit, wondering why this individual had not responded to his knock. "Excuse me."

The spring-loaded door closed slowly, providing him with a glimpse inside. Three black bags, about four feet in length, lay on three gurneys. The strong odor of chemicals that wafted out suggested autopsies. His thoughts started swirling.

"Lieutenant Dawson." The sharp voice of the scientist sliced into his eardrums like a scalpel. Recognizing the Russian accent, he realized it must be Doctor Droznin.

"Yes, ma'am."

"We've reported your intrusion to Admiral Samuels."

*Intrusion?* "I'm here to check on Lily Meyers."

"I have no update for you."

"Doctor Droznin?" He waited for her to indicate he was correct. Instead, she just stared. "Whatever you can tell me would be helpful. Lily's roommate is worried about her, and I assured her I would check on Lily first thing."

An accordion of crinkles appeared in Doctor Droznin's forehead. "Is Tabatha Williams exhibiting any symptoms?"

Dawson rocked back on his heels. "No."

"As I told you, I have no update."

From having served eight years in the U.S. Navy, Dawson knew a bureaucratic stonewall when he hit one. He could argue all day with Doctor Droznin and get nowhere. His next step was obvious, and the doctor had apparently already done him the service of alerting Admiral Samuels.

He thanked her because protocol called for it, and then exited Medical Clinic 17. Walking away from the building, he revisited the scene he'd glimpsed. Logic told him the BDU was still clearing apartments in the Yellow and Red Zones, and the scientists had an insatiable curiosity to study the effects of the bacteria that had claimed so many two years earlier. Neither rational thinking nor the fresh air did much to clear his churning mind.

~ ~ ~

Five hours later, Lieutenant Dawson entered HQ at Trump Towers. Ensign Parker saluted him and he returned it. If it weren't for the uniform Parker wore, Dawson might have mistaken him for a Colony East cadet. He wondered if the ensign had started shaving yet. Dawson even detected a trace of acne under the ensign's left ear. He must have enlisted right out of high school and, lucky for him, selected submarine duty.

Parker had raised Dawson on the radio earlier, informing him that both the admiral and Doctor Perkins wished to see him. Good, he had thought, kill two birds with one stone.

Dawson sat ramrod straight and thought it strange that the ensign was avoiding eye contact. The only other occasions when Parker wouldn't look him in the eye were the times he had made furlough requests to the admiral.

Admiral Samuels stepped out of his office. With his crew cut, barrel chest, and permanent scowl, he reminded Dawson of a squat bulldog. True to the breed, the admiral's bite was as fearsome as his bark.

Parker gestured. "Go on in." The ensign seemed to find the items on his desk too interesting for him to look up as Dawson passed.

Samuels and Perkins made quite the pair. With canines on his mind, Perkins reminded Dawson of a greyhound wearing a maroon bowtie. He had a long thin nose and sunken cheeks. He mostly liked to sit back, quiet and observant, but when he decided to give a speech, he rambled on at breakneck speed, mixing poetic metaphors with the sterile vocabulary of the sciences. Dawson wasn't alone in missing the deeper meaning behind many of Doctor Perkin's soliloquies.

The chief scientist adjusted his wire rimmed glasses on the thin bridge of his nose. "Good afternoon, Lieutenant. I appreciate your taking time out of your busy schedule. Your efforts to support Generation M have not gone unnoticed. Company leaders play an important role in nourishing the seeds of the new society."

Dawson nodded. "Thank you, sir." He knew when to keep his comments brief.

Admiral Samuels sat behind his huge mahogany desk, drumming his fingers. After a moment, he walked around the desk and half-sat on a corner. "Mark, just what were you thinking? In Colony East, we lock doors for a reason. Medical Clinic 17 hadn't opened yet."

Dawson realized he might get only one chance to speak his mind. He'd better make it good. "Sir, last night a CDC quarantine team took one of my cadets, Lily Meyers. As far as I can tell, I received no prior notification. Nor did I receive a status update in the daily memorandum. This morning, I decided to see how she was doing. I want to keep my cadets informed of Lily's condition."

A vein in the admiral's neck popped out like a rope. "Did you ever think of asking me? Wouldn't that have been the easier course to take, the right course?" He glared down on Dawson, roasting him like a pig on a spit.

The rising heat Dawson felt inflamed his cheeks and his pounding heart indicated the admiral's technique was working. He'd think twice before exploring Medical Clinic 17 on his own again.

Doctor Perkins nodded to the admiral. "I can sympathize with the lieutenant. My Q-teams can be aggressive at times. The team should have informed him. I'll reprimand them so this unfortunate situation doesn't repeat itself."

Admiral Samuels grunted. After serving for five years under the admiral's command on the *USS Seawolf* and a year at Colony East, Dawson still couldn't read that grunt.

Perkins now faced him. "I'd also like to apologize for Doctor Droznin's abruptness. While polite discourse sometimes eludes her, we have no better steward for the seeds of the new society. Doctor Droznin's ability to analyze data is absolutely critical to the success of the colony."

Just warming up, Doctor Perkins tented his slender fingers. "Lieutenant, I learned an important lesson as a postdoc at Princeton. Never publish a paper prematurely. Make sure your research is thorough and rock solid. Collect all your data before you reach a conclusion." A shadow of concern spread across Perkins' face. "We've identified a new illness. We have some theories on what's causing it, but that's all we have, a hypothesis. We'll share what we know, but only after we have made our conclusions." The shadow lifted and he practically beamed. "Lily Meyers is very important to all of us. She can help us solve a piece of the puzzle." Doctor Perkins turned his eyes into deep pools of wisdom. "Many people believe science moves forward in leaps and bounds. Nay, Lieutenant Dawson, not true. Ever since the ancient Greeks plotted the heavens, science has marched forward in tiny, incremental, systematic steps. We are like a slug creeping up a blade of grass; we comb through data as slowly as a bivalve filters seawater for nutrients. Deliberation and thoroughness are the bedrock of science. Lily, as an incubator of the illness, should help us in our quest. You have to trust that we're utilizing her appropriately. She offers a key to the survival of Generation M."

Dawson felt the admiral's glare, which he knew meant only one thing. Salute and move on. He turned his head slightly, removing Admiral Samuels from his peripheral vision. "Thank you for explaining that, Doctor Perkins. Can I see Lily? I'd like to let her know everyone in Biltmore Company is pulling for her."

"I'm sorry, that won't be possible," Perkins said. "We've transferred the subject to the Atlanta Colony where we have a more sophisticated research lab."

Dawson fought the wobble in his knees. "Can I write to her?" The admiral moved back into his field of vision, and Dawson sensed he was none too pleased.

Perkins' face lit up. "That's a wonderful idea. It should lift her spirits. Deliver your letters to the liaison office. Doctor Levine will make sure they're put on the next transport flight."

"Is that all, Lieutenant Dawson?" The admiral asked, expecting only one answer.

"Yes, sir."

"Good. Dismissed."

# CHAPTER FOURTEEN
## CASTINE ISLAND

*Lucky Me*, Jordan's destination, was at her mooring in the harbor.

He leaned forward in the rowboat and dipped the oar blades into the water. Keeping his arms straight and elbows locked, he pulled back and completed the stroke by bringing the handles to his chest. With a powerful thrust, the boat glided away from the dock. A steady breeze out of the southwest, typical for early May, kept him cool as he worked the oars.

Only the captain was on board *Lucky Me*. Jordan had made sure of it before setting off.

While Nikki was getting her strength back, the gypsies had quickly settled into the rhythms of island life. Monty and Stone were staying in Jordan's room. Last he'd seen the boys, they were testing their skateboarding skills on Mount Melrose. The crew members, Alisha and Todd, slept in their berths at night, but they loved bowling by candlelight so much, they had practically moved into Castine Lanes.

The captain had volunteered to work in the garden, and it was during a weeding session that Jordan had told her how much he loved sailing, how he had always wanted to join the Navy. He learned that she loved the sea and sailing as much as he did.

Halfway between the dock and schooner, Jordan rowed in a circle. Someone watching him might have thought he was operating a rowboat while drunk. He was drunk—with doubts and indecision. What would he tell Abby? How would Touk react to his leaving?

He kept rowing in circles until his arms became heavy. Then he aimed the bow at *Lucky Me* and took slow, steady strokes until he cut through the schooner's reflection on the surface.

The captain appeared at the rail.

"Permission to come aboard. There's something I'd like to ask you."

She tossed him a rope. "I've been expecting you."

~ ~ ~

Abby followed Monty up Melrose Street. Having just finished a run, he was walking up the street, carrying his skateboard under his arm. She watched him pump his fist and shout encouragement to his brother, ten-year-old Stone, who zoomed by him on a skateboard.

A foot shorter, Stone was a smaller version of Monty. Both boys had shaggy brown hair that was turning into dreadlocks from a lack of shampooing. They also seemed to share a love of thrills and spills. Every day on the island had resulted in new scrapes appearing on their knees and elbows. They wore their wounds with pride.

After two days of following Monty around, Abby thought this might be her best chance to speak to him without Jordan around.

The changes she saw in her brother worried her. At first, she was happy to see him more energetic and talkative, like the Jordan of old. A month ago, he never got up before noon—some days not at all. Now he was out of bed before 8 a.m.

He'd been spending a lot of time with the captain, and recently, Monty. Whenever Abby approached the two boys together, it was obvious they changed the topic of their conversation. Now, Abby was about to have her own conversation with the gypsy boy, a heart-to-heart talk about something very important to her.

Monty reached the crest of the hill, and she jogged up to him. "Better than Rockefeller Center?"

He pulled up his sleeve to show off his latest road rash. "Way better!"

"How'd you become a gypsy?"

"When I got out of the colony, I was worried the adults would change their minds and come after me. I thought the best thing was for me and Robbie to leave New York."

She raised her eyebrows. "You mean Stone."

Monty rapped his head with his knuckle. "We went to the New Haven Trading Zone. There were a couple of gypsy ships moored. I figured we should start with the biggest one, and that turned out to be *Lucky Me*. I told Jenny my story, and I've been seasick ever since."

Jenny was the gypsy captain. All the crew called her by her first name.

"You really get seasick?" Abby asked.

He nodded with a grin. "The minute we leave a harbor. Other than that, Nikki talking in her sleep, and Stone stinking up the cabin with his farts, I love it."

Abby raised her eyebrows. "It sounds crowded."

"Actually, we have an open berth. Bruce left us in New Jersey. He was the best sailor we had. We really miss him during storms."

Abby tried to ignore the sick feeling in the pit of her stomach, fearing that berth had Jordan's name on it.

Just then, Stone trotted up the hill carrying his board.

"Awesome ride, dude." Monty punched his brother in the arm.

"Thanks, dude," Stone punched Monty back.

"Love you, bro." Another punch.

Stone punched him back again. "I love you, too."

With their fists, they traded several more expressions of fondness for each other. Abby shook her head, pondering the mysterious nature of boys.

Stone hopped on his board and rattled down the hill. "Bend your knees," Monty shouted.

Stone bent his knees.

Monty whooped and turned to Abby. "It's so cool when he listens."

"Usually, younger brothers stop listening to you after they turn six. I guess you really missed him when you were at Colony East."

"Totally."

"Families are important," she said. "Sticking together and all that."

Monty nodded. "Yeah, all that…" he paused, giving her a strange look, like he was about to say something he shouldn't. Something Abby wasn't supposed to know. "Every situation is different."

Abby wasn't going to let him go until she pried the secret out of him. "I think families are the same everywhere."

Monty shifted side-to-side and his mouth squirmed. Slapping on a fake smile, he hopped on his board and pushed off. "Catch you later." He hadn't said it, but Monty's eyes had confirmed her worst fear. Watching Monty fly down the hill, Abby knew she had to stop Jordan from making a terrible mistake.

# CHAPTER FIFTEEN
## COLONY EAST

Lieutenant Dawson reviewed Lily Meyer's folder, looking for a nugget he might use to cheer her up. The folder contained information obtained from interviews with Lily and from whatever public records the scientists could find.

She'd been gone for just over ten days, and Dawson wanted to make sure she received a letter every three days.

He read that she was born and raised in Brooklyn. Her father had worked for a bank. Her mother had taught high school biology. Lily's grandmother on her mother's side died of lung cancer, and her grandfather died of a heart attack at sixty-seven. There was no mention of her paternal grandparents. Lily had been a top student in her first-grade class at the Teunic Bergen School, PS 9, when the epidemic struck. She had listed her hobbies as coloring, playing piano, and digging up worms.

Dawson picked up his pen, wondering what it was about this particular cadet that had inspired him to sneak around Medical Clinic 17. Something about Lily tugged at his heart.

*Dear Sarah*

He stared at the paper until the words blurred. Then he folded it and started with a fresh sheet.

*Dear Lily,*

*I hope you are feeling better. Everyone in Biltmore Company can't wait to see you again.*

*You'll never believe how fast we assembled this morning. Eighteen minutes, thirty-two seconds. Yes, a new record!*

*We got our first squash, asparagus, and cucumbers from Central Park Farm. Incredibly, a chicken laid a blue egg at the United Nations.*

Once more Dawson started over, thinking it wasn't a good idea to mention food, given the symptoms of the illness. He copied the first part and continued:

*Don't tell anyone, but tonight I am going to conduct a surprise inspection. I'm worried some of your fellow cadets are getting a little sloppy making their beds.*

*I hope you get better soon.*

*Lieutenant Dawson*

He sealed the note in an envelope, addressed it, and placed it in his satchel. Tomorrow, he would deliver it to David Levine in the CDC liaison office, who would place the letter on the next flight to Atlanta.

# CHAPTER SIXTEEN
# CASTINE ISLAND

Expecting Jordan to arrive any minute, Abby pressed her back against the boulder. She'd overheard her brother telling Timmy that he was going mushroom hunting. This spot was the worst-kept secret on the island. Everyone knew Jordan came here to cry.

Out of respect for him, Abby had never come here before. It would be intruding in Jordan's personal life. How he grieved for Emily was none of her business, and since he had never wanted to talk to her about it, she knew better than to approach him. With the gypsies leaving in the morning and Jordan's duffel bag packed, though, things had changed. This was family business. His actions would affect her and Toucan as much as they would him.

She saw how Jordan had brushed away pebbles to make a place for the wildflowers he left here. She twirled a flower between her fingertips and imagined her brother's sadness locked inside the stem, the same way he kept it locked inside himself.

Doubt crept into her mind. Who was she to tell Jordan that he couldn't leave? He was fourteen. He could make his own decisions. If he didn't want to stay here with them, she couldn't force him to.

Abby knew she still had time to go home before he arrived. She could walk along the water and cut through the woods to the place she hid her bike, but instead she pressed harder against the boulder as if to glue herself in place.

Her heart beat faster at the sound of rocks clacking. Jordan was walking over the layer of polished stones, coming closer. She stood.

Startled, he jumped back and quickly moved his hand behind his back, but not before she saw the tiny bouquet of flowers. Her heart roiled hard in her chest.

Jordan's face reddened. "What are you doing?"

Abby pretended not to notice him stuffing the flowers down the back of his pants.

"Jordan, are you going with the gypsies?"

He scrunched his face. "No!" He paused a moment. "Yes."

"You're a really good sailor." Abby had thought about and rehearsed what she planned to say even down to the friendly tone. "I think you'd make a great news gypsy, but you should wait a year or two. The mainland will be much safer then. Maybe, you and Eddie could go together."

"Abby, you worry too much."

She was ready for that comment. "Yeah, I guess. You have to admit, there are some scary things happening on the mainland."

He interrupted. "What, like kids using solar panels? Some dumb kid crashing a plane he could barely fly? Come on, Abby!"

They dueled back and forth. She listed the dangers of the mainland. He countered with positive things they'd heard about.

"What about the Pig?" Abby cried.

He smirked. "I bet more kids have died from peanut allergies."

She locked eyes with him. If he doesn't care about himself, let's see if he cares about the rest of his family. "Touk and I need you. We've survived because we've helped each other."

"You guys are fine. Have you seen Touk bossing Timmy and Danny? Abby, she takes after you. I mean that in a good way. She takes charge. Hey, just because I leave doesn't mean we're not a family."

She shook her head. "It's not a good time to go."

His turn to act warm and friendly. "I'm not leaving forever. I bet I'll be back by September. I'll miss you and Touk, but c'mon, three months is no big deal."

"It's Emily isn't it?" Abby blurted. Jordan turned pale and took a step back. Several wildflowers dropped from his pant leg. Abby felt her face growing hot. She wished she could take back what she said. Emily's death was too sensitive to bring up. Maybe it was even mean on her part to use it as her ultimate weapon to keep him here. "I know what you're going through," she added, improvising. "We're all sad about Emily. We loved her. I miss Kevin, too." She rested her hand on his shoulder. He swatted it away. "Jordan, you let things build up inside of you and then you explode and want to do something crazy. Leaving the island isn't going to make you feel better. You can't run away from your problems."

He turned. "Mind your own business."

"Jordan, I care about you. I want to see you happy again, but you're being selfish. You're not thinking about us."

He spun around. "Did you care about Mandy?" Anger burned in his eyes.

Abby rocked back on her heels. "Mandy?"

"Mel told me what you said. You put a guilt trip on her. You told her how much Timmy belonged here. Were you really surprised when she came to the yacht club? If she and Timmy had gone to that lake in Maine, she'd be alive today. If you had minded your own business… " He kicked a rock and faced the water.

Abby's head started spinning. She slumped down until she sat on her heels and hugged her knees. Tears ran down her cheeks and splattered on the polished pebbles between her feet. It was incredible to think that for the past year Jordan had blamed her for Mandy's death. Did Mel think that too? Up until now, Jordan had not mentioned Mandy once. Yes, she was willing to admit that she wanted Mandy and Timmy to go to the island, but she didn't think Mandy's death was her fault.

A new thought crossed her mind, one that took her by surprise and stole her breath. She was the one being selfish. Maybe Jordan should go with the gypsies.

When Abby looked up to tell him that and apologize, he was already gone.

# CHAPTER SEVENTEEN
## COLONY EAST

Gunshots rang out. *Pop pop. Pop pop pop.* Lieutenant Dawson knew that ensigns patrolling the East River were firing warning shots at kids getting too close to the perimeter.

He kept a careful eye on Cadet Billings, walking alongside him, and debated whether he should reschedule their fly-fishing lesson. Pier 15, where he planned to take Jonzy, offered an unfettered view of the patrol boats. The admiral, Dawson thought, would frown upon a cadet having a front row seat to the colony's security measures.

He decided to wait and see if the gunfire subsided. After all, it wasn't every day someone showed interest in the art of fly-fishing.

*Pop. Pop. Pop.*

"Question for you, Billings. How much fishing have you done?"

"My grandfather used to take me fishing in Prospect Park. We used bobbers and worms."

Having studied Jonzy's profile, Dawson knew that Jonzy grew up in Brooklyn, close to Prospect Park, and his grandfather's first name was Lemon. Lemon, who was the first African-American Professor of Physics at Brooklyn College, had lived with Jonzy and his mother at the time of the epidemic.

"Any luck?" he asked.

Jonzy beamed. "I caught a five-pound bass."

Dawson whistled. "Sounds like a fish story to me."

They cut through Rockefeller Center. It was Saturday at noon and the plaza was filled with kids biking, skateboarding, roller blading, or just hanging out. The sidewalks were empty of both cadets and adults alike when they entered the Yellow Zone. Cars and buses, on the other hand, clogged the streets of the area that to Dawson seemed like an outdoor museum, memorializing the chaos that followed the night of the purple moon. Someday, the expanding colony would utilize the Yellow Zone, but first the Body Disposal Unit had a ways to go, with thousands of apartments and condominiums to inspect. Only then, would Navy crews focus on clearing the metal graveyard in the streets.

He and Jonzy skirted a police cruiser blocking the sidewalk and stepped around a city bus lying on its side.

Dawson led the cadet toward Herb's Fin and Fur. "Careful, there's a lot of glass." He had discovered the small shop of fly-fishing supplies months ago after he had searched the city's more prominent sporting goods stores. The empty shelves at those stores hadn't surprised him. He imagined fishing equipment had helped survivors of the epidemic obtain food, and they had cleared out the big stores. Herb's had suffered only minimal looting.

The front window of the shop, like every other storefront on the block, was smashed.

"Behold!" Dawson stepped up to the unbroken display case inside that offered a wide assortment of colorful flies. "The art of master craftsmen."

"Wow!" Jonzy put his face close to the case, fogging the glass when he exhaled. "How do you know which one to use?"

Dawson chuckled at the question. Fly fishermen had been arguing over that since the first Scots wet flies in the 17th century. "It depends on the color of the sky, fish species, time of year, the river current, water temperature, and what insects are hatching. Bottom line, you need to outsmart the fish."

The corner of Jonzy's lip curled. "What if the fish is smarter than you?"

"The fish wins. Simple as that."

He advised Jonzy to select a wasp fly, which should do the trick nicely on a hot day in May. Thirty minutes later, they were on Pier 15, ready for the first cast. Thankfully, the Zodiacs were well down the East River, and the ensigns skippering them were not firing any more warning shots.

Dawson demonstrated the proper casting technique. Thinking it was best to learn by doing, he handed over the gear to Jonzy and retreated a safe distance.

Sitting cross-legged, he watched with a combination of pride and dread as Jonzy landed the fly in the water, one out of every three casts.

Proving his tenacity, Jonzy could eventually place the fly in the river with consistency—not far enough from the pier, but a step in the right direction.

"You know what my father told me, Billings? Never give away your secret fishing spot."

"Ha. Too late, Lieutenant." Jonzy winced. "I bet your dad was strict."

Dawson smiled to himself. "Why do you say that?"

All of a sudden, his star pupil seemed to develop fly-fishing amnesia. He flicked the rod tip side-to-side and caught the pier three casts in a row.

"Say what's on your mind, Billings."

Jonzy hemmed and hawed, finally spitting it out, "Sir, you're super-strict. I figured you learned that from your dad."

He smiled. Yes, he had learned a lot from his father, Commander Dawson. "Rules are made for a reason."

"You've got to admit, some rules are really dumb."

Dawson burst out laughing. "You want dumb rules, join the Navy. But we can't pick and choose which ones to follow. The system would never work."

Jonzy took a step toward him and looked him in the eye. "What if Martin Luther King had followed the law? If he hadn't broken the rules, African Americans might not have had the same rights as other people."

Dawson had to agree. "For all our sakes, we should be thankful that Doctor King wasn't in the Navy."

Jonzy took another step. "Would you ever do that? I mean, break a dumb rule. Let's say the rule might hurt millions of people."

He tensed, wondering if Jonzy knew. No, he thought, that was impossible. Admiral Samuels, of course, knew, and he was certain the CDC with its penchant for keeping profiles on everyone, had documented the nitty-gritty details of his failure. Should he tell the boy? He couldn't think of a reason for keeping it a secret.

"I disobeyed an order once that I thought was dumb, and I regret it to this day."

Jonzy put the fly rod aside and sat down before him to listen to the story about an event that would likely haunt Dawson forever.

"When the CDC developed the antibiotic, they gave it to us first, the surviving adults in the Navy, so we could help distribute the pills. My first assignment was to work at a pharmaceutical manufacturing plant in Atlanta where they made millions of pills. Then I received orders to drive a shipment of pills to Washington, D.C.

"My commanding officer, Captain Tanner, told me that if I couldn't get through on the highway, I should turn around and come back, they'd find a new route for me. I didn't take him seriously. The whole time I was thinking, nothing is going to stop me.

"So, we set off. I drove a postal service truck, and Ensign Foster took a jeep. I was carrying the pills and drums of gasoline for both vehicles. The jeep had a winch. Foster's job was to pull away any wrecks blocking the lane.

"The trip was six-hundred miles, and the first two-hundred miles were easy. Then we hit a stretch with a ton of wrecks. It took us three days to go twenty miles. Every hour of delay burned in my gut because I knew more kids were dying.

"We came to one spot that had an eighteen-wheeler on its side. The highway beyond it was clear, and there was almost enough room for the truck to pass, but one slip and you'd tumble into a ravine. Foster and I talked it over. I told him I wanted to try to get the truck through."

Dawson raised his shirt, and Jonzy's eyes widened at the sight of mottled scar tissue covering his chest.

"The shoulder of the road collapsed," he continued with a growing tremble in his voice. "I rolled the truck into the ravine. The gasoline exploded. Foster somehow managed to get me out and back to Atlanta. I woke up in the hospital.

"Because I disobeyed an order, fifty thousand kids never received the antibiotic."

He paused, staring at the Brooklyn Bridge. There was nothing more to the episode than that. Children had died because of his insubordination. He'd carry the burden to his grave.

"You did the right thing, Lieutenant," Jonzy said. "You tried."

How he would love to believe that. Only he couldn't. He had acted irresponsibly and thousands died as a result. All he could do was go forward and obey the orders of his superiors, trusting they operated with greater wisdom.

Just then, a burst of gunfire erupted across the river. "C'mon, Cadet. Let's pack up. Lesson's over. The fish will live to swim another day."

# CHAPTER EIGHTEEN
## CASTINE ISLAND

Jordan slammed his bedroom door shut. He figured Monty, Stone, and the captain should all be back on the boat by now. He'd said good-bye to them half an hour ago. *Lucky Me* would sail in the morning without him.

Feeling as empty as his duffel bag, which he had just unpacked, Jordan flopped on his bed. Abby's reaction hadn't come as a total surprise. He never expected she'd lead a marching band as he sailed out of Castine Harbor, but after all they had been through together since the night of the purple moon, he wished she had given him her blessing instead of making him feel guilty. She just didn't understand.

Angry heat flushed through his body. His bossy sister stuck her nose into everyone's business. Maybe Abby should start worrying about her own life.

Jordan cringed at what he had said about Mandy. He didn't believe that Abby had caused Mandy's death. He had said it to hurt her.

Someone knocked on the door. Not wanting to see anyone, especially Abby, he glanced at the window, thinking he could open it, step onto the porch roof, and climb down the trellis.

*Rap, rap, rap.*

"I'm busy," he shouted.

"Jordie, I have something for you." It was Touk.

He breathed a sigh of relief. "Give it to me later."

The door opened. When he saw both his sisters, he shot up and headed for the door. They blocked his escape. "Get out!" he snapped angrily.

They refused to step aside.

Toucan held out a music CD. "It's for you. From me and Abby."

Seeing the crazy colors, he knew right away it was "Sgt. Pepper" by the Beatles, but he kept his hands by his sides.

"You're going to be at sea a lot," Abby said. "We thought you'd want something to listen to."

He swallowed hard and took the CD. Was this a joke? No, he realized they were coming to say good-bye. The adventure was on and that frightened him. Then he felt a sudden sadness. He wanted to jump in bed and pull the covers over his head.

"The captain told me there's a boom box on *Lucky Me*." Abby handed him a paper bag with batteries. "You can thank Toby. Be safe."

Toucan wrapped her arms around his leg and squeezed. The top of her head came just above his waist. "Be safe, Jordie."

As his eyes filled with tears, Jordan looked away, but with Touk holding on tight, he couldn't escape. He trembled all over as a fountain of sounds gushed up from deep inside. It was a strange mixture of sobs and giddy laughter.

After a moment, he sat on the bed and dragged his sleeve across his eyes. "Abby, I didn't mean what I said. I'm sorry."

She nodded. "I didn't mean what I said, either."

Touk sat on his left, Abby on his right, and they each inched closer. It was a Leigh-family sandwich and he was the bologna. Nobody spoke, as if words might break the magic of their precious last minutes together.

# CHAPTER NINETEEN
## COLONY EAST

Waiting for Sandy at Rockefeller Center, Lieutenant Dawson sat at the edge of the reflecting pool. He unfolded the aluminum package to reveal carrot sticks, french fries, and Swedish meatballs. There was not a cloud in the sky, and warm alpine gusts whistled through the broken windows high above. In the pool, ducks paddled by, dipping beaks to munch on algae.

Dawson pinched off pieces of a meatball and absentmindedly fed them to the ducks, thinking his first picnic with Sandy had everything but ants and a blanket. The fantasy of them enjoying a real picnic together without a care in the world tugged at him, but the reality of the moment jerked him back.

Earlier that morning, in the officer's mess, she had told him with a deeply furrowed brow that she had news from Doctor Droznin about the mutated germs. She had whispered, "Highly confidential."

He had suggested they meet later to talk in private, nobody would think twice about two company leaders sharing a late afternoon snack in the colony's most public setting.

The second free period had just begun and the sidewalks were clear of cadets, most of whom were attending a lecture on amphibian life cycles at Carnegie Hall. A scientist, identifiable by his Hush Puppies, walked across the plaza, deep in thought.

Ten minutes later, Sandy arrived. "Sorry I'm late. When I went to medical school, I never imagined I'd be training sailors to be doctors." Tension filled her voice.

"Go Navy," he said, trying to lighten her mood. She smiled, but her eyes showed grave concern. He held out a fry. "Better than Mickey D's." She waved it off.

Taking a seat beside him, she lowered her voice. "Most of what I'm about to tell you we'll get in tomorrow's memorandum. We're going to Code 9."

"Nine!" That meant every cadet must carry a germ mask, and the scientists would position quarantine vans around the colony. He'd review the manual later to refresh his memory on the other required measures. "What happened to Codes 5, 6, 7 and 8?"

She inched closer. "Their theory was correct. Solar energy is accelerating the mutation of AHA. The new strain, AHA-B, is widespread near the equator."

A chill rippled through Dawson, knowing what an epidemic meant for regions in Africa and South America. Developing nations lacked the resources to staff advanced infection labs, such as the Max Planck Institute for Infection Biology in Germany, the Pasteur Institute in France, and, of course, the CDC. "What about the kids who live near the equator?"

Sandy's face turned pale before his eyes. "Doctor Droznin told me that about thirty to forty percent of the people exposed to the new strain will contract the illness and die."

Strangely, this news bolstered his spirits. He had assumed the percentage would have been much greater. He chose to view the statistic as a survival rate of sixty percent, a figure that was still numbing, but ever since the night of the purple moon, the way the survivors considered the mortality rates of epidemics had changed.

"They made a shocking discovery," she continued after a long pause. "They took infrared images of several areas and determined a population decrease of ninety five percent."

Dawson tasted bile in the back of his throat. "Why so high? You said thirty percent."

"They think that food riots broke out. The hypothalamus gland becomes so stimulated that victims will do anything for food."

He dropped his head. "And the other survivors will do anything to stop them. The germs kill thirty percent and the rest… "

They sat in stony silence, each of them dwelling on the widespread suffering that was occurring thousands of miles away. A strand of thinking, unforgiving as barbed wire, wended through his mind. Maybe AHA-B had run its course and the final fight to the death for diminishing food supplies had put an end to the suffering for many.

Finally, Dawson lifted his chin and pulled his shoulders back. "Are the scientists close to developing an antibiotic?"

Her eyes brightened a bit. "They're running three trials now. Droznin told me that one antibiotic looks very promising."

He quietly pumped his fist. "Yes. Did she mention Lily?" A sudden wave of guilt washed over him. He had just learned about a large swath of the planet ravaged by a new germ and survivors killing survivors, yet his concern focused on one cadet; one girl in a million who was being taken care of by some of the smartest scientists in the world. That's how the brain copes, he told himself. When the scope of the devastation was incomprehensible, you needed to reduce it to a single person. Lily was his face of AHA-B.

Sandy nodded. "Doctor Droznin told me that all the test subjects are still alive."

*Test subjects.* The sterile, scientific phrase burned a hole in his gut. Even so, he was overall thankful they were all alive. Lily was alive. He clenched his jaw and repeated to himself that Sarah was alive, too.

"Mark, there's something else they're not telling us now. They don't want to cause panic." Dawson braced for the next round of bad news, something he had become quite accomplished at doing. "The number of cases north of the West Indies is relatively small. The germs came here in the air currents in the upper atmosphere. It was just a fluke that Lily and Max became exposed. But that's going to change when hurricane season arrives."

Dawson's heart stopped. Every sailor knew that hurricanes formed near the equator. In the Atlantic Ocean, they started as seedlings off the coast of

Africa. A single storm born in the tropics, he realized, would suck up the mutated bacteria and blanket the germs over the United States.

"Hurricane season officially starts June first," he said. "That's two weeks away, but the first storms usually don't hit us until September, sometimes later. That gives us two or three months. What can we do?"

Sandy reached out and squeezed his hand. "Pray the scientists find the right antibiotic."

# AHA-B

# CHAPTER ONE
## DC TRADING ZONE

Jordan felt like he was inhaling swamp water with every breath. Not even Miami had been this stifling.

Longing for cool, Castine Island fog, he squinted at the Washington Monument. It rose like a white shadow in the blinding haze. Someone had decorated the spire by pouring a bucket of purple paint from the observation area at the peak.

Sheets of sweat streamed down his forehead and stung his eyes. "This has to be the biggest zone we've visited."

"And the hottest," Monty chirped.

"Compared to the last time we were here it's a ghost town," said Jenny, the captain of the *Lucky Me*. After spending six weeks together in cramped quarters, Jordan and the captain were now on a first name basis. He and the entire crew were family.

For the past hour, Jordan, Monty, and Jenny had been camped on the grass next to the Lincoln Memorial, awaiting the trading delegation from the White House Gang.

"Where is everyone?" Jordan asked, meaning traders and shoppers. About a third of the people wore germ masks.

"The Pig," Monty whispered, his eyes going wide.

Jordan punched Monty in the arm. "The fear of Pig is spreading faster than the germs."

Monty punched him back. "Are you afraid?"

"I'm thirsty."

"Last time we were here," Jenny said, "the traders gave us iced tea."

Monty closed his eyes as if closing his eyes could shade the blistering heat from his brain. "If you knew someone had the Pig, and they drank from a bottle of cold iced tea, would you drink from the bottle?"

"No," Jenny and Jordan said at the same time.

Monty licked his lips. "I would."

"Mind if I do the deal?" Jordan asked Jenny. He knew it might be his last chance to lead a trading session. He had not yet told them he planned to leave *Lucky Me* once they returned to Castine Island.

Jenny smiled. "Think you're ready?"

"After watching you?" He gave her a big nod.

"Here's what you should know. After the night of the purple moon, the White House Gang found a large warehouse with canned goods and freeze-dried foods. They eat well." She pointed out a chubby trader. "He's probably an associate."

"Or has the Pig," Monty interjected.

Jenny ignored the comment. "Whatever you do, don't mention that our friend came from Colony East. Otherwise, they'll have a million questions and we'll be here all night."

Monty punched Jordan in the arm. "Listen to the captain."

Jordan punched him back. "C'mon, they'll invite us to the White House. Do you want to sleep in the West Wing or in the Lincoln Bedroom?"

"Only if they have air conditioning and iced tea."

They agreed not to mention Colony East. Fifteen minutes later, the crowd parted as the delegation of three kids appeared: a girl with red dreadlocks, a skinny boy, and a boy with muscular arms. They appeared to be fourteen or fifteen years old, but it was hard to tell since they were wearing germ masks. Dreadlocks led a dog, part pit bull terrier, part something equally menacing. Jordan eyed the rope leash, hoping it was strong. Skinny Boy held a beach umbrella under his arm, and Biceps carried a backpack, likely containing payment for the news they were about to receive.

Dreadlocks greeted Jenny and introductions followed. Dreadlocks was Low, Skinny Boy was Single Cell, and the one with the muscular arms, Bombie.

Single Cell pitched the umbrella, and the delegation, along with the dog, sat in the shade. Jenny waved for Jordan to begin.

"We've sailed from Maine to Florida." Jordan listed all the trading zones they had visited. "In North Carolina, drought wiped out most of the corn and potato crops."

Low held up her hand. "We're only interested in two things today: our competition and what you've heard about the Pig."

Jordan jumped ahead to their only news on gangs. "A tank at a fuel depot exploded in Charleston, South Carolina. We saw black smoke on the horizon. It took us all day to reach port. By the time we got there, the fire had burned out. One witness told us the Grits were responsible."

Single Cell lifted his eyebrows. "Grits?"

Jordan explained that three motorcycle gangs in Georgia had combined forces and the new super gang called themselves 'Grits.'

The delegation members eyed each other with concern. Low addressed her companions. Then she asked Jordan, "Did they use guns?"

Jordan shrugged. "The witness didn't say anything about guns."

Several traders inched closer to eavesdrop. Bombie shot them a dirty look and they moved back in a hurry.

Jordan paused to see if they had more questions about the Grits before he moved on to the next topic. They didn't.

"At every zone, we've heard about kids dying from the Pig," he said. "There were a few cases in New Jersey and one in Delaware, but most of the cases are south of here. Miami had more than fifty cases. The total number is seventy-two. The kids were all ages. Forty of them died from the illness. Seven died from getting beat up after they tried to steal food."

Low scratched the dog behind the ear. "Add fifteen from here."

Jenny asked for clarification.

"Ten died from a fever. We chased five away. I don't know what happened to them."

Jordan's stomach knotted, thinking that the faster they wrapped up the session and sailed away the better. A crowded trading zone seemed like a breeding ground for the Pig. "Ready for the big event?"

Low, Single Cell, and Bombie all leaned forward.

Jordan took a snort of soggy air and began, "In Atlanta, adults in hazmat suits were looking for kids who had the Pig."

"Why?" Bombie blurted.

Jenny jumped in. "Several witnesses saw them take two kids away in a van." She should have held her comment until Jordan, the lead negotiator, had finished, but he didn't mind. Jenny caught herself and nudged Jordan. "Sorry."

Nodding that he was fine with the interruption, he continued, "There's no way to know why they took the kids. One witness told us the adults wanted to find a cure for Pig, but that was just a guess on her part."

"I hope they do a better job of passing out pills than last time," Single Cell remarked.

Bombie flexed his right arm. "This time, we have guns. The line to the airport won't be long for us."

"When are you coming back to the DC Zone?" Low asked.

Jordan gestured to Jenny and she replied they planned to return in three or four months.

The delegation stood. Bombie left his pack on the grass. Single Cell uprooted and collapsed the umbrellas. Then the crowd magically parted and the three of them and their dog headed back to the White House.

"Nice job," Jenny told Jordan. "You do the honors."

He reached into the pack. "It's cold," he cried to Monty. "I think it's iced tea!"

"Oh my God," Monty exclaimed.

"Not," Jordan smirked. Before Monty could punch him, he lifted out the next best thing. A pack of germ masks.

# CHAPTER TWO
## CASTINE ISLAND

Biting her lip to hold back tears, Abby gently stroked Touk. A layer of fat covered her sister's once knobby elbows and bony arms. Toucan's cheeks had filled out too. Because of her appetite, she had gained twenty-five pounds over the past month.

The flickering light from the lantern next to the bed showed she had opened her eyes a crack. "Want some water," Abby whispered, fearing dehydration.

Toucan lolled her head on the pillow. "French fries."

Abby ran her fingers through Touk's curls, parting the damp hair to feel heat radiating off her scalp. "Touk, you've had enough to eat for now."

Her sister mumbled something, and Abby deciphered that she wanted chocolate. She picked up the glass of water from the table and held it before Toucan. "You need to drink."

She thrashed her arms. "Chocolate."

Abby gritted her teeth, knowing she might have to restrain Toucan for her own safety. When Toucan continued flailing and shouting for french fries, Abby took her by the wrists and held her arms firmly against her body. Despite her fever, Touk found an untapped source of strength and struggled to break free. Abby pushed down harder, seeing a crazed look in her sister's eyes that frightened her. She wrapped her arms all the way around Touk and hugged her tightly until their accelerating heartbeats reached a peak and then started to slow.

"Just rest," Abby whispered and eased her grip as Toucan stopped fighting. "Try to sleep. We'll be leaving in the morning." She let go when Toucan finally settled.

Doubts wafted through Abby's mind for the hundredth time. Questioning her decision to take Toucan to Colony East, she squeezed the blanket until her fist cramped. There were so many unknowns. Did the danger of traveling on the mainland outweigh the risk of Pig? Touk's fever might break. Abby had seen kids with high fevers, lying in bed one minute and playing outdoors the next. But those kids had a cold or the flu.

And if they reached Colony East, could they get inside? The odds were against them, but Abby worried that if they did nothing, the chances of Toucan dying were greater.

At the foot of the bed, Cat licked her paw. Counting Cat, it was just the three of them in the house. Mel had moved out three weeks ago, offering a lame excuse. "Abby, I'm going to stay with Derek. I'll have a bedroom with a good view of the water. I'll be able to spot gypsies better."

Abby couldn't blame her friend. The fear of Pig had the island firmly in its grip. When kids walked by the house, they moved to the other side of the street as if the germs might jump through the wall.

After Mel left, Abby arranged for Timmy and Danny to move in with Eddie. The boys needed constant supervision and she had her hands full.

Only one person had stood by them the whole time. Toby brought them food and water. He arranged for Eddie to take them to Portland in the whaler, and he told Abby he was working on a way to get them from Portland to Colony East. She didn't know what they would have done without him.

When Touk kicked into a rhythm of steady breathing, Abby grabbed the lantern and went downstairs. Gusts buffeted the window, and she expected rain soon as a storm moved in. She'd been checking the barometer as much as Jordan would have. The pressure was dropping. Not an ideal time to cross the strait to the mainland, but with her sister's condition worsening, they couldn't afford to wait any longer.

In the kitchen, she sat at the table with pen and paper. If something happened to her or Touk, she worried that guilt would eat Jordan alive.

*Going with the gypsies was the best thing you ever did. We are so proud of you. Love, Abby and Touk.*

When Jordan returned to the island, Eddie would fill him in. By that time, maybe she and Touk and Toby would have returned. They'd have stories to tell about their adventure visiting the adults of Colony East. And if they never returned, Abby hoped her note might help her brother find peace.

# CHAPTER THREE
## COLONY EAST

Lieutenant Dawson waited for Sandy to join him in the officer's mess. "I have good news," he had told her on their walk to Grand Central Station, but he wanted to wait until the voices of two-hundred chattering cadets ensured privacy. She had shown little interest. In fact, she had hardly spoken a word.

Sandy arrived at the table with a distant look in her eyes. Adding to his concern, she only had a small wedge of melon on her plate. Doctor Perkins had given a lecture to the colony's officers on depression. "The stomach is a beacon," he'd said. "If the brain's neurotransmitters convey a sensation of apathy and sadness, the beacon dims. A lack of appetite is quite often the first sign of depression."

Dawson's plate, heaped with boiled potatoes, poached eggs, and sausages, indicated that his beacon was burning brightly. He could hardly contain himself. "Want to hear my good news now?" He waited for her to snap out of her trance. "I spoke to Colonel Murray. He flies C5 transports and is one of our best pilots. He told me he's getting a new assignment. He'll be making daily flights to the tropics to collect weather data."

With her fork, Sandy pushed at her melon wedge. He thought she was listening to him, but he couldn't be certain. He considered the news he had was like a nugget of uranium that could brighten the darkest day.

174

"Space dust destroyed all the weather satellites, so they have to find a new way to track storms," he continued. "Surface ships will take barometric pressure measurements, and if they see something interesting, they'll send the planes in for monitoring.

"Here's what I learned from the Colonel. The meteorologists believe we'll have a mild hurricane season. Since the epidemic, the ocean's cooled a quarter of a degree. That's a huge change. They think it's even possible we won't get a single storm. Sandy, we might dodge the bullet!"

When she nodded, a tear dribbled down her cheek. "Yeah, that's really good news."

He leaned forward. "Okay, are you going to make me guess what's wrong?"

"With so many people suffering, I'm embarrassed to say."

He nudged her foot under the table. "What?"

"I'm getting a promotion."

Dawson whistled. "In the history of the military, I think you're the first person to get teary-eyed over a promotion. Major Hedrick?" He winked. "Lieutenant Colonel Hedrick?"

"Mark, they're transferring me to Atlanta."

He dropped his fork.

"The admiral called me to his office last night. Apparently, Doctor Perkins is impressed with my training program. They want me to launch 'Doctors of Tomorrow' at the Atlanta Colony."

Dawson muttered, "Don't they have enough doctors down there?"

"PhDs in microbiology, genetics, immunology, chemistry, evolutionary biology. There are only two medical doctors."

He used his napkin to wipe his mouth, and dabbed his eyes while he was at it. "A few months in Atlanta will be over before you know it."

Sandy shook her head in a way that froze his insides. "When I finish up in Atlanta," she said, "they're sending me to Colony West."

The noisy din of the cadets pushed down on him like a heavy stone, and he struggled to draw air into his lungs. "When are you going?"

She looked down, and he thought she might be crying. "Maybe early September. I'll know for sure in a few weeks." Her voice trembled.

He sighed in relief, at first fearing that she might have said a few hours. The Navy, as a whole, moved at the speed of a slug, but individual transfers often happened in a snap.

Dawson pulled his shoulders back and plastered on a fake smile. "Ours is not to reason why." He raised his metal cup filled with fresh milk from the Lower East Side dairy herd. "To Major Hedrick."

When Sandy kept her eyes lowered, he knew for sure she was crying.

# CHAPTER FOUR
## AT SEA

Jordan kicked back and propped his feet on the rail. After sailing through squalls for much of the day, the seas were calm. The crew was below deck, all fast asleep. They had turned in early. He felt good, like he owned the night.

He gazed at the full moon. Yellow was the color the moon ought to be. Pale yellow, white, or even blood red was fine too. Anything but purple.

The breeze out of the southwest rustled his hair and kept the sails taut. Despite their heavy load, *Lucky Me* sliced through the water at twelve knots or faster. Jenny had acquired five hundred gallons of gas in a trade with a fuel king at their last port of call, the Trenton Trading Zone, and the cans were piled everywhere on the deck.

Colony East was off the port side. A light flashed atop the Empire State Building and the moon outlined the city skyline. Jordan chuckled, thinking the "seeds of the next society" were safe inside their hotels, tucked in bed. He wouldn't trade places with them for anything.

Around midnight, the wind shifted and the temperature jumped several degrees. The breeze was blowing offshore. Jordan popped Sgt. Pepper into the boom box and sang along with 'Lucy in the Sky with Diamonds' and 'With a Little Help from My Friends'. It was even better, knowing he'd be singing those songs on the island before long. He'd surprise Abby and

Touk, and he couldn't wait to see their expressions. Jordan lowered his voice to avoid an irate crew yelling for him to shut up.

An hour later he adjusted course, moving the boat closer to shore where the wind was blowing slightly stronger. He pulled the mainsheet to trim the sail, making sure he was using the breeze to his full advantage. For every extra knot of speed he could coax out of the wind, he figured he'd arrive home that much sooner. As he held the line that controlled the sail, he marveled at the ropes of muscles rippling in his forearm. He'd left Castine Island strong and depressed. He'd return very strong and feeling much better about himself.

Jordan secured the mainsheet and took a moment to admire the frothy wake of moonlit bubbles *Lucky Me* left behind. Then he flicked on the flashlight and consulted the navigation chart. He figured they were passing the tip of Long Island. When he thought the danger of underwater rocks had passed, he changed course again, heading for the northern Connecticut shore.

Sometime later, the sound of an outboard motor caught his attention. He grabbed the binoculars and scanned the shoreline. A sleek boat sped on a course to intercept them. His heart raced. Should he wake up the crew?

Jenny had warned him about traders who might approach them at sea, hoping to get a better deal. "Don't trade with them," she'd instructed. "They arrive at the zone before us and trade our news. I've been burned too many times."

Jordan lowered the binoculars. He'd let the crew sleep. He'd handled aggressive traders before.

With its two powerful outboard engines purring, the boat motored alongside the port side. Jordan played out the mainsail to slow *Lucky Me*. The moon sat low on the horizon and because the hull blocked the light, Jordan couldn't make out the skipper in the dark shadows.

"How big is your crew?" the skipper shouted.

"Five, including me," Jordan replied. "We have nothing to trade."

"How many life jackets do you have?"

"We don't need any life jackets." Jordan grabbed the flashlight.

"Put on your life jackets and abandon ship."

Jordan gripped the rail to steady himself. A pirate was attempting to take command of *Lucky Me*. He needed to wake the crew. When he trained the flashlight on the motorboat, he nearly fell overboard in shock. The pirate was a young boy. The ski mask did not hide the fact the kid was ten or eleven years old.

Just then, two other kids, also wearing masks, threw back the tarp they'd been hiding under and rose to their knees.

A smile crept over Jordan's face. A crew of baby pirates had ordered him to jump overboard. Should he shout "boo"?

He quickly sobered. Each kid was aiming a rifle at him.

"Hurry up," the skipper shouted.

"Jump," one of the masked bandits squeaked in a shaky voice.

He raised his hands, thinking that if he stalled long enough, one of the crew might wake up, or the pirates might lose their nerve and leave. He wanted to avoid a confrontation that could result in someone getting hurt, including one of the misguided ten-year-olds. "What do you want?"

"Are you stupid or deaf?" one of the kiddie-pirates mocked.

He swallowed his anger. Thoughts raced through his mind. Should he dive for cover or crawl to the wheel and try to ram them? The crunch of wood smashing into fiberglass would get the crew up fast, and the confusion of two booms swinging above the pirates' heads might send them on their way. Then he remembered the flare gun attached just inside the bulkhead door.

Keeping his hands raised, Jordan took a step toward the cabin. "I'll get the captain. She'll give you whatever you want."

Something hot slammed into his leg as the crack of a rifle ripped through the air. The force of the impact knocked him across the deck. He couldn't believe he'd just been shot. It felt like he was moving in slow motion as he flew through the air, crashed into the railing, and flipped overboard.

The shock of the icy water sped time up and flushed air from his lungs. He quickly became numb except for the searing heat inside his right thigh. Fearing he was losing blood, he cried out, but nobody could hear him. *Lucky Me* was sailing away.

Jordan quickly assessed his chances of surviving, and they did not look good. He did not have a life jacket. The wind was blowing offshore. If he didn't bleed to death, he would probably die of hypothermia.

He slid his hand down his right side. The tear in his pants indicated the bullet had entered the outside of his thigh. If he stood any chance of making it, he'd have to expend as little energy as possible. He tried to relax. Dawn was an hour away. He set a goal. See the sunrise.

All of a sudden, *Lucky Me* came about. The crew must have awakened and discovered him missing. They were coming to rescue him. He watched anxiously as the pirates motored around the schooner like a shark circling its prey.

Jordan surged with excitement as a brilliant ball of white arced from *Lucky Me*. The flare, dropping sparks and trailing wisps of smoke, soared over the pirate's boat and fizzled in the water.

The bow of the pirate boat reared up as the skipper moved it to a spot out of reach of the flare gun.

With the schooner bearing down on him, Jordan waved his arms, but he didn't think they could see him. Then shots rang out, and the crew on *Lucky Me* dived for cover. Bullets struck the wooden hull with heavy thuds, and others tore through the canvas sails sounding like a whip snapping.

The bow passed within arm's reach, and Jordan lunged in vain to grab the rudder.

Someone from *Lucky Me* fired another flare. It landed just short of the pirate boat. The pirates quickly answered with a fresh hail of bullets.

A moment later, the twin outboard motors whined loudly and the pirates headed straight for *Lucky Me* at top speed. Someone fired a flare from the schooner, but the fiery ball landed to the left of the motorboat.

As the pirates veered hard right, one fired a flare at *Lucky Me* from point-blank range. It struck the after-sail and dropped to the deck as the crew scrambled to put it out with a fire extinguisher.

The pirates made another run, firing two more flares. The first crossed the schooner's bow and landed in the water. The second flare hit the forward sail. This time, a hole opened in the canvas, forming a rim of flames. That flare, too, dropped onto the deck. Fanned by the wind, the flames licked upward and soon the upper half of the sail was ablaze.

With the fire illuminating *Lucky Me*, Jordan's heart sank at the sight of Monty and Jenny struggling to lower the sail in a desperate attempt to save the schooner.

The pirates watched from a distance of thirty yards as flames leaped from sail to sail.

Suddenly, a huge fireball erupted, engulfing most of the main deck and sending a plume of pink smoke into the air. More explosions followed an instant later. The booms of cans of gasoline igniting rolled over the water, like cracks of thunder. *Lucky Me* twisted upwards into a single tornado of flames and then the flames faded as she sank into the black water.

The pirates sped off.

Hot tears filled his eyes as he floated in a silence broken only by the sound of debris splashing around him. Now, more than anything, Jordan wanted to live so he could hunt down the pirates. They would not get away with this, he vowed.

Needing something to help him stay afloat, he spotted a can of gasoline twenty yards away. He fixed his eyes on the can and swam toward it as *Lucky Me* exploded over and over again in constant replay in his mind.

It took him several attempts, but he finally grabbed the can. Hugging it desperately, he sank. Cursing, Jordan knew he had to empty the can before it would float. His fingers were frozen, and it seemed to take forever to unscrew the cap. Holding the can upside down with his arms extended, he slipped beneath the surface, but the pain of the frigid water forced him to come up after only a few seconds. He had to do the maneuver two more times. He cried out in despair when he thought he had let go of the cap. Then he saw it, lodged in his clawed, numb hand. He screwed the cap back on, and this time, he and the can floated.

Fearing he would become separated from his flotation device and drown if he passed out, he undid his belt. He fed one end through the handle and then looped the belt under his chin and tied a knot. Commanding himself to go limp, he was able to keep his nose and mouth out of the water.

Jordan guessed the shore was about two and a half miles away. With the wind blowing offshore, he was being pushed further away from land. Out of strength and ideas, he closed his eyes and said a prayer for his friends on *Lucky Me*. If there was life after death, he would see them soon, or else, he'd settle next to them at the bottom of the ocean. Either way, he'd be joining them. Suddenly, Abby and Toucan appeared in his mind, urging him not to quit. Despite that he was already numb in the frigid water and the wind was blowing him away from land, his sisters refused to leave him alone. They persisted—stubborn Touk and bossy Abby—chiding him not to give up.

He fought to open his eyes and keep them open.

# CHAPTER FIVE
## CASTINE ISLAND

Abby pulled Toucan closer when she heard a knock at the front door. Her sister mumbled groggily in response. The door creaked open downstairs and soon heels clicked on the wooden steps.

A moment later, a flashlight beam shone through the darkness and reflected on the window as Toby stuck his head in the bedroom. "Ready?"

Abby's heart jumped into her throat. It was her last chance to change her mind. No, she thought, Colony East offered the only hope for Toucan.

She climbed out of bed and put on her sneakers. Next, she wrapped Touk in a raincoat and pulled a wool cap over her head.

Toby struggled to lift Touk. "She's burning up," he exclaimed before carrying her downstairs and out to the Jeep parked in the driveway.

Abby grabbed their packs of food and water and followed. Toucan cried out when the rain hit her face. In the passenger seat, Abby held on to her and gently wiped the water off her forehead. "In twelve hours, you'll be in the hospital." She tried to sound more convincing. "A real doctor will take care of you." Her tone still sounded fake. "Touk, I love you."

"Where's Eddie?" Abby asked Toby as he climbed behind the wheel. "He can help us carry her to the boat."

Toby started the engine. "Eddie's not coming." He paused a moment. "Do you want the real reason or the reason he gave me?"

Abby imagined a metal box deep inside her mind where she kept her fears and wishes stored away. She lifted the lid and packed her disappointment inside. Eddie, Jordan's best friend, had failed her and Toucan in their greatest hour of need. Abby closed the lid of the imaginary box. The only thing that mattered to her was reaching Colony East.

She quickly discovered that Eddie wasn't the only one afraid of catching the Pig. When they pulled into the parking lot at the harbor, Abby had expected at least a few friends to show up and see them off, albeit from a safe distance. The lot was empty.

She jostled Toucan. "Wake up." Her sister didn't stir. "If you get up, I'll give you a piece of chocolate."

"Two," Toucan murmured.

Abby smiled sadly at her sister's effort to negotiate. "Okay, two."

They didn't need the flashlight. The sky had lightened enough to reveal solid gray cloud cover and the jetty, lying low and long against the horizon. Together, she and Toby half-carried, half-dragged Toucan across the parking lot and out onto the slick dock. With the rain coming down in sheets and the wind howling, Abby didn't want to think about the strait— the twenty miles of open ocean they were about to cross.

She climbed down the dock ladder and stepped into the whaler, cursing the water that had pooled in the boat, rising just above her ankles. Toby handed Toucan to her and returned to the Jeep for their supplies.

She covered herself and Touk with a tarp. Inside their dark cave, she gave her two small pieces of chocolate.

"More," Touk cried.

Abby grabbed her wrist just in case. When Toucan curled into a ball instead of thrashing, Abby wrapped her arm around her, trying to comfort her as best she could.

Toby fired up the outboard, and Abby soon sensed the motion of the boat as he pulled away from the dock. She knew from the smooth ride they were still in the protected harbor.

Beyond the jetty, Toby drove the boat hard, skittering over the wave tops. Abby hugged Toucan, hoping the whaler's ability to handle rough seas would offset Toby's lack of experience.

Gripping the rail with one hand, she found the rhythm of the boat as it pounded the waves. She cradled Toucan's head before each impact.

The further from land they went, the bigger the waves. Every bruising crunch, Abby told herself, put them closer to their destination.

The bow crashed into a rising wall of water, slamming Abby from her position, jostling Touk. The next wave caught Abby off guard and knocked the wind out of her when she landed stomach-first on the fiberglass bench. Toucan burst into tears as icy water drenched her clothes.

At that moment, the engine quit, and the boat swung around, now taking the waves broadside. They rolled violently side-to-side, water pouring over the port and starboard gunwales, rising to Abby's shins, then her knees. She clutched Touk to absorb the brunt of the blows. Fearing they would capsize, Abby ripped back the tarp and gulped at the sight of Toby trying to insert the gas spout into the outboard's tank. With the boat bucking up and down, gasoline splashed everywhere.

He forced a smile. "Part of the plan." He finished filling the tank and pushed the starter button. The engine sputtered. Toby cranked the motor without pause. She didn't think that was part of the plan. If it didn't catch soon, he'd drain the battery. Abby's stomach twisted in panic. Stranded halfway between the island and the coast in stormy conditions, the list of ways for them to die was long.

Toby kept his finger welded to the starter button.

Abby remembered her dad teaching her how to start a lawn mower. "Sometimes the engine gets flooded with gas," he had explained. "Move the lever to the highest speed. The gas will flow through."

She grabbed his arm to get his attention. "Toby, give it full throttle."

He shook his head and kept cranking and cranking the motor.

Wondering at what age boys might actually start to listen, Abby reached out and pulled the throttle lever toward her, full on. The motor coughed blue smoke and hummed to life.

"Thanks," Toby muttered with a sheepish grin. Avoiding her eyes, he revved the motor and headed off in the direction of Portland.

When they entered Portland Harbor an hour later, the rain had thinned to a mist and clouds were breaking up to the west, showing a patch of blue.

Abby watched Toby steer for a slip at the trading zone that was reserved for lead negotiators.

Once he had tied up the boat, together they moved Toucan to a park bench. At first, Abby thought it was strange that traders and shoppers, some wearing germ masks, cleared a wide path for them. She shuddered when she realized how sick Touk must look. She had witnessed her sister's gradual decline. If these kids were this afraid, Touk might be sicker than she thought. They had no time to waste.

Toby gathered their supplies from the boat and told Abby to wait at the bench while he finalized the deal for their ride to Colony East.

With Toucan slumping against her shoulder, Abby kept a wary eye on her surroundings. Activity at the zone picked up. A fishing trawler, looking like it was towing a flock of hungry gulls, motored toward a dock. Kids shouted out their wares. Puma sneakers, smoked deer meat, even baseball cards. Just about anything could be traded. The blast of a horn caused quite a stir as the crowd surged toward a fuel truck in the parking lot.

She wished Toby would hurry up.

Abby closed her eyes and thought about Jordan. A sudden shiver passed through her. The feeling made her uneasy. She wished he were here. If her brother had skippered the whaler, they would have avoided their near death experience in the strait.

Once more, Abby lifted the lid of the metal box deep in her mind and placed in it her fantasy that Jordan would sail into Portland Harbor on *Lucky Me*, and they would go to Colony East together.

# CHAPTER SIX
## MYSTIC

*A blade of fear twisted in Jordan's stomach as the growl deepened. He took a step back in the dark shadows. The throaty vibration wound tighter and tighter like a spring ready to snap.*

*Then the dog pounced. It had a broad chest and a flat head and blank eyes. Pushing off its back paws, it hurtled at Jordan, strings of saliva flying from open jaws.*

*The dog smashed its throat against his thigh, choking off its air supply, which enraged it even more. Then it clamped its jaws until teeth met bone.*

Jordan screamed and then blinked as bright light drilled into his brain through his eyes. Wondering if he had just jumped from one nightmare to the next, he saw he was in a bed, facing a window where leafy branches swayed outside, creating dancing shadows on the teddy bear wallpaper.

Trying to clear his vision, he focused on a bag of clear liquid hanging from a metal pole next to the bed. A tube ran from the bag to the top of his hand with white tape holding the needle in place. He realized he was awake and hooked up to an IV.

He saw bandages on his thigh and it all came back to him. Horrific images flooded his mind. Pirates attacking. Getting shot. *Lucky Me* vanishing in flames. The exploding cans of gasoline were land mines buried deep in his heart. He remembered struggling in the cold, dark water. He cried out as he plunged deeper into grief.

All of a sudden, it felt like someone was hammering a spike into his thigh. Each blow in sync with the beat of his heart. He screamed again.

Two girls rushed into the room. The shock of seeing them silenced Jordan. There was one his age who had straight black hair that came to her shoulders and very dark eyes. When she gazed at him their eyes locked, and he forgot about his pain for a second. He decided then, to try not to scream so loudly. The other girl was younger, probably around twelve. She also had black, straight hair, but her expression was far less serious than the older one. It almost seemed as if she had just told herself a private joke and was stifling laughter. Jordan saw nothing funny about his situation. The girls spoke to each other in a foreign language.

The younger one put a blood pressure cuff on his arm while the older one took his pulse. The lightness of the girl's fingers on his beating pulse, while her serious eyes darted from his wound to her wristwatch and back, made him forget his anguish again for a fleeting moment.

Jordan lifted his head, but the searing pain it caused in his leg convinced him to lie back. "Where am I? A hospital?"

The girls traded glances. He didn't know what they were communicating except this was no hospital.

"You're lucky," the older one said. "A fisherman found you floating."

"Where?"

"This is Mystic, Connecticut," the younger one said.

He tensed. The pirates had attacked them off Mystic. What would they do if they learned there was a survivor? Something else concerned him. He worried about Abby and Toucan. If the pirates boasted, the news of the disaster on *Lucky Me* would spread. The pirates would not know the name of the boat, but a two-masted schooner was rare. His sisters would hear about the boat sinking from other gypsies. They'd think he was dead.

"I live on Castine Island," he blurted. "I need to get home, now."

The older girl produced a syringe. "First, you need to get better. How does your leg feel?"

Unable to speak in the grip of pain, his contorted face answered for him.

The girls again spoke to each other in a language he didn't understand. Then, together, they rolled him onto his side. He grunted in agony as they wedged a pillow underneath his back to keep him propped up. The younger girl scrubbed a spot on his butt. The older girl snapped her finger against the syringe.

He felt the pinch of a needle, and a moment later, the brilliant sunshine and leaves outside held greater interest than his throbbing thigh.

# CHAPTER SEVEN
# PORTLAND TRADING ZONE

"Hey!"

Hearing Toby's voice, Abby blinked in the bright sunshine and saw him standing before her with another boy. Coming out of a deep sleep, she panicked before realizing Touk was snuggling in the crook of her arm.

Toby nodded to his companion. "This is Spike. He's our driver."

Spike had a wispy mustache and a constellation of purple moon tattoos on his upper arms. Abby guessed he was fifteen or sixteen. She introduced herself and Toucan. When he scrunched his brow, a look Abby had seen a hundred times after mentioning her sister's name, she added, "Her real name is Lizette."

Spike grinned. "My name's Arthur, but call me Spike."

"Can you carry the girl?" Toby asked him.

Spike stepped forward, and with little effort, scooped Toucan up as if she were made of straw. "Whoa, she feels like she just came out of the oven."

Toby shrugged. "It's just a bad cold."

Abby held her breath, fearing they would lose their ride if Spike decided Touk's fever was from the Pig. She exhaled in relief when he walked off without dropping her sister like the hot potato she was.

Spike opened the passenger door of a red Mini Cooper, flipped the seat forward, and gently laid Toucan in back. Abby climbed in next to her, crinkling her nose at the strong odor of gasoline. She found the source: two five-gallon cans in the cargo section behind her. She wasn't about to complain.

With Toby next to him in the passenger seat, Spike drove with one hand on the wheel, the other hand resting on the barrel of a shotgun.

They headed south on Route 95, weaving around the abandoned cars and trucks. Abby craned her neck left and right, taking in the sights. They passed corn and wheat fields, and bicycle convoys that rolled along in the breakdown lane. Her jaw dropped when Spike drove on the median strip to pass a slower moving fuel truck. She looked up into the rearview mirror, catching him smirking at her.

A few miles into New Hampshire, four motorcyclists roared up behind them. Abby gasped at the sight of rifles slung on the backs of the two lead riders.

Just then, one of the bikers sped up and rode alongside them. She peered into the car and grinned when she saw Spike. After giving him a thumbs-up, she raced ahead and the other bikers followed.

Spike winked at Abby in the mirror. "Nobody messes with Martha's property."

"Spike works for Martha," Toby explained. "She's the fuel king who controls Portland."

Abby knew of Martha.

They stopped in view of the Welcome to Massachusetts sign, which was covered in graffiti, much of it purple. Toting his gun, Spike got out and took a leak behind a bush. Abby broke out snacks and water. She gave a few crackers to Touk and passed apples to the boys.

"More," Touk demanded.

Drawing in a sharp breath, Abby placed her sister's head in her lap. "Shhh."

"Please, Abby, another cracker."

Preparing to hold her arms if she started flailing, Abby dribbled some water on Touk's forehead and blew on it to cool her down. "Try to rest."

"She's got the Pig, right?" Spike asked.

Toby crunched his apple. "Nah. It's the flu."

"I want a cracker," Toucan screeched.

Hugging Touk, Abby locked eyes with Spike in the mirror. It was obvious what was wrong with Touk. Should she tell him the truth? Her heart hammered in her chest as she held his gaze, but she said nothing. A flash of sadness crossed his eyes and then he started the engine. As they drove off, Abby wondered if the Pig had claimed someone close to Spike.

They approached a roadblock south of Boston, where a group of older boys and girls were collecting tolls.

Toby held a diamond in his hand. "This should get us through."

Spike scoffed. "Put it away." He pulled up to the collector and simply said, "Martha." The boy waved them through.

Spike patted the shotgun and snared Abby's eyes in the mirror. "Where Martha's influence ends, this takes over."

A pit formed in her stomach. Violence made her sick, but she kept her mouth shut. She would have to deal with whatever got them to Colony East.

Just over the Rhode Island border, Spike turned on the radio. "Listen up y'all, Jamey can't get enough purple," DJ Silver intoned. "That's cool with me, and I'm sure it's cool with a lot of you out there. Mix a little red and blue, you get purple. No big deal, right? So here you go, Jamey, 'Purple Rain' by Prince."

Abby shot forward. "Wow. The Port comes in so clear. We can only pick it up at night."

"This far south it comes in during the day," Spike said. "The station's in Mystic, Connecticut."

"I can't believe kids figured out how to run a radio station."

"The adults got it running for them. Martha told me. She knows the fuel king who supplies diesel for the station's generators." Spike slapped his hand on the steering wheel to keep the beat and sang along with Prince.

Abby was curious to know more, but she didn't want to do or say anything that might agitate Spike and cause a delay. The easiest way to minimize agitating him was to keep her mouth shut.

Later, the Providence skyline came into view. Abby had last seen the city three years ago when she'd accompanied her mom on a visit to a friend in

Newport, Rhode Island. She remembered her mother pointing out the gold-domed state capitol building, which now looked like it had burned to the ground.

"End of the line." Spike pulled to the side of the road and stopped in front of a Greyhound Bus. The rubber tires splayed out from the rims, and a pile of empty cans and a metal drum used for cooking indicated the bus had once served as shelter.

Abby shot forward. "What?"

Toby glared. "Abby, I'll handle this."

"Your friend only paid for me to bring you to Providence."

She sat back, gritting her teeth.

Toby turned to Spike. "You want to take us all the way to Colony East? Ten crates of shrimp."

"Bro, it's not shrimp season."

"I'll owe you."

"Twenty," Spike countered.

"Fifteen."

Abby's head spun. Twenty crates of shrimp was nothing. The comet had put an end to overfishing and the stocks of fish were rebounding. During shrimp season, February to April, fishing trawlers leaving Castine Harbor routinely harvested hundreds of crates of shrimp in hours.

"No deal," Spike said.

Toby opened the passenger door. "Thanks for the ride."

Abby felt like she had entered a bad dream as she watched Toby get out of the car.

"The girl's got the Pig," Spike said. "You really want to get out here?"

Toby ignored him and turned to Abby. "Let's get Touk out feet first."

Heat flared on her cheeks. She couldn't believe that five crates of shrimp were all that was keeping them from continuing to Colony East.

"Okay, fifteen crates," Spike said.

Toby paused, thinking. He studied the bus, the sky, the metal drum. He narrowed his eyes and nodded to himself.

Abby wanted to scream, "Take it". She managed to keep her mouth shut. She had to trust Toby. And should he prove himself untrustworthy, she would have no choice but to wring his neck.

Toby faced Spike. "Five crates, that's my final offer. Take it or leave it."

Abby turned into a pressure cooker of hot steam ready to blow.

Spike jerked his thumb. "Get in."

They drove on with Abby slowly returning to a solid state, too shocked by what just happened to think. Why had Toby offered such a low number? It was as if he had wanted them to get kicked out. Even stranger, Spike had accepted a low-ball offer after turning down higher offers. Abby told herself she could live with the strange mysteries of boys as long as they were heading to Colony East.

At the New York state border, Spike stopped for gas and filled the tank from the two gas cans stowed in back. Before they started out again, he gently placed his hand on Touk's head. "Hang in there, kiddo."

Abby swallowed hard, caught off-guard by the tenderness of his gesture. "Spike, you knew someone who had the Pig?"

"Yep." He took a deep breath, and his shoulders sagged in defeat as he let the air out. "My cousin Jimmy. I took care of him since the night of the purple moon. He was twelve." Spike's voice choked with emotion. Abby reached out and touched his arm.

He wiped his eyes, cleared his throat, and his mischievous smile returned as if he needed to change the topic. "Toby must really like you. He traded your Boston Whaler for this trip."

Abby's jaw dropped. She had always assumed that Eddie or someone else from the island would hitch a ride on the fishing trawler and drive the boat back. When she saw Toby squirming in his seat, she knew what Spike said was true.

Spike read her expression. "You didn't know? This is a one-way trip for your lead negotiator. He gave the boat to Martha in return for a ride to Providence. Toby knew if he offered me too many crates of shrimp to go to Colony East, I'd never believe him. So he held his ground." Spike faced Toby. "You're good dude. I just hope you can negotiate your way into Colony East."

Spike turned on the radio and drove on. DJ Silver dedicated songs that played and ended, but the words and the music sounded distant through the thick fog of Abby's swirling emotions. Toby had traded away more than a boat to help Touk. He had sacrificed his life on Castine Island. The boy whose father had beaten him, whom nobody loved growing up, whom Abby had tried to avoid a thousand times, humbled her.

She looked at him in the front seat and he avoided looking back. She kept looking and he finally turned. Even if she knew what to say, it was too soon to say anything. She made eye contact and gave a tiny nod. She saw his eyes grow glassy, knowing her eyes were already that way. Toby gave her a slight nod and looked away.

They crossed the White Stone Bridge into Brooklyn, paying the toll with one of Toby's rubies. The toll collector, a girl wearing a New York Giants cap, and missing a few front teeth, had scoffed at the offer of a diamond. Spike stopped at the first gas station they came to. Kids using pick axes and shovels had dug a hole to reach the underground tank long ago, but he was after a map.

"Bingo," Spike said, holding out a street map of Brooklyn he found in the office.

With Toby reading the map and giving directions, they got plenty of stares in the red Mini from the local kids who predominately walked, bladed, or boarded.

They decided the base of the Brooklyn Bridge would be the best drop-off spot, but six blocks away Spike had to stop because buildings on both sides of the avenue had collapsed and deposited a mountain of bricks in the way. Then they discovered the side streets were also obstructed by downed power poles, crumbling buildings, and makeshift encampments.

Spike turned in his seat. "End of the line." Abby recoiled in shock when he tried to hand her the shotgun. "Take it," he implored. "If your sister steals food, people are going to want to hurt her. They tend to back off when you aim a double-barrel at them."

She shook her head and spoke through jaw muscles cramping with tension, "She'll be with us."

Spike balanced the gun on his palm, as if serving it to her on a platter. "My cousin, Jimmy, snuck off and nearly got himself beaten up when he stole apples."

"Spike, I appreciate the offer, but I can't shoot anyone."

He broke open the shotgun. "Me neither. Look, it's empty."

"Abby, take the gun," Toby said.

Spike grinned. "Spoken like a true negotiator. You can trade it."

Abby put her hand on Spike's arm. "Keep the gun. Thank you for everything."

Spike reached out and gently squeezed Touk's hand. "Lizette. I really like your name."

# CHAPTER EIGHT
## COLONY EAST

Too anxious to sleep, Lieutenant Dawson climbed out of bed and paced in his living quarters. His excitement had started when Admiral Samuels had put out a request for volunteers to accompany scientists outside the fence. "They're looking for children infected with AHA-B." Of course, Dawson had volunteered immediately, and now he couldn't wait to get the daily memorandum to see if the admiral had honored his request.

At three o'clock, he heard footsteps padding down the carpeted hallway. He knelt and grabbed the memorandum as soon as the ensign fed it under the door.

Dawson's heart thumped as he read his orders: Report to Ferry Terminal 7 at 0900. Chief Petty Officer O'Brien will assume command of Biltmore Company until 1700.

He arrived at the terminal building ten minutes early. It was located on the East River, two blocks south of Pier 15. Here, Navy mechanics tended the fleet of Zodiacs. The building also housed a ferry that, prior to the epidemic, had transported pedestrians across the river. Dawson had heard a rumor the admiral wanted to return the vessel to active service for moving supplies. He believed the rumor. The old man had a sense of nostalgia for things that were once a normal part of life.

The corner of Dawson's lip curled at the sight of Sandy standing in a group assembled on the dock. She, too, had volunteered to accompany the scientists. He harbored a wish that someone higher up the food chain, above Admiral Samuels and Doctor Perkins, might decide to transfer one of the medical doctors from Colony West to Atlanta instead of Sandy.

Approaching the group, Dawson lost the bounce in his step when he spotted Doctor Droznin. The Russian scientist didn't like him and the feeling was mutual. Despite his issues with Doctor Droznin, he told himself he would never let his personal feelings get in the way of the mission.

He noted that a second scientist, whom he didn't recognize, was also part of the group. The woman, in her thirties, wore a white lab coat with short sleeves, revealing the sinewy arms of a rock climber. Most of the scientists at the colony looked like the heaviest thing they lifted was a box of beakers, but every now and then an athlete slipped in among the white coats. The sailors included patrol boat skippers, Ensign Pickering and Ensign Jackson. They had both served with him on the USS Seawolf. Pickering, a sonar technician, was into online gaming. From Pickering's perpetually long face, Dawson wondered if the ensign found a world minus online games almost as bleak as one minus adults. Pickering was the one who, on Admiral Samuels' orders, had modified the room radios, ensuring the cadets could only pick up the boring drone of the CDC robot. Ensign Jackson, a machinist mate, was a member of the Hopi Tribe, the only Native American at Colony East, and, at age twenty-six, the oldest Native American in the country. How Jackson had managed the transition to a claustrophobic sub from the expansive vistas of the Arizona desert he would never know. Dawson knew that both ensigns enjoyed the respect of the admiral, which was likely the reason they were escorts today.

Doctor Droznin introduced her colleague, the athletic Doctor Gowan, as a microbiologist with the CDC field team. "We're looking for cases of AHA-B," Droznin told the group. "We want to procure an infected subject who has a healthy sibling. We'll break into two teams. Doctor Gowan and I will split up, so we can assess symptoms and make a decision on who to bring back to Medical Clinic 17."

Ensign Pickering gave pointers on what they could expect after passing through the gate into Brooklyn. "We received quite the welcome yesterday, and we should see bigger crowds today. All of you will have a radio and a Taser, and you'll be accompanied by either me or Ensign Jackson. We're both armed. If you become separated, call in your location and stay put."

"How long do we have?" Dawson asked.

Droznin stepped forward. "Get in. Get out. We're not tourists, Lieutenant."

Sandy inquired about the request for siblings. "Do you want brothers, sisters, or both? Does age matter? Should the younger one or older one be infected?"

Doctor Gowan replied, "We're conducting Phase IV antibiotic trials, and we need to establish a control group with DNA matches. Age doesn't matter. We can have any combination, they just have to be siblings."

Doctor Droznin sighed impatiently. "Anything else?" Nobody spoke up. "Good. Let's get going."

Ensign Pickering broke them into teams, Alpha and Bravo. The bad news for Dawson was that Sandy was on the other team. The good news was that Doctor Droznin was also on the other team.

They suited up and piled into two Zodiacs. Close to the Brooklyn shore, Ensign Jackson, seated beside him, said, "Lieutenant, smell that?" The hazmat face shield muffled her voice.

Dawson drew in a breath, mostly smelling the plastic of the suit, but also detecting a faint odor of roasting meat. "A barbecue," he exclaimed.

"Rat barbecue," she said. "You won't see a lot of pigeons flying around, either."

Dawson pulled his shoulders back, trying to prepare himself mentally for the desperate conditions they would encounter.

Alpha team beached ahead of them. Ensign Pickering punched the security code at the gate and shouted at the throng of children on the other side, "Back up. Clear out." Pushing with both hands and then putting his shoulder into the effort, he managed to open the gate wide enough for the Colony East party to squeeze through.

Dawson stepped through it and stared in wonder. Kids played soccer, using the open door of a police cruiser as one of the nets. Child vendors sold water, fish, and bicycle parts. Meat roasted on spits over coals in metal drums. Rat? Pigeon? Whatever it was, it sure smelled good. Purple cabbages grew in rows of raised garden beds. Those cabbages, he noticed, were growing faster than the ones planted in Central Park Farm. He marveled at the resilience of the human spirit.

Led by Doctor Gowan, Bravo team headed north, the crowd swelling around them. Rather than shrink away from the tall people wearing white suits, the kids crushed closer. Pickering's flustered voice crackled over the radio. "Create a perimeter as you move." Dawson saw the reason for the ensign's frustration. Alpha team had become bogged down to a standstill in a quicksand of heads coming up to their chests.

Gowan pointed up ahead. "Over there."

Dawson caught a glimpse of the small girl before the seam in the crowd sealed. Rattily dressed, she sat on a curbstone, alone, head in her hands. He swallowed hard, thinking that his daughter, Sarah, could be sitting on a curbstone in Mystic at this very moment, forlorn and infected with AHA-B. He picked up the pace, trying to banish that image from his mind.

Closing in on the girl, he and Ensign Jackson created space by barking commands. "Let us through. Everyone back up. Now!"

Dawson scanned the surroundings. The child sat before a fish market, Ribbentrop Fish carved in a wooden sign. Kids camped inside the market, and the cardboard that covered the smashed window had a message painted in bright purple: ADULTS PLEASE SHARE! Something deep inside him kept his eyes glued to the plea.

"Lieutenant!" Ensign Jackson needed help peeling a boy from her leg.

Doctor Gowan knelt beside the sick girl. She took her temperature with an electronic ear thermometer and then inspected the girl's arm, poking and squeezing it the way one tests for a ripe cantaloupe. "A-H-A-B," Gowan announced for the benefit of Bravo Team. She said to the girl, "Do you have a brother or sister?"

Dawson held his breath, praying this girl had a healthy sibling so they could take her back to Colony East and enter her into the drug trial. Billions had died, but something about this girl tugged at his heart. All of a sudden, his head swam. He knew he could not leave her, no matter what. If she didn't go to Colony East, he wouldn't return either. Dawson wondered if he was losing his mind.

The girl moved her lips and Doctor Gowan positioned her ear as close to the girl's mouth as her white hood allowed. The girl spoke again.

Gowan nodded and looked up. "She's got a sister and a brother."

Dawson tried to wipe his eyes, surprised when his gloved hand scraped the plastic shield.

A teenage girl pushed forward and he held his arm out to stop her. Except for her torn clothing and awful stench from not bathing, she was like any of his third-floor, female cadets. They locked eyes. He saw fear and fatigue in her gaze. "I want to see my sister," she said. "She has the Pig."

"Pig?" Of course, he thought, AHA-B stimulated the appetite. "Go on."

The teen hugged her little sister. Then Doctor Gowan performed the same tests on the older sibling, taking her temperature and squeezing her arm. Nodding to herself, Gowan brought the two-way radio to her face shield. "Alpha team."

"This is Droznin. Go ahead."

"We have a confirmed case of A-H-A-B. The child has a temperature of one hundred and three degrees. Fat content is high."

The crowd of children pushed closer, straining to hear every word spoken by the adult.

"Does she have a sibling?" Droznin asked.

"Roger," Doctor Gowan replied. "Brother and sister. The sister's with us. Fifteen years old. Not infected."

"Bring them in."

"Lieutenant, can you carry her?" Gowan asked.

Dawson responded immediately, scooping up the child in his arms. "I'm Lieutenant Mark Dawson. Who are you?"

"Elsie," she whispered hoarsely, gazing up through feverish eyes.

He hurried, knowing every second counted.

# CHAPTER NINE
# BROOKLYN

Toby burst through the front door and slammed it behind him. "Adults. I saw adults!"

Abby sat up on the couch, trembling from the loud and sudden intrusion. Touk hardly stirred in her arms, delirious with a high fever.

Toby shifted from foot to foot. "Abby, they were from Colony East. Hurry up, we have to go. They're looking for kids who have the Pig. They want siblings. You and Touk."

He started pacing, which stirred up clouds of dust. Sunlight streaming through the window showed the particles swirling in the air. Last night, after Spike had dropped them off, they had entered the brick house on Livingston Place, concluding it was uninhabited because of all the dust.

"Please, sit," she told him and adjusted the pillow under Touk's head. "Look at her. She can't even stand on her own." Abby's voice pinched when it hit her how much her sister's condition had worsened over the past couple of hours.

Talking fast, Toby filled her in on his trip to the river. Just six blocks away, he'd seen adults wearing hazmat suits take two kids back to Colony East. "I heard them talking over two-way radios. One adult said the kid had A-H-A-B."

Abby scrunched her brow. "Ahab?"

He shot to his feet. "It's their name for the Pig. Let's go. They're coming back."

At first, Abby thought Toby couldn't possibly know what the adults were planning to do. She also knew they were running out of time. They had nothing to lose and everything to gain by taking Touk to the spot where Toby had seen the adults.

"Hey, sleepy." When she stroked her head, she noticed Toucan's teeth chattering. Abby wanted to scream. The fever chilled her sister one minute, drenched her in sweat the next. She packed couch cushions around her for warmth, careful not to rile up too much dust.

"How are we going to carry her?" Abby asked. "Remember what it was like to get her in and out of the whaler."

"What if we make a stretcher?" Toby suggested. "We could use a door."

"A door's too heavy," she replied.

They discussed other ideas. Lug her using a lawn chair, a folding card table, a hammock. Push her in a wheelchair. Do the fireman's carry, taking turns to put Touk over their shoulders. All might have been good ideas if they were stronger, if they had time to look for a wheelchair, if they were lucky, if, if, if…

Abby walked to the window. "We could ask someone to help us. While you were away, I saw kids go by on skateboards."

"We have nothing to trade." Toby reached into his pocket and produced his five remaining gems. "I tried to trade these for news. Nobody wants diamonds. Somebody flooded the market with fake diamonds, and rubies are worth half what I can get for them in Portland."

"Kids might help us because we need their help."

"Abby, they don't think like you."

"We can ask."

Toby held up his hands in frustration. "They'd see Touk has the Pig and run the other way. Look what your friends did."

"Spike helped us," Abby reminded him before realizing that Spike was the exception, and that Toby was right.

He placed the gems in her hand. "I'll stay with her. If anyone can convince the adults to come here to get your sister, you can."

Abby knew he was right again. Besides, it was also her responsibility. Suddenly, an idea popped into her head. "Toby, you said they wanted a brother or sister of someone who has the Pig? Maybe they'll take a brother and sister?"

Toby twisted his face. "They'll never believe I'm your brother."

"Yes." She felt her idea taking root. "We can be twins!"

He rolled his eyes. "Give me a break."

"Johnny Black and his sister, Mady, are twins. They don't look anything alike."

"Who?"

"They're from Cambridge. We have nothing to lose. I'm going to tell you some things about my family. You can make up the rest. You're good at making stuff up."

"Thanks. I think."

After giving him a quick history of the Leigh family, Abby moved beside Touk on the couch. Realizing it might be the last time she saw her sister, she started to shake all over. Then she forced that thought from her mind. Her best chance to help Toucan was to strip away her fear and sadness and focus on the job ahead. Abby whispered, "I love you."

Toby was a different story. She stepped up to the boy who had done so much for them. If this was to be their last time together, she wanted to leave him with something that had been on her mind. She placed her hands on his cheeks and looked into his eyes. Her pulse quickened and she felt a funny feeling spreading throughout her body. She gently kissed him on the lips long enough for Toby to get over the shock and kiss her back.

# CHAPTER TEN
## MYSTIC

Fearing the shockwaves of pain that would result from sneezing, Jordan pinched his nose and held his breath. Making even the slightest movement triggered a searing jolt in his thigh. The urge to sneeze passed and he exhaled.

A snippet of conversation drifted through the walls, though he couldn't make out the words. He desperately wanted to know where he was—exactly where. He recalled the two girls had said Mystic, Connecticut.

He vaguely remembered the older one coming into his room a number of times to change his bandage, take his blood pressure, give him a shot. Her last trip, he thought, she had taken away the IV setup.

How long had he been here? Was he in danger? When could he leave? He stared at the ceiling, trying to turn off the stream of chatter in his mind that made him more and more agitated.

He grimaced in frustration, which set off a chain reaction of muscles twitching and skin stretching, making him cry out from the sensation that felt like someone peeling the flesh off his femur.

The older girl entered the room and rushed over to him. "Does it hurt?"

*Hurt?* Jordan grinned in disbelief. "Yes, but I'll feel a lot better if you'll answer some questions."

205

He saw a sparkle in her eye. "We want all our patients to feel better." She pulled up a chair and sat beside him. "What would you like to know?"

Jordan couldn't take his eyes off her. He felt himself drifting in a breeze of sweet perfume that was only the scent of minty antiseptic soap coming off her hands.

"I'm Jordan Leigh."

"Hello, Jordan. I'm Wenlan Lu. My sister is CeeCee."

"This is Mystic, Connecticut?"

She nodded.

"I think I heard you and your sister talking to each other in a different language."

"Our parents came from Taiwan. CeeCee and I try to speak Chinese so we don't forget it." She gave him a little grin. "You didn't imagine that."

He winked, "So I'm not going crazy?"

"You talk a lot in your sleep, but I don't think you're going crazy."

He thought Wenlan had moved closer to him, but then realized that her dark eyes had pulled him closer to her. "Is this a hospital?"

"Not exactly. When I was in sixth grade, the teacher, Mrs. Griffin, had a boy named William sit next me. She told me William was shy, and she wanted to put someone friendly beside him." She pointed to herself. "Mrs. Griffin loved me because I was friendly and I never goofed off. So I talked to William. I didn't know it at the time, but that would change my life.

"After the night of the purple moon, shy William became a fuel king. Now he has a large gang and controls the entire state. When he wanted to open a medical clinic to treat the members of his gang, he remembered that my mother had been a doctor so he asked me if I wanted to run the clinic."

"Did you want to be a doctor when you grew up?"

Wenlan whistled softly. "Are you kidding me? My mom never stopped working. She'd get calls in the middle of the night. My father was an accountant. I think I might have tried that."

"William must have figured a doctor's kid would know at least a little something about it," Jordan said.

She nodded. "He was probably right. He makes sure our generators run, and he gets us all the medicine and supplies we need."

Jordan debated whether he should ask if the pirates that sank *Lucky Me* were part of William's gang. Not just yet, he decided. He wanted to learn more.

"How do you know how to treat people?"

"CeeCee and I study the *Physicians' Desk Reference Manual*. It's a fat book with lots of diagrams. There's also a lot of trial and error."

Jordan's heart pumped harder. "Am I your first gunshot victim?"

She paused a long moment as if she were trying to decide how much to say. "Unfortunately, no. You're very lucky. The bullet missed the main artery in your leg."

"Do you know what happened to me?" Jordan heard the anger rise in his voice.

She rested her hand on his arm. "I don't know exactly, but you're safe here."

Just her touch drained some of his anger away. "I'm not a member of William's gang. How can you take care of me?"

She narrowed her eyes, pretending to look fierce. "I'm the last person William wants to have an argument with." She wagged her finger at him. "Remember that."

Jordan wished she hadn't pointed at him like that, because it meant she had to take her hand off his arm. "Yes, doctor," he smiled and immediately paid for making a physical gesture with a stabbing pain in his leg.

"Is this talk making you feel better?"

His leg was killing him. "Much better. Can I ask you a favor? I live on Castine Island. My sister is going to worry about me. If I write her a note, could you have someone take it to a trading zone? If they give it to a gypsy traveling north, maybe she'll get the note."

"Of course I can. Is Emily your sister?"

Jordan felt his heart stop, and he turned his head towards the wall away from her.

"You kept mentioning Emily in your sleep," Wenlan added.

He looked at her. "She was my girlfriend. She died in the epidemic."

Wenlan squeezed his hand. "I know what it's like to lose someone close."

When neither of them spoke for a long moment, Jordan knew they would leave it at that.

"My sister is Abby," he said finally.

The glow returned to Wenlan's eyes. "Abby. I like that name. I'll get you a piece of paper to write your note."

# CHAPTER ELEVEN
# COLONY EAST

Alone in the company leader's office, Lieutenant Dawson read over his note to Lily.

*Dear Lily,*

*Tomorrow, your fellow cadets are going to get a big surprise. After dinner, they'll be served the first batch of Colony East ice cream. The flavor is vanilla!*

*By the time you get back, I hope they figure out how to make chocolate ice cream. That's my favorite.*

*Well, we hope to see you soon. Tabby keeps asking about you.*

*Lieutenant Mark Dawson,*

*Biltmore Company Leader.*

Thinking this breezy news would cheer up Lily, he sealed the letter in an envelope and delivered it to David Levine in the CDC liaison office.

Levine paled the moment he entered the office. Dawson thought it was strange the scientist's hand shook as he took the envelope.

"Thank you," Dawson said.

Levine lowered his eyes and turned away without a word.

The scientist was shy and awkward around people, but something seemed to be troubling him. It was not long before Dawson understood the source of Levine's anxiety. In the air command pilot's room, he picked up the latest weather fax and drew in a sharp breath. The first tropical storm of the season had formed off the coast of Africa. They had named her Athena, and she could be very bad news.

So much for a quiet hurricane season, he thought. The map showed the storm at position, 18.4 N 126.3 E with gusts maxing out at fifty miles per hour. The meteorologists projected Athena would track toward Cuba, and gave it a fifty percent chance of strengthening into a hurricane. What direction Athena took from that point on, or whether she grew or fizzled, was anyone's guess.

He considered Levine's concern as a very bad omen. The scientist likely knew the latest results of the antibiotic trials. An early season hurricane combined with a delay in producing the antibiotic would create a disaster of epic proportions.

Dawson struggled to keep his chin up and shoulders back as he left the pilot's office.

# CHAPTER TWELVE
# BROOKLYN

"Nineteen Livingston Place," Abby kept repeating to herself, not wanting to forget the place where Toucan and Toby were staying. When she met the adults, she'd tell them that Toucan and Toby were at Nineteen Livingston Place, please pick them up.

Scuffing her feet from fatigue, she approached the area where Toby had said he'd seen the adults in hazmat suits. Abby counted five kids sprawled on the sidewalk in front of Ribbentrop Fish Market, all appearing as sick and listless as Touk. She figured they were suffering the advanced stages of the illness. Several of the victims had friends or family with them. Word must have spread that the adults had come to this spot, and now they were all hoping the adults would return and take them to Colony East. Abby eyed the sick kids with compassion, but also as competition.

Then she spotted a large metal gate a block away, so she walked over to it to get her first close-up glimpse of Colony East. Pressing her face against the bars, she gaped in amazement. On the other side of the river, a truck drove along a road. There were boats that motored back and forth, fifty yards off shore, and she could make out adults in them, though none appeared to be heading for shore.

Abby paused to think how far they had come. She considered it nothing short of a miracle that she, Toby and Touk had made it from Castine Island to the edge of Colony East. It was a miracle that Touk was still alive and that Toby had witnessed adults looking for kids with the Pig. She realized, though, that all those miracles would amount to nothing if this was as far as they got. Less than a mile away were doctors who might be able to save Toucan, but the final leg of the journey seemed much further than that. Abby felt as if she were standing at the edge of the ocean, with Colony East as far away as the horizon.

"There should be a lot of trash at high tide." Abby spun around. The filthy boy who spoke had a friendly face, wore two pearl earrings, and from what she could tell, appeared to be close to her age.

"Trash?"

"You're not from around here," he said, sizing her up.

"I'm from Maine."

"Cool," he beamed. "Tonight the moon is full, so the tide will be extra high. The adults dump all sorts of good stuff in the river. Last week, I got a bunch of uniforms the kids over there wear. They just had a few rips."

Abby hesitated, leery of saying too much to a stranger, especially on the mainland. Then she reconsidered. Toucan was dying and the time for playing it safe had passed. "I don't want trash. I'm waiting for the adults. My sister has the Pig."

In an all too familiar reaction, the boy took a step back. It was somewhat promising, though, that he hadn't walked away.

He nodded. "The adults have come two days in a row, looking for kids who have the Pig. They're coming back to get more kids tonight."

Abby's pulse raced. She wondered how he knew that, but she didn't want to come across as a naive stranger who asked dumb questions. "Where's the best place to wait?"

He crinkled his eyes. "The best place is the hardest place to get to." He reached his arm through the bars of the gate and pointed. "Right there. You want to meet them when they get out of their boats. On this side, it's a free-for-all. Everyone wants to touch them and talk to them. The mob'll push you out of the way."

Abby's heart sank as she peered up at the cinder block wall, three times taller than she was and topped with curly barbed wire. "You can climb over that wall, right?"

"Yeah, I know a way," he said, "but it's hard and dangerous. That wire will slice you to bits if you don't know what you're doing. Coming all the way from Maine, you don't want to bleed to death."

Abby pleaded. "I need to get over there."

"Forget it. You'll get hurt."

"Please," she begged. "My sister is very sick. If she doesn't get help soon…"

The boy hesitated. "Well, okay then. My friend has a ladder and rope. We climb up, throw a blanket over the barbed wire, then lower ourselves down on the other side."

Something about the boy's sudden change of heart alerted Abby. She wondered if he wanted something from her. "I can do that," she said, pushing caution aside.

He narrowed his eyes. "No offense, but I don't think you're strong enough to hold the rope. Look at your arms. Where are the muscles?"

Abby straightened, aware that she had misread his intentions. He really was concerned about her safety. "Listen, I can do anything."

The boy stared across the river, thinking. Abby held her breath. She made two fists, hoping he noticed the muscles in her forearms.

He finally let out a sigh. "What do you have to trade?"

She fished the gems from her pocket.

"That's it? Those diamonds are fake."

She felt the blood drain from her face. "Please."

He pursed his lips and looked away. He nodded to himself, starting to speak, and then stopped himself. He made a clicking sound with his mouth. "All right," he said finally and plucked the three rubies, leaving her with two diamonds.

Abby's eyes welled with tears. "Thank you."

"If you get hurt, it's not my fault," he said and led her along the wall for fifty yards. "Wait here." He disappeared into the crowd before she could ask him how long he would be. After four hours, with darkness falling, Abby balled her fists in anger, knowing the boy had tricked her.

Abby clenched her jaw and told herself she would find a way over that wall. She picked herself up and headed toward the gate, her mind whirling with ideas, fueled by the furious urgency of Toucan's imminent death.

Before the boy had known anything about her, he had mentioned trash. More than likely, he had thought the idea of picking trash from the river would bait her. Others must collect trash from the river, she thought. How did they get over the wall?

She stopped and listened for any noises coming from the other side of the wall. It was difficult to hear anything above the noises coming from this side. Kids played soccer, tag, they sang, laughed, ate, hung out around fires in barrels, rode bikes. It was as lively a gathering as any place she could remember before the night of the purple moon, a new type of society thriving. Unfortunately, all that was missing from this carnival of survivors were doctors who could help her sister.

Abby continued to the gate and peered out. Her pulse raced at the sight of the red and green running lights of boats that were closer to shore than earlier. After a minute, she realized the boats were only patrolling back and forth.

She headed north toward the Brooklyn Bridge, which, in the light of the full moon, looked like a broken skeleton. She hadn't gone far when she heard voices. Up ahead, a flashlight flickered at the base of the wall. Moving closer, she saw a kid disappear into a hole in the ground. Abby picked up her pace, knowing that a tunnel must lead to the other side of the wall and beyond that, Colony East. To Abby, crawling through a hole certainly seemed smarter than trying to climb over razor sharp barbed wire ten feet in the air.

Abby sized up the hole and got on her hands and knees. She was about to worm into it, when all of a sudden, two girls marched up to her. One positioned her foot an inch from Abby's hand. The other girl shone a light in her eyes. They both wore shorts and black leather boots, and the one with the flashlight had on a policeman's hat. She waved the light and hissed, "Are you going to pay, or what?"

Then the one who had nearly stepped on her fingers widened her stance in a menacing way. "Pay or get out of here."

Abby dug the two diamonds from her pocket and held them in her palm. Both girls laughed. "That's all you got?" one sneered. "It's high tide. You know how much trash you'll get?"

214

"I don't have anything else to trade," Abby said, stopping before telling them that Touk was dying, sensing that sympathy would not buy her the privilege of crawling through the muddy hole. She also had another plan taking shape in her mind and it was best to conceal the real reason for wanting to get to the river's edge.

The girl with the flashlight kicked some dirt at her. "Move on. Now!"

Abby thought fast. She had never negotiated before, but she had watched Toby enough times. "I'll give you fifty percent of the trash I get. You choose what you want."

The girls traded glances. Finger stomper gave a little snort. "Seventy percent."

"Forty percent," Abby shot back.

"Sixty-five," flashlight girl countered.

Every cell in her brain and in her heart screamed for her to agree to that number. But she had seen the best in action. She trusted Toby. In a calm voice, almost apathetic, like she didn't care what they would say, she said, "Thirty percent. That's my final offer."

The girls burst out laughing. Then they stepped away and conferred privately. They returned.

"Go on. We get to choose what we want. And don't get shot."

Abby quickly crawled through the hole before the girls could change their minds, and emerged on the other side. Along the bank, kids waded to their knees and fished snippets of trash from the river using long poles with hooks.

Colony East rose up before her like the Emerald City, it gave her cold chills. Gazing at the city, Abby remembered that Dorothy encountered a few obstacles before she got to see the Wizard of Oz. She resolved that nothing was going to stop her from getting to the adults.

She kicked off her shoes and stepped into the water. The silt squeezed between her toes as her feet sank in the mud. Compared to the icy water of Castine Island, the East River was a steamy bathtub. She sensed the trash collector kids stop and gape at her as she waded deeper. Imagining Touk on the edge of death and requiring urgent care, Abby slipped all the way in and took her first stroke toward Colony East.

# CHAPTER THIRTEEN
## COLONY EAST

Dawson's two-way radio crackled with the voice of Admiral Samuels. "Dawson, come in, over."

Strange. The admiral ordinarily left the mundane task of communicating over the radio to Ensign Parker. It was even stranger the admiral would raise him this early in the morning. Reveille was not for another thirty minutes.

"Dawson, over."

"Get to my office, on the double. O'Brien will cover for you."

Dawson couldn't read anything into Admiral Samuels's gruff, irritated tone, because he always sounded that way.

Ten minutes later, as rosy clouds boiled on the horizon, Dawson stood before Trump Tower. Before facing the admiral, he recited the sailor's refrain—Pink sky at night, sailor's delight. Pink sky in morning, sailors take warning.

Ready for stormy seas, but hoping for the best, Dawson raced up to the fourth floor, discovering Ensign Parker had yet to arrive and the door to the admiral's office open. He stepped inside and snapped off a crisp salute.

Seated behind his deck, Samuels waved a hand. "Have a seat, Mark." Then he leaned forward. "Abigail Leigh."

"Sir?"

"Do you know her? L-E-I-G-H."

Dawson didn't recognize the name. "Is she a cadet?"

"They picked her up on a windmill stanchion in the East River. She swam from the Brooklyn side and flagged down Ensign Mathews in a Zodiac. Do you know Mathews?"

"No, sir."

"She's a real go-getter. They call her 'torpedo'. Just arrived from Colony West. She was a weapons specialist on the *Virginia*. Ms. Leigh informed the ensign that her sister has Ahab."

"Ahab?"

"A-H-A-B. She called it the Pig. She said she knew we were looking for kids who were sick, who had siblings, and she gave an address where her brother and sister were staying."

Dawson exhaled a sharp puff of air. The will of survivors amazed him. This girl breached the wall and made it halfway across the East River, all in a desperate attempt to save her sister.

"Normally," the admiral continued, "Mathews would have taken the girl back to Brooklyn, but Abigail Leigh said she knew you."

Dawson choked. "What?"

"So Mathews called me and asked what to do. I called Doctor Perkins, and he told me they were still looking for test subjects so I sent a team to pick up her brother and sister."

"Abigail Leigh?" Dawson shook his head. "Doesn't ring a bell."

"Sister is Lizette, brother is Toby."

"Admiral, I have no idea. I…" All of a sudden, he felt his throat clamp shut. What if Abigail Leigh had come from Mystic? She might have been his neighbor. Kids of all ages had lived in their neighborhood. His wife had known all their names. They had joked they would never have trouble finding a babysitter for Sarah. How in the world had this girl found him? Easy, he thought. The CDC had broadcast that submarine crews had survived the epidemic, and Abigail Leigh might have known he was in the Navy serving on a submarine. She might have assumed they had assigned him to Colony East because it was close to Mystic. That assumption would have been dead wrong, but she had made it here nevertheless. This girl might have information about his daughter. It was his lucky day.

The admiral furrowed his brow. "Abigail and Toby are being processed at the hospital. Their sister is on her way to Atlanta. We're not sure that we got to her in time. She was quite sick. I'm assigning the older siblings to Biltmore Company. You can meet them once Captain Hedrick and Doctor Droznin are through with them."

Dawson decided to double down on his luck. "Sir, when the scientists develop the antibiotic, I'd like to volunteer to help distribute the pills."

The admiral waved him off. "Go on, meet your new cadets."

Dawson stayed put. "I'll do it right this time," he blurted. "You can count on me."

"Dismissed."

Heat gushed up his neck and burned the tips of his ears. "If you don't think I'm fit..." he paused, knowing he was flirting with insubordination. "Admiral, I want to. I want to complete the mission."

The admiral stared at him for a long moment. He knew all too well how Admiral Samuels could wilt the toughest officer with his glare. This time was different. The admiral was looking through him. The old man finally lowered his eyes and shuffled some papers. "Good luck with the Leigh children, son."

Dawson, recognizing a stonewall when he met one, saluted and left, suddenly not sure that he wanted to learn the fate of his daughter.

# SEEDS OF A NEW SOCIETY

# CHAPTER ONE
## COLONY EAST

With the knot in her stomach cinching tighter, Abby sat on the examination table in the emergency room. What would the adults do when they learned she had lied? She feared they would kick her, Touk, and Toby out of Colony East.

Last night, too exhausted to swim any further, Abby had climbed the ladder at the base of a windmill halfway across the river and flagged down a patrol boat. She told her story to the skipper, a woman with harsh eyes, who seemed more concerned that Abby had made it so far without detection. "You're going back where you belong," the skipper said in a cold tone. Then Abby remembered the name of a company leader that Monty, the gypsy kid, had mentioned; the only one she had remembered, thanks to her mom's favorite TV show, Dawson's Creek. Abby blurted out that she knew Lieutenant Dawson. The skipper made an urgent call on her radio; one thing had led to another, and they had brought her here to the hospital.

A doctor, who had told Abby to call her Sandy, stepped closer, holding a cotton swab in a gloved hand. Ensign Royce, who had taken Abby's blood earlier, had referred to Sandy as "Captain Hedrick".

Abby liked Sandy, who really seemed to care about her, unlike the patrol boat skipper who had treated her like a piece of trash that had floated too far from the Brooklyn shore.

"Open wide, please. One more test," Sandy said, smiling.

Abby opened her mouth, and Sandy rubbed the cotton swab back and forth inside her cheek then sealed it inside a tube. "That's all the prodding and poking for now."

"Can I see Lizette and Toby?" Abby asked.

When Sandy lowered her eyes, a cold wave of dread washed over Abby.

"Your sister is very sick," she said in a concerned tone. "Let the doctors do their jobs first. Okay?"

Abby bit her lip at that, reminding herself how incredibly lucky they were to make it this far, and for Toucan to receive care from the adults at all.

"How do you know Mark?" Abby's heart skipped a beat. *Mark?* Sandy looked at her inquisitively for what felt like minutes but was probably only seconds. "Lieutenant Dawson?"

Abby couldn't have responded to that if she'd wanted to. Her mouth was as dry as dust and fireworks of fear were exploding her mind. She gripped the edge of the table and tried to slow her breathing, worried that she might pass out. She no longer felt the individual beats of her heart; it was a steady hum inside her chest. Finally, she shrugged and looked away. Another eternity passed.

"Well, you'll see him soon enough."

Abby breathed a sigh of relief. It was as if they had lined her up before a firing squad and all the bullets missed. She knew, though, they would reload and once more take aim.

Sandy gave her a change of clothes and sneakers and led her to the bathroom. The sneakers were brand new and fit perfectly, and Abby cracked a smile—her first in Colony East—when she stepped into the pair of clean underwear.

She looked at herself in the mirror, wishing she could stay in the bathroom until Touk was healthy again. Trouble lurked outside the door, probably starting the minute she met with Lieutenant Mark Dawson. Why couldn't she have shouted out the other name that Monty had mentioned to them, the friendly company leader? Monty said that Lieutenant Dawson was the strictest. Well, none of that mattered now.

She used the toilet and flushed. How long had it been since she saw a toilet that worked? The water swirling down the bowl hypnotized her. Then she turned the sink tap off and on several times, and held her hands in the hot water that poured out until she couldn't stand it anymore. She brought her soapy hands to her nose, closed her eyes, and inhaled. The perfumed scent carried her away to a field of flowers where they were having a picnic. Just the three of them: Jordan, Touk, and Abby.

Someone rapped on the door, ripping her from that imaginary place.

"Abigail, are you okay?" It was Ensign Royce.

"I'm fine. Be right out."

Back in the emergency room, Ensign Royce brought her a bowl of chicken soup, which she devoured, and then told her she had an appointment with a CDC scientist. He asked her to sit in a wheelchair. "I know you can walk," he apologized, "but it's a regulation. You'll find Colony East has lots of rules and regulations."

While he was pushing her down the hall, she thought how Ensign Royce reminded her of a grizzly bear, a gentle, clean-shaven grizzly bear. He was tall, wide, and had enormous hands the size of paws, but despite his chubby fingers, he had drawn her blood with the delicate touch of a butterfly.

He pushed her outside the hospital where she had her first glimpse of the colony in the daylight. Working traffic lights flashed red, and caused a line of cars and trucks to form at the intersection. A group of kids with garden tools, all wearing the very same overalls she had on, walked by on the sidewalk. Every boy had a short haircut, as did all the men in the hospital. Strangely, more than anything else so far, it made her think of the colony as a prison.

Ensign Royce chirped when he wheeled her into the building next door, "End of the road. Medical Clinic 17. We walk from here." He escorted her to an office on the second floor and left her to wait alone. She studied the plaques on the wall. Doctor Droznin had earned a PhD in Computational Biology from Princeton University. She remembered Monty had mentioned Doctor Droznin, but couldn't remember if what he had said was good or bad. The other certificates were in a language she didn't understand.

The only brightly colored objects in the room were a diminishing line of nesting dolls on the desk. The family of hand painted dolls included parents and three children. Abby picked up the mother.

Just then, a woman entered so Abby quickly returned the doll to the desk. The woman had rust-colored hair pulled severely back in a bun, and black-rimmed glasses. Abby could smell an odor of chemicals on her white lab coat.

"I'm Doctor Droznin," she said in a thick accent. She stepped beside Abby and starting with the smallest doll, packed each child into the older one, the children into the mother, and the mother into the father. Doctor Droznin turned the single doll in her hand. "Look how they fit together. Yet there's no more room. Just like at Colony East."

Even though Abby was unsure what the doctor meant, she nodded vigorously.

Doctor Droznin took a seat at her desk and peered up. "We maintain a file on every individual at Colony East. I'm going to ask you some questions."

Abby had a thousand questions of her own, but she decided she would speak only if spoken to. She thought the best way to postpone the inevitable, getting kicked out of Colony East, was to be polite and agreeable.

Doctor Droznin picked up a pen. "Let's start with Lizette."

Trying to stifle a yawn, Abby did her best to answer the first of many questions about Touk's symptoms. She realized she had only slept a few uneasy hours over the past three days, and her exhaustion was making it difficult to understand the scientist's accent. Abby either asked Doctor Droznin to repeat herself or made a guess at what she meant, over and over again.

Doctor Droznin flipped a page in her notebook. "Let's talk about your parents."

"When can I see Lizette?" Abby didn't care how she came across.

"That won't be possible. We transferred her to Atlanta this morning."

Abby lurched forward. "Atlanta, Georgia? Why didn't anyone tell me?"

"We're entering her into a drug trial," Droznin replied in a matter-of-fact tone.

A shiver passed through Abby. "Will she be okay?"

Doctor Droznin snapped her pen on the table as if the question agitated her. After a long pause, she said, "You and your siblings are quite important to us. All of you are being monitored closely."

Taking that as good news, Abby sat back, knowing there was nothing she could do or say that would change anything for Touk.

Prompted by the doctor, Abby continued answering questions. Doctor Droznin wanted to know everything about her parents and grandparents. Professions, educational degrees, medical histories, then the causes of their deaths, "My mom and dad died the night of the purple moon," Abby said tiredly.

Doctor Droznin scribbled away without looking up. "Ages?"

Abby suddenly worried what Toby would say, if, for some reason, Doctor Droznin asked him the same detailed questions. She told herself everything would be fine. If anyone could pull off the ruse that he was her twin brother, it was Toby. "I can't remember," Abby said as a precaution.

Doctor Droznin made a notation, seeming unconcerned by the response.

By the time the topic shifted to her, Abby could barely keep her eyes open. She mumbled where and when she was born, where she had lived, grades in school, and then described her childhood illnesses. During a pause in the questioning, Abby drifted to sleep and was promptly jolted awake with the doctor's next question.

An hour later, Doctor Droznin closed her notebook. "How do you know Lieutenant Dawson?"

"I don't remember." Abby's heart pounded at such a stupid response.

"I understand. You're probably still in shock."

She blinked in disbelief as the doctor raised a walkie-talkie to her lips. "I'm finished with one—one—oh—two." Abby had noticed the number stitched on her sleeve: 1102. If Doctor Droznin said she was in shock, believing that was the reason she had no recollection of Lieutenant Dawson, then Abby would remain in a state of shock.

Ensign Royce wheeled her back to the hospital, where she stood in the lobby and followed him down a hallway to another room. "End of the road, again." He rapped on the door and pushed it open.

A man, sitting in a chair next to the bed, jumped to his feet and stared at her. "Come in," he said. Something about his nose caught her attention. It was slightly crooked beneath his eyes. He had dark wavy hair and stood ramrod straight. Feeling her knees wobble, she stared back, knowing this must be Lieutenant Dawson. "Did you grow up in Mystic, Connecticut?" he asked.

She swallowed hard and shook her head.

He stepped closer. "Have you ever been to Mystic?"

"No," she barely whispered.

Her responses seemed to seriously disappointment him. She suddenly wondered if this might be someone other than Lieutenant Dawson.

He took another step toward her, and she could definitely tell now that his nose had once been broken. "Do you know anything about Mystic?"

Abby nodded, relieved that she finally had something to say other than no, no, no. "There's a radio station there called The Port. DJ Silver plays songs and dedicates them to the survivors." Seeing his eyes brighten, she quickly added. "I've only seen the antennae for the station as we drove by it on Route 95."

He blinked several times. "I'm Lieutenant Dawson. How do you know me?"

Abby took a deep breath. The moment had arrived, the biggest decision of her life. It was time, she thought, to be partially truthful. Besides, they had already sent Touk to Atlanta. "I live on Castine Island. It's off Portland, Maine. Three months ago, news gypsies visited us. One of them had lived at Colony East, and he told us about you."

He cocked his head, confused. "News gypsies?"

"They trade news for supplies."

"Why did you say you knew me?"

She thought it was strange the lieutenant showed no interest in who had mentioned his name. "My sister had the Pig. AHA-B. My brother, Toby, and I knew she had to see a doctor, so we brought her here. I tried to swim—"

"And Ensign Mathews was going to take you back to Brooklyn, so you mentioned my name."

"I'm sorry I lied," she whispered to her brand new sneakers.

The lieutenant curled his lip into a small smile, but Abby saw the same sadness in his eyes that she saw in so many survivors.

"I'm glad you told me the truth," he said. "I value honesty above all else. How many children live on Castine Island?"

Abby's muscles turned to mush and she almost crumpled to the floor from relief. It seemed like she had just passed a big hurdle. They weren't going to kick her and Toby out of Colony East. At least not today.

"After the night of the purple moon," she explained, "there were only seventeen survivors on the island. More kids moved to the island because it's safer than the mainland. They were the lucky ones who got the pills." He shuddered and his face turned white. Wishing she hadn't mentioned the pills, she quickly added, "Almost two hundred kids live there now."

"What ages are the youngest?"

Abby paused to think. "Clive is two and a half. Chloe is a month older."

The lieutenant's brow furrowed. "So they were babies at the time of the epidemic?"

She nodded. "Yeah, we searched the homes where we knew babies lived."

He nodded to himself and smiled again. The change was dramatic. The way his face lit up and his eyes crinkled at the corners conveyed an overall expression of hope. Then he surprised her with a salute. "Welcome to Biltmore Company, Cadet Leigh. I'm your company leader."

Abby paused, unsure of what to do. Finally, seeing no harm, she brought her hand to her brow in her first salute, ever.

# CHAPTER TWO
## MYSTIC

Beads of sweat dribbled down Jordan's face and chest as he positioned the foam pads of the crutches under his arms. Wenlan had told him he needed to walk for two hours a day to promote the healing of his wound. "Doctor's orders!" The memory of her alluring eyes and finger wagging in his face was fresh in his mind.

He planted the rubber tips on the floor ahead of him and swung forward. When he touched down on the foot of his good leg, he jarred his other leg, sending flames of pain out from his thigh.

He glanced at the clock. In one hour, fifty-nine minutes, and forty-five seconds, he could return to his bed where the pain was tolerable if he remained perfectly still.

Grimacing, Jordan hobbled from his room to the hall, and then down the hall and into the waiting room to check on the other patients. There was a boy holding a bloody rag against his head, and a girl, who on the removal of her boot revealed a swollen ankle. Either one, or both of them, he realized could be part of the pirate crew that turned Lucky Me into an inferno and killed his friends. The third patient in the room, a chubby boy with flushed cheeks, looked like he had the Pig.

None of the patients paid any attention to him, and none were in any condition to hold the door open for him. Jordan fought the urge to scream out in agony as he wedged the door and wiggled his way through.

He rested on the front porch as the breeze cooled his face, which was wet with perspiration from exertion and anxiety. A pick-up truck sat idling in front of the clinic, the driver listening to *Sympathy for the Devil* by the Rolling Stones.

Jordan pressed onward and learned how difficult it was to navigate down three steps with crutches. He took a quick breather on the front walk, and then headed for the street.

The song ended, and Jordan nearly toppled over when he heard a familiar voice. "Dudes and dudettes, do you dig the Stones? Let's shout it out. Do you positively, absolutely, go freaking nuts over the Rolling Stones? I sure hope so." It was DJ Silver. "We're going to keep it rolling. Ashley, this is for you, 'Paint it Black'."

Homesickness flooded through Jordan as he plodded onward.

That evening, as he was resting in bed, he lied to Wenlan, telling her he had walked for two hours when he had only walked half that, secretly resting just a block away from the clinic, out of her sight. He didn't feel the least bit guilty.

"I'm really proud of you," she said. "You are my favorite patient. Keep it up, and you'll be walking in no time."

Suddenly, feeling guilty, he changed the topic. "You'll never believe what I heard. The Port. We used to listen to The Port every night on Castine Island. We could never get the station during the day because the signal was too weak."

Wenlan stepped to the window. "Come here."

The distance to the window from the bed was about ten feet, but with his leg feeling relatively at peace, he wanted to stay put. "Describe what you want me to see."

"Don't be a baby."

"I'll look tomorrow."

"You can see the antenna of The Port."

Jordan hopped on his good leg like a frog. The antenna rose like a needle spire. "That's The Port?" he exclaimed, disregarding the tidal waves of pain pounding him into oblivion.

She nodded. "The home of DJ Silver. The most egotistical boy I've ever met."

Jordan stared out the window, knowing how he could tell Abby he was alive and well: DJ Silver would tell her for him.

He gave Wenlan a hug, which surprised her. She wrapped her arms around him and held him for a few long seconds, which surprised him even more.

# CHAPTER THREE
## COLONY EAST

Unpacking the clothing and toiletries she had received before leaving the hospital, Abby paused and pinched herself to prove she wasn't dreaming. Lieutenant Dawson had assigned her a room on the third floor in the Biltmore. She wasn't dreaming, but it didn't seem real, either.

She placed three pairs of gray overalls in the dresser drawer, thinking of herself as "lucky person 1102", the number stitched on her sleeve.

In the bathroom, she wet her toothbrush and squeezed out a dab of green gel onto the bristles. She had brushed her teeth twice already this morning, and soaring in a cloud of peppermint, she let the taste linger on her tongue and gums until the coolness subsided. The toothpaste tasted good enough to eat.

Abby tapped the bathroom light switch on and off several times. She imagined her thrill at being able to produce instant illumination was equal to that of Thomas Edison, the inventor of the light bulb.

In the main room, she sat back on the luxurious king-size bed and bounced a few times before reaching for the radio. She pulled her hand back, though, still feeling like a visitor in a stranger's house.

She opened the mini-fridge and rubbed her finger on the surface of an ice cube. She wondered if she would ever tire of experiencing the small conveniences of the life that she had once taken for granted.

She admired her wristwatch with the luminous hands and dial. "Everything runs on time at Colony East," Ensign Royce had told her. She wished that time would stop at Colony East, and in Atlanta, too, placing her and Toucan in a state of suspended animation, and that the germs ravaging her sister's body would simply freeze in their tracks.

Abby backed out of her fantasy and walked to the window. Peering out, she saw an alleyway three stories below. The building next door blocked much of the view, but she could see a wedge of Lexington Avenue that ran in front of the hotel. Some cars and trucks drove by, while a woman in a white coat pedaled a bicycle.

"Cadet Leigh."

Abby turned and teared up. Toby and another boy stood next to Lieutenant Dawson. It was her first time seeing Toby since she'd left him with Touk at 19 Livingston Place. Both Toby and the other boy wore the same grey overalls she did.

"I'd like to introduce Cadet Billings," the lieutenant said. "His living quarters are next to your brother's on the fourth floor. Mr. Billings volunteered to give you and Toby a tour of Colony East. For future reference, please address me as Lieutenant, Lieutenant Dawson, or sir. I'll refer to you as Miss Leigh and Mister Leigh, or simply, cadet."

Toby rolled his eyes.

"Yes, Lieutenant," Abby replied, shooting her 'brother' a hard stare-a look that told him not to blow it.

"Billings will brief you on the other rules and regulations," the lieutenant said. "We run a tight ship at Biltmore Company. Billings, be sure to show them Central Park Farm."

Cadet Billings beamed. "Aye-aye,sir."

"And pay attention to them, too," the lieutenant added. "We can all learn from the Leighs. They had their own community on Castine Island."

Toby's head snapped her way. All Abby could do was shrug back. Apparently, what she'd told the lieutenant impressed him.

Lieutenant Dawson excused himself from the trio.

Cadet Billings closed the door and dropped his voice to a whisper. "Call me Jonzy. Rule number one, don't trust anyone."

Abby rocked back on her heels. She figured the expression of shock on Toby's face likely mirrored hers.

"Can I trust you two?" Jonzy asked with a shrug, not looking for an answer. "I have to take that chance. Time is running out, and I need your help."

Abby's chest tightened and it was hard to breathe. "Please, just show us around," she implored. After it took a miracle for them to make it here, why jeopardize their delicate situation?

Toby held up his hand. "Abby, let's hear him out."

Jonzy walked to the window and shut the drapes. "Two months ago, as a test, I told several friends that I was building a radio. We're not supposed to listen to any unauthorized communications, like The Port. Do you know about the teen station?"

Toby brightened. "We drove by it, and we listened to it every night back home."

His enthusiasm was troubling. For all Abby knew, this was an elaborate set up to test their loyalty, and Toby was falling for the trap. The smartest thing was to leave. Leave now.

"I told my friends where I hid the parts," Jonzy continued. "The next day the lieutenant searched my room and knew right where to go. Don't trust anyone, okay?"

Abby took a step toward the door, not wanting to hear any more. "Toby, let's go!"

He wasn't ready to go anywhere. "Why do you need our help?" he asked Jonzy.

"Every night, CDC headquarters in Atlanta communicates with the scientists at Colony East and Colony West."

Toby frowned. "Colony West?"

"It's in Los Angeles. Atlanta Colony is the biggest. Colony East is next, then Colony West. I listen to their conversations on the radio."

"How?" Abby challenged, her curiosity getting the better of her. "You said Lieutenant Dawson took your radio parts."

Jonzy grinned. "Those were for a cheap radio. I have a police radio which scans a wide range of frequencies."

Abby's level of anxiety spiked when Toby took a seat on the bed. "Where did you get it?" he asked.

Jonzy sat in a chair. "A police cruiser in the Yellow Zone. It's part of the colony where you need an adult escort. I snuck out and went there at night."

With her hand hovering near the doorknob, Abby wondered if she should just walk out and hope Toby followed.

"What would have happened to you if you had gotten caught?" Toby asked.

"Doctor Perkins would have kicked me out. He's the chief scientist."

Abby's eyes met Toby's. Monty had told them that Doctor Perkins had kicked him out of the colony for just delivering a choice phrase at the council meeting. "Do you want to get us kicked out?"

Toby crinkled his eyes, thinking, and then he ignored her question. "When do you listen?" he asked Jonzy.

"I keep the police radio in the restaurant on the fortieth floor. The reception is better up there. It's lights out at eight o'clock. I go up after everyone is sleeping."

Abby shook her head, thinking Jonzy was the type of kid who made up fantastic stories to sound important. Even though he was probably harmless, she still wanted nothing to do with him.

"If a topic is really important," Jonzy said, "Doctor Perkins participates in the discussion. He's been on the radio a lot lately."

Good, she told herself. The taller his tales, the sooner Toby would wake up and they could start their tour.

Jonzy put his finger to his lips, opened the door, stuck his head out, and then closed it again. "You never know who might be listening. The scientists know a new epidemic is coming"

Speaking in a low voice, he told them how the bacteria that caused the first epidemic mutated, mostly close to the equator, and how the scientists thought a hurricane would spread the deadly strain across the country. Despite her burning desire to run from this boy as fast as she could, Abby moved closer to hear him. His story troubled her for two reasons. It seemed too crazy to make up, and many parts rang true from her observations of Toucan's illness.

Toby started pacing. "Abby, did the scientists ever say anything like that on the CDC station? Have they given any warnings?"

"Toucan caught the Pig," she said, "but Castine Island is two thousand miles from the equator."

"Who's Toucan?" Jonzy asked.

"Her sister," Toby said, and then quickly corrected himself. "Our sister."

Jonzy lit up. "Lizette."

Abby tensed, but quickly relaxed, thinking Lieutenant Dawson must have mentioned her to Jonzy.

"She's in drug trial C," he added.

Abby swallowed hard. "What does that mean?"

Jonzy shrugged. "Another kid they sent to Atlanta, Elsie, is in drug trial B."

"Huh," Toby blurted. "They sent Touk to Atlanta?"

Abby nodded. "Doctor Droznin told me."

"Who's that?"

"She asked me questions about our family."

Toby winked at her. "Doctor Levine completed my profile, so it's all good." Then he turned back to Jonzy. "What else have you heard?"

"They want to develop an antibiotic that works and ship it here before the first hurricane hits, but they haven't said anything about passing out pills outside the colony."

"I'm sure they're going to help everyone," Abby said confidently and opened the door. "I'm not going to sneak around and get in trouble. Toby, are you coming?"

"You and Toby are part of a control group." Jonzy said.

Abby stepped into the hall and headed for the fire exit door. She was curious to know what a control group was, but not curious enough to stop. Not hearing footsteps behind her, she nervously turned. The hall was empty. Equally dumbfounded and mad, she sighed in frustration and set out in search of Central Park Farm.

# CHAPTER FOUR
# MYSTIC

With The Port's radio antenna less than five hundred yards away, Jordan stumbled to the side of the road and collapsed in the shade, where he leaned against a stone wall. Painful rashes had blossomed in his armpits from the uphill and downhill slogs on the crutches. Exhausted, he let his arms flop to his sides, sighing in relief as air circulated up into his short sleeves.

Wenlan's "one mile" had turned out to be more like four miles. He'd left the clinic at dawn and now the sun was overhead. Still, he was pleased with his progress, considering that two weeks earlier the pirates had left him for dead.

Jordan watched with envy as an ant crawled up his wrist with ease. It swiftly scaled the vertical cliff of his skin, navigating through a forest of hair follicles, and reached a peak fifty times its height.

He fixed his gaze on the tower. The final leg of any journey, it seemed, was always the hardest. The road's grade to the station, while not that steep, was all uphill, making him wince at the thought of the pain that was to come.

One thought spurred him to stop envying the ant and sit up. Abby would get the surprise of her life when she heard DJ Silver announce over the radio that her brother was doing well and would be home soon. If she didn't hear it personally, someone on the island would.

Hearing a car, Jordan struggled to his feet. Scanning the stretch he had just inched up, he saw a Jeep round the bend. The underarm pads of his crutches scorched his armpits like sizzling branding irons as he hobbled to the shoulder of the road.

He stuck out a crutch, hoping to flag the vehicle.

The driver pulled alongside him and stopped. The passenger window powered down. A boy with a Mohawk, around twelve, was behind the wheel.

"Where are you going?" the boy asked.

Jordan's stomach dropped. That voice. He was certain it belonged to the pirate, the boy behind the mask who, along with his fellow murderers, had nearly killed him and sank *Lucky Me*.

He refused the ride with a shake of his head and pressed onward, a surge of adrenaline blunting his pain.

Inching forward, the Jeep kept pace. "I'll give you a ride. Get in."

All of a sudden, Jordan wasn't sure the boy was the pirate. Many boys that age had high-pitched voices that cracked.

"C'mon," the boy urged. "I don't have all day."

Not wanting to chance it, he shook his head again and continued.

"Suit yourself." The back tires kicked up gravel as the boy sped off.

An hour later, Jordan stood in the parking lot of what he realized might be the only kid-operated radio station in the world. A few cars were in the lot, but with every tire flat, he assumed they had been here since the night of the purple moon.

The building was low and squat, with tongues of ivy licking the brick walls. A bronze plaque beside the glass door said: 'The Port – FM 101'. The radio antenna—the target he had aimed for over the past six hours—was bolted to the bricks.

A generator chugged away nearby with a fat electric cable running into the building from it. He counted ten large metal drums. Diesel for the generator, courtesy of the fuel king, William, Jordan presumed.

Above the generator's hum, he heard a truck in the distance. It drove by about two hundred yards to his left. He figured that was Route 95, which ran all the way to Maine to the north and to Florida to the south. When he finally felt strong enough, he could try to hitch a ride to Portland if he couldn't find a sailboat or a spot on a gypsy boat sailing north.

With some difficulty, he managed to open the door and step inside to what appeared to be part reception area, part elephant cage. Peanut shells littered the carpet. Other signs that someone camped out here included a rumpled sleeping bag on the couch and a few empty water bottles on a coffee table. A framed certificate announced that The Port was a member-in-good-standing of the Rotary Club, Mystic, Connecticut. Jordan smiled to himself, thinking he would have had to turn around and go back to the clinic if The Port were a member-in-bad-standing.

Jordan recognized the music blasting out of a speaker mounted on the wall as the voice and guitar licks of Jimi Hendrix.

Below the speaker, the station's control room was visible through a rectangular glass window. Inside, a boy kicked back in a chair, his feet propped on the console. He wore sunglasses, a thick braid of gold chains around his neck, and a New York Yankee baseball cap.

Chuckling that he would gladly set aside his loyalty to the Boston Red Sox in return for Abby hearing that he wasn't dead, Jordan rapped on the glass and entered through a door on the right. Music played from a speaker here, too. "Are you DJ Silver?"

The boy swiveled around in the chair just as the song ended. He moved close to the microphone.

"Hey, survivors, you musta loved that. Jimi Hendrix, 'All Along the Watch Tower.' First played in twenty-five BC."

Jordan was now certain it was DJ Silver. He had never heard anyone else use the term BC—Before Comet.

"Next up, we got something slow and mellow." The DJ's eyes glanced to a notebook on the desk. "This is from Alison going out to Tim. I want all you survivors to keep it slow and keep it locked here." He punched a button and Beyonce came over the speaker.

Jordan grinned. DJ Silver's only competition was the robotic voice of the CDC station telling survivors how to avoid toenail fungus, and other gross and boring tidbits of information. Maybe the adults at Colony East kept it locked on FM 98.5, but he couldn't imagine anyone else listening to the CDC station voluntarily.

DJ Silver lowered his sunglasses. "And who are you?"

"Jordan. I'm from Rhode Island."

He had concocted a whole story to explain his wound, thinking it best not to mention that a pirate shot him.

"With that accent? Yeah, right. What can I do for you, Jordan-who's-not-from-Rhode-Island?"

"I had a bad bike accident."

DJ Silver looked like he believed that about as much as Jordan's earlier comment. "Tipped over your tricycle?"

Jordan plowed onward, "My sister doesn't know what happened and I know she's worried. Can you make an announcement that I'm okay?"

DJ Silver tapped his sunglasses back in place and slowly shook his head. "I guess you're not from around here. We don't do news on The Port."

"Why?"

DJ Silver bobbed his head. "Listen, dude, if I started giving news, two things would happen. One, the adults would shut me down. Two, I would go ape-crazy because they'd shut me down. DJ Silvy is like a geyser of creative vibes. I got to spread the love or I'll explode. I hope you're cool with that."

"Why would the adults shut you down?"

The DJ shrugged. "Beats me. That's the way it rolls around here. We only play music. You feel me?"

The crunching defeat Jordan felt rattled him harder than the rocket of hope that had thrilled him when he first learned The Port was close by. He had to make DJ Silver understand. He started by making a pact with himself. He would stay here until one of two things happened: DJ Silver tossed him out, or the DJ agreed to announce that he was alive. If he tossed him, Jordan would just pick himself up and hobble back inside.

Then he had an idea that might avoid a lot of wasted time and intense pain. "Could you dedicate a song for me? 'Here Comes the Sun by the Beatles.' Say it's to Abby and Toucan from Jordan."

DJ Silver gave him a thumbs-up. "Now you're talking cheesy whiz. You're too smart to be from Rhode Island." He slid a notebook toward him. "Write it down, brother."

Jordan flipped through page after page of dedications, and then wrote what he wanted DJ Silver to say. "The best time is tonight after sundown." He returned the notebook.

DJ Silver threw his head back and laughed. "Tonight? Try two months from now." He fanned the pages. "First come, first serve."

Jordan looked around for a place to sit. He considered pleading but knew that DJ Silver would tune him out. Jordan thought the only thing DJ Silver didn't tune out was DJ Silver. That's it, he thought. He would make an appeal to his ego.

Bursting with excitement over his own cleverness and certainty that his plan would work, Jordan waited as the DJ dedicated and cued up another song.

"I really come from Castine Island. It's in Maine, off the coast of Portland. About six hundred kids live there." Jordan tripled the number of kids on the island because DJ Silver's ego was three times bigger.

The DJ yawned.

"We can pick up The Port, but only after sunset. Every night, kids go to Toby's house to listen to you. Toby's the only one who has batteries."

Intrigued, Monty sat forward, fiddling with his silver chains. "Six hundred fans live there?"

Jordan gave him a big nod. "Standing room only at Toby's. Everyone loves you, dude."

His eyes widened. "Standing room only?"

"If you don't mind, I'd like to get your autograph."

"Dude, I don't mind at all." He scribbled his name and handed the paper to Jordan. "Jordan-from-Castine-Island-Maine, I got you covered. Abby and Toucan—what is that, some type of bird—will get tired of hearing 'Here Comes the Sun.' DJ Silver takes care of his fans."

Jordan hobbled toward the station room door and stopped before leaving. About to speak, he bit his tongue, thinking that any insult he hurled at the New York Yankees might only confuse the DJ. "You are the man! Rock on!"

# CHAPTER FIVE
# COLONY EAST

Lieutenant Dawson laced up his jogging sneakers and peered out the window of the company leader's office.

At 15:30, Admiral Samuels exited Trump Tower and turned north on 5th Avenue. Every day, regardless of the weather conditions, the admiral took an afternoon stroll, his course as predictable as the time he began his walk. Taking a brief detour through the outer gardens of Central Park Farm, he went east on 62nd Street, south on 3rd Avenue, west on 53rd, then back on 5th Ave. for the home stretch.

Dawson gave the admiral a ten-minute head start. Then he jogged south on 5th and east on 53rd. Slowing to a walk, he intercepted him halfway down the block. "Permission to join you?"

"Fall in, Lieutenant."

"Quite a heat wave we're having, sir."

The admiral grumbled, "What's on your mind, Dawson? Spit it out."

"Sir, at the Academy, I earned a top grade in logistics, and the summer after my Plebe year, I was assigned to the USS Enterprise, where I supported the munitions supply officer. I have a good mind for supply distribution."

The admiral nodded with interest. "You have a good mind for distributing supplies."

For an instant, Dawson was annoyed that Admiral Samuels was paraphrasing him, the same approach he used for the cadets of Biltmore Company. Then he realized he had learned the trick from the admiral.

"Yes, sir," he said. "I can do it all, soup to nuts. I can come up with a plan, and I can execute the plan."

The admiral grinned and shook his head. "Mark, if this is your roundabout way of asking me to reassign you from serving as a company leader, forget it."

"No, sir. I love being a company leader."

He cuffed Dawson on the shoulder. "Good, keep it that way. That's an order."

The admiral saluted an ensign who rode by on a bicycle. "You know why I walk down 3rd Ave." Even though the admiral paused, Dawson knew he didn't want an answer. "It's one of the least traveled streets in the colony, so I don't have to salute every five seconds. There's a lot to be said for walking alone. It helps clear the mind."

Dawson felt the cold bore of the admiral's stare, like staring down the barrel of a gun held by a farmer who wanted you off his property, pronto. He had to speak fast before the admiral shooed him away, so he could finish his walk in peace.

"Sir, I'd like to volunteer to distribute the antibiotics. The tropics are heating up. Athena fizzled, but they're worried about Tropical Storm Burt. Though the storm's moving erratically, they say there's a fifty percent chance that Burt will become a hurricane." He sucked in a lungful of hot, dry air. "I'm sure the CDC is working hard to finalize the antibiotic, but the time to start planning the distribution of the pills is right now."

"Denied," the admiral barked, plowing forward like a cutter through choppy seas.

Keeping pace, Dawson snapped angrily, before he could rethink it. "Is it because of what I did in Virginia?" He had never before dared to use such an angry, demanding tone to a superior officer.

The admiral, who was just as certainly unaccustomed to being addressed in such a tone, stopped.

"Sorry, sir," Dawson said. "I feel strongly about this."

Admiral Samuels had a look that Dawson had never seen before—a look that all admirals learned to keep under wraps—indecisiveness.

"Yes, Lieutenant. It's because of what happened in Virginia. I don't want you to bring this matter up again. Understood? And next time you jog, find a different route." Giving Dawson no chance to respond, the admiral continued south on 3rd Avenue.

Dawson felt his shoulders melt forward, and it had nothing to do with the heat of the day.

# CHAPTER SIX
## MYSTIC

Hypnotized by the leaves twisting outside his window, Jordan was lost in thought. Just then, he saw Wenlan, casting a long shadow from the setting sun, walking across the clinic's backyard and sitting on the stone wall. He held his breath, hoping that CeeCee would not join her, and headed outside.

CeeCee liked to make fun of him for some unknown reason. It seemed that every time he was around the sisters, CeeCee would say something in Chinese and giggle. Wenlan would then respond angrily, also in Chinese. Jordan had no idea what they were saying, but he picked up on their feelings. Laughter and anger were universal.

Wenlan was still alone, so he approached her, trying to hide his limp. The last thing he wanted was for her to order him to exercise more.

He had a question he wanted to ask her, one that he had postponed asking several times, afraid he knew what she would say. Jordan realized he might chicken out again. Maybe it was best if he started with a joke?

Keeping a straight face, he sat on a flat rock beside her. "Slacking off?" Patients had streamed into the clinic non-stop since the morning; this was probably Wenlan's first break of the day. When her eyes widened in shock, he forced a grin.

Sensing his sarcasm, she grinned, too, and shook her head. "Why do accidents happen in bunches? Two broken ankles, one burn from a cooking stove, a concussion, and oh, the craziest of the day, a goat bit Skinny Urban."

"Doctor Wenlan and Doctor CeeCee to the rescue," Jordan beamed.

A corner of her lip curled. "Stay away from goats. I refuse to treat any more patients bitten by their pets."

The question burned at the tip of his tongue. Jordan shielded his eyes from the sun, still not ready for the disappointment he was sure her response would cause. He said instead, "Does it ever bother you that you're only supposed to treat members of William's gang? You know, other kids get hurt and sick and could use your help too."

Wenlan took a deep breath. "My mother worked in a hospital with two hundred other doctors. There were two bigger hospitals nearby with five hundred more doctors. Now there's just CeeCee and me. It used to bother me, but we can't help everyone. You see what it's like here."

"I guess," he said, thinking about Colony East. Maybe Abby had been right. How could a few thousand adults look after millions of survivors? He should cut the adults some slack.

Jordan's heart beat faster. He had to ask Wenlan now. He had spent too much time fantasizing that she and CeeCee would return with him to Castine Island. No matter what she replied, he needed to hear the hard truth and move on.

"My sister is the first medical responder on the island," he began.

"You mentioned that. Abby turned the barber shop into a clinic."

Jordan cleared his throat. "Would you and CeeCee want to go back with me? Abby would love to get more help." He heard a tone of defeat in his voice.

Wenlan paused a long moment, which he took as a good sign. The invitation touched her. She also seemed sad, and that, Jordan thought, was a bad sign.

"I can't leave Mystic," she said finally. "I'm needed here, and I love what I do." She gave a little smirk. "Trust me, you don't want to spend three days in a little boat with me and CeeCee."

Jordan turned away, blinking back his tears. "Hey," he said, wanting to change the subject, "why is your sister always laughing at me?"

Wenlan chuckled. "She's laughing at me."

Jordan leaned back. "You?"

"Do you remember what it was like to be twelve? CeeCee makes fun of me because I like you. She says I get all nervous around you." Jordan's jaw dropped. Then, a little more softly she said, "I wish you wanted to stay in Mystic."

Wenlan had jolted him twice in as many seconds, and he froze as his heart and mind engaged in a debate.

She hopped off the rock and stood before him. The sun crowned bright orange around her silky black hair and made her eyes even darker. He felt the heat rising in the shadow she cast on him. He didn't move and hardly took a breath, because maybe this was a dream, and he didn't want to awaken, but mostly because he was about to give her an answer. The heart spoke best in perfect stillness.

"I think I do," he whispered. "Yes, I want to live in Mystic, but I have to go back to check on my sisters."

Wenlan eclipsed the sun as she moved closer to kiss him. He closed his eyes, shutting out all the light, and kissed her back. They were now together on their own private island.

When Jordan opened his eyes, he got his third jolt in as many minutes. CeeCee was standing outside the clinic covering her mouth with her hands.

# CHAPTER SEVEN
# COLONY EAST

The lieutenant's voice boomed from the speaker in the ceiling. "Rise and shine, cadets. You are seeds of the new society, Generation M. You have an exciting day ahead of you… "

Abby shot up in bed, barely paying attention to the droning announcement. The highlight of the day was that Sheraton Company would perform the musical, *Brigadoon*, at Carnegie Hall.

After the national anthem, she turned on the radio and listened to the CDC station while making her bed.

"Do you know that UV rays can penetrate clouds? The CDC offers the following tips to protect yourself from the harmful rays of the sun… "

Abby snapped it off, finding it incredible that the CDC had not once mentioned AHA-B over the past twenty days, at least during the times she had listened which was in the morning right after reveille and again after lights out, lying in bed with the volume low. Just one official word about the illness was all Abby wanted to hear. Then she could talk some sense into Toby. She could tell him the CDC was letting kids know about the new epidemic, just as they had done after the night of the purple moon.

She worried about Toby not only for his sake, but for her's and Touk's as well. The boy she had a crush on was acting recklessly. If he got caught, who knew what would happen?

Toby had taken more foolish chances than she could keep track of, all under the influence of Jonzy Billings, a boy she wished would just go away. Toby always had a gleam in his eye when he described his escapades. She thought he enjoyed the thrill of sneaking around the adults most of all. Abby abhorred violence, but she had to resist punching Toby in the nose on more than one occasion for his antics. He and Jonzy had made a nighttime trip to the Yellow Zone and spent countless hours eavesdropping on radio transmissions from the top floor of the Biltmore. Toby had even bragged that he and Jonzy liked to kick back and listen to The Port at night in the hotel's former restaurant.

Finished making her bed, she stepped into the flow of cadets streaming by her door and followed them down the stairway to the hotel lobby, where boys and girls poured in from every floor. As she waited in the logjam, her eyes darted to the sign above the suggestion box: All Ideas Are Good Ideas!

She had a good idea. Abandon her peaceful nature and pop Toby a good one in the eye. Maybe then he'd stop playing with fire.

The members of Biltmore Company formed rows in the middle of Lexington Avenue. After Abby took her spot, she saw Toby step outside with his sidekick, Jonzy. Toby craned his neck, looking for her. A chill went down her spine when she saw his troubled expression. Usually he greeted her with a little wave and silly smile, unable to contain himself, eager to tell her about his latest adventure with Jonzy. Something serious was on his mind this morning.

The lieutenant jogged out and everyone snapped to attention. He glanced at his watch, and then scanned the crowd. Abby felt a strange tension crackling among the cadets.

"At ease," he barked.

After a moment's pause, he thrust a triumphant fist skyward. "A new record! Fifteen minutes, twelve seconds."

Cheers erupted around her. With her sister a thousand miles away, Jordan's whereabouts unknown, and Toby bursting at the seams with some horrible news, Abby couldn't summon any excitement over breaking some stupid record to assemble in front of the Biltmore. She clapped only to act like a part of the crowd.

"Company, DIS...MISSED."

Toby came over to her and together they walked toward Grand Central Station. Because of their schedules, it was the only time of the day they could speak to each other privately. To the casual observer, Abby thought they would have looked like a couple of goofball siblings, whispering and smiling to each other, but their feigned behavior masked contentious arguments.

"Tropical Storm Caity blew out to sea," he told her, "but Tropical Storm David just formed. The scientists think it will turn into a hurricane. It might hit us."

Abby sighed in relief, hoping that was the worst news he had. Tropical Storm David would probably disappear just like the other tropical storms. She imagined a week from now, two weeks from now, Toby would be bringing up future tropical storms Evelyn, Frank, Gabby... whatever they named them... with the same level of fear. And if one did turn into a hurricane and bring the germs here, the scientists would be ready for it. Deep in her heart, she knew the adults cared about everyone.

Toby narrowed his eyes. "Abby, did you hear what I said?"

She gave him a dismissive shrug. "I'm not deaf."

"Have you listened to the CDC station?"

She looked away. "Maybe."

"It's the same old BS."

"Toby, after the night of the purple moon, they didn't announce the distribution schedule until two weeks before they sent the pills to the Phase I cities."

"They told us they were working to develop pills," he stammered.

Abby geared herself up for this argument, one they had often. She was able to predict everything Toby would say and she could spit back her responses without having to think.

"Abby, I have news about Touk."

Struggling to breathe, Abby felt her knees wobble. When she stopped, a girl bumped into her from behind. The fifteen-year-old cadet whispered something to her friends and they laughed at Abby as they passed by.

"I have news about us too," Toby added. They continued walking. "You know how we're part of a control group? Last night, Doctor Droznin talked with a scientist from Atlanta on what they were going to do with the control groups. If Touk survives, they want to know if it was because of her natural immunity or the antibiotic. They'll infect us with AHA-B to find out."

"What?" she exclaimed.

"If Touk lives, they'll give us the Pig to see if we have natural immunity to it. If Touk dies, they'll give us the antibiotic. Abby, we're a couple of lab rats."

It took a moment for his words to sink in. Abby tried to imagine her reaction to receiving an antibiotic that would cure her. It would mean that Toucan was dead. It would be easier for her to accept them infecting her with AHA-B on purpose, for that would mean Touk was alive and well, but this involved Toby; he too, would be infected, in his words, like a lab rat.

"They wouldn't do that!"

"Trust me, they would. They're adults."

"We should go to Lieutenant Dawson."

"Are you kidding me? He's a company leader. He knows what they're going to do."

"Maybe…"

He mocked, "Maybe this is all a big dream. You're going to wake up and your mommy will be cooking breakfast for you, and your daddy will want to do something fun with you. Well, you better wake up for real. Tonight, Jonzy and I are exploring the subway tunnels."

Abby's heart stopped. Still reeling from the news about Toucan, she felt the meanness of his words burning like acid. Just because his father had beat him and his mother had abandoned him, he didn't have the right to take it out on her. Then he had casually announced he was going into the tunnels.

"The tunnels are a good way to move around the colony," Toby added. "We have to find a way to escape."

"Escape? What for?"

"We need to tell everyone what the adults are doing."

She raised her voice, "What if they catch you?" She lowered it when several cadets looked their way. "Toby, you are not going into the subway tunnels."

"We have to try something." He stared in space briefly. "I'm just not sure what."

"Listen to me," she whispered frantically. "Stay away from Jonzy."

"This isn't the time for your bossy routine."

Rage exploded inside her chest, triggering a tsunami of anger that swept through her brain. Abby somehow resisted her first impulse to shout at the top of her lungs. Gritting her teeth and clenching her jaw, she hissed, "Toby, I hate you."

Hurt painted his face and his bottom lip started trembling. He looked at the ground and walked away from her, blending into the line of kids about to slingshot through the revolving doors at Grand Central Station.

Every cell in her body urged her to race after him, apologize, tell him she had spoken out of fear; she didn't hate him. Abby swallowed hard. She loved Toby. She had to hold herself back so he would understand how serious she was. He needed time alone to think about his behavior. Abby doubled over as tears dribbled off her face, dropping like pearls and splashing on the pavement below. She wanted to go to him so badly.

# CHAPTER EIGHT
## MYSTIC

Jordan hauled in the mainsheet and *Mary Queen of Scots* heeled on her side. It had been a month since he'd been shot, and while his thigh was still sore, the wound had healed well enough for him to make the trip to Castine Island. He felt he had good mobility in the sailboat. Pulling the rope more, he tipped the boat even higher, noticing a trickle of water bleeding between the hull and railing. Not a big deal.

He was sailing the boat hard to make sure she would make it all the way. Better to fix a problem in Mystic Harbor than out at sea.

He had found the twelve-foot Day Sailor—*Mary Queen of Scots* painted on the stern—on her side in a sandy cove. The boat, along with many other sailboats, had long ago broken away from its mooring. With no one to help him launch the boat, Jordan dreamed up a brilliant idea. He secured several burlap bags, which he had seen while biking to the harbor, to the side of the hull, and then filled them with rocks. Bracing himself with his good foot, he tilted the boat until it rolled upright. Next, he dug a moat in the sand. After three days of digging, the tide came in, the moat filled, and he pulled *Mary Queen of Scots* into deeper water like she was on wheels.

Jordan shifted his weight and put *Mary* high on her port side. No leaks. He pulled the tiller toward him, so the bow turned away from the wind, and he jibed. Jordan ducked as the boom swung around. Letting the sail flair wide, he ran with the wind to his back. He spotted a few tiny holes in the canvas. They weren't a problem, he judged. The two metal stays holding the aluminum mast in place, he thought, appeared sturdy, and the same for all the winches, hasps, and hooks. He rammed the tiller back and forth, and to his delight, the steering mechanism remained in one piece. Deeming *Mary Queen of Scots* seaworthy, he headed for shore.

At first, the distant whine of the motorboat sounded like a mosquito buzzing in his ear. As it grew louder, the roar of the engines became chillingly familiar. He craned his neck. Against the rosy anvil-shaped clouds of a thunderstorm, far out at sea, a speedboat raced into the harbor.

Jordan had seen other motorboats zip across the harbor over the past week. Every one of them had conjured images of the pirates, but all were false alarms.

With his head throbbing from a cocktail of adrenaline and bloodlust, he watched the skipper throttle back and pull into a slip at the dock. The boat was a whaler. In the dying light, three kids hopped out of the whaler. Two boys and a girl. They skipped along the dock, their laughter, carrying across the water. They crossed the street and entered a house.

Jordan lowered the sail and secured the sailboat in water up to his waist. It was dark when he stood before the house across the street from the dock. Light flickered from lanterns on the second floor. Before the night of the purple moon, the house had been an ice cream shop. You could order cones outside at one of three windows or go inside where there were tables and a counter with stools.

He walked out to the end of the dock, feeling prickly all over, and peered into the whaler. There was enough moonlight to reveal a tarp bunched up at the stern. He climbed into the boat and poked around, looking under the tarp. Unable to see in the darkest corners, he patted his hand along the deck and jabbed his finger on a fishhook. He sucked his finger and spat out the blood.

Hearing a noise behind him, he spun around. It was just the hull groaning as it rubbed against the mossy dock piling.

His nerves fraying to the breaking point, Jordan sat behind the wheel and opened a dry well. He skated his hand over a laminated chart. When his fingers stabbed soft wool, he knew immediately he had found the pirates. The well held three ski masks.

He pedaled back to the clinic and tiptoed up to his room. The lights in Wenlan and CeeCee's bedroom were off. He lit a candle and crept into the kitchen. From a drawer, he took out three long knives. He ran his thumb over each blade. Better than nothing, but none were sharp. He wanted better.

Visiting the room where the girls performed minor surgeries, he weighed a surgeon's scalpel in his hand. The metal handle was about as thick as a pencil. The one-inch blade at the tip was razor sharp. He scraped the blade along his arm, and it sheared off the hairs with ease. There were four scalpels. He didn't think Wenlan or CeeCee would miss one.

A large book on the shelf caught his attention. *Grey's Anatomy*. He took the book to his room, flipping through the pages in the yellow candlelight until he came to a drawing of the neck. The artist had peeled back the skin to show the throat muscles and blood vessels. He found the carotid artery, a thick vessel that feeds blood to the brain, running vertically between the Adams Apple and the ear. He checked the location in the diagram, then arched his neck and probed with his fingertip.

Knowing where the pirates lived and knowing where to cut, Jordan had everything but the murderous will to exact the revenge he had promised himself. He closed his eyes and pictured the crew of *Lucky Me*. "Jenny, Monty, Stone, Nikki, Alisha, Todd." Whispering each name, he saw their faces, heard their voices and remembered their quirks. As they vanished in a swirl of flames, he found the will.

# CHAPTER NINE
# COLONY EAST

Ensign Parker's voice crackled over Lieutenant Dawson's two-way radio. "Lieutenant Dawson, come in." Parker's tone had an edge of urgency.

"This is Dawson, over. Standby." He stepped outside the Grover Cleveland Conference Room and lowered the volume to make sure their conversation was private. "Go ahead."

"Emergency CEC meeting, oh one hundred hours. You and Toby Leigh. Wilson will cover for you."

"Parker, what's up?"

"Oh one hundred hours, Lieutenant."

"Roger." Dawson signed off his radio and sighed, wondering what Cadet Leigh had done now. For Admiral Samuels and Doctor Perkins to hold an emergency council session, he couldn't begin to imagine.

Leigh seemed to have a lot of anger toward authority figures, regardless of rank, affiliation, or job function. Dawson had received countless reports of the boy's insolence from everyone from Navy cooks to farm bosses. Toby was so different from his sister.

Dawson figured the parents were to blame for his rude behavior. Of course, that didn't explain why Abigail was so respectful and followed every rule. Perhaps that was normal in a family. One good apple for every bad one.

Ten minutes later, Chief Petty Officer Wilson arrived to take over trigonometry.

Wilson was an old salt, career Navy, maybe a year or two older than Admiral Samuels. Wilson liked to joke that he'd served when "the ships were wood and men were made of steel." Wilson's experience and versatility earned him every odd job in the colony. The last time Dawson had seen the chief petty officer, he was taking a group of seven-year-old cadets on a nature walk along the Hudson River.

Dawson saluted Wilson and told him the chapter to cover.

Then he put in a call to the liaison office to locate Cadet Leigh. Soon he was standing outside the Thomas Jefferson Conference Room. He spotted the boy in Lieutenant Masters' History Class. He thought briefly about waiting for the period to end, but then decided he didn't want to risk being late for the council meeting. He entered and whispered to Masters.

"Toby, please go with Lieutenant Dawson," Masters instructed.

Dawson made eye contact with Abigail Leigh, three seats from her brother. She turned pale. He wished he had something positive to tell her, but whatever her brother had done, he had brought it upon himself.

"Follow me," Dawson told the cadet as they stood in the hall outside the class.

"What's up?"

Dawson gritted his teeth. He'd save his breath. Leigh had already heard his spiel on the importance of the chain of command, showing respect, following orders. "Let's go," he snapped. "We have an appointment."

"With who?"

"With whom, sir?" He gave Leigh a threatening look and that got him moving. They walked in silence to Trump Tower. Cadet Leigh maintained a dismissive scowl the whole way.

When they started up the stairs, the boy finally spoke. "Where are we going, sir?" His voice trembled. The insolent veneer was cracking.

"Colony East has a council that meets once a week. It's chaired by Doctor Perkins and Admiral Samuels. We've been asked to attend an emergency session."

"Why do they want me there?" Leigh hesitated. "Sir."

He could see the boy was shaking. "If I were a betting man," Dawson told him, "I'd say they're not giving you a letter of commendation. If there's anything you want to tell me, now's the time."

Leigh's shoulders folded over like taffy in the warm sun and he addressed the tips of his shoes. "Abby had nothing to do with it, sir."

"Nothing to do with what?"

The boy shook his head and remained in a posture of defeat. After a moment, Dawson figured the cadet was not going to tell him anything.

"Let me be honest with you, mister. If I'm asked for an opinion of your behavior, I'll give it to them straight. From the day you stepped foot in Colony East, you've shown disdain for the rules and regulations. And you've been insolent to the men and women obligated to enforce the rules. Think about it, would your behavior make your father proud?"

Toby choked out a sob.

Dawson knew he'd gone too far. His pent up frustration with the boy was leaking out in a corrosive way. Leadership demanded control. He lowered his voice and changed his tone. He wanted to be upbeat, without being effusive. "Here's some advice my father gave me. When you're facing a tough battle, don't give in. Throw your shoulders back, lift your chin high. Show pride and courage in the face of your enemy. Especially, if that enemy is fear. I think you have that spirit inside of you Cadet. I know you do."

Leigh wiped his eyes and replied to his pep talk with a hard stare. The boy clearly had serious issues.

"Suit yourself," Dawson said. "So much for sharing a word to the wise."

They entered the council meeting room, and after brief formalities, he and Cadet Leigh sat opposite Admiral Samuels and Doctor Perkins, and, to his surprise, Doctor Droznin.

Doctor Perkins tilted his head down, peering above his glasses at Leigh. "Son, what's your name?"

The cadet stared into his lap.

The chief scientist slipped into his expression of wisdom the way one puts on a windbreaker one sleeve at a time. The smarmy smile came first. Then he somehow made his eyes look like deep pools of knowledge. "It's not Leigh, is it? Did you think you could maintain your charade forever?

There's a reason we scrape cheek cells for every cadet. We just received your DNA results, young man. Precision is the poetry of science, and your genetic fingerprint informs us that you are not related to Abigail and Lizette Leigh. Is your name really Toby? Or did you make that up, too?"

A heavy silence poured into the room. Dawson checked on the admiral. He was contemplating his craggy fingers folded before him. Droznin seemed to be contemplating equations on her scientific calculator.

"Toby Jones," the cadet said after a long moment.

Doctor Perkins let out a sigh. "We're in very troubling times and it pains me to think of the choices we must make. Unfortunately, we have limited resources. Imagine you have one glass of water and ten thirsty individuals. You can give every one of them a sip and they'll still be thirsty. Or you can select two and quench their thirsts. In the former situation, nobody wins. In the latter, we take the most responsible action. Such is our intent with Generation M."

After hearing Doctor Perkins deliver this theme many different ways, Dawson knew the meaning behind his convoluted words all too well. Now, though, he was more consumed with the shocking news that Toby and Abigail were not brother and sister. That's what Toby had meant in the stairwell when he said Abby had nothing to do it. But she did know! Abigail Leigh, he realized, was aware of the deception from the beginning. She had made herself an accomplice by withholding the truth, by her silence.

"It was my idea," Toby blurted out, as if he had read Dawson's mind. "I told Abby to pretend I was her brother. She didn't want to do it."

Doctor Droznin looked up from her calculator and interjected, "Abigail Leigh is still useful to us."

"Mr. Jones," Doctor Perkins said, "in light of the circumstances, I'm afraid we must expel you from Colony East."

Admiral Samuels looked up. "Lieutenant Dawson, what's your take on Cadet Jones?"

On one side of Dawson, Toby Jones hung his head. Across from him, Admiral Samuels jutted out his jaw and fired laser beams from his blue eyes. Doctor Droznin had returned to her calculations, and Doctor Perkins sat in calm repose.

Expelling Toby Jones was potentially a death sentence for the boy, Dawson realized. The meteorologists had reported Tropical Storm David was now Hurricane David. The hurricane was bearing down on Cuba, and there was a fifty-fifty chance it would swing north and make landfall on the east coast. Dawson was unaware of any plans to distribute the antibiotic outside the colonies, though he still held a sliver of hope the higher-ups had something up their sleeves.

"As Biltmore Company leader, I'm happy to offer my assessment of Cadet Jones. Jones has been a model cadet. After a brief adjustment period, I've come to admire him for his assertiveness and leadership skills. He gets along well with the other cadets. He shows respect to those who command him. I'd be honored to have him remain a member of Biltmore Company."

Dawson had witnessed many flavors of expression on Cadet Leigh, all variations of rebellion, smirks, sneers, pouts and the like. Now he saw a new expression. Shock.

"Thank you for that report, Lieutenant," Doctor Perkins said. "I should remind everyone at the table, we have many thirsty individuals and only one glass of water. We're obligated to nurture the seeds of the new society." Perkins looked to his right, his thin nose swinging like a weather vane in a cold wind. "Admiral."

Admiral Samuels paused a long moment. "Parker," he barked finally.

Ensign Parker and two sailors walked over to Toby and told him to stand.

Toby Jones pulled his shoulders back and lifted his chin high. Dawson could feel the boy's courage rising. Then Jones faced him. His eyes were clear and bright. "There's something you need to tell Abby." His voice was steady and strong. "Tell her I know she didn't mean what she said." He grinned and gave him a wink. "Sir."

Dawson sat in stunned silence as they led the boy away.

# CHAPTER TEN
# MYSTIC

Jordan rolled onto his side, his back, his side again. Too restless to sleep, he lit a candle and entered the bathroom where he looked at himself in the mirror. "Jenny, Monty, Stone, Nikki, Alisha, Todd." Their ghostly faces floated across his.

With his resolve to avenge their deaths restored, he carried the candle back to the bedroom and blew it out. Pressing his palms against the windowsill, he looked up at the stars and once again whispered the names of his friends. He didn't know if they were among stars or in the bellies of sharks, but memories of the *Lucky Me* crew would always be part of his heart.

At dawn, Jordan rolled a strip of paper around the scalpel and slipped it into his sock. Wedged inside his sneaker, the handle bit into his ankle, but he found it oddly comforting. He knew the scalpel was there.

He slung his pack over his shoulder, hopped on the bike and pedaled to Mystic Harbor where he busied himself on *Mary Queen of Scots.*

Splicing line, he kept his eye on the whaler tied up at the end of the dock, and on the ice cream house across the street.

An hour passed and then the boy with red hair ran from the house and onto the dock in his bare feet. Ten or eleven years old, he wore a T-shirt and jogging shorts. Yesterday, Jordan had mostly seen this one in the company of the girl with stringy blonde hair.

His heart raced as he watched the pirate climb into the whaler. Jordan couldn't decide what he wanted most: for the pirate to fire up the boat and speed off, or for him to stay put.

When it seemed the pirate wasn't going anywhere, Jordan waded ashore and eyed his bike. It was not too late to hop on it and pedal back to the clinic. Forget everything. Spend his final days with Wenlan before sailing to Castine Island.

"Jenny, Monty, Stone, Nikki, Alisha, Todd... " Jordan spoke their names and took a step toward the dock. Then another. Even with a limp, he moved as quietly as a leopard. His strength had returned. His right arm felt especially strong. He stopped for a moment and stared into the sun. The fireball that had ended the lives of his friends had been just as brilliant. The explosions from that night of horror rocked his memory.

The pounding in his head lessened and his mind cleared as he approached the dock. On the wide planks, he bent down and pretended to tie his shoe.

He saw no activity at the pirates' house. In the opposite direction, the redheaded pirate had tossed a few life jackets on the dock. The pirate was cleaning the whaler. Jordan transferred the scalpel to his back pocket and gave his T-shirt a tug to make sure the blade stayed hidden.

A moment later, he stood on the dock above the pirate, an executioner lording over the condemned. "Hey, awesome boat." The pirate may have pillaged and plundered, but he must have eaten like a bird. His shirt was baggy where his chest belonged, and whoever put those purple moon tats on his forearms didn't have much room to work with.

He eyed Jordan suspiciously. "You from around here?"

"I'm staying with my cousins: Jenny, Monty, Stone, Nikki, Alisha, and Todd. Do you know them?"

"Nah."

Jordan's eyes darted from the pirate's nest of tangled hair, to his freckled cheeks and sunburned arms. He avoided his neck, fearing the intensity of his thoughts would telepathically give his intention away. "Bet you can go really fast."

"Sixty-five," he boasted.

"Knots?"

"Miles per hour!"

"No way!"

The pirate grinned. "Want to go for a ride?"

Jordan whistled softly. Avenge the deaths of his friends at sea? That was more than fitting. "Is it safe?"

"Gimme a break."

"All right." Jordan climbed into the boat. "Don't go too fast. I don't want to get hurt."

"I'm Billy."

"Jordan."

Not wanting to know anything else about the pirate, Jordan settled into the passenger seat and sat with his back straight to keep the tip of the scalpel pointing up.

A girl cried out, "Billy."

Jordan tensed, but quickly settled when he saw she was only six or seven years old. She raced across the playground and onto the dock.

The pirate grumbled, "My twerpy little sister."

Soon the girl stood above them, gawking at Jordan. She had the pirate's rusty colored hair and knobby knees and elbows. "Who's that?" she asked shyly, twisting back and forth.

The pirate fired up the motors. "None of your business. Amy, get lost."

Her face brightened. "Can I come?"

"Don't bug me. Untie the rope."

"Please," she begged.

The pirate untied the mooring line himself. "Stay out of trouble! Promise me!"

Amy pouted. "No."

The pirate smirked at Jordan. "Like I care." He nudged the throttle and they pulled away from the dock, leaving his disappointed sister behind. Jordan wondered what her reaction would be when her brother washed ashore. He put Amy out of his mind.

Well clear of the dock, the pirate shouted gleefully, "Hold on," and rammed the throttle lever all the way forward. The twin outboards roared and the nose of the whaler lifted so fast that Jordan saw nothing but blue sky. From the force pushing him back in the seat, he worried the scalpel blade might snap off. He slipped the weapon out of his pocket and held it by his side, out of the pirate's sight.

Whooping and laughing, the pirate drove the boat hard, a boy playing with a powerful toy. The hull pounded and skittered across the waves. They hit one wave and flew through the air, the props whining like dentist drills. They landed with a thud. Jordan sensed the wave was groundswell from a large and distant storm.

"You want to drive?"

They were cruising slowly three hundred yards from shore, tossing side-to-side in the chop. Many miles away, the white sail of a gypsy boat was a tiny speck. Jordan saw the pirate's eyes lock onto it for a second.

"Really?"

The pirate slid out of the seat. "Go for it, dude."

Jordan reached over and killed the engines.

"What the—?"

Before the pirate could utter another word, Jordan snatched his wrist, a cobra striking its prey. Twisting his arm, he forced the pirate to his knees. The pirate struggled, but with Jordan's adrenaline pumping, he easily overpowered him. He caught a faint whiff of ammonia and musk. It was the odor of fear coming off the pirate. He locked his fingers on the back of the pirate's neck and pushed his face against the deck. Then, he rolled him over and pinned his shoulder down with his knee. The pirate made little grunts as Jordan's knee drove harder into him from the rocking motion of the boat.

Jordan brought the scalpel to his mouth and scissored the paper with his teeth. He unraveled it and gripped the metal handle in his sweaty palm.

"Remember *Lucky Me*? The two-masted schooner you attacked. That blew up. That burned." His heart hammered in his chest as he spoke. The pirate's eyes showed confusion at first, darting and narrowing, then suddenly, they widened. "Jenny, Monty, Stone, Nikki, Alisha, Todd. This is for them." Jordan pushed the pirate's chin back with his left hand and held the scalpel against his neck.

While he only had to push a few millimeters to puncture the pirate's skin, a canyon opened up inside him, which he couldn't cross. He was not a murderer. A sick feeling sloshed in his stomach and rose up in his throat. He leaned back, breathing hard.

"I knew someone who did some terrible things and she changed. Her name was Mandy. You can change, too."

The pirate sneered. "Screw you."

Rage exploded in Jordan's brain and seized control of him. He grabbed the pirate's hair and yanked his head as he brought his hand back. A frightening beast had risen from the deepest, darkest part of his soul and fed on his pent up anger. The muscles of his shoulder stretched tight. Hand and scalpel were one. He grunted as he whipped his arm forward and down. Yet, something in him altered the trajectory—something stronger than the beast. He drove the blade into the hull where it snapped off. He would honor Mandy and his friends from *Lucky Me*, not by killing this boy, but by putting an end to this senseless cycle of violence.

Billy was crying. He had melted into a frightened ten-year old. Would he rob and kill again? Jordan drew in a sharp breath and got off him, thinking the answer was probably yes. But just maybe the boy would change.

Too exhausted to feel, much less think, Jordan moved to the skipper's seat and headed for shore. About twenty yards from the dock, he told Billy to jump.

"I can't swim."

Jordan tossed him a life jacket and threw him overboard with one hand.

Then he made a wide sweeping turn with the whaler, and when the boat was aiming straight out to sea, he nudged the throttle forward and leapt out.

Jordan dived under the water and held his breath until his lungs ached. The ocean coursed through his veins and washed away his oily sick feeling and dissolved his rage. He broke the surface and took a huge gulp of fresh air, ready to begin a new life.

# CHAPTER ELEVEN
## COLONY EAST

Abby anxiously scanned the faces at Grand Central Station. All four companies were here for evening chow and there was no sign of Toby. Abby had a sick feeling ever since the lieutenant had taken him out of History Class. She feared they'd caught him outside the Biltmore, but if so, it didn't explain why Jonzy was still there. Unless the boys had split up and Jonzy got away. She waited until Jonzy was returning his tray to the galley and moved beside him. "Where's Toby?"

"I don't know," Jonzy replied. "I'm worried."

They both kept their eyes straight ahead.

"Worried," she snorted. "This is your fault."

Abby broke away from the line and headed for the door. Outside, fleeing to the Biltmore, she had nearly reached the hotel when the lieutenant caught up to her on Lexington Avenue. "Come with me, Cadet Leigh."

Shivering from his cold tone, she followed him into a meeting room next to his living quarters. There, he smiled and asked her in a pleasant tone to take a seat. The anger welling in his eyes belied his attempt to pretend he was friendly.

"Abigail, when you first arrived, you admitted to me that you lied. You told Ensign Mathews that you knew me. I admired you for your honesty.

265

Do you recall me saying I valued honesty above all else? Care to be straight with me?"

Her thoughts swirled madly. Should she admit that she knew Toby was going outside the Biltmore? Her heart thundered in her chest, the echo of each beat throbbing in her head.

After a long moment of her silence, the lieutenant leaned forward. "Toby Jones."

Abby dropped her chin to her chest. Then she looked up and matched his stare with one equally intense. "It was my idea. When my sister got sick, Toby was the only one on the island who would help us. He made it possible for us to make it here. He risked everything, and after we reached Brooklyn, he saw the adults take a girl who had the Pig." Abby noticed the lieutenant lean back as if hit with a little puff of wind. "Toby heard them say they were looking for healthy siblings. He wanted just me and Touk to go. I mean, Lizette. I begged him to pretend he was my brother. Before I swam here, I told him about my family. If anyone should be punished, it's me."

"Too late, Cadet. We went before the council today. Toby Jones was expelled from the colony. Don't worry, he received a week's supply of food and water. From what you told me, I'd say he's an industrious young man."

Abby took breath after deep breath. Her mind was so clogged it felt blank.

"Abigail, you'll be allowed to remain in Colony East, if that's what's concerning you."

She barely registered his words. Then, the dam burst and a flood of raw emotion swept through her. She boiled in a quiet rage. If what Toby had told her was true, they had expelled him knowing that a deadly epidemic was on the way. Clenching her fists in anger and too shaken to look the lieutenant in the eyes, she fixed her gaze on the bump on the bridge of his nose. "When we first met, you were curious about what happened to the babies after the night of the purple moon. We took care of them because it was the right thing to do. Was it right to kick Toby out of Colony East?"

His head jolted back, this time as if struck by an unexpected gust of wind. With the color draining from his face, he pulled his shoulders back and lifted his chin. "Ordinarily, I'm not at liberty to discuss the specifics of what happened at a council meeting, but I'll make an exception. Cadet Jones wanted me to inform you that he knew you didn't mean the last thing you said to him."

Abby felt the sob coming, and she fought with every ounce of willpower to keep it contained. "May I be dismissed, sir?"

"Dismissed," he said in a distant tone. The color had yet to return to his face.

Abby suddenly knew what she had to do for Toby, for Jordan and for every survivor outside Colony East, Colony West, and any other colonies the adults ran. She did her best to suppress the pulse of anxiety that came with her newfound determination. "Thank you, sir," she said in a respectful tone, giving a crisp salute.

# CHAPTER TWELVE
## MYSTIC

At the Mystic Harbor playground, Jordan sat next to Wenlan on the swings. Nearby, *Mary Queen of Scots* floated in five feet of water. With the tide going out, Jordan figured he had thirty minutes before he had to sail—before the hull would sink into the soft mud and delay his departure for another six hours.

The mainsail luffed in the stiffening breeze, and he had more than enough food and water stowed in the boat to make it to Castine Island. Wenlan had even packed him a germ mask. Everything was ready. Almost everything.

He reached out and took Wenlan's hand. He slipped his palm against hers and cradled her slender fingers. Giving him a sweet smile, she squeezed his hand briefly as she pushed with her toe to start a gentle swaying motion.

"You and CeeCee would love Castine Island."

She gave him a sidelong glance.

Jordan gave her a playful bump. "Hey, I'm allowed to try."

He tried to imagine Abby's reaction when he told her he planned to return to Mystic. If her initial reaction to his leaving with the gypsies was any indication, he knew she'd put up a lot of resistance, especially after he told her about Lucky Me. Jordan held out some hope that Abby and Touk might want to join him in moving to Mystic.

The clatter of halyards striking the mast caught his attention, as if *Mary Queen of Scots* was calling out to him to hurry. The boat rocked side-to-side in three successive waves.

"Those are set waves," he said. "They're coming from a big storm at sea."

Alarm filled Wenlan's eyes. "Is it safe for you to go?"

How he wished that storm was barreling down on Mystic. It would provide the best reason to postpone his trip, to stay with Wenlan another day, another month. But the wave maker was still a ways off. He estimated the storm, whether a Nor'easter or possibly a hurricane, would hit in four or five days, giving him ample time to sail home safely. "Yeah, no problem."

He worried more about the storm that was battering his mind. The last time he had left a girl he loved, a chain reaction of events had started that ended in her death. Superstition had kept him in Mystic as much as the longing he knew he would feel the moment he set sail.

Glancing over at Wenlan, his heart wrenched. A solitary tear ran down her face.

Jordan stood up and turned to face her. Not wanting to see any more tears, he took her other hand in his and pulled her body close. "I'll leave at the next high tide."

Wenlan shook her head. "No. You're leaving right now. The sooner you go, the sooner you'll come back."

As her tears dried, he realized she was right, and he felt a pressure building in his chest. His throat thickened. His tears were about to begin.

Giving Wenlan a quick goodbye kiss, he ran to the shore and into the water, making splashes as he pumped his knees high, racing against the falling tide. The short-lived competition would go a long way towards helping him postpone his hard sobs until he was out of sight.

# CHAPTER THIRTEEN
## COLONY EAST

Lieutenant Dawson inched the vase until it sat dead center on the table. He had almost settled for an arrangement of squash flowers from Central Park Farm before scoring a bouquet of Queen Anne's Lace. He had picked the wild flowers along the East River, during an inspection of the shoreline as part of the readiness preparations for Hurricane David.

The food he had set out for the evening—corn on the cob, beets, lettuce, string beans—was also compliments of the hurricane. Admiral Samuels had issued an order to pick all the crops before the storm hit.

Completing the table setting, Dawson had swiped a linen tablecloth from the hotel's restaurant along with fancy silverware and plates. He had briefly considered inviting Sandy to the rooftop for a candlelit dinner but opted instead for his living quarters. He did not think it was the time or the place for a celebration on the rooftop, with Hurricane David barreling down on the east coast.

There was also a practical matter for dining in his living quarters. While *Major* Hedrick had been relieved of her duty as Hilton Company Leader, Dawson was still responsible for the Biltmore cadets who, he hoped, would give him and Sandy a little peace this evening.

He found her transfer maddening. Promotions and transfers were part of the military's DNA, always executed with one thing in mind: the mission.

Maybe the higher-ups should consider relationships for once. He wouldn't hold his breath on that one.

Dawson collapsed in his chair and sighed. Why had he waited this long to tell her what she meant to him—the evening before her departure to Atlanta Colony. He supposed he should consider himself lucky. To beat the hurricane, they might have bumped up her flight even earlier.

He opened his dog-eared copy of *Twenty Thousand Leagues Under the Sea*. As a young boy, the words of Jules Verne had planted the seed in his mind to command a submarine someday. Later, cruising near the bottom of the ocean, Dawson found the fictional adventures of the Nautilus helped take his mind off home. Now, he hoped reading about the stern, though good-hearted Captain Nemo could temper his nervous anticipation of Sandy's arrival.

At the sound of footsteps in the hall outside, he sprang to his feet, and at the first rap, swung the door open with a whoosh.

He felt his stomach drop at the sight of her puffy cheeks and red-rimmed eyes. She'd been crying.

"Mark, I'm so sorry."

The anguish of her tone rocked him back on his heels. He knew immediately she was referring to some tragedy he was unaware of. Clutching her elbow, he steered her inside and noticed the package she held in the crook of her other arm. "What's wrong?"

She handed him the bundle. Recognizing his own handwriting, he sucked in his breath as if someone had kicked him in the stomach. They were the letters he had written to Lily. All unopened.

"Doctor Perkins spoke to me," her voice halting. "Lily died three weeks ago. David Levine didn't know what to do or say, so he kept taking your letters. If I had known…"

Sandy rested her hand on his arm. The support helped him stay on his feet.

"Doctor Perkins said that Lily made an important contribution to the development of the antibiotic," she continued, trying to sound upbeat. "He says he's going to recommend that they name it after her."

What the CDC called the antibiotic mattered little, Dawson thought. Lily, the girl who had liked to dig for worms, whose unseen struggle had been a source of inspiration and strength for him, was dead.

He struggled to catch his breath against the pressure of sobs buried deep inside his chest. They felt like hot lava, ready to erupt. How could anyone live in a world drowning in so much tragedy? He closed his eyes and his mind conjured a vision of his tiny Sarah floating by like a mirage. If he reached out for her, she'd vanish. "Shoulders back," he told himself. He had to go on for his daughter, and his cadets needed him too. His shoulders disobeyed the feeble command, and he remained hunched, crushed by a thousand pounds of sadness.

Suddenly aware of the lightness of Sandy's touch, he opened his eyes. Tears streamed down her cheeks. He wrapped his arms around her and the scent of her vanilla shampoo wafted all around him. He felt like they were together in the time and space between heartbeats of sorrow. He started to speak, but instead let his thoughts fade. He closed his eyes again. Just holding her in a stolen moment of tenderness said more than words ever could.

# DAVID

# THREE DAYS LEFT

First to arrive for the emergency company leader session, Lieutenant Dawson took his seat at the table. He thought the location was unusual. They were meeting on the fifth floor of Trump Tower in the Gregor Mendel Conference Room where Doctor Perkins held CDC meetings.

Newly minted Lieutenant Mathews strutted in next and took a seat next to where Perkins would sit. She opened a notebook, and gave Dawson a curt nod, "Lieutenant."

"Welcome," he said.

Dismissively, she dropped her eyes and started writing.

"Lieutenant, *junior grade*," Dawson muttered to himself. Last week, Ensign Mathews was patrolling the East River, firing warning shots at children who waded too far into the water. Now, the former weapons specialist was the new leader of Hilton Company. The Hilton cadets, he imagined, were experiencing culture shock from the change of leadership styles. In some ways, Mathews reminded Dawson of himself three years ago, eager to make an impression and climb the ranks. He wasn't sure that he liked what he saw.

A moment later, Lieutenant Masters and Lieutenant Murphy sauntered in, followed by Admiral Samuels. Doctor Perkins and Doctor Droznin came in next.

Standing, the admiral leaned forward and propped himself on the table with eight knuckles. "David just became a category three, but they expect the storm to strengthen to a category four or five. The eye is a hundred miles off Bermuda at this time. The meteorologists think landfall will be northern Virginia. Landfall ETA for Colony East is four days. Effective tomorrow, we're canceling all classes and activities. The storm's going to pound us pretty hard in more ways than one. Doctor Perkins and Doctor Droznin would like a word with you." The admiral jutted out his jaw and paused, as if he had more to say, but instead clamped his molars together and took a seat.

Doctor Perkins tented his delicate fingers. "We all know the story of Noah's Ark. Whether you believe there really was an ark, or you consider the tale a metaphor, there's an important lesson for us. God told Noah to build an ark because of a catastrophic flood." Perkins raised his hands, pretending he was God. "Noah, I command you to gather two of every living creature." He swept his gaze around the table, pausing at each attendee, so the gravity of his words could sink in. "God didn't tell Noah to gather ten of every creature. Because God understood that Noah had limited resources. Noah only had his two hands to build the ark." Doctor Perkins curled his lip with the subtlety of a Chinese brush-painting master. "We all know the outcome. After forty days and forty nights of rising flood waters, life began anew."

Lieutenant Mathews nodded vigorously as she scribbled away. The other company leaders stared straight ahead with dazed expressions. Masters and Murphy always let the doctor's ramblings go in one ear and out the other. Dawson's stomach had warped into a tight coil, and, as usual, he had no clue what Admiral Samuels was thinking. The admiral owned the ultimate poker face.

Doctor Droznin spoke next. "We have successfully developed an antibiotic that fights AHA-B."

"Meyercilliun," Doctor Perkins interjected, seeming pleased he had convinced the higher-ups to name it in honor of Lily Meyers.

Heat flared in Dawson's cheeks in reaction, but he was also relieved to hear the scientists had developed an antibiotic.

Mathews leaned forward. "Doctor, how do you spell meyercilliun?"

Perkins spelled it for her, delighting in every letter.

"They're ramping up production in Atlanta," Doctor Droznin continued. "Unfortunately, they're behind schedule. We will receive the first batch of pills tomorrow for CDC and Navy personnel. We'll distribute any extra to Generation M. The second batch will be for the remainder of the colony, and will come as soon as we can get a flight in after the hurricane. Because of our ongoing research of AHA-B, we'll also hand out special dosages to the subjects in our control group. I'll contact you with a schedule."

Both scientists stood, ready to leave.

Dawson raised his hand. "What's your plan for passing out pills outside the colony?"

Perkins cleared his throat, as if to say, he'd handle this one. He rubbed his chin in contemplation, then nodded to himself, furrowing his brow. Finally, he looked over at Dawson with an expression of concern. "All our hearts go out to survivors everywhere, and we will do what we can, when we can. Like Noah, we have limited resources. Our greatest tragedy would be for the flood to wash away the seeds of the new society."

Dawson's stomach coiled tighter as the words also washed away his hope.

Mathews underlined the note she'd just taken as the two scientists excused themselves.

"Thank you," she called out. "That was extremely informative."

"Dismissed," Admiral Samuels sighed.

⁓ ⁓ ⁓

Abby pulled the covers up to her chin. It was lights out, and Lieutenant Dawson had just told them over the intercom that a hurricane was going to make landfall in three days. "We'll batten down the hatches and ride it out," he'd said. He had also reminded them that they were the seeds of a new society, which almost made Abby sick to her stomach. Soon she heard him working his way down the hall to bid them good night in person.

"Good night, Cadet Leigh," he said in a pleasant tone, as if he'd put Toby's expulsion from the colony behind him.

277

She answered him just as cheerily, "Good night, Lieutenant." She didn't want him to suspect anything.

"Sleep tight," he said and moved on.

An hour later, all was quiet on the third floor. Abby hadn't heard a peep out of her neighboring cadets for forty-five minutes. With adrenaline jetting through her veins, she couldn't wait any longer. Earlier in the day, she had whispered to Jonzy, "We need to escape." He had whispered back, "Eleven p.m., my room, fifth room on the right."

She crawled out of bed and stuffed towels under the blanket. From the door, she turned and studied the lump. Someone passing by the room in the dark would think nothing was amiss, but if she was going to make these nightly excursions a habit, she'd better come up with a better looking dummy.

She stepped into the hall, knowing she had to be careful. If the lieutenant caught her outside her room, he'd report her to the council. She didn't worry they'd kick her out of the colony because of their ongoing experimentation. She feared they'd lock her up in Medical Clinic 17 instead.

Abby walked lightly, in bare feet, down the hall and into the fire exit stairway where she climbed up the cold metal stairs to the fourth floor. She entered the wing of the fifteen-year-old boys for the first time.

Her skin prickled as she crept down the hall, passing rooms of slumbering cadets—seeds of the new society—dreaming. She entered the fifth room on the right.

"What...?" Jonzy whispered.

"Let's go."

"No, it's too early!"

"I'll wait." Abby moved to the side of Jonzy's bed, away from the door, and stretched out on the floor.

He swung his feet beside her. "Toby said you can be bossy at times."

There were times when you needed to be assertive, she thought. *Like right now!*

Already dressed in overalls, Jonzy packed towels under the covers to fashion a dummy that Abby thought looked only slightly more realistic than her effort. He grabbed his glasses and nodded for her to follow him.

They huffed and puffed up thirty-six flights of stairs to the restaurant on the top floor.

"Is it safe up here?" she whispered.

"Totally," Jonzy said, speaking in a normal voice to emphasize his point.

"Jonzy, I'm sorry I blamed you for what happened to Toby. He's not my brother." She summarized the conversation she'd had with the lieutenant two days ago.

"Toby told me you weren't his sister."

"When?" It surprised Abby that Toby would have let his guard down like that.

"One time he said he really liked you, and I told him that was kind of weird."

Pieces of Abby's heart tore off and fluttered away.

"Don't worry about Toby," he continued. "We always knew one of us might get caught. So we came up with a plan. He'll stay near the colony. There's a fish market in Brooklyn, just across the East River. That's where we can find him."

"I know where it is."

Jonzy gave her a panoramic tour of Colony East, pointing out some landmarks, but mostly the security measures the adults had taken.

Green and red lights dotted the East River. "They doubled the number of patrols since you swam to the windmill."

He led her to a dinner table where he lifted up the tablecloth and gestured to radio equipment hiding behind it. "Communication central!" Sitting cross-legged, Jonzy punched a power button and twisted a nob. "I can pick up conversations between the patrol boat skippers."

A voice crackled, "Pork chops smothered in gravy." The man had a southern accent.

"I'll take a Starbucks," a woman said.

A new man chuckled, "Dunkin' Donuts. America runs on Dunkin'."

"Before or after the comet?"

"Ha ha."

"Shut. Up."

Abby sat back, puzzled. "Are they serious?"

Jonzy lowered the volume. "All they do is argue and joke with each other. Sports, food, coffee."

She shook her head in dismay. "These people are going to sit around and joke while a hurricane infects millions of kids with the Pig."

"Abby, you have to be careful." Jonzy's tone sent a chill down her spine. "Last night, I heard Doctor Droznin talking to Atlanta. They're shipping some pills here before the hurricane, but they're also sending pills for the control group. Tomorrow, the lieutenant is supposed to take you to see her."

Abby swallowed hard. "Did they mention Touk?"

Jonzy shook his head.

She felt a cloud of cold mist spread inside her chest. "I hate Colony East. No matter what happens tomorrow, I'm going to try to escape. I need to get pills for Toby and Jordan, my real brother."

Jonzy turned on another radio. "Maybe he's listening to The Port right now on Castine Island?"

Abby heard a song play. *Here Comes the Sun.* It reminded her of the CD she and Touk had given to Jordan.

"The scientists don't talk until midnight," Jonzy said. "When I get bored, I listen to DJ Silver. I hope you'll take me to Castine Island."

Abby punched him in the arm, because boys understood a shot of pain as an undying seal of truth and honor. "You better come to the island with us! But first, we have to get out of here!"

Jonzy turned off the radio, and they moved to the window overlooking the East River, where they discussed their escape plan.

"The storm's hitting in three days," he said. "We have to wait until they get the second shipment of pills. They won't arrive until after the hurricane clears out."

"Agreed," Abby said. "How do we get the pills?"

"Droznin is passing them out."

"I've been inside her office," Abby said.

Jonzy rubbed his arm where she had punched him. "I bet she did that bit with the dolls? Fit them all together and say there's no more room in Colony East."

Abby gave him a nod. "Yep. Weird. Medical Clinic 17 will be locked, but we can break the glass."

Jonzy smirked, "Too noisy."

"Not if we hold a blanket against the glass, then smash it with a rock."

"How do you know that?"

"Cuz I'm smart," Abby said.

"Okay, if you're so smart, how do we hide from the video camera aimed at the door?"

Abby shrugged. "We go through a window. Once we're inside, we might need a crowbar to pop open Doctor Droznin's door. Got a crowbar?"

Jonzy spread his arms. "New York City used to be the shopping capitol of the world. There's a crowbar for sale somewhere out there."

"When do we go shopping?" she asked.

"Tomorrow night."

"Is it safe?"

Jonzy shrugged. "They haven't caught me yet. What else do we need?"

"Gems," Abby said. "Diamonds are worthless, but we can trade rubies and pearls for rides, food, information."

"I have two walkie-talkies and a gun," Jonzy said.

Abby's stomach dropped. "No gun."

Jonzy frowned. "I could have had a hundred guns. I went to an apartment building on the Upper East Side. Everyone owned a gun."

She drilled him with a hard stare. "No."

"Okay, no gun."

"Thank you. We need plastic containers to keep things dry, like the pills and the walkie-talkies. There might be flooding after the hurricane."

"Food is easy," Jonzy said. "Every day, take something in your pockets from Grand Central. Stuff that won't spoil, like rice and potatoes."

"We need maps. Especially a street map of Brooklyn."

Jonzy said he would get a Yellow Pages phone book so they could pick out the stores they needed to visit. "Every room in the hotel above the fourth floor has the Yellow Pages."

Then the conversation turned to finding a way out of Colony East.

To the north, Jonzy explained, armed guards patrolled the Red Zone. That perimeter also had an electric fence. The underground subway tunnels leading to Brooklyn, the Bronx, Queens, and New Jersey had all been sealed off, as had the Holland Tunnel and Brooklyn Battery Tunnel. The only bridge left standing was The George Washington, and it had a barricade that would require dynamite. Abby nixed Jonzy's idea of adding dynamite to the shopping list. Finally, he told her that both the Hudson and East Rivers were crawling with patrol boats.

Despite the long odds, Abby felt the excitement that comes from making decisions and taking action, knowing she could live with the consequences. Over the past several weeks, she had started seeing herself less as "lucky person 1102" and more as "prisoner 1102." A prisoner ready to escape a formidable, high-security prison.

"I vote we swim," she said.

"Too many patrol boats," Jonzy blurted.

"When I swam to the windmill, I had to shout and wave my arms to get the attention of Ensign Mathews."

"I have a fear of the water."

"Jonzy, I have a fear of being electrocuted on a fence."

"Seriously, Abby, when I was five, my uncle tried to teach me to swim by throwing me in the deep end of a pool." She heard the rising panic in his voice.

"All right, we'll keep thinking."

Something caught Abby's attention. The lights of the patrol boats all swerved in one direction and formed a line, like ants returning to their nest. "Look. Where are they going?"

"Shift change," Jonzy explained. "The skippers go to the ferry terminal and a new crew takes over."

"So for a moment, the river is completely free of boats?"

"Abby, there's something else we need. Sleep. I've been up late every night for the past three weeks. Today, I fell asleep in physics class. Lieutenant Dawson will get suspicious if my teacher reports me."

"Jonzy, how long before the boats come out again?"

"Ten minutes."

"So the river is free and clear for a full ten minutes?"

"Maybe nine minutes." He paused. "Or less."

Abby had a new item to add to the shopping list, but she didn't think now was the time or place to disturb Jonzy with her idea.

# TWO DAYS LEFT

Lieutenant Dawson picked up the mic and flipped the on switch. "Cadet Leigh, please report to the lobby, on the double." He preferred reserving the public address system for comments made at reveille and lights out, but Leigh wasn't in her living quarters and he didn't want to be late for their meeting.

A minute later, Abigail entered the lobby.

"Where were you, Cadet?"

"Playing cards with Cadet Billings, sir."

"We have a meeting with Doctor Droznin."

He saw the blood drain from her face. They walked to Medical Clinic 17, making small talk, her voice shaky at first. From her overall friendly tone, Dawson thought Abigail was adjusting well after the incident with Toby Jones. He found it curious, though, that the normally inquisitive girl hadn't asked any questions about their meeting with Droznin.

The waiting room was crowded with ensigns, sailors, and several scientists. Abigail was the only cadet.

A girl's frightful scream inside Doctor Droznin's office caused a stir outside. Chins lifted, eyes narrowed. It sent a chill down Dawson's spine. When he looked over at Abigail, she was trembling and gripping the arm of the chair, her knuckles white.

Then Lieutenant Masters and a cadet emerged from the office. It took Dawson a moment to recognize the cadet. Her name was Gracie, and she was the older sister of Elsie, the sick little girl they had picked up in Brooklyn. Gracie was shaking and crying as Masters tried to console her.

Droznin stepped to the door and said in a cold flat tone, "Royce."

Ensign Royce entered the office and re-emerged in less than a minute.

"Dawson and Leigh," Doctor Droznin called from the doorway.

Dawson sat next to Abigail as Doctor Droznin made some notations in a book at her desk. Then Droznin opened a desk drawer and removed a bottle of blue pills. She put on a glove, knocked a pill into her palm, and passed it to him. "Chew or swallow. Do you need water?"

He shook his head and crunched the pill.

Next, Droznin removed a bottle from the same drawer. It had far fewer pills, and they were pink. Similarly, she placed a pink pill in her hand and held it out to Abigail. "Chew or swallow it. I have water if you need it."

"What is it?" Abigail asked politely.

Dawson was wondering the same thing.

Droznin extended her hand further. "You saw my waiting room. We don't have all day."

"I want to know what it is," the cadet demanded.

Droznin addressed him. "Lieutenant, please inform Ms. Leigh we can do this the easy way or the hard way. If necessary, we can restrain her and administer the dose rectally."

"Doctor Droznin, I think you owe it to her to tell her what she's taking."

Droznin shot him a glare. "Should I have Doctor Perkins contact the admiral?"

Dawson clenched his jaw. "Yes, that might be a good idea, Doctor." He kept his tone measured and calm.

"How's my sister doing?"

Both he and Doctor Droznin turned to Abigail. Strangely, in Dawson's battle of wills with the doctor, he had almost forgotten she was there.

"Did her drug trial go well?" Abigail added.

"Yes, Lizette responded well to the antibiotic," Droznin said. "She has made a full recovery."

Abigail held out her hand. "Give me the pill, please."

Cadet Leigh crunched up the pink pill, and Droznin called the next patient. Dawson had no idea what just happened.

~ ~ ~

Jonzy threw down a card. "How do you feel?"

Abby picked up. "I'm not hungry, if that's what you mean. But I only took the pill an hour ago."

They had resumed their pretend game of Crazy 8's in Jonzy's living quarters.

"Gracie went before me," Abby added. "I think Doctor Droznin told her that her sister died."

Jonzy lowered his eyes briefly. "So Droznin gave Gracie the antibiotic?"

"Yeah, probably the blue pill. I got the pink pill."

He smiled, but there was sadness in his eyes. "I'm really happy about Touk."

Abby bit her lip and nodded. "It's the best news ever."

Jonzy gave a little snort. "I can't believe Lieutenant Dawson just sat there while Doctor Droznin infected you with AHA-B."

Abby shook her head. "It's strange, but I don't think he knew what I was taking."

Jonzy picked up a card. "He's a company leader. He has to know. If Admiral Samuels told the lieutenant to jump off a bridge, what do you think he'd do?"

"I'm not sure anymore."

"He'd jump," Jonzy said. "Trust me."

Abby glanced at the door to make sure nobody was snooping outside. Lowering her voice to a whisper, she traced the outline of the bridge that connected Medical Clinic 17 to the hospital. "There are two windows, here and here. If we go out the hospital window, we can crawl across the top and smash the window in the clinic." She winked at him. "Are you afraid of heights?" Abby had found that sometimes joking around helped a person with their fear.

Jonzy stared at her, saying nothing. Apparently, he wasn't ready to joke about his fear of water.

He finally put down a card and picked one up. "That looks like a good way to get into the clinic. We have to be careful using the two-way radios. If we get separated, keep the messages short. Assume that someone will hear us. The best time to communicate is midnight, that's when the adults are doing their own communications, so we need code names. I'll be Lemon."

Abby grinned. "Lemon?"

"That was my grandfather's name."

"You mean his nickname."

"Nope, he showed me his birth certificate. Lemon Billings. What's your code name?"

Abby shrugged.

"I got one for you." Jonzy winked. "Bossy."

"Bossy? Well, okay. But you'll never have to call me that."

"Because?"

"We'll never get separated!"

⌐ ⌐ ⌐

Close to midnight, Abby entered the stairwell, ready to go shopping in the Big Apple. She found Jonzy waiting for her. They each carried packs with supplies they would need for the nighttime excursion. They had both memorized the stores they planned to visit from the Yellow Pages.

"Hungry yet?" he asked.

"Let's go," Abby whispered, realizing the gnawing sensation she felt in her stomach was more than a simple craving for a midnight snack.

They descended the stairs and moved through the dark lobby to the front door. Peering both ways, they saw it was all clear and stepped outside.

They moved east on Lexington Avenue, nearly hugging the buildings and storefronts to stay out of the pale moonlight. Even though the shift change had occurred an hour ago, Abby remained wary. She felt vulnerable on every street and intersection they crossed. She imagined it was how a prairie dog felt running from hole to hole while hawks circled overhead.

"Is your heart beating as fast as mine?" Jonzy asked after reaching the other side of Tenth Street.

Abby pressed her palm against his chest and felt a steady hum of beats. "It's a tie."

They arrived at their first destination without incident. The Triple A office seemed to be one of the few places in New York City that survivors had not bothered to raid. Travel planning services, Abby thought with a wry grin, were not of much use since the night of the purple moon.

She held the pillowcase against the glass door as Jonzy took aim with a rock. Later on, they hoped to get a hammer, but for now, the fist-size rock from Central Park Farm was all they had. When he adjusted his glasses, she prayed he'd be accurate. He reared back and swung his hand forward. Abby closed her eyes and heard the glass shatter in muted tingles. It amazed her that such a thin piece of cloth could muffle the sound so well. She trained the flashlight on the breech, and Jonzy carefully reached through the opening he'd created to unlock the door.

She scanned the office with her flashlight. Purple dust sparkled on the floor just inside the doorjamb. A family with two parents and two kids, sitting in a car with the Grand Canyon behind them, smiled down from a large poster on the wall. 'The Best Way to See America', the caption read.

With the image of the family firmly emblazoned in her mind, Abby took Jonzy by the hand and led him to a rack of maps. They grabbed a bunch and settled behind the counter. She cupped her hand over the flashlight and turned it on. Just enough light squeaked between her fingers for them to appraise their haul.

Jonzy found a street map of Brooklyn, and, from an atlas, Abby tore out maps of Maine, Massachusetts, New Hampshire, Connecticut, and New York.

Their next stop, Macy's, was a gold mine. The large department store was more typical of a post-comet store. Hundreds of survivors, if not thousands, had at one time camped on every floor. Some sections, like Bedding, had been totally trashed. Other areas looked as if they could open for business tomorrow. Abby found a red wig on a display, which she thought would go a long way toward improving the authenticity of her bed dummy. After smashing the jewelry case with the rock, she filled her pockets with pearls and gems for trading.

Jonzy found a hammer and crowbar in the tool department and retired the rock.

Not surprisingly, the kitchen section had no knives, pots, or pans, but plenty of blenders, food processors, toasters and electric coffee grinders. On a counter filled with plastics, they were happy to find two containers which would keep the walkie-talkies and pills dry.

The department kept on producing. Abby picked up a plastic cutting board with a hole cut in one end.

"What's that for?" Jonzy asked.

Abby wasn't ready to tell him it would make a good paddle for the rafts they were going to construct. She shrugged as she slipped two cutting boards into her backpack.

He made a strange face, but asked no further questions.

Leaving Macy's, they headed to a stop that Abby had put on the itinerary, a supermarket on Madison Ave. She hoped to find bottles of bleach or vinegar. Emptied of their contents, the plastic jugs would make good rafts. At the supermarket's address, though, they found a pile of rubble and ash. The building had burned down long ago.

She spotted an art supply store across the street and suggested they check it out. The windows were broken, but there were no signs of kids ever living in the store. With graffiti a popular art form following the near extermination of the adult population, spray paint was a hot item, evidenced by the empty Krylon and Montana racks. Abby flicked on the penlight as she strolled down an aisle. A bolt of joy rocketed through her at the sight of plastic gallon jugs of acrylic paint lining two shelves.

"Jonzy, we can make two rafts with plastic jugs. Help me pour out the paint."

"Forget it."

"The East River has no boats for ten minutes at the shift change." She removed a cutting board from her pack and demonstrated how it could be used as a paddle.

"You're crazy." Jonzy watched as she poured paint from five or six jugs, and then, in an encouraging sign, he pitched in to help. Soon they had sixteen empty jugs which Abby placed in a garbage bag from the Biltmore's cleaning supply room.

"We need a way to lash them together," she said.

Jonzy shined the light on a spool of twine. "I guess we could use that."

"Great idea," Abby exclaimed, wanting to make him feel part of the plan.

Jonzy pulled off what he thought was enough twine to lash the jugs together to make two rafts.

Abby suggested they take the jugs to the vicinity of Pier 15, tie them together, and then hide the rafts. He agreed reluctantly.

As they were heading toward the river, Jonzy pinched her sleeve to stop her. "I know a place where we can get inflatable life vests. It's in the Yellow Zone."

They had to return to the Biltmore before three o'clock, which was when ensigns visited each company leader to drop off the daily memorandum. But so much of their plan depended on Jonzy's ability to overcome his fear, the added risk of getting the life vests was worth it, she thought.

One hour later, after walking seven blocks out of their way, they stepped into Herb's Fur and Fin. By then, Abby knew that Lieutenant Dawson had brought Jonzy here before. The moment Jonzy told her that, she thought back to the way the lieutenant had responded to Doctor Droznin in her office. She really believed he hadn't known that she was being infected with the Pig.

Jonzy removed two life vests from a rack on the wall. "Yank this string, the vest inflates." The way his eyes lit up, Abby realized the detour had been worth it.

With Jonzy carrying the garbage bag with the paint jugs over his shoulder, and Abby carrying both their packs, they headed toward the river. The Brooklyn Bridge had just come into sight when Abby heard a motor. She turned and spotted headlights rounding the corner two blocks back. They had to hide fast.

Jonzy faced her with wide eyes, frozen in terror. In one quick motion, she planted her shoulder into his chest, wrapped her arms around his waist, and drove him forward with her legs. She threw him on the pavement and landed on top. He grunted on impact. She smothered him until the truck sped by.

"Sorry," she said, helping Jonzy to his feet. She hoped he wouldn't freeze like that during their escape attempt.

They resumed walking and she led them along the river through weeds that came up to their chests. She went to the water's edge and dipped her fingers in. "Feel how warm it is."

Jonzy kept walking, "I believe you."

He pointed out Pier 15 ahead of them. Abby eyed the East River, thinking it would be very difficult to paddle a raft made of paint jugs to the Brooklyn shore from the pier in ten minutes, but unless they came up with a better plan, they would have to try.

Jonzy led her to a trash dumpster across the street, half filled with construction materials—broken boards, pails, twisted metal, and a ratty, torn plastic tarp. Given the lateness of the hour, they agreed that he or she or both of them would return the next night to lash the bottles together. He tossed the bag of bottles inside and covered it with the tarp.

Thirty minutes later, at 3:20, Abby pulled the covers up to her chin in her bed. Reveille was three hours away, but the way her heart was racing, she thought sleep was as improbable as escaping Colony East.

# ONE DAY LEFT

Perched forty stories above Colony East, Abby shook her head to clear away the image of hot pancakes dripping with butter. She resisted the urge to raid their food supplies.

The two packs, hidden under the table next to the radio equipment, contained rice and potatoes, as well as their tools, maps, flashlights, inflatable life vests, plastic tubs, and two-way radios.

Jonzy had gone to Pier 15 to lash together the empty paint jugs to make two rafts. He'd conceal the rafts in the dumpster. Abby was proud of him for facing his fear head on.

She concentrated on the task-at-hand. Peering through binoculars, she counted the number of patrol boats in the East River closest to the Brooklyn Bridge. She noted the time, 10 PM, and recorded her observation in the notebook. She counted boats in other sections of the river and wrote down those numbers too.

The data in the notebook told a troubling story. The number of patrol boats had increased. She knew her next observation would determine if they should stick with their plan to cross the East River. How many minutes would the river be free of boats during the eleven o'clock shift change?

Abby panicked briefly at the thought of a delay. It might take a week or longer to scout out a new section of the East River or even the Hudson. They'd have to move supplies and make repeated observations. She couldn't wait that long. It shocked her how the Pig had progressed in her over the past twenty-four hours.

With an hour to wait for the shift change, Abby paced around the perimeter of the restaurant. The airport was quiet, all planes grounded until Hurricane David passed. The light flashed atop the Empire State Building, and heavy cloud cover concealed the moon and stars.

She quietly tuned in The Port. *Purple Rain* was playing. The song ended and DJ Silver came on. "This next song is a shout out to Abby and Toucan. You heard me right. Toucan. That, survivors, is a little girl, not a bird with a big beak. Jordan says all is good. He's getting better every day. I've seen him with my own eyes." 'Here Comes the Sun' started.

Abby breathed so hard and fast she worried she might pass out. Had she imagined that? Some victims of the Pig experienced hallucinations. But that was during the latter stages of the illness. No, she had heard DJ Silver say her name for real. Jordan was sending her a message. He was near The Port. In Mystic, Connecticut. Maybe *Lucky Me* had sailed into a nearby harbor. He, of course, assumed that she and Touk were still on the island. Boy, did they have some catching up to do.

Abby dug the maps out of her backpack and traced a route to Mystic. It was on the way to Castine Island. It made sense to stop there.

She floated back to the window, the hunger pangs getting more painful, but she didn't care. For the first time, she felt hopeful. Toby was hanging out near the fish market, and Jordan was in Mystic. The packs and rafts were ready.

At eleven o'clock, Abby watched as the patrol boats formed a line and headed for the ferry terminal. Eight minutes later, they were patrolling the section of the river that she and Jonzy planned to cross. With adrenaline as her fuel, Abby figured she could cross the river in five minutes if need be. She was ready to go.

# LANDFALL

Lieutenant Dawson stared at the window ledge. M Y S T I C. Someone had traced Mystic in the dust on the ledge. The window overlooked the East River and his former home was beyond that. Someone, he figured, had chosen this time and place, this ledge, for a reason.

He pondered the possibilities as his heart thundered in his chest. Was someone sending him a message? If so, what was it? Why Mystic? Why now?

Only a handful of people knew about his connection to the city. Sandy was in Atlanta. Admiral Samuels? He almost laughed, but the seriousness of the matter doused the faint humor of the old man hoofing up forty flights to write Mystic in the dust.

The CDC knew that he and his family had resided in Mystic. They knew everything about every sailor and officer in the colonies. In fact, the scientists probably knew more about him than he ever imagined. But it was inconceivable that any white coat hush puppy was the mystery scribbler.

Dawson jolted. He had mentioned the town of Mystic to Cadet Leigh, and she might have told others. He exhaled, shaking his head. He refused to accept that Abigail Leigh, or any Biltmore cadet, had come up here. He bristled at the idea of his cadets sneaking around under his nose, but he could think of no better explanation.

Figuring out the 'who' was only half his problem; learning the 'why' was what intrigued and troubled him more.

He eyed the horizon. A vein of dark grey clouds ran between the ocean and pale blue sky above. The leading edge of Hurricane David would block the sun for all of today and much of tomorrow. The storm was at their doorstep. Soon the winds, laden with deadly germs, would lash Colony East, and Mystic, and vast parts beyond.

~ ~ ~

Abby had never experienced such hunger. Her mouth watered at the slightest thought of food. She had faced starvation before, but her mind had allowed her to turn off its cravings. She'd read later that her response was a design of nature, a trait carried forward from the early days of man, when survival required clear and focused thinking during times of famine. Now, she could think of nothing but food. Foamy saliva dribbled down her chin from her endless fantasies of cake, burgers, hot buttery popcorn...

In her dark living quarters, she pulled the covers up to her chin and tried to pay attention to Lieutenant Dawson delivering his final messages of the day over the intercom. "Expect the storm to worsen. If any windows blow out, report them to me immediately. You are the seeds of a new society. Tomorrow..."

The lieutenant's voice suddenly cut out as the hallway lights went out. Abby flipped her lamp switch. Nothing. She realized the power must be out in the building. As she crept to the window, gusts bowed the glass in and out and raindrops struck like a round of buckshot. Peering out, she saw that the streetlights and traffic lights on Lexington Ave were out. She tingled with excitement. If the power outage extended throughout the colony, it would give them an incredible opportunity. She and Jonzy must leave— tonight. Doctor Droznin had the first shipment of antibiotic pills in her office. There weren't enough pills for everyone Abby knew, but probably enough for the people she loved. She had to believe that.

She jumped back in bed and waited. After six weeks in Colony East, she could predict what the lieutenant would do next. He'd pay a visit to every cadet to explain what happened.

Five minutes later, right on schedule, she heard his voice and saw the dancing flashlight beam as he worked his way down the wing.

He stuck his head in her room. "Batten down the hatches. We've lost power."

"Just Biltmore Company, sir?"

"Everyone."

Not wanting her curiosity to spark any suspicion, she asked meekly, "Are we safe, sir?"

"A little wind and water never hurt anyone."

Wind, water, and billions of germs, she thought.

"Cadet Leigh?"

"Yes, sir."

The lieutenant paused for a long moment, and she began to wonder if something was wrong. Had he sensed something in her voice? "Good night," he said finally, and moved on.

When she was certain he was on the second floor, she got dressed and arranged the wig on the pillow. "Sleep tight," she whispered to the bed dummy. "When you wake up, I'll be outta here." Then Abby laced up her sneakers and went to Jonzy's room.

"Jonzy, let's go now."

"No way!"

She led him into the bathroom, shut the door, and they debated in low voices, his filled with fear, hers with desperate hope.

Jonzy worried about the dangers of the hurricane. Flooding. Flying debris. The East River. "Abby, we'll drown."

She understood his concerns. Hurricane David was dropping a trillion tons of water on them, and Jonzy had a fear of even wading up to his ankles. She hoped that her logic would help him gain an upper hand on his fear.

"How many boats will be in the river? Zero. Will the security cameras be working at Medical Clinic 17? No. Will anyone hear us breaking glass? No. Have all the pills arrived? No. But Doctor Droznin has enough in her office for you, me, Jordan and, Toby, with some left over. The storm is a gift, Jonzy. Colony East has no power. Come on, we have inflatable life jackets and rafts. We'll bob like corks."

"Abby, I can't."

She found his hand in the dark and held it. "Jonzy, I need to take a pill. The dose of Pig that Doctor Droznin gave me must have been very strong."

She held her breath in the silence. She felt that her ears were about to pop from the low pressure of the storm. She was moving her finger to the flashlight button when he squeezed her hand.

"OK, let's do it, Cadet," he said.

When she snapped on the penlight, she saw craziness in his eyes. It was the type of daring look, Abby thought, well suited to someone who couldn't swim... who was about to jump into a river during a hurricane.

～ ～ ～

Lieutenant Dawson lit a candle and opened *Twenty Thousand Leagues Under the Sea*. He stared at the page, unable to concentrate on the words.

In the flickering light, his eyes fell to the photo of his daughter beside him. He blew out the candle, but Sarah's image still burned brightly in his mind. Even if she were dead, there were thousands more her age being exposed to AHA-B. And if she were alive, she would be one of the millions of children the CDC seemed willing to ignore.

Dawson's throat suddenly thickened and he felt his face flushing. He needed fresh air. He needed to shout into the wind, even knowing what seeds the wind sowed.

～ ～ ～

Abby held on to Jonzy's hand and had to tug repeatedly to move him down the stairs from the top floor where they had gone to get their packs. The burning madness in his eyes had extinguished, replaced with the wide-eyed look of a lamb being led to slaughter.

While Jonzy's mind seemed willing to attempt an escape during Hurricane David, his body resisted. Abby hoped that once they stepped outside, and he experienced the full force of the storm, it would energize him, though part of her worried he might seize up completely.

Just before they entered the lobby, he stopped and whispered in her ear.

"Abby, let's go through The Red Zone. With the power out, we can cut the electric fence. We'll get wire cutters on the way."

She paused, thinking it was late to make such a drastic change to their plans. But hadn't she just done that? True, the power failure presented an incredible opportunity, yet she had hatched the idea to leave during the storm instantly.

"Let's do it, Cadet," she said, feeding Jonzy back his line with a half-smile.

Jonzy almost yanked her off her feet, leading her across the lobby to the door. Like a dog musher, all she had to do was hang on, and Jonzy would drag her all the way to Mystic.

He reached for the door handle and pulled. The clinking sound triggered a shudder of fear in her chest. It was locked!

The shudder passed, as Abby reminded herself they had come prepared. Neither of them had thought the Biltmore's door would be locked, but Abby had been expecting the unexpected.

As she was lifting the flap of her pack to get the hammer and pillowcase, a pale wedge of light reflected on the door. She quickly turned. Someone with a flashlight was approaching the lobby from the first-floor hallway.

They raced to hide behind the lobby counter. Footsteps clicked on the tile floor. Keys jangled. They heard the front door open. The hurricane roared inside the lobby. Then the door closed.

Abby peered above the counter. Lieutenant Dawson stood outside the door. He seemed to be shouting to someone, but she couldn't see who it was. Who else would be outside now? "The lieutenant," she whispered to Jonzy.

"Should we go back upstairs?"

"No. Wait." Abby patted the area beneath the counter with her hands and felt shelving of smooth, polished wood. Her arm sank to her elbow. It was deep enough, wide enough, and high enough for them to squeeze into, a perfect hiding place. She grabbed Jonzy's hand and guided it to the shelving closest to him. "Crawl in."

"You first."

Face up, Abby shimmied her way onto the shelf. Jonzy pushed her knees down, getting her legs to fit. Then he shoved a pack between her belly and the top of her shelf, which compressed her diaphragm and forced her to take half breaths.

Just then, the door opened. Jonzy froze in response. The blast of the hurricane spiked and muted. The lieutenant's footsteps grew louder. It sounded like he was approaching them.

Wedged like a sardine, Abby felt that her pounding heart might blow out her eardrums. She took baby breaths. Jonzy remained perfectly silent and still. When the flashlight beam reflected off the ceiling, she saw that he had plastered himself against the shelf, a pack beside him, her pack.

Keys clicked on the counter. The lieutenant had placed his keys six inches above her nose. Chills rippled down Abby's spine and into her legs before they bounced back to the crimp of her knees. Jonzy was exposed. All the lieutenant had to do was look down to see him. Abby heard him put down the flashlight. She heard keys jangle. She could tell he was inserting a key into a lock, a padlock. The padlock clicked open. She couldn't believe that he had chosen this moment to look inside the suggestion box. *All ideas are good ideas.* The words jumbled in her mind. She heard the lid creak open and close. Paper rustled. The flashlight beam shifted on the wall, splashing light that threatened to reveal Jonzy. The lieutenant chuckled to himself, likely reading a note. She thought he might be leaning against the counter, and worried that he might feel the vibration of her thundering heart through the wood.

After a long moment of silence, she watched the beam move to the floor behind the counter, like a bloodhound sniffing for a scent, then it zeroed in on the pack.

"What in the…?" the lieutenant exclaimed.

Jonzy jumped up. "Sir, it's me."

"Billings," the lieutenant shouted. "What are you doing? What's in that pack?"

Jonzy picked up the pack and quickly stepped away from where Abby was hiding. "I can explain, sir."

"You better have an explanation, mister. What's in the pack?"

"I have to use the bathroom."

"Give it to me."

"Sir, I have to go really badly."

"Let's go," he grumbled.

When she could no longer hear their feet clicking on the tile, Abby counted to ten then squiggled out of the shelf. She grabbed Jonzy's pack and hurried to the door, fumbling for the hammer in the pack. Her blood turned cold as her fingers brushed the unmistakable shape of the gun. She withdrew her hand in revulsion, gritted her teeth, and continued her search. Finding the hammer, she gripped the handle with both hands, and swung it against the glass in the door. The steel head just bounced back. So Abby gripped it harder, placed her feet wider, clenched her jaw, then swung at it again and again, chopping, chopping, chopping away until she finally made a hole big enough to slip through.

As she crawled into the jaws of Hurricane David, a single thought dominated her mind—cake with vanilla frosting.

～ ～ ～

From the cadet's pack, Lieutenant Dawson removed water bottles, a screwdriver, a wrench, rope. An inflatable life vest? He rubbed his jaw, wondering where the boy got these things. He doubted Billings had found them in the Biltmore, which meant he had left the building without authorization.

"Billings," he barked. "Hurry up." The cadet was still in the bathroom.

He reached deeper into the pack and produced two maps. One was a street map of Brooklyn, the second map was of Connecticut. Incredibly, he thought the cadet was attempting to leave the colony. In a hurricane! What was Billings thinking?

A route traced on one of the maps caught his attention. He directed the flashlight beam onto the map of Connecticut and immediately felt as if someone had kicked him in the gut.

The line in pencil ran to Mystic.

～ ～ ～

Abby used her hand to shield her eyes from the blast of wind and rain. She squinted to make out the strange, dark shape next to the sidewalk on

300

Lexington Avenue. She inched closer until she realized it was a quarantine van crushed by a massive hunk of concrete and bricks. The vehicle looked as if a giant had flattened it with a sledgehammer. She suspected the van had no occupants, or else, rescue crews would have been trying to do whatever they could, which would not have been much.

She jumped when another heavy chunk suddenly exploded in the street ten feet away. A building was being torn apart piecemeal by the roaring winds fifty stories above her. She hurried on her way, leaning hard to the right just to go in a straight line.

The stinging rain and wind diminished significantly once she crossed Lexington Ave and reached Broadway, where the buildings acted as a buffer.

The streets and sidewalks were empty of foot patrols and vehicles as far as she could tell. Once the streetlights flickered, but they never fully lit.

Abby moved to a spot across the street from the hospital and kept watch. After a minute, she raced across the street and entered the dark building.

She cupped her hand around the head of the flashlight and turned it on. The light shone like red lines between her fingers. She climbed the steps to the second floor, using this red lantern to find her way up.

Soon, she was standing before the window that looked out on Medical Clinic 17. She opened the window easily and looked down. The annex roof was three feet below. Abby needed Jonzy now, but she tried to put him out of her mind.

She climbed out of the window and onto the roof. Crawling toward the clinic, she dipped her right shoulder into the crosscurrent of howling wind. If she fell from here, she'd break a leg, or worse. When a sudden gust pried her up, she dropped to her stomach and pulled herself forward with her elbows.

She reached the end. Made of thick plate glass, the clinic's window was taller than she was and wider than her outstretched arms. She removed her backpack—Jonzy's pack—and slipped her leg through the shoulder strap to keep the pack from blowing away. She retrieved the hammer, thinking the roar of the storm was a blessing. It would drown out any noise she was about to make.

On her knees, she gauged the best spot to strike the glass, the window's center. The rain blurred her vision, but she had a large target that would be impossible to miss. She reared back and swung for the bull's-eye as hard as she could.

She flicked on the penlight and saw fissures had spread out in all directions, right to the window's edges. It reminded her of a spiderweb of frost. She turned off the light, gripped the hammer tightly, and reared back again.

This time the hammer won and the window broke apart in large and small pieces. Shards dropped like the blades of a guillotine and lethal slivers whistled away in the wind.

Being careful to avoid the sharp edges of glass stuck in the frame, Abby placed the pillowcase over the window ledge and lowered herself inside the clinic.

She hoped she'd find the antibiotic pills on the second floor, one floor below her, but what really dominated her mind was the possibility she'd discover a cafeteria on her way to Doctor Droznin's office.

~ ~ ~

Lieutenant Dawson wondered why Billings was taking so long. He drew in a sudden breath. Prior to now, Billings had obviously left the Biltmore to acquire the contents of his pack. The cadet had also snuck up to the fortieth floor and traced Mystic in the dust. He wouldn't put it past Billings to try to weasel out from under his nose. Had he duped him and climbed out the bathroom window?

In a spike of panic, Dawson ripped the door open and charged into the bathroom.

Startled, Cadet Billings jumped back from the sink where he was washing his hands.

Dawson stomped past him and checked the window lock. It was engaged.

"Let's go," he barked and instructed the boy to sit on a couch in the central area of his living quarters. Dawson paced, feeling a vice of tension gripping his neck and jaw. "Were you trying to leave the colony?"

"Yes, sir."

Dawson stopped, struck dumb by the cadet's candor. "Why, Billings? Why leave Colony East?"

"Sir, you know why."

"Enlighten me, Cadet."

"The hurricane is bringing billions of germs from the tropics. The scientists developed an antibiotic, but they're only passing it out to the three colonies. The survivors should know about the new epidemic. They should know what you and the scientists are doing."

*Him?* Dawson dragged a chair across the room and sat before Billings. His ears were ringing and he felt numb all over. He briefly wondered if he could produce sounds with his vocal chords. "Where did you learn this fairy tale?"

"I listen to conversations between Colony East and Atlanta. Doctor Perkins and Doctor Droznin talk over the radio all the time."

"Radio!" Dawson challenged.

"Six months ago, I got a two-way radio from a police cruiser in the Yellow Zone. I set it up in the restaurant on the top floor."

Dawson's head spun. He knew what the cadet had just admitted would result in an immediate expulsion. But what Billings had reported troubled Dawson just as much as the cadet's bold infractions. Where did the facts end and the fiction begin? He swallowed hard at the possibility everything Jonzy had said was the truth.

Suddenly, Dawson had to know something. He looked the boy in the eye, "Jonzy, why did you trace Mystic in the dust on the top floor?"

His eyes widened, informing Dawson he knew nothing about it.

Billings shook his head. "Mystic? I don't know anything about Mystic, Connecticut."

Dawson knew he was lying. "A mystic is someone who sees the future. Who said anything about Connecticut?" The boy squirmed. "Is anyone else involved in your harebrained scheme?"

"No sir. That's the truth."

With a sinking feeling that he knew exactly who else was involved, Dawson shot to his feet. "Stay put," he ordered and raced toward the third floor.

~ ~ ~

As Abby moved away from the smashed window, all she could hear was the soft pattering of water dripping on the floor from her wet clothing.

She slipped the flashlight from her pocket and turned it on just long enough to see the stairway exit sign. Dragging her fingertips along the wall for guidance, she moved down the hall to the stairway door, entered, and groped for the railing. In the dark, she climbed down the steps to the landing and then stopped. Buried deep in the lab, surrounded by brick and glass and steel, she could no longer hear the raging hurricane.

Feeling that her insides were swirling as fast as the winds, she crept down the next flight of stairs and stepped into the second-floor hallway. She briefly flicked on the flashlight. Room 202 was opposite the stairway door. Soon she was standing before Doctor Droznin's office, Room 214, halfway down the hall.

Abby's temples throbbed as she gripped the knob. She paused to say a prayer. The knob turned. She let out a huge sigh of relief and thanked her God, and all the other gods, just in case, and even gave a quick nod of appreciation to the random energy of the universe that spun up hurricanes.

Abby stepped into Doctor Droznin's office and closed the door behind her. She flicked on her flashlight and went straight to the drawer where Doctor Droznin had kept the bottle of tiny blue pills. The drawer was empty. Then she opened the drawer below it. In it was a bottle containing three pink pills, the type of pill she had taken, which had infected her with AHA-B.

Abby rifled through every drawer in the desk, but didn't find any blue pills. She began a systematic search of the office. She ripped open filing cabinet drawers and looked under stacks of paper. She frisked the pockets of a lab coat hanging on the hook. In a moment of mad desperation, Abby shook the nesting dolls, thinking Doctor Droznin might have hidden the pills there.

She checked her watch. It was midnight, and the building had five floors, perhaps two-hundred offices and labs. Abby decided she would search for the pills until two a.m. If she didn't find anything by that hour, she would have to head for the East River. Crossing the river in darkness

304

offered her only chance of success. Abby knew the personal risk she would take to leave empty-handed, but staying inside the colony posed a bigger risk. Outside the fence, she might die from the Pig or else get beaten up, or worse, trying to satisfy her insatiable appetite. Despite all that, something bigger was at stake. The survivors had to know what the adults were doing. Unsure of Toby's condition, she might be the only voice who could tell them. She had to make it across the river and spread the word for as long as her strength held up.

The door opened and a powerful flashlight beam blinded Abby. Her adrenaline surging to every extremity, she was ready to kick, claw and scratch her way past the guard.

"I followed the drips of water." The accent removed all doubt of the identity of the individual shining the light.

Abby shielded her eyes. "Doctor Droznin, please give me antibiotic pills. I only want three."

"Three? Everyone in Colony East is receiving a pill. Or are you thinking of leaving the colony? You swam here. I suppose you think you can swim back to Brooklyn."

"Just three pills. Please."

"Abigail, I won't give you a single pill. You are part of my control group. But you should know that statistics are in your favor. The mortality rate of AHA-B is thirty-four percent. Inside Colony East, there's a sixty-six percent chance you will make a full recovery. Outside is a different story. Other variables would come into play."

Doctor Droznin lowered the blinding light, a sign that Abby considered a positive gesture.

"I encourage you to stay," the scientist continued. "What Doctor Perkins decides to do with you after he learns you broke into the clinic, of course, is unpredictable, but I think he might be impressed. He admires intelligence and courage. You and Lizette would make a significant contribution to the gene pool. Doctor Perkins might consider you an important seed of the new society."

Abby's eyes darted to the two-way radio Doctor Droznin held in her hand, and she started inching toward the doctor's desk, where she had placed her pack. "What happens to the kids outside the colonies who get AHA-B?"

"That's a variable we understand quite well from data we've collected near the equator. There will be widespread looting of food supplies. We project a population decrease of ninety to ninety five percent."

Despite the bile that Abby tasted in the back of her throat, she felt her stomach growl in hunger. She moved closer and closer to her pack. Then she rested her hand on the desk, the backpack now within reach. "How do you feel about that Doctor Droznin? That ninety percent of the kids outside the colonies will die."

Droznin paused a long moment. Abby couldn't see her face in the shadows, just the outline of her body. "I feel terrible," the scientist said. "I have not slept well since we received the first infrared imagery from the equator."

Abby heard a softer, more caring tone in her voice and she began to wonder if Doctor Droznin might give her a pill. She decided she would take three or none. It would be the negotiation of her life.

Doctor Droznin scraped Abby's face with the harsh beam of light and illuminated the nesting dolls. "The beauty of scientific inquiry is that it strips away emotion. Our population modeling shows that a hundred scientists cannot possibly sustain millions of survivors while at the same time advancing society. I may sleep poorly, but I have the conviction we are following the right model."

Abby swallowed hard and slipped her hand inside the pack. Her fingertips touched the plastic container and worked their way deeper. "Doctor Droznin, who are you to say what society should look like? Millions of kids working together can do a lot."

Doctor Droznin chuckled. "I hope your natural immunity protects you, Abigail. I like you." The suddenness with which she brought the radio to her lips stunned Abby. "Headquarters, this is Droznin."

Abby gripped the cold metal handle and pulled the gun from the pack. She pointed the barrel at Doctor Droznin. Her mind felt like a pond with minnows darting this way and that. She had a thousand thoughts, but she couldn't focus on a single one.

A man's voice crackled through the two-way radio. "Go ahead doctor."

Doctor Droznin blinded her with the flashlight beam.

Shielding her eyes, Abby took a step toward her. "Drop the radio."

"Doctor, go ahead, over," the man said.

"You want a pill?" Droznin asked.

Abby tightened her grip on the gun's handle and rested her index finger on the trigger. Sweat trickled down her brow and stung her eyes. "I want three pills."

"Doctor Perkins has the pills in his office which is locked. Honestly, Abigail, I wouldn't give you half a pill even if I had the key. I have dedicated my life to science."

"Doctor Droznin!" The radio dispatcher spoke with a new urgency. "Please report in, over."

Abby stared in disbelief as Doctor Droznin brought the radio to her lips and opened her mouth. With conviction and a steady hand, Abby aimed and pulled the trigger.

~ ~ ~

A projectile struck the window as Lieutenant Dawson peered into Cadet Leigh's room. All seemed to be in order. He wondered if he should disturb her sleep to ask if she had written Mystic in the dust. He tiptoed over to her bed to see if she might be awake.

"Code Red. Gunshot heard at Medical Clinic 17."

Dawson jumped at the dispatcher's voice over his two-way radio. Code Red meant he must do bed checks for every cadet and report back to HQ ASAP. "Code Red. Gunshot heard at Medical Clinic 17." Dawson lowered the volume.

All of a sudden, he realized it was a wig on Abby's pillow. He picked it up and flung it across the room.

~ ~ ~

Abby slipped out of the front door of Medical Clinic 17 and heard the 'be bo be bo be bo' of an approaching Q-van. The ferocity of the storm muted the siren. Feeling as if the wind might lift her off her feet and send her flying down the avenue, she ducked behind the bushes along the front of the building. Realizing what had just happened, she started to tremble uncontrollably.

Doctor Droznin was in a lot of pain, but she would live. Abby had aimed the gun low, and the bullet had ricocheted off the floor and struck her knee. The scientist fell to the ground, shouting in Russian and bleeding from the wound. Abby responded immediately, relying on her experience as a medical first responder. She told herself the situation with Doctor Droznin was no different from caring for Derek, who had hooked himself in the ear with a triple-pronged bluefish popper. She bottled up her panic and went to work, making a tourniquet from the sleeves of a lab coat and the crowbar she'd packed. She twisted the crowbar until the bleeding stopped. She told Doctor Droznin to hold the crowbar and apply pressure. By that time, the scientist had quieted and had a strange look in her eyes, maybe thinking she had failed to account for the variable of getting shot. Abby had fled when the radio dispatcher said he was sending a team over.

The siren grew louder and soon a Q-van with red flashing lights pulled up in front of Medical Clinic 17. Sailors, carrying flashlights, piled out of the van and charged toward the door. Abby lay flat, spread out on the ground, pressing her face into a bed of wet pine mulch as boot heels thundered within feet of her head.

Because of the shooting, Abby knew she was public enemy number one at Colony East. Her only allies were Jonzy, who couldn't do much for her, and Hurricane David. The driving rain and howling winds would make it easier for her to move without detection.

Crouching, she kept her eye on the van, thinking someone might be behind the wheel. When she realized the van was empty she ran across the street and started for the East River, ducking from alley to alley. Enough moonlight leeched through the shifting shades of gray clouds to let her distinguish large objects through the blur of water in the air.

Every few minutes a Q-van drove by, the driver sweeping a spotlight on both sides of the street. She had yet to see anyone on foot, but she imagined adults were fanning out from the clinic.

She waited in an alley for an approaching Q-van to drive by. Raindrops flew horizontally, and torrents of water rushed down both gutters of South

Street. When the van had passed, she scurried to the sidewalk and thought she saw an entrance to the subway on the corner, a block away. The wind shear nearly knocked her off her feet as she raced into the street.

She gasped at the incredible sight. It was a subway entrance, though it bore more resemblance to a sinkhole draining a lake. A waterfall cascaded down the wide steps. A thought flashed across her mind. The only good thing about Jonzy's capture was that he had luckily avoided this deluge.

~ ~ ~

Lieutenant Dawson got right in Billing's face. "You lied to me!" Shaking with rage, he put his finger an inch from the cadet's nose. "Someone fired a gun at Medical Clinic 17. Mister, you better pray that has nothing to do with Abigail Leigh."

Dawson stepped back to breathe and slow his racing heart. Tears streamed down Billings' cheeks as he cowered in a corner of the couch.

"Okay," Dawson said. "This is your last chance. Tell me what's going on."

Billings looked up, and Dawson drew in his breath at the sudden change. Anger, not fear, filled the boy's eyes. The cadet sat up straight and pulled his shoulders back.

"I'll tell you what's going on. They infected Abby with AHA-B. But you probably already know that. Because her sister survived, they want to see if the antibiotic saved Lizette or if it was her immunity.

"You're the one who lied, Lieutenant. You feel guilty that you couldn't help fifty thousand kids. Now you're killing millions. But I'm glad you're following orders."

The words hit Dawson like a baseball bat. "Jonzy, where is she going? Where?"

Jonzy folded his arms and glared. The boy was now the only true leader in the room.

Dawson grabbed the map he'd found in the backpack and saw Pier 15 circled. With no time to spare, he raced out the door.

~ ~ ~

Abby descended into the darkness of the New York City transit system, trying to get her bearings. Her ability to pick the right subway tunnel— heading in the direction of Pier 15 could mean the difference between escape and capture.

She reached the first landing, flicked on her flashlight, and saw that she could go left or right. She went right, and from there, straight to an escalator. The pitch was steeper than the first set of steps and the opening narrower. A torrent of water funneled between the sides of the escalator, so she gripped the rail to maintain her footing and headed down.

At the bottom, Abby gulped when she discovered the tunnel had flooded. The entire transit system must be filling up with water. A black, oily river rose to within a foot of the platform. She watched a traffic cone float by at a good clip. At the same time, it was strangely peaceful. The only sound was the rush of water.

The momentary sense of calm evaporated as Abby wondered if she was trapped. She wasn't about to swim in that black, oily mess, and climbing up the escalator, against the raging rapids, seemed a daunting task. Then she spotted a narrow metal platform that ran through the tunnel at the same height as the top of the trains. She'd guessed the platform had been built for maintenance crews. As long as the water didn't rise much higher, the platform offered a way from station to station.

Training the flashlight beam, she approached the mouth of the tunnel. The walkway was two feet wide, and appeared easy to climb up to, and easy to navigate in the dark. There was even a railing.

Would it be difficult to climb out at the next station? Probably, but she'd worry about that when she got there. For now, the walkway offered the fastest way to put distance between her and Medical Clinic 17.

Turning the flashlight off to save batteries, she took baby steps at first. Then feeling more confident, she picked up the pace.

After several minutes, Abby clicked the light on and froze. Pairs of pink and red eyes sparkled ahead. Rats had also sought the safety of the platform.

"Go!" The silence smothered her shout. The glowing jewels remained fixed in the dark void.

Abby realized that she was in their underworld domain, and it would take more than shouting to scare the rats away. Cursing herself for ditching the gun, she rifled through her pack and wrapped her fingers around the hammer. She banged it against the rail. The vibration traveled up her arm as a twang rippled away into the darkness.

Abby waved the light to see if the noise had frightened any of them. She shuddered. It wasn't two or three rats she had to deal with, but hundreds. They perched on the walkway for at least as far as the weak flashlight beam revealed, a constellation of sparkling rubies.

Gripping the hammer in one hand and holding the light, she approached the first rat. Its pink, whip-like tail curled on the grate. Two teeth jutted up from the lower jaw. Light-headed and numb, Abby had reached such a level of terror that she doubted she had the ability to command her muscles to move.

She swung the hammer and landed the blow an inch from the rat's snout, much closer than she intended. The rat jumped and made a splash when it hit the water. It swam into the darkness.

Forging ahead, she cleared the next two rats the same way. She feared her heart might explode because it was beating so fast and hard. She confronted rat after rat. Some she scared into jumping by banging inches from their snouts. Others she had to poke. Several scrambled up her leg. She grabbed their tails and flung them into the air. The first one had elicited a scream. She dispensed the second rat with a quick grunt. The third, four, fifth, sixth and seventh rats were simply nuisances, and she kicked, tossed, and whacked them aside without a peep.

Abby finally reached the next station. Were it not for her race against dawn, she would have crumpled into a fetal position and slept. With daylight approaching, she returned the hammer to her pack and put the flashlight into one of the watertight containers.

She battled her way up the escalator, upstream the whole way. The smell of fresh air and bellow of howling wind informed her that the storm had not abated and she was getting nearer to the street level. Through a revolving door of metal bars, she spotted what she thought was the East River. If the Brooklyn Bridge was to her left, she had further to go, if it was to her right, she'd overshot the pier.

Incredibly, the bridge was to her left, but she might as well have been a thousand miles away from Pier 15. The revolving door wouldn't budge. It was locked or rusted.

She faced two choices. She could battle the rats and return to the first station or she could battle them and try the next station, hoping it offered a way outside. This close, she decided to go for a new station.

She retraced her steps and groaned in disbelief. The walkway to the next station was on the opposite side of the tracks. The flashlight showed a ladder rising up to the platform. Between her and the ladder was a moat filled with the most disgusting water imaginable. Unidentifiable disgusting blobs floated down the rat river.

Something snapped inside of her. She was going to reach the ladder on the other side if it was the last thing she did. Abby removed the life vest from the pack, put it over her head, and yanked the string. The air bladders puffed out. She returned the flashlight to the plastic tub and cinched the pack tight on her shoulders.

Backing up to get a good start, she put her head down and charged forward. She misjudged the number of steps and tumbled into the tunnel river, choking on a mouthful of greasy, salty, putrid water.

She clawed, dog paddled and scratched her way forward, but her fingers slipped off the ladder, and the current swept her into the tunnel.

Abby tried to see the the bright side. Being carried downstream was a lot faster than inching her way along the platform.

~ ~ ~

Lieutenant Dawson sprinted down Broadway, one block east and parallel to Lexington Avenue. If Cadet Leigh was going to Pier 15, Broadway was the most direct route. He glanced left and right, thinking she might huddle in an alley to hide.

With the wind at his back, he felt like he had wings. Rain saturated the air, and he found it useful to breathe through his mouth with his lips puckered. It broke up the larger drops.

The Prospect Street intersection was two blocks ahead. Prospect led straight to the pier. As he crossed Avenue U, he saw movement out of the corner of his eye. The vehicle was on top of him in a flash, and he dived for safety. Fully outstretched, he hit the ground and slid, grunting as the friction of the pavement punished his stomach and face. The speeding armored personnel carrier missed him by inches.

He tasted blood. Dawson wiggled his jaw, figuring it was bruised but not broken. He ran his finger along his upper and lower teeth. No chips. He was most certainly bleeding somewhere other than his mouth, but it was impossible to know how badly with the rain hosing his wounds. He hopped to his feet and continued, exercising greater caution at intersections.

The sight at the corner of Landry Avenue and Prospect Street stopped him figuratively and literally. The force of the hurricane had blown apart a tall building.

He scrambled up and down the pyramid of bricks and steel girders in the road and raced toward the East River, hearing the roar before he saw it. He moved as close to the raging water as he dared go. The Brooklyn shore was dark, as was all of Colony East.

He thought Abigail was too smart to attempt to cross the river. Then he considered her state of mind. Doctor Droznin had infected her with AHA-B. The cadet was desperate. She had fired a weapon, and there was no telling if she had shot anyone. Dawson decided to comb the bank between here and the bridge, expecting to find her quivering like a frightened rabbit in the weeds.

~ ~ ~

With the life vest keeping her head above the water, Abby drifted in the underground river. She knew she was moving because the *ploink ploink ploink* of drips grew louder and then faded as she floated by leaks from above.

Where would she end up? The subway tunnels stretched for miles. Was there some end? Or many ends? Or did the tunnels form an infinite maze, looping around and crisscrossing? She feared becoming a soggy rat meal.

Without the ability to see, Abby had to rely on other senses to guess at her location. She sniffed and was reminded of low tide, the rot of dead clams and tang of salty kelp. She inhaled slowly, drawing in fetid airy tendrils of oil and gasoline. She opened her mouth and wagged her tongue. Her taste buds helped paint a fuller picture of the odors. She remained alert for fresh air, which would signal she had entered a station. But how would she know which way to paddle to reach the platform?

"Yo!" After shouting, she listened for the faint echo. Bats, she had read, operated by echolocation. They chirped and relied on the sounds bouncing back to navigate. As soon as she detected a change in the ceiling's height, she'd dog paddle in that direction.

"Yo. Yo. Yo." She counted to three between shouts, straining to hear subtle differences in the echoes.

Floating in the darkness warped her sense of time. Sometimes she felt like her entire existence in the subway river had yet to reach a single second. Other times, it felt as if she had been in it forever.

Her brain lit up like a neon sign when she caught a whiff of fresh air. Real or imagined, Abby could almost taste the hurricane. She plucked out scents carried in the winds: exotic African spices, sweet coconut, the perfume of flowers stripped from stems.

She called out more frequently. "Yo… Yo… Yo…"

All of a sudden, she experienced a cathedral of emptiness soaring above her. The void swallowed her shouts. She kicked and paddled to the right and soon bumped into something hard. She beached her torso on the platform ledge, hooked her left knee on the landing, and then levered up the rest of her body. Stretched out on the smooth cement, she congratulated herself for pulling into the station.

~ ~ ~

Lieutenant Dawson leaned into the wind, fighting his way toward the Brooklyn Bridge. His radio crackled with reports of the hunt for Cadet Leigh.

"Charlie Tango, sweep of Central Park Farm complete, over."

"Roger Charlie Tango. Head north. Movement reported."

"Zulu Foxtrot, Times Square clear, over."

"Roger Zulu Foxtrot."

"CDC all-points bulletin." It was Doctor Perkins. "Code Purple. If the suspect is injured or killed, bring the body to Medical Clinic 17. Repeat, if the suspect is injured or killed, bring the body to Medical Clinic 17. Perkins out."

Dawson angled his posture lower and drove his legs harder into the teeth of the wind. Flecks of debris plastered the flashlight, dousing the beam. He wiped them away until he realized the flashlight was useless. He pocketed it.

He reached the bridge without spotting anything that resembled a person. Unfortunately, he realized he might have stepped over Cadet Leigh and not seen her.

He spun around to identify the source of a sudden deafening groan. Above the roar of the rushing water, it sounded like the grind of metal on metal, something twisting to the point of breaking. The eerie screeching sent chills inward to his core, as if the cold raindrops were soaking through his skin and into his blood.

A crack, loud as thunder, brought his attention to the middle of the river. He blinked and held his arm up to shield his eyes from the buckshot of debris blasting through the air. Fifty yards away, the freighter, which had wedged itself against the bridge abutment before the colony had opened, rolled over. There was just enough light to show the enormous hull shifting. All of a sudden, the raging current swept it away like it was a toy boat.

Dawson paused in awe. Then he started back toward Pier 15.

~ ~ ~

Confident in her ability to navigate in total darkness, Abby skipped digging the flashlight from her pack and waded through the knee-deep water. She traversed the subway platform, zeroing in on the sound of rushing water.

She reached the base of the escalator. Trying to climb up, she strained to push her legs forward against the waterfall cascading between the handrails. The force drove her back.

Abby stepped aside and took a moment to rest. With new resolve, she placed her hands on the two rails and started upstream, pulling with her arms while pushing off with her feet. Pummeled by a torrent that threatened to take her legs out from under her, she inched higher, little by little. The higher she climbed, the weaker the force of the water became. Her progress boosted her morale and that, in turn, gave her added strength. She reached the top.

Stopping to catch her breath, Abby saw steps ahead of her leading up to a dark gray sky. Water cascaded down them, but it was dispersed, and she climbed up with relative ease. Nothing blocked the entrance. Nothing stood in her way to the outside. At last, she exited her free ride through the New York City transit system.

From the color of the sky, she guessed the sun had risen. Even though the storm raged on, the wind and rain seemed to have lessened. Something suddenly smacked the back of her arm hard, twisting her. A sheet of plywood blew by, skittering along the ground and then lifting into the air like a candy wrapper. Abby's elbow throbbed from the impact, but she was thankful a sharp corner of the wood hadn't struck her head. Wary that Hurricane David had more punches to throw, she continued cautiously.

Abby gulped in terror at the sight of the East River, a churning, angry torrent of rapids that seemed to defy gravity. The waves crested higher than her head. She spotted the tops of the windmills, their spinning blades a blur. She blinked in disbelief as a patrol boat tumbled downriver.

In the half-light, the surroundings looked vaguely familiar, but Abby didn't know exactly where she was until she spotted the Brooklyn Bridge. With a lot of resolve and some luck, she had managed to land in the perfect location. All that remained for her to do was grab the rafts from the dumpster and launch herself from Pier 15. Then she realized that was a very bad idea. The river was out of control. Her inflatable vest and raft notwithstanding, the East River would silence the only voice that could announce what the adults were doing. She would drown. Instead, she'd hide in the dumpster throughout the day and make her escape that night.

She was startled by a flashlight beam. Forty yards away, the ghostly eye danced back and forth as the adult carrying the light ran toward her.

Abby bolted for the dumpster. Running with the wind, she flew five feet or more with every stride. She concentrated on where she planted each foot, trying to avoid paint cans, bricks and other obstacles.

"Abigail." Her name whizzed by like a bullet. She turned and saw Lieutenant Dawson chasing after her. "Abigail, stop!"

She leaped onto the dumpster, and her forward momentum folded her over the horizontal metal lip, the force puncturing her life jacket's air bladders. She scrambled for a toehold and got one. Gasping, she reached down and flipped up a corner of a tarp. The wind did the rest and the blue tarp sailed away. The rafts, each made of eight bottles, lashed together, were right where Jonzy had told her they would be. She grabbed a raft in each hand and jumped down. Landing in a crouch, she whipped her head back and forth, looking for the lieutenant.

She gasped. Only thirty yards separated them, a distance shrinking by the second. The river was also thirty yards away, and Abby picked an angle she hoped would keep her just out of the lieutenant's grasp.

"Abigail. Stop. Please. Stop."

Gulping air to feed her lungs, she choked on raindrops and choked harder when she realized Pier 15 was gone. It had washed away. Out of the corner of her eye, she saw the blur of the lieutenant, and before her rose the blur of the river and an uprooted tree that it had tossed ashore. Struggling to carry the two rafts, she feared they were slowing her down and let go of one. The roar of the river made her take a firmer grip on the other.

She cleared her mind of all thoughts because she would have tripped over a single doubt. Abby had to put her fate in the arms of the hurricane.

The lieutenant was closing in fast, less than twenty feet away, on a course to intercept her at the water's edge. She angled slightly to the right. Digging deeper into her last reserve of strength, she flung herself forward with abandon.

The lieutenant leaped at the same moment. Abby saw his expression of desperation, arm extended, fingers straight, back arched, ready to grab her. She felt the bump of him striking the bottles in her left hand. She let go and fell sideways into the river. The world flipped upside down and turned dark green and then brown.

~ ~ ~

Dawson scrambled to his feet. He kicked off his shoes, ready to jump in. He scanned downriver, watching for her head to pop up. "Abby," he shouted. "Abby." The wind pulled her name apart and scattered the letters.

Frustration shredded his insides as he calculated her likely position, his eyes darting back and forth over the writhing rapids. He saw hundreds of objects that looked like arms and legs and heads, but it was only debris swept into the raging water. Tree branches, chunks of wood, beards of white foam.

Gripping the crude flotation device, he raced along the bank and waded up to his knees, struggling to keep himself rooted. Pebbles and grit blasted his legs. He knew that too much time had passed. The volume of water was too great, the surge and suction too fierce. By now, her body would have carried to the bridge, if not beyond.

Spears of anger shot through him as he questioned his actions. He should have run faster, taken a different angle, jumped sooner. A sudden thought exploded into a thousand icy splinters. What if he had stopped? Abby might have stayed out of the river.

Dawson took off running again, lifting his knees high, pumping his arms. The plastic bottles tumbled apart and whipped together again with every stride. Running served no purpose other than to prevent him from plunging into a well of grief.

Lungs burning and legs throbbing, he stopped and dropped to his knees. The sob rose from deep inside his chest and tears filled his eyes. He collapsed forward, his forehead bumping the pavement. He pushed his cheek into the mat of wet weeds and cried.

～ ～ ～

Abby broke the surface and took a sip of air. Only a sip, because the river quickly sucked her back under. She spun and rolled as her arms and legs stretched at a force she felt might pull them from their sockets. Unable to control herself, she tried to breathe every chance she got, guzzling and snorting and huffing air each time her nose cleared the water.

She opened her eyes and kept them open. A deafening roar accompanied the blurry flashes of objects. She saw the pylons of the Brooklyn Bridge. A moment later, she flew by the pilings of the Williamsburg Bridge. Between momentary observations, her world was silent and black with a searing ache spreading inside her chest as her lungs scrounged for precious molecules of oxygen.

Abby took a deep breath of air and faced what appeared to be a mountain in her path. In the split second before she went under again, she saw the river coursing up the side of the mountain. The rising wall of water sheared near the mountain peak, creating two massive fountains. One cascaded to the left, one to the right.

When she was pulled down this time, Abby felt herself swept up and lifted higher as if the East River had changed course, and its mouth was in the clouds. A moment later, she hung suspended between sky and river. Then she started to fall, riding a waterfall, accelerating.

The thud came without warning, turning her world black and silent.

~ ~ ~

Lieutenant Dawson was still numb from exhaustion and from having let Abigail slip from his grasp when he stood. The sky had lightened to gunmetal gray and the rain and wind were easing up. He blinked and took deep breath after deep breath.

Fifteen minutes later, Dawson faced Trump Tower. The storm had blown out several windows on the upper stories. Shards of glass, bricks, and trash littered the street. It seemed that half the vehicles of the colony were here, the hub of the search activities.

He entered the building and on the fourth floor walked past Ensign Parker, who had his ear to a radio.

"Lieutenant," Parker called out. "What happened to your shoes?"

Realizing he was barefoot, but not caring, Dawson entered Admiral Samuels' office. Both the admiral and Doctor Perkins studied him. Samuels was out of uniform and had the red, watery eyes of someone lacking sleep. Perkins wore a crisp white shirt with his maroon bowtie firmly in place.

"Cadet Leigh jumped into the river. I'm afraid she drowned."

"Parker," the admiral barked, "Call off the search."

"Yes, sir," the ensign shouted back.

Doctor Perkins lowered his eyes and shook his head. "I'm sorry to hear that, Lieutenant. We invested significant resources in Abigail Leigh. I wish we could have monitored her vitals. She would have played an important role in our understanding of AHA-B."

Dawson bit his tongue so hard he tasted blood.

Doctor Perkins directed his next comment to Admiral Samuels. "Can we recover the body? We can glean valuable information from an autopsy."

"Lieutenant, what river?" Admiral Samuels asked in a somber tone.

Dawson paused a moment. Then he brought his shoulders back and lifted his chin. He stared at Doctor Perkins. "The Hudson River, sir. Right by the George Washington Bridge."

# DAY ONE

Abby opened her eyes to sunshine. With her cheek pressed against the mud, she saw a terrain of silt and debris washed ashore, including a birdcage and washing machine. The Colony East skyline was also in her peculiar view, as was the river, still running swiftly but nothing like before.

She sat up, gingerly moving limbs and fingers to see if anything was broken, and then saw what had deposited her onto dry land. Half the hull of a freighter sat firmly beached, half of it still in the river. She realized she had gone up it as if it was a giant waterslide. Despite the hard landing that apparently knocked her unconscious, she was grateful that the river hurdled her this way, or else she might be still drifting, or probably drowned.

Abby took stock of her situation. The colony was still very close, two or three miles away at most. No bones broken. One leg of her overalls had torn off, but her backpack straps had held sturdy. Her stomach growled for food, but the thrill of being alive helped take her mind off that. For now.

A group of young kids approached her, and she reached into her pocket, hoping to trade gems for a place to hide and get some rest. She pulled out a fistful of river mud and nothing else.

Abby picked out who she thought was the bravest of the bunch, a girl of five or six, and said, "Can you help me?"

Without asking for anything in return, they formed a circle around her and all pitched in to get her to her feet. Then, they escorted her toward a row of houses. Abby's dad had read *Gulliver's Travels* to her and Jordan. In the story, Gulliver is washed ashore after a shipwreck and becomes prisoner of a race of tiny people, less than a foot tall. Abby felt like Gulliver as the band of kids, whose heads came no higher than her shoulders, led her up the steps of a house. She would soon learn that she was in Greenpoint, not the country of Lilliput. Greenpoint was a section of Brooklyn, a half mile north of the Brooklyn Bridge.

The house was overflowing with kids around the same age as the group who had found her. Nobody seemed to be in charge, but they all seemed to cooperate. A sudden spike of hunger reminded Abby of what Hurricane David had brought. Sadly, the survival and organization skills of these kids were about to be put to the test.

She made her first trade. In exchange for dry clothes and half a boiled potato, she gave them her Colony East overalls, ripped leg and all.

The roof had leaked during the hurricane, soaking a lot of their bedding, but they found a dry place for her to sleep on the floor. Abby checked the contents of her backpack. Inside were six packs of cooked rice and the plastic tub. She gave two packs of rice to the kids, devoured one herself, and removed the two-way radio from the tub. She turned it on and quickly turned it off when she heard the hiss. The batteries were good. The radio had survived Hurricane David. She would attempt to contact Jonzy at midnight, after which, she would try to make her way to the fish market, hoping to find Toby. Her chances of doing the latter were probably much greater than the former. She gulped at the thought of Lieutenant Dawson marching Jonzy before the council. What would Jonzy say about their escape plan, and how would he respond when they told him she had shot Doctor Droznin?

Abby gripped the radio and curled up. She needed to rest and she needed to satisfy an insatiable appetite. Her brain battled her stomach. Exhaustion tilted the balance of power, and she drifted into a deep sleep.

Abby awoke in the dark. It took her a moment to remember where she was and what had happened. All of a sudden, she realized the radio was gone. The luminous dials of her watch showed the time was 12:15. In a panic, she quickly stumbled through the room, slowing down only after accidently kicking several kids sleeping on the floor.

She heard sounds coming from the porch. To her horror, kids had the walkie-talkie. They were giggling and passing it around. One kid pressed the button and shouted, "Pears." The next one brought it to his lips and said, "Apples."

"Please, I need that."

Thankfully, they gave it to her.

Abby held the radio, about to ask if they heard anything, when Jonzy's voice crackled. "Bossy, this is Lemon, over."

Abby blurted, "Lemon, this is Bossy." Tears streamed down her cheeks.

"Bossy! How's the fishing?"

"All is well. But I could eat a fish whole. Lemon, how'er things at Treasure Island?"

There was a long pause. The kids crowded around her, straining to hear the strange conversation about fish and lemons.

"Bossy, go to the market, I hear they're having a good sale tomorrow."

He wanted her to go to the fish market. She had a million questions, starting with how Jonzy had managed to keep his radio and communicate, but every word they spoke might be picked up by the adults.

"Bossy, keep your shoulders back."

Abby almost dropped the radio. That was not Jonzy's voice. There was no mistaking who it was.

Then Jonzy spoke. "Bossy, we're signing off for now. We have to go."

From the swirl of confusion, a skim of hope rose to the surface of Abby's mind. Lieutenant Dawson, speaking over Jonzy's contraband two-way radio, had told her to keep her shoulders back. It was his way of telling her to be strong in the face of fear. And Jonzy had said, "We have to go."

Abby ignored the gnawing pit of hunger in her stomach and pulled her shoulders back.

*Posting a review of Colony East at your favorite online book retailer is always appreciated.*

# GENERATION M – COMING IN 2014

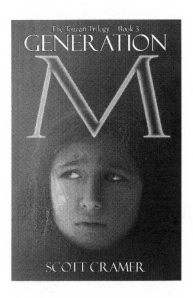

Sign up for the Generation M email notification
http://eepurl.com/DlQMn

# ACKNOWLEDGEMENTS

Writing is a team sport. Perrin Dillon and Otto Ball hung in there with me from the beginning, chapter by chapter. Dr. Roland Stroud is the king of grammar. I am also incredibly grateful for an outstanding group of beta readers who went beyond the call of duty: Karol Ross, Emma Lindehagen, Susan Pett, Megan Sciera, Sue Ryzak Wysocki, John Bickford, Doc Pruyne, Bonnie Tweddle-Shuster, Penny Adair, Eileen O'Neil, Don Cummings, David Roys, Kathe Filbert, Cynthia Sheep, Emily Sposa, Debby Alter, and others. Nanci Rogers proofed the novel and Diane Winger made important edits along the way.

# ABOUT THE AUTHOR

Scott Cramer has written feature articles for national magazines, covered school committee meetings for a local newspaper, published haiku and poetry, optioned a screenplay, and worked in high-tech marketing communications. His pursuit of a good story has put him behind the stick of an F-18, flying a Navy Blue Angels' fighter jet, and he has trekked through the Peruvian mountains in search of an ancient Quechua festival featuring a condor. Scott and his wife have two daughters and reside outside Lowell, Massachusetts (birthplace of Jack Kerouac) in an empty nest/zoo/suburban farm/art studio with too many surfboards in the garage.

LIKE http://www.facebook.com/authorscottcramer for updates and promotions.

31619374R00212

Made in the USA
Middletown, DE
10 May 2016